The
Wedding
Ringer

The
Wedding
Ringer

Kerry Rea

Jove
New York

A JOVE BOOK
Published by Berkley
An imprint of Penguin Random House LLC
penguinrandomhouse.com

Library of Congress Cataloging-in-Publication Data

Names: Rea, Kerry, author.
Title: The wedding ringer / Kerry Rea.
Description: First edition. | New York: Jove, 2021.
Identifiers: LCCN 2021007361 (print) | LCCN 2021007362 (ebook) |
ISBN 9780593201848 (trade paperback) | ISBN 9780593201855 (ebook)
Subjects: LCSH: Bridesmaids—Fiction. | Female friendship—Fiction. |
GSAFD: Humorous fiction. | Love stories.
Classification: LCC PS3618.E213 W43 2021 (print) |
LCC PS3618.E213 (ebook) | DDC 813/.6—dc23
LC record available at https://lccn.loc.gov/2021007361
LC ebook record available at https://lccn.loc.gov/2021007362

First Edition: November 2021

Printed in the United States of America
1st Printing

Book design by Alison Cnockaert

In loving memory of my son, Ciaran Riley Rea.
You are always with me.

1

I never envisioned myself as a twenty-nine-year-old children's birthday party performer, but here I am. Princess effing Sparkleheart. The *effing* is silent. Squeezing myself into a flamingo-pink, Goodwill-clearance-bin ball gown that itches severely, I look like a walking bottle of Pepto-Bismol.

Once upon a time, I was someone else. Everybody was. Before my idol Ruth Bader Ginsburg became the Supreme Court's resident badass, for example, she was just a little girl from Brooklyn with big dreams and a bowl cut. Before Meghan Markle met Prince Harry, she was a B-list actress who got her start as a briefcase girl on *Deal or No Deal*.

But unlike Ruth and Meghan, whose glow-ups transformed them from ordinary people into aspirational figures, my transformation went in the opposite direction.

Weekends as Willa Callister—blogger, Columbus's adventurous "it girl," and fiancée to Max—are a thing of the past.

Today's gig is Chloe Wellington's sixth birthday party, the social event of the summer for central Ohio's under-ten set. I know this because it literally says so on the invitation, a thick piece of white stationery covered in pressed rose petals that each guest had to display before entering. Chloe's backyard garden party, complete with rows of sparkling fairy lights and a shitload of mason jar centerpieces, is a Pinterest board come to life.

Chloe herself, a wiry, gap-toothed kid sporting a fuchsia dress and a tiara I suspect might have actual diamonds in it, is a total asshole.

A key part of my job as Princess Sparkleheart is to keep the party moving. It's been difficult today, given that Chloe has chosen to eschew the usual elements of my routine. I'm supposed to perform a whimsical wood flute number, as well as a sugary-sweet reenactment of how I met and fell in love with Prince Leon the Brave. But she ripped the wood flute from my hand three seconds into "Twinkle, Twinkle, Little Star" and used it to smack a smaller child in the mouth. And instead of listening during story time, Chloe made her dutiful friends crawl around on all fours and make horse noises while she perched lazily on their backs.

"Faster, Kinsley!" Chloe screeches, digging her heels into the sides of the poor kindergartner she's chosen as her latest victim. "Slow horses don't get birthday cake."

Kinsley, a sweet-faced girl in a dinosaur-print dress, lets out a mournful whinny and tries to pick up the pace. But her knee hits a divot in the yard, sending both girls crashing to the ground.

Terrified that Chloe might smash her tiara over her friend's head as punishment, I whistle for attention.

"Gather round, children!" I say in my Princess Sparkleheart voice, which is somewhere between a Minnie Mouse–like squeak and how my normal voice sounds when I'm choking. "'Tis time for Princess Chloe to open her royal presents."

"But I want to hear the story of how you met Prince Leon," a pigtailed child says. She pops a miniature cupcake into her mouth and tugs at my skirt with icing-coated fingers, coming dangerously close to exposing Princess Sparkleheart's private parts.

Princess Sparkleheart never gets angry, I tell myself as the pigtailed kid claws at my skirt and Chloe steps over a crying Kinsley, uttering a string of very unprincesslike words. *Princess Sparkleheart never gets angry.*

"Tell us the story!" the pigtailed girl insists. "Did Prince Leon the Brave rescue you from an evil witch? Were you cursed until you found true love's kiss? Or maybe he was an ugly monster who held you captive somewhere, like in a castle or an attic, until your love changed him and he turned nice and also really handsome?" She claps her hands together and stares at me with wide, hopeful eyes.

"Um, no. Actually, Prince Leon and I met when I saved *him* from the jaws of a hungry dragon." I pause, unable to resist the chance to inject a little feminism into the party. "Besides, love should be a partnership between equals. Relationships should never start out with one person holding the other captive, because—"

"Tell that to Princess Belle," the girl retorts. "But seriously, tell us about Prince Leon. Does he have long hair? And does he wear it in a man bun? Because I'm, like, *really* into man buns."

Chloe rolls her eyes. "Prince Leon isn't real, dummy."

A seed of anger takes root in my chest, and I force myself to take a deep breath and not think about how much I hate children. *Princess Sparkleheart never gets angry.*

Chloe's mother Beth, a raven-haired woman whose T-shirt reads *HOW MERLOT CAN YOU GO?* in sequined letters, doesn't bother to scold her daughter for name-calling. Instead, she pats the pigtailed girl on the head. "It's not story time, Annabelle. It's present time, okay?"

Annabelle groans in exasperation. "But Chloe has, like, eight hundred thousand presents. Can we at least have cake?"

"It's time," Beth insists, "for everyone to sit and *watch Chloe*." She smiles in a vaguely menacing way—a subtle reminder that if anyone draws so much as one photon of the spotlight away from Chloe, she will fuck their world up.

"Goddammit," the pigtailed girl mutters. I give her an apologetic smile and toss a pinch of fairy dust (read: dollar-store glitter) at her in consolation.

"Gather round, princes and princesses," I announce, adjusting my flower crown as the children assemble before me, looking like they'd very much prefer to skip Chloe's present parade and get to the cake. "Let's see what tributes the villagers brought for Princess Chloe on her day of celebration!"

"I brought her an outfit," a redheaded child declares with a shrug. "It's yellow. From Target. She'll probably hate it."

I toss a pinch of glitter at her. "Now, now. A princess is grateful for any gift she receives."

"What shade of yellow are we talking?" Beth asks, narrowing her eyes at the child. "Because anything paler than lemon washes Chloe out."

Before the girl can burst into tears, I grab a present from the top of the pile and present it to Chloe, who perches herself in the golden throne I drag to every party. It's a plastic lawn chair spray-painted gold, and it will come in handy if Princess Sparkleheart ever has to moonlight in an industry requiring lap dances.

I place the gift in Chloe's lap and curtsy. "Here you are, princess. Open your gift and see what treasures await."

Chloe, who seems to have outgrown the fairy princess theme by at least a year, gives me a dismissive glance. "Take it down a notch."

I glance at Beth, but she's busy beaming at Chloe and recording the proceedings on her iPhone. We all watch as Chloe tears open gift after ornately wrapped gift, including a new iPad, a summer's worth of vouchers for horseback riding lessons, and—I shit you not—an Amazon gift card worth three hundred dollars. She tosses the gift card aside with a bored expression, and it takes every ounce of restraint in me not to shed my royal dignity and dive after it. It would take three Saturdays as Princess Sparkleheart to earn that kind of cash.

When the gift-opening marathon concludes, Beth motions for me to follow her into the house. We march through the backyard, my skirt rustling as we pass the pony ride station and the slightly deflated bounce house, where at least one partygoer has vomited up the catered appetizers. In a kitchen that looks like the pages of a Crate & Barrel catalog, I reach into a refrigerator the size of my childhood bedroom and remove Chloe's cake. It's a dreamlike confection that would make Willy Wonka jealous; the cake is castle-shaped, complete with pink buttercream turrets and a chocolate-chip-cookie-dough drawbridge. A tiny edible version of Chloe peers out from the strawberry shortcake balcony, gazing down upon her sugary kingdom with an uncharacteristically benevolent expression.

I feel the weight of the cake in my hands and have the sudden urge to smash it. *Princess Sparkleheart never gets angry*, I remind myself again. It's the mantra I repeat when the parties get overwhelming, or when a child accidentally whacks me in the face during a game of piñata. That happens more often than you'd think.

I struggle not to drop the cake, which weighs about the same as my three-year-old niece, as Beth and I parade back into the yard. Chloe claps her hands in excitement and the other children crowd around us, marveling at the cake and the promise of an impending sugar high. Beth lights the candles one by one as the adults, who have smartly avoided the petting zoo and the gift-opening display in favor of drinking wine indoors, join the outdoor festivities. Chloe's dad snakes an arm around Beth's waist, slurring something about the hors d'oeuvres, and I'm surprised when Beth doesn't light his hair on fire.

"Happy birthday to you," she sings, and everyone joins in in off-key voices, rushing through the lyrics to get to the cake-eating. My biceps burn with the exertion of holding the cake, and I dream of the moment when I can collect my money from Beth and go home to shower off the glitter and unchecked commercialism and drink myself to sleep.

"Happy birthday, dear Chloe," the woefully out-of-tune group continues. "Happy birthday to y—"

That's when I see her. At the outskirts of the assembled group, next to where Chloe's dad is indiscreetly eyeing a guest half Beth's age, stands Sarah. She's scrolling through something on her phone, so her face is turned away from me, but it's her. I'd know her any-where. I recognize her outfit: a coral, sweetheart-neckline jumpsuit from Express that we'd picked out together. She thought the color was garish on her pale skin, but I'd convinced her it was just the unflattering fitting room lighting. And I was right. Here, at Chloe Wellington's sixth birthday party, with a bottle of Perrier in her hand and a slim gold bracelet around her left wrist—the one she broke when we were eight and tried Rollerblading with our eyes closed—Sarah looks pretty.

The shock of seeing her rips through me like a knife through soft, yielding flesh. My stomach lurches as a vision of her and Max together reappears in my mind: their sweaty bodies tangled and moving underneath my plum-colored bedsheets. I shut my eyes as

Beth and the children finish the birthday song, their voices flat and ringing in my ears.

When I open my eyes again, fighting back against the memory of Max's trembling hands pressed against Sarah's pearly-pink nipples, I see her lips opening and closing, forming the words of the song. I know she's not really singing, that she's a terrible singer who lip-synced her way through our fifth-grade choral songbook, just as I know that she hates every single thing about this party, from Chloe's incessant smirking to the monogrammed cloth napkins. I know all this because I know her, or at least I used to. I used to think I knew both of them.

It's only when the group finishes the song with one last, tuneless note and a hearty cheer that Sarah glances up from her phone. Her gaze sweeps past the pony rides and the bounce house and the over-loaded charcuterie table and lands, finally, on me. Her mouth drops open, and I notice her face is less round than it used to be. Maybe her boss at the law firm has her working eighty-hour weeks again, or maybe her on-off relationship with Pure Barre is back on. Or per-haps, in the five months since we last saw each other, since the day I swore to never speak of her again, I'd forgotten what my best friend looked like.

Sarah's face wrinkles with confusion. I imagine how I look from her perspective, with my ridiculous ball gown and too-tight heels and my flower crown wilting in the July heat. I fight the urge to vomit.

She tucks a strand of hair behind her ear. Her nervous tic. "Willa," she says. Her voice is soft, hesitant, the way one might speak to a dog baring its teeth.

And then it happens. My fingers go slack as my body's fight-or-flight instinct kicks in. I try to hold on to the cake and the last of my sanity, but I don't stand a chance.

"No!" Beth screams as I drop Chloe's sugar castle and it splatters on the ground. A turret pops off and rolls into the grass, and the chocolate-chip-cookie-dough drawbridge crumbles. Chloe shrieks as the tiny cookie version of herself gets buried beneath layers of smushed icing, and an opportunist pony who's trotted over from the petting zoo bends toward the collapsed cake and takes a swift, gigantic bite.

"What the hell?" Beth still grips a lighter in one hand, and I step back as she thrusts it in my direction. "What have you done?"

"I'm sorry," I whisper. My head is suddenly pounding, and my body feels lighter than air, as if I could float away at any moment. Beth's face is as red as the merlot mentioned on her shirt, her lips curled into an alarming snarl, but all I see is Sarah's head thrown back in ecstasy as Max thrusts into her, her head slamming the headboard with each wave of motion. All I see is the shock on her face as I drop my purse in the entryway of my bedroom, Max still thrusting, not yet noticing my presence. "I'm so sorry."

"That cake cost three times what I'm paying you." Beth's hands clutch her chest, and I back away in case she decides to grab my throat instead. *"Three times."*

"I'm sorry," I repeat as the pony chomps merrily on the remaining clumps of cake and icing. I bend toward the ground to see if I can salvage any of it, and the pony licks a bit of glitter off my head.

"Get up," Beth demands as a sobbing Chloe is surrounded by a circle of concerned friends.

I do as instructed, pressing my fingernails so roughly against my palms that I draw blood. "I'm so sorry, Beth. I can run to Costco and get a sheet cake—"

"Costco?" Beth presses her face so close to mine that I think she might spit on me. "Cut the bullshit. I only hired you because our Elsa impersonator came down with the flu, and look what happened." She

motions to the cake, where another industrious pony has joined the first in licking frosting off the grass. "You've ruined Chloe's party."

Princess Sparkleheart never gets angry, the better angels of my nature remind me. It's more a desperate prayer than a mantra. *Princess Sparkleheart never gets—*

"Willa," Sarah calls. "Willa!" She crosses the yard toward me in swift steps, weaving through the crowd of children weeping over the decimated cake.

"Just leave," Beth orders.

I've never wanted to disappear as much as I do now. My skin itching from my dress and the sting of humiliation, I grab my golden throne and wood flute and head for the street. One of my heels comes off in my haste, but I press on, leaving the shoe and a crowd of crying children in my wake.

"Willa!" Sarah's running as fast as her jumpsuit will allow, which isn't very fast at all, and I'd laugh if my whole world weren't such a shitshow. "Just talk to me for a minute. Please."

I grip my wood flute so tightly I think it might snap. If it weren't for what Sarah did, I'd still be Willa Callister, popular Columbus blogger and functional human being. I'd live in my charming Short North town house instead of my sister's spare bedroom. I'd spend Friday nights with other late-twenty-somethings instead of marathoning *The Golden Girls* and fantasizing that I was the girls' fifth roommate.

If it weren't for what Sarah did, we'd still be Sarah and Willa. I'd still be me. But we aren't, and I'm not.

"Willa, please," she says. She's a sea of coral coming at me, and I quicken my pace. "Please."

It's the third *please* that pushes me over the edge. I fling my throne into the grass, hard, causing one of the flimsy legs to snap off. Sarah winces as if I've struck her.

"My name," I say, gritting my teeth, "is Princess Sparkleheart."

"Get out!" Beth screeches.

When I bend down to pick up the throne and its dismembered leg, I hear a burst of throaty laughter behind me. The noise prickles my skin and makes my stomach contort. What kind of monster could possibly find my humiliation funny? Enraged, I whip my head up to see a dark-haired man nearly doubled over in laughter next to Beth's white picket fence. He clutches a beer in one hand, and I can hardly stop myself from grabbing the bottle and dumping its contents over his head.

When his laughter dies down enough that he can breathe properly, the man straightens up and takes a long, deep inhale. He has handsome features, with brown eyes and a jawline that a younger Princess Sparkleheart might have described as panty-dropping. He looks clean-cut in slacks and a blue oxford shirt with the sleeves rolled up to reveal muscular forearms.

Fury pulses through my veins, and the better angel of my nature abandons ship.

"Something funny?" I ask Mr. Asshole, clutching the broken leg of the throne like I might shank someone with it. It takes a second for me to realize that I probably look like a deranged '80s prom queen, and I let the chair leg fall to the grass.

Surprise flashes across the man's face when he realizes I've been watching him.

"No," he answers, but the sound comes out as a choked laugh. He coughs and pounds a fist against his chest. "No, sorry. I'm not—I'm not laughing at you. It's just . . . I choked on my drink." He hoists his beer up as evidence, revealing a Roman-numeral tattoo on his right wrist, and tries to subtly wipe away a tear trailing down his cheek.

"You're an asshole," I say, my voice trembling. "And a bad liar."

I hoist my poufy skirt up toward my knees and hobble one-shoed toward my car, leaving Mr. Asshole and Sarah and any remaining shreds of my dignity behind.

My chest heaving with the work of fighting back tears, I scramble for my car keys. I unlock my slightly dented Toyota Corolla with trembling hands and scurry into the safe cocoon of my car, slamming the door shut behind me. My tulle skirt gets stuck in the door, but I fire up the engine regardless, desperate for escape.

"Willa!" Sarah emerges from the backyard, clutching my abandoned shoe. She waves the high heel around wildly, and I half expect her to chuck it at my car to get me to stop. "Wait!"

I slam my foot against the gas pedal and peel away from the curb, nearly destroying an innocent patch of purple hydrangeas in the process. The neat, tree-lined streets and matching gray mailboxes of Beth's neighborhood whiz by me, and a visor-sporting woman in a minivan blasts her horn as I pass. The only thing that stops me from pulling over and dissolving into sobs is the knowledge that my bed and a bottle of wine await me at home.

They, at least, make everything better. Because Princess Sparkleheart might never get angry, but she sure as hell gets buzzed.

2

My sister Stacey lives in a sprawling four-bedroom home in Dublin, Ohio—Columbus's most popular new-money suburb. The egg-white Colonial house she shares with her wife Glory and my nieces sits on a one-acre lot and borders a lush golf course. During my first week living here, I was drinking my morning (read: one p.m.) coffee on the back patio when an errant golf ball zoomed past me, missing my right temple by mere inches. Looking back, getting struck by that ball would have been a blessing. Death by sports mishap would have saved me from performing at Chloe's party, which, in turn, would have prevented my sister from wanting to kill me. Stacey, who's my boss in addition to being my landlord, owns Celebration! Events, an event-planning company she built entirely on her own. The exclamation point in the title is very important to her. As is the principle that Princess Sparkleheart doesn't destroy birthdays, which means I'm totally screwed.

I tiptoe onto Stacey's front porch and press my ear to the wood-paneled front door, listening for any sounds of activity in the living room. Stacey and Glory are rarely home on Saturdays, so I think I'm safe, but I can never be too careful. Once Stacey hears about my disastrous day as Princess Sparkleheart, she's probably going to end me, and I'd prefer to be at least slightly tipsy for the encounter.

When I don't hear the blaring of the TV or the squeals of my nieces from the living room, I unlock the door and step inside. Luckily, the foyer is empty except for the family's four-year-old Irish setter, Nala, who's resting in a patch of sunlight streaming through the window. She wags her tail when she sees me, and the thump of her tail against the cherry-wood flooring loosens the knot in my stomach.

I remove my flower crown and kneel to scratch the mahogany fur behind Nala's ears. "Hi, girl. Wanna get drunk with me and pretend today never happened?"

Nala wags her tail harder and clambers up from her spot on the floor. With my four-legged partner in crime trailing behind me, I cross the foyer and head for the kitchen. Even though I've lived in this house for four months, I'm still getting used to it. Stacey and I grew up with our mom in a cramped ranch home with chipped paint and a shower that spat hot water only on occasion. Stacey's mini-mansion, with its vaulted ceilings and basement wet bar and sparkling granite backsplash, makes me feel like a little girl playing house.

Nala and I shuffle into the kitchen, and I have to blink a few times to adjust my eyes to the blinding white. Everything except the blooming purple orchid on the windowsill is the color of fluffy cotton. I open the pantry and survey the contents, desperate for comfort food. Unfortunately, Stacey and Glory are as zealous about healthy eating as they are about Pottery Barn kitchen accessories, and the best option is a half-eaten bag of lightly salted rice cakes.

Sighing, I pop a rice cake into my mouth and toss one to Nala, then grab a bottle of Moscato hidden behind the dry goods. Red wine would be better, but then again, so would getting knocked into a coma by a golf ball.

"And now, we hide," I whisper to Nala. Her paws smacking the hardwood, she scampers out of the kitchen and follows me through the foyer and up the curved staircase that leads to the second floor. The spare bedroom where Stacey and Glory let me crash sits at the end of a long hallway, next to my nieces' playroom. Nala and I are halfway down the hall, almost in the clear, when I hear the play-room door bang open.

"Willa." My sister's voice stops me cold. Even though Stacey's only five years older than me, her displeased-mom tone makes me scramble to hide the Moscato.

"Stace!" I smile brightly and hold up the rice cake bag in greet-ing. "Happy Saturday! How are the children?"

In her weekend uniform, a pair of leggings and a loose T-shirt that says MAMA BEAR in gold cursive, Stacey looks comfortable but overworked. The faint circles underneath her eyes reveal a lack of sleep. Her honey-blond hair sits in a messy bun atop her head, and she hasn't applied any makeup yet, so the freckles on her nose are on full display.

"Your nieces are fine," she says, crossing her arms over her chest. "Unlike poor Chloe Wellington."

Fuck. I'd hoped I could at least figure out how to spin the day's events in my favor before facing my sister. I pop another rice cake into my mouth to buy myself some time, and Nala nuzzles her head against my hand in solicitation. "About that. Things didn't go as planned."

"According to the phone call I just had with Beth Wellington, that's putting it mildly." Stacey sets her jaw in a firm line and raises her eyebrows, giving me the same look she gave my oldest niece, Kaya, when she fed her hamster a hot dog out of pure curiosity. Looking at my sister is like looking at a longer, leaner version of myself. We have the same round cheeks and wide-set, hazel eyes, but Stacey is half a foot taller than my five-two frame. Her height came in very handy for her when we were kids; she would dangle the TV remote just out of my grasp, refusing to let me watch *Clarissa Explains It All* until I begrudgingly fetched her Pringles from the snack drawer.

Nala whines, and I feel the tears I fought on the car ride home threaten to erupt as Stacey's gaze bores into me. "I didn't mean to drop the cake," I half whisper. "And I certainly didn't mean for the ponies to eat what was left of it. And I didn't mean for Chloe to cry, or for Beth to—"

"Willa," Stacey says, letting her arms fall to her sides. "What happened?"

A combination of shame and rage churns my stomach. I can't tell Stacey that seeing Sarah in her coral jumpsuit was like seeing a ghost, that hearing her familiar voice call my name made my stomach ache like a feral animal was trying to claw its way out. If she knew the real reason why I'd lost control of myself at the party, she'd try to understand. Stacey would stroke my seriously-overdue-for-a-wash hair and feed me chicken noodle soup and whisper into my ear that I was strong and brave and better off without Sarah and Max. That's what she did five months ago, right after The Incident when my world exploded.

But I can't tell Stacey the truth about the party. A week after The Incident, after I canceled the final wedding vendors and deleted my registry and vomited so much I lost six pounds, I vowed to myself never to speak of Sarah or Max again. Not to anyone, no matter what. And I keep my promises, even if neither of them did.

"Nothing happened. I just didn't expect the cake to be so heavy, and it slipped out of my hands." The lie causes a wave of guilt to crash over me. I shouldn't lie to Stacey, who's the only person in the world who has my back anymore. And I shouldn't discount the damage my fuckup could have on her business. Celebration! Events was Stacey's baby before she had actual babies. She works harder at growing her company than anyone I know, and it's the reason she can afford this house and my nieces' private-school tuition and the fourteen trips to Starbucks she makes every week. It's also the reason she can give me free room and board while I put my shitty life back together.

The possibility that I've single-handedly destroyed my sister's empire makes my skin prickle, and I tug at the itchy collar of my dress. "How bad is this?"

The firm line of Stacey's jaw relaxes, and she brushes a stray lock of hair from my face. "One bad party isn't the end of the world, kiddo. But it is the end of your relationship with my Moscato." She reaches around me and wrenches the bottle of wine from my grasp. Sometimes we're exactly the same as we were as kids, except we wrestle over alcohol instead of the last pack of Dunkaroos. "Beth Wellington gave us a one-star review on Yelp, but it'll get buried under the good ones," Stacey continues. "No one will take her opinion seriously, anyway. Her only other review is of Disney World, and she gave it one star for being too crowded."

I snort-laugh. "It figures that she wouldn't like mixing with the common folk. You should have seen her face when I uttered the words *sheet cake*."

Stacey laughs, but it's not the characteristic braying laugh she's famous for. It's more of a polite chortle, the kind you'd reserve for an annoying airplane seatmate who won't stop telling dad jokes.

"Willa," she says, her voice so full of concern that it makes my throat ache, "don't take this the wrong way, but with Chloe's party today, and the piñata situation last week . . ."

I cringe. At seven-year-old Timmy Erten's birthday party, I took my eyes off the kids for a single instant to admire his handsome uncle. That was all the time it took for a rowdy child to smack the birthday boy straight across the face with the piñata bat.

"That wasn't entirely my fault," I protest. "The kids at the party said Timmy is a known girlfriend-stealer. He kind of had it coming."

Stacey raises her eyebrows. "Is it your fault you were less concerned about Timmy's broken nose than whether or not his hot uncle was single?"

"His nose was bruised, not fractured. And give me a break on the uncle. He looked like Tom Hardy, and you know how much I love *Mad Max*."

Stacey sighs so loudly that her nostrils flare out like a cartoon bull's. "I'm not saying that you're the worst Princess Sparkleheart I've ever hired," she says in the kindest tone she can muster. It's the same overly patient voice she used when I was six and decided to cut my own bangs with a pair of zigzag-bladed safety scissors. "But I'm not saying that you're not."

"I really am trying." My voice rings with desperation, and I swallow hard to get rid of it. It's hard to admit that some days, just getting out of bed and putting dry shampoo in my hair feels like a major accomplishment. It's hard to face the fact that five months ago I had a career and an upcoming wedding and a really good credit score, and now I'm about to be fired from a job that a sixteen-year-old could do. Fired by my own sister, no less. "I'll try harder. I promise. No more broken noses, no more cake dropping. Five-star Yelp reviews from here on out." I raise my hand to give her a little salute.

Stacey nods. "Okay. But I'm still keeping the wine." She opens her mouth like she wants to say more, closes it, and opens it again. "I know you don't want to hear this, but I just think if you started trying to write again, maybe a blog update here or there, you'd feel better. A Willa who doesn't write is like a Nala who doesn't bark. It just doesn't work."

A ball swells in the back of my throat. Stacey doesn't know that I've tried to start writing again. But every time I sit in front of my laptop, determined to pour the contents of my broken heart onto the screen so I can piece it back together, I draw a blank. I haven't found the right words to describe my pain, and I'm not convinced they even exist. The loss and loneliness I've experienced since The Incident can't be summarized in a neat, clickbaity blog post. Even if I could write instead of staring at a blinking black cursor on the screen, no one would want to read it. The former readers of *Willa Leads the Way* expect cheery, aspirational posts about my top five date-night restaurants and my ice cream tour of the Buckeye State. They don't want to read mournful ramblings from a woman who ruins birthday parties and feels dressed up when she puts on leggings instead of sweatpants.

The new me can't deliver what they want anymore. But I don't know how to make Stacey understand that.

"You're right," I tell her. "I don't want to talk about the blog."

Stacey lets out a frustrated huff, but before she can resume her well-intended lecture, the front door opens and a tornado of activity sweeps into the house. I glance over the stairwell to see my sister-in-law Glory crossing the threshold, her dark waves gathered on top of her head in a pineapple bun. She carries a canvas bag stuffed with pears in one arm and my eight-month-old niece Lucy in the other. Lucy, wearing a purple dress with rocket ships on it and clutching a half-eaten graham cracker, is busy trying to yank Glory's hair from the bun. My other nieces, three-year-old Maeve and six-year-old Kaya, trail behind them. Kaya, carrying an overloaded bag of apples in her tiny arms and singing "Baby Shark" at the top of her lungs, trips over the rug that borders the entryway. She tumbles to the ground, the apples spilling across the floor. Maeve wastes no time grabbing a fallen apple and taking a giant bite out of it.

Glory lets out a little yelp as baby Lucy succeeds in ripping a chunk of hair from her bun, and Kaya takes one look at the newly formed scratch on her knee and bursts into tears.

"Stace!" Glory exclaims. "Rescue me. Please." Her shoulders sag beneath the weight of Lucy and, I assume, the crushing exhaustion of motherhood. It occurs to me that I'm not the only one who might enjoy getting knocked out by an errant golf ball.

Stacey springs into action, hurrying downstairs to the foyer. Nala lets out a hoarse bark and gallops after her, abandoning me for the promise of dropped graham cracker crumbs.

"Willa," Stacey calls as I start to head for my bedroom, grateful for the opportunity to escape her watchful gaze. "We aren't done with our conversation. We really need to—"

"My knee is BLOODY," Kaya wails, saving me from a continued lecture. Red-faced and teary, she clutches her knee to her chest and rolls around on the carpet like she's been shot. "It won't stop BLEED-ING. I'm gonna need a turn kit! I'm gonna need an ampertition!"

Stacey gives her wife a questioning glance.

"Girl Scouts," Glory explains. She tears her hair free from Lucy's chubby fingers and sighs in exasperation. "First aid lessons."

"Ah." Stacey pulls a sobbing Kaya into her arms and presses a kiss to her temple. "You don't need a tourniquet or an amputation, sweetheart. You're going to be fine."

Kaya just cries harder. "But at Girl Scouts—"

"Fuck the Girl Scouts," Glory interrupts, causing my sister to shoot her a look that could freeze hell. "Sorry," Glory mutters, wincing as Lucy moves onto another chunk of hair. "Long day at the farmers' market."

"So, anyway," I say as Nala gently steals the apple from Maeve's outstretched hand, then trots off to enjoy it in peace. "I'm going to take a nap. Good talk, Stace. Hi, Glory."

My sister-in-law lifts a hand in greeting. "Hey, don't disappear on us. We're going to be terrible parents and use screen time to calm the girls down. Wanna watch a movie? We'll probably go for something brand new, like *Frozen* or *The Incredibles*." She winks at me and lifts Stacey's Moscato bottle to her lips, pretending to chug it. "C'mon. Nobody makes popcorn like Aunt Willa."

I smile at her offer because I know I should. My three nieces are my favorite people in the world, and Glory loves my sister enough to tolerate me, so they're a good crowd to hang out with. Besides, nothing warms my heart faster than Maeve shouting "Yucky!" every time we watch *Frozen* and Prince Hans graces the screen.

But I can't ignore the feeling that I'm basically the grown-up version of the short, chubby kid who only gets picked in gym class because the popular girls feel bad for her. I've already commandeered a bedroom in Stacey's house, not to mention the fact that her generosity—and willingness to overlook the fact that I'm a horrendous Princess Sparkleheart—is the only reason I'm employed.

I might be a friendless twenty-nine-year-old with a missing shoe and a recycled ball gown, but I'm not a complete idiot. I know better than to intrude on precious family time.

"Thanks, but the party today wiped me out." I motion to my sweat-stained dress and singular bare foot and shrug.

Glory and Stacey both start to respond, but Kaya starts howling again, and Maeve screeches when baby Lucy abandons her mom's bun in favor of grabbing Maeve's tightly coiled hair. I seize the opportunity to escape to my bedroom and close the door swiftly behind me, shutting out the sound of crying children.

I collapse into my bed and burrito myself in the soft comforter, not even bothering to undress. The silence and bareness of the bedroom soothe me. When I moved out of the town house I shared with Max and into my sister's home, Stacey encouraged me to decorate my space as I pleased. But what pleased me was getting rid of everything that reminded me of Max and Sarah and my former life. I have no framed photographs on the walls, no knickknacks from past beach vacations or hiking trips to the Smokies. I have no rustic-looking *Live, Laugh, Love* sign on the wall because I'm not laughing or loving, and because those signs are cheesy bullshit.

I don't need a well-appointed bedroom. I don't need Stacey and Glory's pity, as well-intended as it is.

The old Willa—the *Buckeye Buzz* lifestyle reporter and definitely *not* self-titled Columbus Instagram influencer, the woman with confidence and friends and the ability to run a seven-minute mile—is gone. New Willa is here instead, wrapped in her sister's comforter and staring very hard at the ceiling, trying not to cry.

And despite what Stacey thinks, New Willa doesn't want to restart her life here.

She wants to escape.

3

Since I don't have enough money saved to get the hell out of Dodge, I have to settle for making the most of my current situation. Which means meeting Zachary, the hot uncle who distracted me long enough for Timmy Erten to injure his nose, for coffee. Coffee wasn't my first choice. I suggested drinks at my favorite tiki bar Huli Huli, because I love the Painkiller, their spiced rum and pineapple cocktail, and because I'm not looking for deep conversation with Zachary. I want to have a few drinks, make flirty conversation, and then go back to his place for some adult playtime. (We can't exactly go back to mine, unless his idea of a good time is listening to an endless loop of "Baby Shark" and discussing the intricate plot points of *PAW Patrol* with Kaya and Maeve.)

But Zachary—who insists on being called Zachary instead of Zach, which seems like a bit of a red flag—suggested coffee instead. This means he's either a cheap date or looking for something serious, neither of which appeals to me. But he really is a Tom Hardy look-alike if I squint hard enough, which is sufficient motivation for me to put on mascara and suffer through an actual date.

Besides, I can't get the vision of Sarah hurrying toward me in her coral jumpsuit out of my mind. And I can't get rid of that other image, either: of Sarah and Max in my bed, eyes closed, mouths open, hands everywhere. Since Chloe's disastrous party on Saturday, I feel even worse than usual. Thanks to Stacey's confiscation of the wine, I didn't drink over the weekend, but I have all the symptoms of a killer hangover—a raging headache, persistent waves of nausea, and a full-body weariness that makes my limbs feel like lead. I spent all Sunday afternoon playing Candy Land with Kaya while Maeve practiced somersaults and Lucy tried to devour the colored cards, but the visions won't relent. I need a distraction, and Zachary just might be it.

So at eleven thirty on Monday morning, I plod into the kitchen wearing a striped pair of leggings and a tight-fitting cami. It screams "not relationship material." Just in case Zachary got the wrong first impression. I've lost some weight over the last few months, so the leggings fit a bit looser than they used to, but they're enough of a step above sweat pants to make me feel okay wearing them on a coffee date. I raked a palmful of mousse through my hair to give my black curls a chance at surviving the thick July humidity, and I skipped a full-face makeup routine in favor of foundation, mascara, and lipstick.

The late-morning light streams through the kitchen window as I rub Nala's ears and grab an apple from the bowl on the counter. I open the refrigerator door to get a bottle of water and notice a chocolate-frosted Bundt cake resting on the shelf.

Before I can even consider making a move on the cake, Glory eyes me from across the room. She sets down her newspaper and raises an eyebrow at me. "Don't even think about it." She sits at the kitchen table with her legs tucked beneath her, her glasses resting on top of her head and a pencil tucked behind one ear. With her deep brown eyes, voluptuous figure, and long, silky hair, Glory reminds me of Salma Hayek. Whenever she gets annoyed with me, which is semiregularly, I remind her of this. Flattery goes a long way.

"Salma, good morning," I chirp. "I loved you in *Frida*."

Glory rolls her eyes good-naturedly and takes a bite of what's probably a kale-flax-seed-quinoa salad. "Brownnose all you want, but that cake is for game night. Ruthie will kill you if you eat a single bite beforehand."

Stacey and Glory's next-door neighbor Ruthie, a spry eighty-three-year-old who wouldn't be caught dead in a cardigan, hosts her weekly game night on Mondays. Attendees include the members of her bridge, book, and gardening clubs and the select few neighbors she likes—which in recent months includes me.

Glory picks up the *Columbus Dispatch* and studies it for a moment before glancing at her Apple Watch. "It's eleven thirty, Willa. What are you doing up so early?"

It occurs to me that I'm now living a life where the fact that I'm upright and conscious before noon strikes someone as unusual. I briefly consider slamming my head between the refrigerator doors, but I opt to take a bite of my apple instead.

"I have a date with a guy named Zachary. We're meeting at Espresso 22 for coffee. So if I go missing today, tell the cops the suspect bears a stunning resemblance to Tom Hardy. And make sure CNN uses a cute picture of me. Semicute, at least."

My recent underemployment and glaring lack of a social life have given me ample time to listen to every episode of every crime podcast in existence, so I'm half-convinced that Zachary could turn out to be a serial killer. In any case, I've tucked a canister of pepper spray into my purse. Better safe than sorry.

Glory stares at me the way one might look at a bird with a broken wing. "You're going on a date at noon on a Monday? Wearing yoga pants and a tank top?"

"Zachary's a pilot. He works odd hours. And these are my nice yoga pants," I argue. "They're from Lululemon."

"Odd hours mean he's married. Leggings in summer mean you haven't shaved your legs. Not that there's anything wrong with not shaving. You do you." Glory stuffs another forkful of kale into her mouth. "Just skip the date and come to the zoo with the girls and me. We're going to check out the gorillas."

Glory, a pediatric dentist, takes Mondays off in the summer to spend more time with the girls, and I occasionally join them on their adventures. Today, however, I'm on the hunt for a distraction, and dragging my nieces' Radio Flyer wagon around the crowded zoo in ninety-degree weather doesn't sound like a good solution.

"And pass up the chance to bang Tom Hardy? I think not."

"You know he's not actually Tom Hardy, right? Besides, are you really in a good place to be dating?" A consummate multitasker, Glory takes another bite of her salad and meticulously straightens the breakfast stool next to her. "True happiness comes from oneself, Willa. You have to water your own garden before you can bloom."

I narrow my eyes at her. Glory's enthusiasm for metaphorical advice is roughly on par with that of the '90s cartoon character Daria, and I'm tempted to press a hand to her forehead to ensure she isn't febrile. "What bullshit podcast did you hear that from?"

"Not a bullshit podcast. A bullshit book." Glory grimaces and lifts a book from the table, hoisting it up for me to see. "Your sister's making me read it."

The book, a glossy volume bearing the image of a beaming forty-something woman cradling a baby, is titled *Mommy Mindfulness: Watering Your Inner Garden to Let Your Mommy-Flower Bloom.*

"Oh my God," I say. "I'm never having children."

"Right? I told Stacey that 'mommy-flower' sounds downright Freudian, and she didn't even crack a smile."

My sister, the ultimate overachiever, probably owns every popular self-help book published in the last two decades. She regards Glennon Doyle's *Untamed* as her personal bible and attends at least two women's empowerment seminars every year. When I moved in after The Incident, she loaded the bookshelf in my bedroom with annotated editions of all her favorites, including *What Color Is Your Parachute?* and the old classic *The 7 Habits of Highly Effective People*. I was more interested—still am—in pretending like the past never happened than reading fiercely upbeat essays, and I skimmed a few highlighted passages from a couple books before ignoring them completely. I still don't know what color my parachute is, and I don't need a bestseller to tell me that most highly effective people probably aren't out there dropping cakes and ruining children's birthday parties.

"I'm serious, though." Glory brushes her hair off her shoulders and studies me carefully. "You didn't leave your room on Saturday, and you've been walking around like a zombie all weekend. Maeve asked me if Aunt Willa was sick."

The thought of my nieces noticing my misery jolts me. Their tiny little shoulders shouldn't bear any of my burden. I need a distraction so that I can feel better, and I need it bad.

"Just a bit of a funk," I answer. "Nothing a little solo time with Zachary the pilot can't cure." I give Glory my most winning smile in an attempt to appear convincing, but it feels like I'm wearing a mask made of my own skin.

She studies me for a second before nodding. Unlike Stacey, Glory isn't one to push. It's a quality I've grown to appreciate over the last five months. "If you say so. But you can't escape your problems with hot pilots, Willa. Or Moscato. Or even by watching every episode of *Golden Girls* on repeat. You have to face the hard stuff sometime."

I roll my eyes. "It's one hot pilot. And I don't watch every episode on repeat. I skip the one where the girls spend the night in a homeless shelter. It's corny and depressing."

Before Glory can press further, Maeve traipses into the sunny kitchen. Her blond, coiled hair sticks out from her scalp like an adorable halo, and she cradles a neon-orange Nerf gun in her small arms.

"Aunt Willa," she says, her little-girl voice deadly serious. "Come on. It's time to hunt dinosaurs."

"Aunt Willa has plans, sweetheart. She'll hunt dinosaurs with you later," Glory says.

"That's right." I lift Maeve into my arms and press my forehead against hers. "You're going to the zoo with Mommy, and then it's dino hunting time. Bet we can catch a triceratops tonight."

"Or a T. rex!" Bending her non-Nerf-wielding arm into a little claw, Maeve lets loose a high-pitched roar and presses her teeth to my neck.

"Hey, no biting," Glory says. "You're hunting dinosaurs, not vampires."

Maeve roars again, and I kiss the top of her head before putting her down. I don't want to be late to meet Zachary, and I definitely don't want Glory peppering me with any more saccharine self-help mottos.

"Remember what I said," Glory says as I discard my apple core in the trash and head for the door. "You have to water your own garden before you can . . ."

"Bloom," I remind her, knowing she's already forgotten the Mommy-Flower advice. "Before you can bloom."

Glory winks at me, and I grab my purse off the counter and head for the door. I may not be watering my own garden, but I'm sure looking forward to watering Zachary's.

4

Zachary's late. Not that I mind terribly, because his tardiness gives me a chance to survey the muffin selection. Espresso 22 is a small, quaint coffee shop located in Powell's historic district, just a few miles' drive from Stacey's house in Dublin. The café's exterior is a cheery blue with white trim, and yellow umbrellas shield the outdoor tables from the midday sun.

Inside, wooden tables and white metal chairs take up most of the available space. Two overstuffed chairs and a bowl of orange flowers line the far window. At the counter, I inhale the rich aroma of coffee and cappuccino and waver between choosing a warm croissant or a lemon muffin.

I order the lemon muffin with a frozen mocha and settle at a table near the front windows. The occasional grinding purr of the espresso machine soothes my nerves, and I sip my mocha and people-watch while I wait for Zachary. I take a bite of my muffin, considering what Glory said to me. It's easy for Stacey and Glory to dole out advice when their lives are damn near perfect, with their annoyingly healthy relationship and adorable—and adoring—children, six-figure incomes, and *Better Homes & Gardens* profile-worthy house. Their earnest attempts to advise me on my dumpster fire of a life only serve to piss me off. Don't get me wrong, I'm happy for them and appreciate the fact that I'm not homeless. But they don't know anything about facing problems; to do that, they'd need to have them in the first place.

The café door opens. I glance up to see if it's Zachary, but it's just a surly-looking teenager with a skateboard tucked under his arm. I check the time on my phone and wonder if he's standing me up. He's only ten minutes late, but if we'd met at a bar like I wanted, I'd be a cocktail deep by now, making flirty banter with a potential backup guy.

I'm about to text him when the door chime jingles again. This time, a red-faced woman barrels into the café, nearly smacking the skateboarder in the face with the door.

"Sorry," she mutters when he gives her a dark look. "Caffeine emergency." The woman straightens the collar of her blue tie-waist shirtdress and wipes a trail of sweat from her brow. Then she taps her foot against the floor once, twice, three times, as if she's a nervous rabbit signaling danger.

My phone buzzes with a text from Zachary: Sorry, be there in 15. Stuck on a work call. I fire off a quick response, and when I look up from my phone again, the rabbit woman is standing directly in front of my table.

"Is this seat taken?"

It takes me a moment to register that she's talking to me. Up close, the woman is sweet-faced and pretty, the kind of friendly-looking stranger you'd turn to for help when caught without a tampon in a public restroom. Her auburn hair falls over her shoulders in expert waves, like she really knows her way around a curling iron, and she tucks a strand behind her ear expectantly. I'm distracted by how the put-togetherness of her look—her beachy waves, the expertly applied eyeliner, the fact that she's wearing Keds with a shirtdress and still managing not to look like an overgrown toddler—contrasts with her jittery demeanor. Her green eyes shift between me and the door, like she's waiting for someone else to burst through it.

"Is it?" she asks. "The seat? Is it taken?"

I blink as she rabbit-taps the floor with her left Ked. "I'm actually waiting for someone."

"But they're not here yet, right?" She motions to the empty seat, her sweeping arm almost knocking over my drink. "So it's technically available, right? Do you mind if I sit with you for a sec?"

Before I can answer, she plants herself in the seat opposite mine and rests her purse, a baby-pink Kate Spade tote, on the table. "What kind of muffin is that? It smells citrusy. Is it lemon?" She removes an actual handkerchief from her purse and, like a sophisticated gentleman in a black-and-white movie, dabs beads of sweat from her forehead. "Or maybe it's orange. Anyway, is it good?" Her gaze darts between the door, me, and the muffin. "It looks good."

The flavor of the muffin is the last thing on my mind as she chatters on like we're old friends. Who the hell is this crazy woman, and how can I get her out of my face before Zachary arrives?

"Excuse me," I say as the unhinged lady taps her foot faster, like she's working toward a crescendo. The table shakes from the motion, and it's all I can do not to kick her in the shin to make her stop. "Can I help you with something?"

"No. I mean, yeah. I mean, absolutely, yes. I'd really appreciate if you could help me with something." She fiddles with the collar of her dress again, then extends her right hand across the table. Her nails are painted a soft peach shade, and a silver charm bracelet dangles from her wrist. "I'm Maisie."

I stare at her outstretched hand, wondering if this is all some elaborate ploy to steal my muffin.

"I sanitize my hands regularly, if that's what you're worried about," Maisie says.

It's not at all what I'm worried about, but I don't want to appear rude, so I extend my hand to shake hers. Her skin is soft, but her grasp is strong. A handshake you can trust, my grandfather would have called it. But trusting never got me anywhere.

I pull my hand back and rest it in my lap. "I'm Willa."

Maisie cocks her head to one side and studies me like a curious golden retriever. "You look really familiar."

I scoot my muffin closer to me. "You don't look familiar at all."

"Do you go to the barre studio on Dublin Granville? Maybe I've seen you there."

"No." I use the straw to stir my frozen mocha and avoid eye contact. I used to get recognized in public sometimes, back when my blog was popular. Before The Incident. It continued to happen occasionally after I deleted my social media accounts, but no one has recognized me from my blog in months. Not that I'd expect anyone to—the old Willa actually deep-conditioned her hair and didn't wear a pink poufy ball gown in public.

"Oh. Well, maybe you go to yoga nearby?"

I squirm in my seat as Maisie tap-tap-taps her stupid foot against a table leg. I don't want her to place where she knows me from. I hate being reminded of my old life. I fight the urge to pick up my muffin and hurl it at her perfectly coiffed head.

"Or maybe—"

"I don't do barre or yoga," I interrupt. "Not anymore. I don't know you, okay?"

Maisie blinks as if I actually launched the muffin at her, and her already-pink cheeks redden further. "Of course, right. I'm sorry."

"Listen," I say, trying to sound kinder this time, "I really am waiting on—"

Maisie's purse makes a brief buzzing sound, and her hand flies into the bag so fast it makes me jump. "Oh no," she says when she has her phone in hand. Her eyes go wide as she stares at the screen. "Oh no, oh no. He's almost here."

"Who's almost here?" I eye the skateboarder suspiciously.

Maisie scrunches up her nose and blinks rapidly, like she's about to cry. "Finn. Finn's almost here."

My Spidey-senses kick into high gear, and I scramble to remember all the tips I've learned from my favorite murder podcast, *Crime Junkie*. "Who's Finn? Is he a stalker? A killer? I have pepper spray in my purse."

Maisie looks at me like I'm the weirdo who parked herself at someone else's table. "A *killer*? Oh my God, no. Finn's my fiancé. He's wonderful."

"That's what they all say," I mutter. I reach for my purse so the pepper spray is handy and knock my muffin off the table in the process. Frustration simmers in my belly and threatens to boil over. Now, in addition to being cornered by this random stranger, I'm muffinless. Screw this.

Before I can reach down to salvage my fallen treat, Maisie reaches across the table and puts her hand over mine. "You have to pretend to be my friend," she says, her tone desperate. "Please."

The pleading in her voice gives me pause. What if Maisie really does need my help? What if she's tangled up with one of those sex-trafficking rings Ruthie's always warning me about? "Listen, I'm all for women helping women, but you need to tell me what's going on. I'm about three seconds away from macing the shit out of the next guy who walks in here."

Maisie tugs at her collar like it's choking her. "Finn thinks I come here every Monday. To meet a friend."

"And you don't?"

She shakes her head.

"So why does he think you do?"

"Because I tell him so."

"So you lie to your fiancé." I can't help the hardness seeping into my voice. After what Max and Sarah did, I have zero patience for cheaters. "Do you lie because you're seeing someone else?"

"Seeing someone else?" Maisie's mouth drops open like the possibility never occurred to her. Like people don't go around cheating on their partners all the time, in their partner's bedroom, with their partner's best friend.

"No. No, it's nothing like that. I tell him I come here on Mondays to meet a friend and do some work. But I actually go . . ." She pauses, and her fingertips dance back and forth across the table as if playing a frenzied piano solo. "I go someplace else."

"Where?"

"It doesn't matter where. What matters is, Finn texted that he's in the neighborhood and wants to treat my friend and me to coffee."

"So say your friend couldn't make it. Or went home sick. Or tell him the truth."

"I can't tell him the truth." Panic fills Maisie's voice. "I want . . . I want him to think I have friends."

The sincerity in her tone gives me pause. "Do you . . . not?"

Maisie shrugs. "I have acquaintances. Neighbors I make small talk with. Co-workers. Sometimes I grab a bagel after yoga with a few of the women from class. I don't have friends like Finn does."

"Can't you just tell him that? If you're marrying him—"

"You don't understand." Maisie stops tapping her foot, and the quiet is almost more deafening than the annoying rhythm. "Finn's not like me. He's got parents who love each other and siblings who get along and a best friend he's known since he was in diapers. He's . . . normal."

"Normal," I repeat, sounding out the syllables like I'm learning a new language. I haven't been *normal* in a long time. "No offense, but I hate him already."

Maisie laughs, showing off the tiny gap that separates her two front teeth. "I'd hate him if I didn't know him. If he wasn't Finn."

The café door opens, and Maisie goes right back to tapping her foot incessantly as a handsome man in a gray T-shirt and running shorts steps inside. He looks to be around thirty, with boy-next-door good looks and a lanky frame.

"Please." Maisie squeezes my hand so hard I think it might break. "I'm not—"

She inhales sharply as the man glances around the café and raises a hand in greeting when he sees her. "I'll pay you," she whispers. "Two hundred bucks."

I pause. I'm generally opposed to accepting money from insane strangers, but my Princess Sparkleheart gig isn't exactly a gold mine. Plus, I have a backlog of student loan debt to catch up on. I lost my job as a reporter at the Columbus lifestyle magazine *Buckeye Buzz* shortly after The Incident, and I'm not proud to say I've defaulted on my loans since. While two hundred dollars is a drop in the bucket of what I owe the U.S. Department of Education, it's still something.

I don't have time to respond to Maisie's offer, because Finn reaches our table in a few smooth strides. He's tall, at least six-one, and towers over Maisie when he leans down to kiss her.

"Finn," Maisie says when he straightens up, "this is Willa. My coffee shop friend."

Finn gives me a warm smile. Up close, his good looks rival Maisie's. His brown eyes bear flecks of gold, and a neatly trimmed beard lends his face an open, relaxed vibe. He looks like a hot, dressed-down lumberjack. "Hiya, Willa."

As I shake his hand reluctantly, Finn notices my overturned muffin on the floor. "Uh-oh. Looks like we've got a bit of a muffin disaster here. Let me know what you had, and I'll grab you another."

I'm disarmed by his use of *hiya* and *muffin disaster*. Surely a killer wouldn't be so damn nice and folksy. Or maybe that's exactly how he'd behave, to trick me into—

"Willa," Maisie says, looking at me with a pleading expression. "Another muffin?"

"Oh. Sure." I blink as Finn continues to smile at me like a good-natured, grown-up Boy Scout. "It was lemon. Thank you."

I watch as Finn takes Maisie's order—a macchiato and a honey-wheat bagel—and strides toward the counter.

"Thank you," Maisie whispers when he's out of earshot. "Thank you so, so much."

I bristle at the assumption that I'll go along with her plan. "I haven't agreed to anything," I retort, although I do appreciate the re-placement muffin. With my bare-bones budget, little indulgences are rare for me.

"I'm not even a good actress," I continue, remembering my many terrible performances as Princess Sparkleheart. "I'm atrocious."

"But it's not really acting. We *are* at a coffee shop, and we're sort of friends now."

"We are *not* friends." I don't know this bizarre woman, and I don't want to. Besides, I don't need friends. I don't *want* any. Friends make you feel safe and warm and wonderful, make you laugh until your sides hurt. And then they rip it all away by banging the love of your life.

"Right." Maisie ducks her head like I've wounded her, and a wave of regret washes over me. Maybe she really is crazy, or maybe she's just lonely.

And *lonely* is something I can relate to. *Crazy* might be, too.

"Lemon muffin, round two." Finn reappears with a tray of baked goods and sets a brand-new muffin in front of me.

"Thanks," I say as he settles into the seat beside Maisie and takes a sip of coffee.

"It's nice to finally meet you," he says, smiling at me with that good-guy smile. I bet he helps old ladies across the street and holds doors open for moms with strollers. Not that it matters; Max used to volunteer at the Broad Street Food Pantry, and he still turned out to be a douche.

Maisie watches me expectantly, but I have no clue how to respond to Finn, so I just stuff my mouth with muffin.

"I was in the area for work and thought I'd stop by and say hi," Finn continues. "You've been meeting Maisie here for Monday coffee for what, a year?"

"Almost," Maisie replies, her gaze darting between her fiancé and me as I cough on my mocha. "We love the muffins."

"We do," I chime in midcough, figuring I can't play mute forever.

Even though I haven't finished my last mouthful of muffin, I take another nervous bite and give Finn a thumbs-up. "Mmm, muffin." Realizing I've just done a modified Homer Simpson impression, I cover my mouth with my hand and finish chewing. "Nice to meet you, too."

"You never come this way for work," Maisie says. "What a nice surprise."

Finn takes her hand in his and rubs her knuckles with his thumb. "I work from home most days," he tells me. "Unless I have to meet a client."

"What do you do?" I ask, praying he doesn't reply with a serial-killer-type profession like taxidermist or circus clown. But when Maisie's eyes widen in alarm, I realize I've already goofed up. If she and I were friends who met every Monday for a year, I would know what her fiancé does for a living. Wouldn't I? "I mean, Maisie's told me a little bit about your work," I continue, trying to cover my tracks. "But I'd like to hear more about it."

"It's IT stuff mostly, with a bit of data analysis thrown in. Nothing as interesting as Maisie's job."

"Yes," I agree. "Maisie's line of work is very interesting." Considering I have no clue what Maisie does—*she* could be the taxidermist, for all I know—I think I'm doing a damn fine acting job.

"What about you?" Finn asks. "I don't think Maisie ever told me."

I pause midchew. If someone had asked me that question five months ago, I'd have had an answer I was proud to deliver. *I write for* Buckeye Buzz, *I'd say. I have a blog, too, where I write about Columbus restaurants and events and everything that makes the city tick. You should check it out.* Now, however, I have to confess to my current stint as Princess Sparkleheart.

"I work in the . . . entertainment industry," I say after a long, awkward pause.

A look of mild surprise crosses Maisie's face. I realize the vagueness of my answer, paired with my reluctant tone, might give Finn the impression that I'm a stripper.

"I'm not a stripper," I add quickly. "Not that there's anything wrong with being a stripper. I'm all for women doing whatever they want with their own bodies. And men too. Because men can also be, you know, strippers."

I feel myself shrinking in my chair as each word ekes out of my mouth. Clearly, it's been so long since I've socialized with anyone besides Stacey, Glory, and my nieces that my brain's forgotten how.

"So you're not a stripper," Finn repeats, but his smile exudes warmth, not mean-spiritedness. "We have that in common. I did dance to Ginuwine's 'Pony' at a summer camp talent show once, though."

"He did," Maisie agrees. "His brother showed me the video. He wore a fedora and everything."

"I got second place, so I'm kind of famous."

I can't help but relax at their banter. "I actually work for my sister's event-planning company. There are no fedoras involved, usually, but it keeps me busy."

It doesn't actually keep me that busy, as evidenced by the fact that I spent the last month watching every episode of *Hoarders*, but they don't need to know that.

"Event planning sounds like fun," Finn says. "Is it mostly weddings?"

"Weddings are just the start of it. My sister also does birthday parties, bar mitzvahs, divorce parties, everything you can think of. Last month she organized a puppy shower. Like a baby shower for a puppy."

"That's the best idea I've ever heard," Maisie says. She squeezes Finn's hand. "We should have had a puppy shower when we rescued Pippa. Talk about a missed opportunity."

"There's always her next birthday," Finn points out. "Three is a big year."

Despite my firm belief that people are garbage and never to be trusted, I find myself liking Maisie and Finn.

"Three is twenty-one in dog years," I say. "Which means she can have her first drink."

"We should have margaritas," Maisie suggests. "Pippa's definitely a tequila kind of girl."

Finn nods in agreement and sips his coffee. "Speaking of event planning, Willa, I'm sure Maisie's told you about the recent wedding drama?"

I try to glance at Maisie furtively, but Finn's eyes are on me.

"Um, yes," I stammer. "I've heard. From Maisie. About the recent drama. It's all so . . . dramatic." I take a giant slurp of my mocha as an excuse to stop talking, but it's so cold that I think my throat might freeze over. I toss back a chunk of muffin and hope for the best.

Finn nods like I've given an entirely normal answer. "When we heard Angela couldn't make it to the wedding, Maisie was so bummed."

I nod as if I have any clue who the hell Angela is. "Yeah, I felt bad that she was so bummed," I echo. "Like, the most bummed."

"Definitely the most bummed. And then the whole disaster with the venue roof. But that's why we decided to move the ceremony to my parents' backyard. No roof necessary." He smiles while I nod along like an idiot.

"And since we're having it at Finn's parents', Pippa can come, too," Maisie adds.

"Wonderful." Pools of sweat start to gather under my arms, and I wish I'd applied an extra layer of deodorant. "Hurray for Pippa."

"Do you have any pets, Willa?" Finn asks.

"I have—" I was about to say I have a dog named Duckie, but I don't. Duckie, the eight-year-old beagle mix Max got when we were in college, used to be attached to my hip. I haven't seen him since The Incident. The thought of his warm doggy breath and the little groan he made when I scratched his belly stabs right through my chest where my heart used to be, and I swallow hard.

"No," I try again. "My sister has an Irish setter named Nala, though, so I'm a dog aunt. And a human aunt."

"That's—" Finn's phone rings, interrupting his response. He raises a hand in apology and answers the call while Maisie gives me an encouraging nod.

"Well," Finn says after he ends the brief conversation, "duty calls. I have to go to the office to deal with a virus issue. I'm sorry I couldn't stay longer, but I'm glad I got to meet you, Willa."

"I'm glad I got to meet you, too," I say. It's not a total lie. Maisie might be insane, but she and Finn seem nice. Any couple who wants their dog at their wedding can't be too horrible—even if I don't believe in love and weddings anymore.

"Can I get you two another round of muffins before I leave?"

We decline, and Finn presses a hand to Maisie's cheek and leans down to kiss her. It's a sweet, intimate moment, and I'd feel a little pang of nostalgia if my heart weren't cold and dead.

When the door closes behind Finn, Maisie lets out a long exhale and leans back in her chair as if she's just run a marathon. "Thank you, Willa. Thank you."

I finish my last bite of muffin and dust the crumbs off my lap. "For what it's worth, the truth always comes out in the end. Every single time. You should just be honest with him."

"I know what it's worth," Maisie says brightly, reaching into her purse. She pulls out a wallet and removes a handful of bills. "It's worth two hundred dollars. As promised."

Her brow furrows as she counts out a stack of twenties. "Damn, I only have a hundred and forty. I forgot I bought groceries with cash yesterday."

Before I can tell her not to worry about it, because a little acting practice might actually help my miserable Princess Sparkleheart routine, she presses the bills into my hand. "I'll Venmo you the rest."

"I don't use Venmo." I'd deleted the app in my social media purge.

"You don't use Venmo?" Maisie's eyes widen as if I've sprouted a third boob. "Well, what's your address?"

"This really isn't necess—"

"A deal's a deal, and I keep my word." Maisie raises her chin a few inches higher.

"I really don't—"

"I can't stand being indebted to people," Maisie insists. Her tone carries a note of finality. "I promised you two hundred, and I need to give you that."

I consider my plunging credit score and relent. I don't typically give my address to strangers, but Glory and Stacey have an excellent home security system. Besides, Maisie seems relatively harmless—at least for a coffee shop table crasher.

I narrate my address as she types it into her phone. When I've finished, she stands up and slips her purse over one shoulder.

"Well," I say, balling a napkin in my fist, "good luck with the wedding. Fingers crossed for no more roofing issues. Or Angela ones."

Maisie smiles, and in a rabbity-quick motion, steps around the table to gather me in a hug. I stiffen as she flings her arms around me, the lilac scent of her perfume filling my nostrils. It's been so long since

I've been touched by someone who's not Kaya, Maeve, or Lucy that the sensation of another body against mine feels foreign.

"Thank you," Maisie whispers against my hair. "If we ever have a party for Pippa, you're definitely invited."

Before I can respond, she releases me, grabs her macchiato from the table, and waves as she hurries toward the door. Then, as fast as she appeared, Maisie's gone.

5

It's not until I'm sitting in my next-door neighbor Ruthie's kitchen, helping to arrange a charcuterie board, that Zachary sends me an apology text and follows up with a call. I send the call to voice mail and set my phone facedown on the counter, grumbling. "Screw you, buddy," I say, popping an olive into my mouth. "I've already forgotten you." Maybe I'm not the catch I once was, but even Princess Sparkleheart has too much pride to tolerate a guy who stands her up.

Ruthie, wearing a pair of houndstooth slacks and a white tank top that shows off her wiry arms, grabs an oven mitt. "Forgotten what? Don't say the artichoke dip, because I will murder you." A still-practicing ballet instructor and widow to one of Dublin's most well-respected cardiologists, Ruthie is one of the coolest people I've ever met. She drives a silver Porsche, led a busload of badass seniors to the Women's March, and has three tattoos, all of which she got in the last decade.

"Easy with the threats. No, I didn't forget the dip. Stacey and Glory are bringing it over with the cake. I meant I already forgot about the jerkface who never showed up to our date."

"Well, you're right to forget him. Men are boring, anyway."

"What about Herman?" Ruthie's late husband Herman is one of her favorite discussion topics. He died of a sudden stroke the summer before Glory and Stacey moved in next door, so I never got to meet him, but pictures of him and Ruthie and their two now-grown children fill her home. Unlike elegant Ruthie, whose decades of ballet training and long silver hair have given her exceptional posture and a perpetual air of sophistication, Herman was fond of T-shirts and tube socks. He looked like the kind of guy who spent all his free time fishing and listening to baseball on the radio, and it's a wonder to me that he and Ruthie ever crossed paths.

"Herman was not boring. But he was the exception, you know that." Ruthie removes a sheet of veggie flatbread from the oven, and the aroma of cheesy zucchini fills the air.

"Stupid Zachary is definitely not the exception. And he doesn't look *that* much like Tom Hardy." I pick at the label on the olive jar, peeling it away from the glass. "Herman would never have stood a girl up."

Smiling, Ruthie transfers the flatbreads from the baking sheet to a cooling rack. "No, he wouldn't have. Herman was always on time. And he had the two most important traits a man can have: he was both interesting and kind. You can always find a man who's one or the other, but both? That's the holy grail."

I nibble on a baguette slice. "I thought Spanx were the holy grail."

Ruthie shoots me a look. "Spanx are the holy grail of shapewear, Wilhelmina. Herman was the holy grail of men." She glances at the empty chair next to mine before resuming her work on the flatbreads. "Interesting and kind. That's what you need to look for. *After* you get your life back on track, I mean."

"I'm not trying to date, Ruthie. I'm trying to bang. Banging is a good distraction."

Ruthie shakes her head. "Don't say 'bang.' It's so pedestrian. You are not pedestrian."

I assemble a row of crackers and cheeses on the charcuterie tray. "The highlight of my week was stumbling onto an episode of *The Office* I hadn't seen before. That's pretty much the definition of pedestrian."

"I'd say the highlight of your week was meeting an intriguing stranger at the coffee shop. That's much more interesting than a sitcom episode."

I scoff at her. "Listen, it was the one where Dwight starts a fire in the office. Hilarious. I have no idea how I missed it before."

Ruthie stares at me without blinking until I shrug. "Fine. I guess meeting Maisie was a little bit more interesting. But only because it was bizarre. Who offers someone two hundred bucks to pretend to be their friend?"

"Someone who's lonely, I presume. People will do a lot of things out of loneliness." She goes quiet for a moment, and I wonder what it's like for her to live in this big house all alone, with its six bedrooms and two fireplaces and no Herman.

"Here," I say quietly. "Have a Triscuit."

Ruthie accepts the cracker and nibbles on it. "I think you should write a blog post about it."

"The Triscuit?"

Ruthie rolls her eyes at me. "Don't be a smartass, Willa. You should write a blog post about your meeting with Maisie. Change her name, make her anonymous. I think a lot of people would relate to the theme of loneliness, of being desperate to belong. It's a universal feeling."

Suddenly without appetite, I put down the cheese cubes. I can't stand how Stacey and Glory and even Ruthie hound me about my blog. They all insist that getting back to my writing will help me heal. Move on. But I've *tried* to sit down and write, to take my broken heart and turn it into art like the famous Carrie Fisher quote advises. So far, however, my heart is still shattered, and I haven't written a single word that's worthy of being called art. I'm too embarrassed to post any of my feeble writing attempts on the blog, anyway. Nobody wants to read a series of haikus about my journey into the wonderful world of SSRIs.

"I don't want to talk about the blog. Besides, you know what my plan is. And that's what I really need to focus on."

Ruthie's the only person who knows that as soon as I save enough money to catch up on my loans, I'm moving away from Columbus. I haven't decided where I'll move to, exactly, but it'll be someplace where no one bothers me about my blog. Where I don't have to drive by the Mediterranean restaurant where Max and I gorged on gyros and fire fries every Friday, or the dive bar where Sarah and I played darts twice a month. Someplace where the park Max proposed to me at isn't eight miles from my bedroom, and where the possibility of running into Sarah at a six-year-old's birthday party doesn't exist. Maybe then I'll find my voice again. Maybe every time I sit down to write, dread won't creep into my stomach and leave my fingers paralyzed.

I need to move someplace free of the old Willa. Someplace I can let go of the anguish that's suffocating me.

And preferably someplace with a beach.

"If you truly want to move, I can't stop you." Ruthie leans against the counter and sips her glass of pinot noir. "But you should know that I disapprove."

"You also disapproved of my outfit yesterday, so pardon me for not being shocked."

Ruthie narrows her eyes at me. "You were wearing a T-shirt with Tweety Bird on it."

I shrug. "It was two dollars at Goodwill! And Tweety makes Lucy smile."

"You were wearing it with *sweat pants*, Willa."

"It's loungewear, *Ruthie*," I retort, mimicking her dramatic tone. "It's *comfortable*."

"Nobody gets ahead by being comfortable."

"I'm trying to get away, not ahead. And are we talking about fashion or life in general?"

"Both." Ruthie examines the charcuterie board I've assembled. "Needs more cheese, I think. People can never get enough cheese."

I nod and add another row of yellow cheddar and Brie, then lean back to survey my work. If I still had my Instagram account, my forty thousand followers would have loved my culinary masterpiece.

"Perfect." Ruthie slips into the chair next to mine and crunches down on a slice of green pepper. "You want to know what I think?"

"Not particularly but something tells me I'm about to find out anyway." I laugh as Ruthie, usually the height of sophistication, sticks her tongue out at me. Her hair is pulled back into a neat ballerina's bun, and the wrinkles that line her forehead only add to her beauty.

"I think you should tell Stacey about your plan."

I try not to choke on the half-chewed Triscuit in my mouth. "Are you serious? Telling her I want to move away would be like telling you I'm not gonna vote in the next election."

Ruthie cries out as if I've stabbed her. "Women died for your right to vote, Wilhelmina Callister. They sacrificed their lives for you, and you can't spare ten minutes of your *Hiders*-watching time to get up off your bum and go vote?"

"It's *Hoarders*," I argue. "And of course I'm going to vote. I was just giving an example."

Ruthie takes a series of deep breaths and stares up at the ceiling for a solid ten seconds. "Not funny. I was about to slap you upside the head with one of the flatbreads."

"And that's exactly how Stacey would react if I told her. So you get my point."

"React if you told me what?"

I whip my head around to see Stacey, Glory, and the girls traipsing into Ruthie's kitchen. Stacey balances baby Lucy on one hip and looks at me expectantly while Maeve gallops along behind her.

"Oh, nothing," I say quickly, leaping up from my chair to take Lucy into my arms. "Just a weird encounter at the coffee shop. I'll tell you later."

"Liar," Ruthie whispers. I scowl at her and then cover Lucy's cheeks and forehead in kisses.

"Aunt Willa," Maeve says, tugging at the hem of my shirt, "there's a Littlefoot in the backyard."

"A brontosaurus? In Ruthie's backyard?" I make my eyes go wide with wonder.

Maeve bounces up and down on her toes. "Yes! Will you help me catch him?"

"No, Maeve," Kaya whines, entering the kitchen behind her sisters. She clutches her dad's hand, and I wave to my ex-brother-in-law. "I wanna show Aunt Willa what I got at the zoo."

"Why don't you show me what you got first, and then we'll help Maeve with the Littlefoot?" I suggest, trying to fend off an impending sister showdown.

Kaya proudly reveals her souvenir, an oversized magnifying glass, and we all agree that it's a useful tool for tracking dinosaurs. I usher the girls into Ruthie's backyard, leaving Stacey, Glory, and Nate to enjoy some kid-free time with Ruthie. I usually spend most of Ruthie's Monday game nights playing with my nieces; it gives my sister a break, and I'm a terrible charades player, anyway.

"There it is! The Littlefoot!" Maeve cries. She and Kaya scamper past Ruthie's massive fire pit and toward the willow tree at the edge of the yard, their little-girl limbs a tangle of motion.

"A footprint!" Kaya exclaims, bending toward the ground with her magnifying glass.

"I love you girls," I whisper to Lucy, who ignores me in favor of cooing at a squirrel. "So, so much."

Moving away will be difficult in only one aspect: I won't get to see my nieces every day anymore. I won't wake up to Kaya trying to draw butterflies on my arms with a Magic Marker, or to Maeve crawling into bed with me in the middle of the night, her face tear-streaked from a nightmare. I won't get to read to them every night before bed, Maeve trying to hold little Lucy still while Kaya sounds out the words to their favorite books. I won't get to cuddle them on their good days, or their bad days, or all the days in between.

But I don't want them to know me like this. I don't want them to know an aunt who has depression and anxiety and negative dollars in her bank account. I want to show them that I can bounce back from being betrayed by the people I trusted most. That I can be strong and happy and whole again. I want to be the aunt and sister my family deserves.

But to do that, I have to leave.

6

"Aunt Willa," a tiny voice whispers. "There's a Sharptooth in the living room."

I pull my comforter tighter over my head and try to go back to sleep.

"It's a Sharptooth," she repeats. "Its teeth are very, very sharp."

I open my eyes slowly, letting them adjust to the sunlight streaming through the window. The light isn't harsh, so it can't even be noon yet. "What time is it?"

Maeve, wearing a Little Mermaid T-shirt and no pants, pokes me in the head with her Nerf gun. "Time to get the Sharptooth. Duh."

Sighing, I rub my eyes and push the comforter off me. It's Tuesday, the morning after game night, and I have nothing on my itinerary except watching shitty reality TV and helping Stacey make calls for Celebration! Events.

"Aunt *Willa*," Maeve repeats, exasperated. "Come on!" Her hair sticks out from her head in seven different directions, lending her a striking resemblance to Edward Scissorhands.

"Morning," Kaya calls from the hallway, where she dribbles a soccer ball back and forth. Her purple soccer jersey almost reaches her knees, and she looks so cute in her shin guards and cleats that I almost don't mind when her right foot misdirects the ball and slams it straight at me. Almost. The ball rockets into my abdomen, knocking the wind out of me, and I double over until I can breathe again, counting to ten so that I don't lose my shit at Kaya.

"Sorry. Mommy says you have a visitor," Kaya continues while I rub my stomach where the ball hit me. "She says you need to come downstairs right away."

"A visitor? Who?" I ask with a wince. I scour my brain, trying to think of anyone who might want to visit me this early on a Tuesday morning.

Kaya, ever the helpful child, shrugs and sends the ball sailing into the playroom.

"I told you," Maeve insists. "It's the Sharptooth. It's here to eat you."

I stopped hanging out with all of my old friends after The Incident, so it can't be any of them, and I don't remember entering any Publishers Clearing House contests, so it's probably not someone carrying a giant check. I think of my defaulted student loans and panic.

"Is it a man in a suit?" I ask Kaya, the words running together as my heart rate spikes. "Did he mention anything about subsidized loans or dragging me to jail?"

"Mommy didn't say. She and Glory just said to come get you." Kaya, who doesn't seem to care that I might be arrested and thrown into the slammer, doesn't take her eyes off the soccer ball.

Maybe Stacey and Glory have finally had enough of me and decided to stage an intervention. Maybe the visitor is a therapist, or a representative from some kind of summer camp for adult losers in need of tough love.

"Quick, tell me," I say to Kaya. "Was the visitor carrying a bro-chure?"

"A bro-what?" she asks, wrinkling her forehead. Before I can an-swer, she scampers after her ball with Maeve trailing behind her.

I hurry to the bathroom and brush my teeth as fast as possible, then creep back into the hallway and lean over the stairwell to catch a glimpse downstairs. Unfortunately, the living room and foyer are empty.

"Willa! Are you coming?" Stacey calls.

Realizing I don't have an escape route, I accept my fate and trudge downstairs. I follow voices through the foyer, past the dining room and its gigantic farmhouse-style table that could seat a dozen people, and into the kitchen.

"Maisie!" She's sitting at Stacey's breakfast bar, one leg crossed neatly over the other. A plate piled with pancakes sits on the coun-tertop in front of her. "What the hell are you doing here?"

"Willa! Manners." Stacey scolds me with the same tone she uses whenever the girls try to ride Nala like a horse. My sister, in her daytime business attire of white linen pants, a pink button-down top, and heels, shoots me a look.

"Yeah, Willa. I know it's been a while since you've had friends over, but geez. A warm welcome wouldn't kill you," Glory teases. It takes all my restraint not to pick up a banana from the fruit bowl and fling it at her.

"Oh, it's okay. Willa wasn't expecting me." Maisie shrugs and takes a bite of her syrup-drowned pancake. "Is that cinnamon I taste, or nutmeg?"

"Both, actually. But just a dash of nutmeg." Stacey beams and flips another pancake onto her plate.

"Excellent," Maisie says. "It really enhances the—"

"Maisie," I say to stop her before she gets too comfortable, "can I talk to you? Outside?" I'm not sure what the heck she's doing here, but she can't just barge into my sister's house and eat my sister's pancakes like it's nothing. That's something only a friend should feel comfortable doing, and like I told her at the coffee shop, we are *not* friends.

"Huh? Oh, sure. Yeah." She glances from me to her plate and back to me. "Mind if I bring my pancakes with me?"

"Of course she doesn't mind," Stacey assures her as if I'm a small child who can't speak for myself. "It's nice to have someone up and eating breakfast with us before noon." She raises her eyebrows at me to remind me that I suck.

"Oh, I've always been an early riser," Maisie says. "I can't imagine sleeping until noon."

"Can you imagine wearing a Tweety Bird T-shirt as an adult?" Glory asks, and this time I do grab a banana and toss it at her. She catches it without turning her head to see it.

Maisie picks up her plate and smiles at me like we're the best of friends. "Lead the way, Willa."

"Why don't you head out to the deck?" I open the back door and escort her out, then rush back into the kitchen.

"What were you *thinking*, Stacey?"

Confused, my sister looks up from the strawberries she's slicing. "Was I not supposed to mention the nutmeg? It's not exactly a secret."

I marvel at her obliviousness. "No, I mean, what were you thinking letting that woman into your house?"

Stacey drops another handful of berries onto the cutting board and stares at me. "What do you mean? Your friend rang the doorbell

54

and asked if you were home. She said the peonies I planted out front were pretty. I like her."

"She's not my friend! She's the crazy lady from the coffee shop Ruthie and I told you about last night."

"*That's* the woman who paid you to pretend to be her friend?" Glory peers out the kitchen window, trying to catch a glimpse of Maisie with this new information coloring her perception. "But she seems so normal. Huh. I guess you never really know about people."

"Listen, I'm not saying what she did isn't strange, but it's not like she paid you to drown a kitten," Stacey says, pointing the tip of the knife at me. "Besides, when's the last time you made a new friend? You're not exactly a social butterfly anymore, either."

"I haven't made any new friends because I don't want to. Because people are awful and terrible."

Stacey rolls her eyes. "I love you, Willa, but the woe-is-me routine is tired. Glory and I are people. Are we terrible and awful?"

"You have your moments," I say.

"Maybe Maisie's a little different, but who isn't? I think you should give her a chance. People can surprise you."

I nod, because I know *exactly* how people can surprise you.

"I meant people can surprise you in good ways," Stacey adds softly, reading my expression. "I wasn't trying to be cruel."

"I know you weren't." I sigh and motion toward the backyard patio. "If I'm not back in ten minutes, send Nala out to sniff for my body."

"Will do," Stacey agrees.

"Play nice," Glory adds.

Flashing them both my middle finger, I step out of the kitchen and into the morning sunlight.

7

Like the rest of their home, Stacey and Glory's backyard looks like it belongs in a layout of *Architectural Digest*. Landscaped greenery paired with a set of hammocks makes the space feel like a bohemian dream. Maisie sits at the deck's hexagon-shaped picnic table, shaded by a giant yellow umbrella.

"This yard is amazing," she observes. "I could curl up in one of those hammocks for hours." She swallows a bite of pancake and watches me as I take a seat across from her. "I hope it's okay that I came."

I shrug, unsure of what to say. It's been months since I've had regular, sustained conversations with adults who aren't Stacey, Glory, or Ruthie, and I think I've forgotten how.

Maisie's traded yesterday's tie-waist dress for head-to-toe khaki, including khaki shorts and a button-down. Only a green polkadotted ribbon wrapped around her bouncy ponytail breaks from the onslaught of beige.

She removes a white envelope from her shirt pocket and slides it across the table. "I brought you the sixty dollars I owe you. You can count it."

I glance at the money in surprise. I hadn't expected her to actually mail it, let alone deliver it in person. The fact that she kept her word even when she didn't have to makes me suspicious. I'm so accustomed to people letting me down that Maisie's sincerity unnerves me. "Thanks, but that wasn't necessary."

Maisie nods. "Yes, it was."

She eats in silence for a moment, and I try to remember Glory's instructions to play nice. "Can I ask why you didn't just mail it? And can I also ask why you're dressed like an Eagle Scout?"

Maisie laughs and wipes syrup from her mouth. "This is my work outfit."

"Your job requires you to dress like Steve Irwin? Not that I'm judging," I add quickly. "I loved Steve Irwin. What a guy."

Maisie glances at me in amusement. "I'm a habitat specialist at the zoo. We don't actually have to wear khaki, but it's practical for the work I do. Plus, I also loved Steve Irwin." She pokes at the remaining bits of her pancakes with her fork. "About the money . . . the reason I didn't mail it is that I wanted to see you again."

I half wonder if Maisie's about to admit that she has a crush on me. Maybe she's got a thing for disaffected, down-on-their-luck party princesses.

"As much as I sound like one of those idiot contestants on *The Bachelor*," Maisie continues, "I feel like we had a connection yesterday. Like we could actually be friends, given the right circumstances."

Her comment almost reaches the beating remnants of my cold, dead heart, but I won't let myself get sucked in. I know what friendship can do to me. "I appreciate that, but I don't actually do the whole friend thing."

She studies me with a confused look on her face. "The whole friend thing? Like what, having them?"

"Exactly." I shift on the picnic bench, suddenly uncomfortable. "I had a best friend once. For my whole life. Until she wasn't my best friend anymore. After that, I realized I don't need friends. I have my sister and my nieces and myself, and that's enough."

Maisie sets down her fork. "Forgive me, but that's really dumb."

"Excuse me?"

"I'm not saying *you're* dumb. I'm saying that your approach to friendship, writing it off like that, is silly. I got salmonella from eating romaine lettuce once, but that doesn't mean I'll never eat salad again." Maisie rabbit-taps her foot against the deck.

My body tenses, and I take a deep breath to relax. "Well, I think salad's boring. Besides, who are you to give advice on friendship? It's not like you're exactly swimming in besties." The instant disappearance of Maisie's smile threatens to fill me with regret, but I won't let it. Her sunshine-and-rainbows outlook on friendship is one I shared before The Incident, but I'm not so naïve anymore, and comparing the death of a friendship to food poisoning is a gross oversimplification that pisses me off. Salmonella might steal your lunch for a few hours, but the betrayal of a friend will steal your trust forever.

"You're right," she says after a moment, her voice almost a whisper. "You're absolutely right. I'm sorry. I shouldn't have come. I should have put the money in the mail. That would have been the normal thing to do."

I don't point out that the normal thing to do would have been to not approach me at the coffee shop in the first place.

"I'm sorry," Maisie repeats, standing up from the table so hastily that she bumps her knee against the bench. She winces, and I can't tell if the pain is from her knee or our conversation. I watch as she hobbles away from the table, and I can't stop guilt from washing over me. Her rose-colored-glasses view of friendship might annoy me, but it's not her fault I have crippling trust issues.

"Maisie, wait. Sit back down." I may be a twenty-nine-year-old party princess, but I'm not an asshole. "I'm sorry. I'm not exactly an expert on normal lately. Or friendship. Or being out of bed before noon."

Maisie tucks one arm behind her back and studies me. "You sure?"

Nodding, I motion to the table.

She sits and folds her hands over her lap, not touching her pancakes. "You know, after I left the coffee shop, I realized where I knew you from."

I sigh. "It wasn't yoga, was it?"

Maisie shakes her head. "You're Willa Callister, from *Willa Leads the Way*. I used to read your blog every day. I followed you on Instagram, too. You were, like, the social media queen of Columbus."

An instinctive thrill runs through me before I can quash it. I used to love interacting with my Instagram followers and blog readers. The fact that I could connect with so many people through my writing made the long hours bent over my laptop worthwhile. I miss that connection more desperately than I want to admit, and I miss writing almost as much as I miss having a best friend. But I don't have anything to write about anymore. Nothing that the Maisies of the world would want to read about, anyway. My blog followers knew me as always-up-for-adventure Willa. Planning-the-perfect-wedding Willa. No one has the ramblings of no-friends-besides-Nala Willa at the top of their to-read list.

"Things are different now," I say. "My blogging days are over."

"Why?" Maisie's tone is gentle, the kind you'd use to speak to a frightened animal. "I won't judge. It's just, your posts made your life seem amazing. I can't imagine giving that up."

A rush of images floods my mind: sunny, sepia-toned pictures of Max and me devouring Belgian waffles at the North Market and sipping Guinness at the Dublin Irish Festival. Me outside the White of Dublin bridal shop, holding a glass of champagne and beaming alongside Glory, Stacey, and Sarah right before I picked out my wedding dress. Sarah and me and a cluster of our girlfriends clutching salty caramel cones from Handel's, the ice cream dripping onto our fingers. Carefully edited, patiently filtered images of Sarah and me. Of Max and me. Of Sarah and Max.

And then, nothing. The end of the blog updates and Instagram posts. The end of the old Willa.

I shrug, unable to find the right words to explain to Maisie how my life crashed down around me. "I didn't really have much of a choice. One day, I woke up and I just . . . couldn't do it anymore."

I leave out the rest of that day, refusing to tell Maisie about The Incident, or how the weeks afterward are a hazy blur of sleep and disbelief and Stacey murmuring comforting words into my ear and begging me to get out of bed.

I focus on a bluebird pecking at Stacey's bird feeder and avoid direct eye contact with Maisie. "It's really not something I want to talk about."

She nods. "Okay."

I do a double take. I'm so used to Stacey pestering me to talk about my feelings and leaving copies of *Caterpillar to Butterfly: Letting Your Breakup Transform Your Life* on my bed that I don't know how to process Maisie's reaction.

"What do you mean, 'okay'?"

She shrugs. "I mean okay. Trust me, I have plenty of stuff I'd rather die than talk about. Besides, at the risk of sounding like a narcissist, I didn't come here to talk about you. I came to talk about my predicament."

"Predicament? I thought you just came to drop off the money."

Maisie, having regained her appetite, resumes eating her pancakes. "What I'm about to say is going to sound crazy."

"Crazier than tricking your fiancé into thinking we're old friends?"

Maisie's cheeks redden with embarrassment. "Yes. Significantly."

"If it's anything involving a flash mob, I definitely don't—"

"Iwantyoutobemybridesmaid." Maisie's words, jumbled with the chewing of pancake, are indecipherable.

"Come again?"

She swallows and takes a deep breath to steel herself. "I want you to be my bridesmaid."

My jaw drops in shock. "You *what*?"

"I want you to be my bridesmaid." Maisie drops her fork and taps both sets of fingers on the table, the rhythm nervous and rapid.

"You want me to be your *bridesmaid*?" I repeat, certain I've misheard. There's no way she's asking a stranger to be an integral part of her wedding day.

Maisie scowls. "Well, you don't have to shout like I asked you to help me hide a body."

"Right, sorry." I take a deep breath and try again. "You're aware that we don't even know each other, right? I don't even know your last name or how old you are. I don't know the first thing about you, which is kind of a prerequisite for being in your *wedding*."

"My name is Margaret Eileen Mitchell. Yes, like the *Gone with the Wind* Margaret Mitchell. Hence why I go by Maisie. I'm twenty-eight years old. I love working with animals and I'm vegetarian and I can't wink. So those are a few things about me." Her fingertips drum the tabletop faster. "What else do you want to know?"

I stare at her for a long moment, processing the details of her life that she deems worthy of me knowing. "You really can't wink?"

"That's what you took away from that?" Maisie sighs. "Look, my wedding is in three months, and my friend Angela from work can't be a bridesmaid anymore. She got picked to go to the Galápagos Islands to research marine iguanas, which is amazing, but kind of sucks for me personally."

"So have one less person in your bridal party," I suggest. "Or ask another friend."

"You don't understand," Maisie says, pushing her plate away. "Angie and I aren't even particularly close. I asked her because I like her a lot, and because I really, really needed a fourth bridesmaid to match Finn's four groomsmen. Like I told you at the coffee shop, I don't have a lot of friends. I'm not like Finn."

"Oh right, Mr. Popular." My tone is more sarcastic than intended. "Why don't you just talk to him? Tell him you'll have a lopsided number in your party. Or just ditch the whole bridesmaid/groomsman stuff altogether. It's not the 1950s anymore. You could have your dog officiate the wedding and nobody would think twice about it."

"I did suggest having Pippa as my fourth bridesmaid," Maisie says. "Finn's mom, Mrs. Forsythe, thought that was hilarious. She basically turned purple when she realized I was serious."

"You call your future mother-in-law Mrs. Forsythe? What is she, your headmistress? Does she not have a first name?"

"It's Victoria. Anyway, Finn's parents are pretty traditional. And they're paying for the wedding, so Mrs. Forsythe wants everything to be perfect. So do I, of course."

I remember Max's mother, who once referred to my blogging hobby as juvenile despite the fact that the advertising profits paid half our rent every month. "Well, it sounds like your perfect and her perfect are two different things."

Maisie shrugs. "Finn's family is very close-knit. I want to be close to them like he is. My family is . . . different."

"Most families are different," I say, thinking of my divorced, both-remarried parents, and of Glory and Stacey, and of my sister's harmonious co-parenting relationship with Nate.

"The other women in my bridal party are great, don't get me wrong. There's Lorene, Finn's older sister; Jenna, my friend from barre class; and Rose, who's Finn and Lorene's cousin and my friend, too. But I need someone I can count on, who will be there for me to make sure everything goes perfectly. Someone I can trust to have my back."

I don't trust anyone anymore, but I'm not sure how to tell Maisie that without sounding like an ice-cold cynic. "You don't have, like, a sister or something? A distant cousin? A pal from the dog park you've met more than twice?"

"Willa, please." Maisie's voice rings with desperation, as if she's on her deathbed and begging me to donate a lifesaving kidney. "This wedding has to be flawless, and it can't be if I don't have a bridesmaid I can count on no matter what."

Her dramatic delivery makes it sound like she's planning a heist instead of a wedding, and I study her skeptically. "And you think I, a complete and total stranger with whom you've spent no more than eighteen minutes, am someone you can trust during what seems to be the most important event of your life?"

"Yes," Maisie says. "Because I'll pay you to do it. I'll pay you a lot of money."

I wait for her to start laughing and give away the joke, but her jaw is set in a firm line.

"I'm sorry," I say finally, "but are you a drug dealer? Not that I'm disparaging the all-khaki ensemble, because you pull it off better than I ever could, but I wasn't aware that working at the zoo was a lucrative position."

Maisie gasps like my question isn't valid. "For your information, I make a very decent wage."

"As a drug dealer? Or like, a high-end escort?"

"No, as a *habitat specialist*. Which I already explained to you. I design the exhibits to mirror the animal's natural environment as closely as poss— Anyway, that's not important right now. What's important is that I'm *not* a drug dealer, but I *am* offering you five thousand dollars to be in my wedding."

I cross my arms over my chest in disbelief. "Excuse me? Did you miscount your zeroes?"

"Professional bridesmaid packages can cost up to two thousand dollars. I'm offering you more than double the going rate."

I wasn't aware that professional bridesmaids existed, let alone that they have a going rate. "Pardon my rudeness, but you want to pay me five *thousand* dollars to wear a pretty dress for a single day?"

Maisie sets her fork down and dabs at her mouth with a napkin. "Not just a single day. Besides the wedding itself, I'll also need you at all the traditional bridal events, like the shower, the bachelorette party, the rehearsal dinner, et cetera."

"Let me repeat myself: *five grand?* Are you insane?"

She shakes her head. "No, I'm not insane. I've actually thought about this a great deal. I was going to hire a professional bridesmaid, but then I had the good fortune of meeting you at Espresso. And I think we have good chemistry. I also think we're in a position to help each other. I desperately need a reliable bridesmaid, and you desperately need . . . a change."

"A change? Says who?" I may not be living the life of my dreams, but that doesn't mean I need to pair up with some rich, friendless zoo lady. I don't need anyone's pity.

"Your sister, for one. When I knocked on the door and asked for you, she gave me a high five and said, 'Thank God, an actual friend!' Forgive me if I'm wrong, but sisters don't usually react that way when things are going great."

I curse Stacey and roll my eyes. "Listen, you might think we need each other, but we don't. I don't need anyone."

She reaches across the table to grasp my hand. "That's not true. Everyone needs someone."

I tear my hand away like she burned me. "I don't. Not anymore."

"Okay, fine, so you don't need anyone." Maisie shrugs and rests her hands in her lap. "But I do, and I'm not afraid to say it. I need a bridesmaid, and I'm asking you because I think we'd get along well. And because when I moved here three years ago, before I even met Finn, I found your blog and I read it every day. I'd curl up after work with a bowl of popcorn and read about your life and your job and what restaurant you ate at that Friday night, or what cycle studio you tried, or which Columbus bookstore was your favorite. And I felt like I had a friend. Maybe that's stupid or crazy, but I don't care, because it's true."

That had been the goal of my blog: to connect with other people and share my love of Columbus with them. Even though I'm done sharing my life with the whole of the Internet, hearing that my words meant something to someone—to Maisie—thaws a little of the ice around my heart. "It's not stupid," I say softly. "Or crazy."

Maisie's face lights up like a Christmas tree. "So you'll do it? You'll be my bridesmaid?"

Panic rises in my throat, and I swallow hard to get rid of it. The thought of anything wedding related—the chiffon bridesmaid dresses, the bouquets stuffed with tulips and calla lilies, the endless discussions about signature cocktails and table linens and votive centerpieces—makes me light-headed. The Incident happened only six weeks before my wedding to Max was set to take place. I refuse to discuss it and try not to think about it, but the opening notes of "Canon in D" still make my lungs constrict until I can hardly breathe. My canceled wedding, and all the memories that go along with it, are relics of the old Willa. Relics I'm determined to leave behind.

"I can't, Maisie. I'm sorry."

"But why?" Her face can't contain her crushing disappointment, and she slumps forward like I've announced that the zoo is closing forever. "It's the easiest money you'll ever make, I promise. We can just tell people we're old friends from, like, summer camp, or something idyllic like that and we reconnected at the coffee shop last year. And it might not even be a lie after a while, because I bet we'll become actual friends—"

"I told you, I don't need friends."

"Maybe you don't," Maisie says, letting out a shaky breath. "And that's fine. After the wedding, we can part ways, and we never have to speak to each other again. I'll give you half the money up front, if that's what you want." She runs her fingers through her auburn ponytail and flicks it over her shoulder, her lips twitching like she's on the verge of tears. "Willa," she pleads, "this wedding is everything to me. Everything. And call me crazy, but I think we met at that coffee shop for a reason."

"There aren't that many coffee shops in Powell," I point out. "That was the reason."

Maisie's nervous energy radiates off her, and she taps her foot with such force that the table wobbles. "Please. Please just consider my offer."

"I can't do it. I can't pretend to be someone's friend. I can't stand the thought of lying like that."

"It wouldn't be lying. It would be doing a job. It would be a business relationship. Strictly professional."

I sigh and cross my arms over my chest. Besides the fact that I'm uncomfortable with pretending to be someone's friend, I'm not sure how to explain to Maisie that I'm not blogger Willa anymore. I'm not the shiny, happy Instagram influencer with her finger on the pulse of the city and the follower count to prove it.

I don't know how to tell her that she doesn't want a bridesmaid who only washes her hair once a week. Who avoids going out in public too often in case she runs into someone from her old life. Who wants nothing more than to move away from the city she used to love.

"Maisie, I just can't. I—"

She puts a hand up to stop me. "You don't have to decide now. Just consider it, okay? I'll write my number down, and you can call me anytime."

Ignoring my protests, Maisie fishes a scrap of paper and a pen from her purse. When she's finished writing her phone number down, she slides the paper across the table and presses it into my palm.

"I'm not going to call you," I insist. I don't even remember the last time I made a phone call that wasn't related to Celebration! Events or ordering a sausage pizza. "It's not personal, and I hope your wedding is everything you want it to be. I just can't be involved."

Maisie shrugs. "Then I'll be forced to go with a professional bridesmaid. But I'd rather have you." She gives me a little wave as she stands up and smooths the folds of her khaki uniform.

"Hey, Maisie," I say as she heads back toward the house. "Where do you really go on Mondays?" It's a question I've been thinking about since yesterday.

She pauses with one hand on the doorknob. "Huh?"

"At Espresso 22, you said Finn thinks you meet a friend for coffee every Monday. But you don't. So where do you really go?"

An emotion I can't quite identify—guilt or reluctance or maybe just shyness—crosses Maisie's face. Then, quick as a flash, it's replaced by a coy smile. "I'd tell you, but that's something only a bridesmaid gets to know."

She waves good-bye, but I don't wave back. I can't. All this talk of Maisie's wedding drudges up memories I'd do anything to forget, like hiding under the covers while Stacey whispered into the phone, letting sympathetic friends and relatives and the less-sympathetic florist know the wedding was off. Worse, I remember standing behind Sarah as she tried on sangria-colored bridesmaids' dresses, zipping them up for her and telling her how beautiful she looked in them. Telling her how lucky I was to have her as my best friend. The image of her in the dress we finally picked, a one-shoulder gown with a satin sash, knocks the wind out of me, and I'm filled with such longing for my former friend that I have to squint to stop tears from springing to my eyes.

I sniffle and massage the back of my neck, trying to release the ball of tension that's formed there. I don't need Maisie Mitchell and her wedding drama opening my old wounds, reminding me of all that I've lost. I'm different now. I'm new Willa.

And I'm nobody's bridesmaid.

8

That night, for the first time in months, I don't fall asleep to the snappy, upbeat tune of the *Golden Girls* theme song. In fact, I don't fall asleep at all. I lie under my comforter in a ratty OSU tee and yoga pants, cursing Stacey and Glory for setting the thermostat so low. Despite my best efforts, I can't get Maisie's visit off my mind.

Everyone else is fast asleep, tucked away in their bedrooms, and the only sounds I hear are the buzz of cicadas through my open window and Nala's soft, steady breathing at the end of my bed. I try to sleep, but even the three glasses of pinot noir I drank can't wash away the memory of Sarah in her flowing bridesmaid gown.

Sarah and I met in the basement of Our Lady of Perpetual Help church, where our mothers attended a support group for recently divorced women. The poorly lit basement smelled of mildew and incense, and the deacon who ran the group brought crayons, coloring books, and fruit-punch Capri Suns for us poor little children from broken homes. Sarah and I, the only kids there who weren't old enough to sneak cigarettes outside or dumb enough to eat crayons, hit it off immediately. We spent those Tuesday evenings huddled over matching Lisa Frank sticker books, trading stories about our parents' failed marriages and our older sisters' boyfriend drama. Sarah, who carried a stuffed kangaroo toy in the front pocket of her overalls and wore her red hair in two braids like Pippi Longstocking, was unlike anyone I'd ever met. When the deacon caught us pressing oyster crackers into each other's mouths and pretending it was the Body of Christ, a most sacrilegious grievance, Sarah courageously claimed the idea was hers alone. I got off scot-free while she lost her sticker book privileges, and from then on, we were inseparable.

Our friendship lasted through middle school and high school and all the trials that came with it: the fact that Sarah's boobs came in first while I was flat-chested until I was nineteen; the time freshman year when we both had crushes on Steve Bennett and promised that neither of us would make a move on him, as if we knew how to make moves in the first place; my mother's remarriage to my stepdad, and the four times Sarah's mom got remarried and redivorced. In fourth grade, when I had an appendectomy and was mortified about going to Megan Maltzer's pool party with an obvious scar, Sarah used a red Sharpie to draw a matching line over her own abdomen. And in sixth grade, when gap-toothed Chuckie Thomas made fun of Sarah's occasionally lazy eye, I responded with a left hook to his face. Chuckie never spoke a word to her again, but Sarah later got surgery to fix the eye issue anyway.

When we started college at Ohio State together, me as a marketing major and Sarah studying political science, we shared a shoebox-sized room and the same good-natured circle of friends. Even when we argued over politics or who snored louder or which of us left a giant bowl of chili on top of the mini-fridge over winter break, causing the room to smell like a family had died in it, we were good to each other. I knew the things Sarah was self-conscious about—her fluctuating weight and the torrent of abuse her mother launched at her over it, the fact that she hadn't seen her dad in years, the time she accidentally called her English comp professor "Mom"—and knew how to make her feel better about them. Sarah knew my weaknesses, too: my fervent belief that Stacey, who was always prettier and more athletic and better in school, was my mom's favorite; the time I gave my first blow job our sophomore year of college and my gag reflex caused me to vomit all over PJ Tyren's penis; the fact that I'd blown a guy named PJ.

Sarah and I nurtured the best parts of each other and protected the weak ones. She was closer to me than anyone. Until she wasn't.

Nala kicks me in her sleep, probably dream-chasing after a squirrel. I sit up to pet her soft fur and climb out of bed, needing a change of scenery. After The Incident, I saw a therapist who taught me about exploring different coping mechanisms. But I only went to a few sessions, so the best coping mechanism I've come up with is ice cream. With Nala trailing behind me, I tiptoe downstairs and into the kitchen. Stacey did a deep clean after dinner, so it smells of Windex and Mrs. Meyer's lemon-scented soap. In the freezer, I sort through bags of frozen brussels sprouts and Stacey's twelve varieties of Halo Top until I find a quart of Häagen-Dazs mint chip.

I grab a spoon and carry my dairy distraction into Stacey's office. I flip on the light to reveal the room's simple setup: a glass desk bookended by metal filing cabinets, with a black armchair and gray walls as backdrop. I plop down in front of Stacey's computer and crack my knuckles. Since I can't sleep, I might as well sleuth.

I type Maisie Mitchell into Google and take a bite of ice cream. Scrolling past obituaries for elderly women who share her name, I find Maisie's LinkedIn page and click on it. The page features a beaming Maisie in a blue button-down shirt and lists a series of impressive career accomplishments. According to her bio, she worked as a curator of exhibits at the Potawatomi Zoo in South Bend, Indiana, before starting her work at the Columbus Zoo and Aquarium. She's certainly no academic slouch either, with a master's in animal science from the Ohio State University.

I take another bite of mint chip and click on Maisie's Facebook page. Since we're not friends, my access is limited, but her account looks normal enough. Her profile picture shows her and Finn grinning next to a waterfall in matching sweatshirts, their arms wrapped around each other. Beside them, a perky-eared border collie looks attentively into the camera. *The Three Musketeers at Hocking Hills!* Maisie captioned the shot. Her older profile pictures are equally adorable: Maisie and Finn at Easter, presenting Pippa with a basket of dog treats; Maisie and Finn at Christmas in matching reindeer-print pajamas, an also-pajamas-wearing Pippa resting on their laps; Maisie and Finn and Pippa on vacation, posing in front of the Santa Monica Ferris wheel.

At first glance, Maisie and her fiancé seem like the kind of attractive, fun-loving couple you'd want to team up with at bar trivia night. Hell, even four-legged Pippa looks like she's grinning in every picture, as if she knows she has the most loving parents in the world. It's hard to believe that Maisie, with her excellent hair and awesome job and lemon-muffin-buying fiancé, doesn't have friends.

It occurs to me, a woman who listens to at least three hours of crime podcasts daily, that maybe Maisie has no friends thanks to a seedy criminal past. My heart beating faster, I search Maisie Mitchell felony but come up with nothing. Maisie Mitchell misdemeanor and Maisie Mitchell Most Wanted yield no fruit, either. Half-relieved and half-disappointed, I Google her name again, but the results provide no clues about the cause of Maisie's bridesmaid dilemma. I stumble upon results from last year's Capital City Half Marathon—Maisie runs a badass mile time—and skim through an article in the *Columbus Dispatch* about a new sea lion exhibit at the zoo. "Zoo guests will walk through a glass tube surrounded on all sides by the exhibit," Maisie's quoted as saying. "It will be a completely immersive experience." Not exactly the words of a killer.

Clearly, Maisie's lack of friends isn't due to the fact that she's an arsonist or a fugitive axe murderer. Considering she knows where I live, that's a good thing, but the mystery of her social isolation persists. Now a few inches deep into my quart of ice cream, I raise another spoonful to my mouth and search professional bridesmaid. To my surprise, I get about forty-two million results. Apparently Maisie's not the only bride who needs backup. I click on different websites advertising bridesmaids-for-hire packages. As Nala pants beside me, patiently waiting for a scoop of ice cream to hit the floor, I scroll through glowing testimonials on the benefits of hiring a professional who won't complain about the hideous color of her bridesmaid dress and knows how to seamlessly guide drunk uncles away from the open bar.

In a four-minute video on one website, a bride named Talia tells the story of how her best friend died of breast cancer six months before her wedding. Talia knew that no one in her life could take her friend's place, so she hired Jennifer from Bridal Besties to stand beside her on her big day. With tears in her eyes, blond-haired, blue-eyed Jennifer explains what an honor it was to carry the eight-foot train of Talia's gown behind her as she entered the church, and how they're still friends to this day.

"Friendship is created in all kinds of ways," Talia says at the end of the clip, holding a picture of her deceased friend in one hand and clutching Jennifer's hand with the other. "Sometimes it's born out of happiness. Sometimes it's born out of pain. And sometimes, it's born on Bridal Besties dot com."

The sickly-sweet marketing works its dark magic on me. By the end of the video, when a now-pregnant Talia and her sidekick Jennifer are shopping for baby clothes, I'm blinking away tears.

"Don't look at me, Nala," I whisper, ashamed to be seen like this by any living creature. A sappy piano tune plays as Talia and Jennifer stroll into the distance, and I grab a wad of tissues from the box on Stacey's desk and wipe my face.

I try to tell myself that the sudden rush of emotion is PMS-related, but I know it's something else. It's that thing I never talk about: the gnawing, clawing monster that eats away at me no matter how many episodes of *The Office* I watch or glasses of red wine I drink. That creeps up on me in the middle of the night when I'm wide awake and staring at the ceiling with a heavy dread in my stomach. That finds me when I least expect it, when I'm in line at Target or watching Stacey hug Kaya or accidentally dropping Chloe Wellington's three-hundred-dollar birthday cake. That thing I can't outsleep or outdrink or overcome: loneliness.

It's not a loneliness that comes from missing my ex-fiancé, though that pain caused many sleepless nights, too. It's the loneliness of missing Sarah. Of having a person who knew everything about me, every nook and cranny of my heart, and then losing her forever.

After The Incident, when I left Max and Sarah tangled in my bedsheets and stormed out of my town house crying so hard I couldn't breathe, it was Sarah who ran after me, sobbing as hard as I was, begging for me to stop. It was Sarah who called me every day for months until I blocked her number, who rang Stacey's doorbell over and over until I had my sister threaten her with a restraining order. It was Sarah who begged me to talk, to listen, to forgive. It was Sarah who was sorry.

Despite my better judgment, I type Sarah's name into the Facebook search bar. My stomach in knots, I click on her profile. Her cover picture is the same as it was five months ago, before The Incident. It's a row of pink roses under a trellis at Inniswood Metro Gardens, one of our favorite parks in Columbus.

But her profile picture is new. Instead of the close-up of her at her twenty-ninth birthday party, her face flushed pink with happiness and a party hat slightly askew on her head, this picture has two people in it. Sarah's in a white-and-blue checkered dress with Max next to her in a white ball cap, his lips pressed to her cheek. A firework explodes behind them, dotting the sky with red streaks.

It's from the Fourth of July. Just weeks ago. That means they're still together. My ex-fiancé and my ex–best friend are still together.

I leap up from Stacey's office chair so fast that the wheels almost roll over Nala's tail. I grab what's left of the Häagen-Dazs and fling it into the garbage can, my stomach heaving with nausea. My body tingles with the desire to smash something or someone, and I pace back and forth across the wood flooring of the kitchen while Nala looks on.

I can hear Stacey's voice in my head already: *Write your feelings out, Willa. Go back to blogging. It will help you heal.*

The thought of healing is enough to make me let out a bitter laugh, and I sit back down at Stacey's computer and open a blank Word document. Let's see what the old readers of *Willa Leads the Way* think of my healing process.

Hello, Waywards! I type, smashing the keys like they've wronged me. I bet you're wondering what your old pal Willa's been up to all these months. Well, beloved readers, I've been wasting my life away as Princess effing Sparkleheart. Maybe you've seen the reviews of my work on Yelp. That's right, guys. I spend my weekends handing cupcakes to spoiled, asshole children and wearing a ball gown that gives me a fucking rash. Meanwhile, my traitor of a former best friend and my balding, didn't-go-down-on-me-that-often-anyway ex-fiancé are a happy fucking couple.

Cheers, right?

Nala nudges my elbow with her head, as if to warn me that I'm making a terrible mistake. I sigh and reread what I wrote. If I post that on my blog, Stacey will wrestle me into the car and drive me straight to therapy. I delete what I've written and rest my forehead on the keyboard, defeated.

There's only one way out of this nightmare, and rage-filled blog posts aren't it. I have to leave. I have to get out of Columbus. If I can scrape together enough money to get my student loans in order and pay the first month's rent for a tiny apartment somewhere—*anywhere*—far away from here, I can escape that monstrous thing. The crushing, choking loneliness. I can forget that Sarah and Max are happy without me while I'm a heartbroken disaster without them.

I close out of the Word document and go upstairs to crawl back into bed, but I don't sleep. Instead, I do math equations in my head, tabulating bills and loans and interest rates. I calculate how much money I need to save before I can get the hell out of this city.

Then, my heart pounding, I lean over to my bedside table and grab the scrap of paper on which Maisie wrote her number. I enter the digits in my phone and send her a simple text: This is Willa. I'm in.

Because maybe I'm not the Willa I used to be, but I can be a new Willa someplace else. And Maisie's money will help me get there.

Maisie could be crazy, but so what? I may have lots of reasons to say no to her, but I've got five thousand reasons to say yes.

9

"*Oh my God,*" Glory says when I walk into the kitchen a week and a half after Maisie's visit. "Who the hell are you, and what have you done with Willa?"

Stacey does a double take as she shifts baby Lucy from one arm to the other. "Wow. You look so pretty, Willa. You look so much like . . . *you.*"

In preparation for my first outing as Maisie's pretend bridesmaid—well, actual bridesmaid, pretend friend—I spent two hours getting ready. Maisie invited me to a happy hour to celebrate Finn's birthday at VASO, a rooftop bar in Dublin. Along with Finn and Maisie, I'll also meet some of the other members of the bridal party. It's been so long since I went out on a Friday night that the rituals that were once a bedrock of my grooming routine—painting my fingernails, putting on eye shadow, washing my hair with real shampoo—felt foreign. I was as uncoordinated putting on eyeliner as I am whenever Ruthie tries to teach me one of her ballerina moves.

I cycled through seven different outfits before settling on a pair of denim cutoff shorts, a white tank top with no stains on it, a loose pink cardigan, and a pair of strappy sandals. I haven't willingly worn anything that's not a T-shirt or yoga pants or a Goodwill ball gown in months, so my look feels downright fancy. I'm not exactly excited about spending the evening trying to be a good actress, but my outfit is a nice break from the Princess Sparkleheart ensemble.

"Ready to act your butt off?" Glory asks, somehow reading my mind. "Go ahead, give us your opening line."

"Um, hello," I respond, imagining that Glory is one of Maisie's friends. My pulse quickens, and a pool of nervous sweat starts to form beneath my hairline. "Greetings. Hey there, I'm Willa. I'm friends with Maisie. We're old friends. From childhood. Friendly friends."

"Oh, shit," Glory says. "You're gonna bomb."

"Stop it." Stacey gives her wife's arm a playful swat and shoots me a reassuring look. "You are *not* going to bomb. You're going to do great. Maybe just don't say 'greetings.' It makes you sound like a Martian."

"Who's a Martian?" Kaya asks, traipsing into the kitchen with a basketball between her arms.

"Nobody's a Martian, sweetheart," Glory says, pressing a kiss to the top of Kaya's head. "Aunt Willa's just doing a good impression of one."

The doorbell rings, and I scowl at her and maneuver out of the way so Kaya can dart out of the kitchen to answer it.

Glory grabs a container of Greek yogurt from the fridge and gives me a solemn look. "In all seriousness, don't let your guard down, okay? Maisie seems really nice, but weddings bring out the crazy in people."

"They really do," Stacey agrees. "The wedding industry is a beast. I've planned enough receptions to witness even the most rational of brides be driven to a nervous breakdown."

Memories of planning my own wedding—selecting my off-the-shoulder mermaid gown, agonizing about linen colors, learning that a charger is a decorative plate and not just something that powers my iPhone—wash over me. I shake my arms out a little to relax.

"Whoa, Willa, you look lovely. Did you get a haircut?" Nate asks as he enters the kitchen. Kaya trails behind him with her arms looped around his waist.

I smile at Nate. "No haircut, but thank you."

My ex brother-in-law, in addition to being an amazing dad, is one of the nicest guys on the planet. When I was in college and he and Stacey still lived together in their old house in Hilliard, he never minded when I crashed there during breaks. Whenever I stayed over, he made French toast for breakfast and let me clog up his Netflix queue with trashy reality shows. I worried I would lose my bond with him when Stacey filed for divorce, but Nate is still as kind to me as ever. Unlike everyone else, he never bothers me about the fact that I've spent the past five months hiding from the world. And sometimes, when he drops Kaya off after a weekend at his place, he still makes me French toast.

"If you're wondering what's different about Willa, it's that she *brushed* her hair," Glory teases.

"Shouldn't you be off watering your Mommy Garden, or something like that?" I retort, ducking so she can't loop her arm around me.

"Hey, nobody should be watering anybody's garden in the kitchen," Nate jokes. "There are children present."

While Stacey helps Kaya finish getting ready to go to her dad's for the weekend, I eat a slice of Glory's freshly baked rhubarb pie and try to calm my nerves. I haven't attended a social function that wasn't a child's birthday party since before The Incident, and my heart races with anticipation. I feel like a sixth-grader about to attend her first boy-girl dance.

"I slipped a twenty in your purse just in case you need it," Glory whispers as I prepare to head out the door. "Be careful."

"Glory," I protest, "I don't need—"

She waves me off. "You never know when you'll need cash. Just watch out for any crazy bridezillas, okay?"

I grin as she cuts Nate a slice of rhubarb pie. "Okay. I love you, too."

⁓

VASO is a trendy rooftop lounge in Bridge Park, a cluster of restaurants and apartments that border Dublin's historic district. The lounge is on the top floor of the AC Hotel and overlooks the Scioto River. I park in the Mooney Street garage and walk the short distance to VASO, rehearsing the friendship backstory Maisie and I crafted over a phone call.

If asked, I'm supposed to say that we met as middle-schoolers at summer camp. We lost touch over the years, but fate brought us back together one spring morning last year, when we ran into each other at the Dublin library.

"In the nonfiction section," Maisie clarified over the phone. "In case anyone asks, I was looking for a copy of *Gorillas in the Mist*. You were looking for a book on interior design."

Maisie may be overthinking the level of detail we need to include, but I mentally review my role anyway. According to our story, Maisie and I haven't been able to hang out outside of the coffee shop due to my crazy work schedule—I had a good laugh at that one—but now that I'm no longer blogging, we're eager to reignite the bond of friendship that developed over s'mores and lanyard-making all those years ago.

When I reach the lobby of the hotel, I check my reflection in the glass doors before pressing the elevator button. My pulse races as I wait for the doors to open, and my knees wobble as if I've just run a marathon.

A well-dressed couple enters the lobby behind me, and I take one look at the woman's black maxi dress and wish I hadn't worn denim shorts. Denim is for losers! Denim is for children! Denim is for—

"Ma'am? You headed up?" the man behind me asks, his shiny gold watch catching the sunlight as he motions upward.

I'm so focused on my horrendous outfit choice that I haven't noticed the elevator doors open. "Sorry," I say sheepishly. I consider turning back and running away as fast as my denim shorts will allow, but the couple is already stepping in after me, leaving me no choice but to move forward.

I step into the elevator and contemplate pushing the emergency stop button, but the maxi dress–wearing woman smiles and reaches past me to press the button for the roof. As the elevator ascends, a hint of bile coats my throat, and I wonder if I'm going to vomit. Social situations never used to give me anxiety. Before The Incident, the thought of meeting new people struck me as a fun opportunity, not a reason to hide forever in Kaya's playhouse. A rush of anger buzzes through me, anger at Sarah and Max for turning me into this person.

The elevator dings as the doors open to a bustling restaurant, where glass windows and a sleek bar create an aura of sophistication. Yellow orbs of light dangle from the ceiling, and modernistic white chairs line the bar. Old Willa would have loved this place. New Willa is about to shit her pants and has to get the hell out of here.

The well-dressed couple steps off the elevator, casting me curious glances as I cling to the far wall like a triggered claustrophobic.

"Everything's fine," I assure them in a high-pitched, not-at-all fine voice. "Everything's fine."

The two exchange a look that says *crazy person alert!* and causes my blood pressure to skyrocket.

"I'm not crazy," I call after them, using my cardigan to wipe a pool of sweat from my armpits. "I just hate elevators!"

"I hate elevators, too," a voice across the restaurant lobby says. "That's why I took the stairs."

I turn to see a man around my age watching me, one eyebrow cocked in amusement. With his broad shoulders, smooth cheekbones, and a jawline that could cut glass, he's the embodiment of tall, dark, and handsome. I hate him immediately.

"Good for you. I'll be sure to give you a gold star next time."

He laughs, revealing a smile that's fifty percent boyish, fifty percent suave, and one hundred percent panty dropper. "You know, I've found that yelling 'I'm not crazy!' at the top of my lungs isn't a great way to convince people."

"Oh yeah? And what is?"

He shrugs. "Not being crazy."

I grit my teeth. "I wasn't yelling. I was speaking *forcefully*."

"Oh, you were hard-core yelling. You were like, angry-mom-screaming-at-her-teenager yelling. Christian-Bale-screaming-on-set yelling. Ron-gets-a-Howler-in-*Harry-Potter* yell—"

"I get it," I say quietly. "I was yelling."

He beams as if he's won our little back-and-forth. "You know what might help you not seem crazy?"

"Being a dude? Because somehow it's women, not men, who always get called the c-word." I pause when I realize the double meaning of my comment. "I mean, not *that* c-word. But, you know, c as in crazy. And also the other one. Which is very unfair. So please, mansplain to me how I can seem less crazy. Go ahead. I'm dying to hear your advice."

The man reaches up and scratches the back of his neck, his T-shirt riding up to reveal a well-formed biceps. "I was going to say you'd seem less crazy if you got off the elevator."

I freeze when I realize I'm still huddled against the elevator wall as if hoping to get sucked into it. "Oh," I say after a beat. "Right." I release my death grip on the railing and stand up straight, smoothing the front of my cardigan.

The man crosses his arms over his chest. "That's better."

"I get motion sickness," I lie, trying to conceal the fact that I'm so terrified of meeting Maisie's friends that I'd rather hide inside this steel box. "Like really, really bad. Anywho, nice meeting you."

I cringe at the realization that I've just uttered the word *anywho* and move to step past him before I can embarrass myself further. That's when I see the Roman numeral tattoo on his right wrist. Panic floods me. I recognize that tattoo. I know this guy somehow, but from where? What if he's one of Max's old friends, a buddy I only saw occasionally? What if I know him from that time Stacey made me go to a relationship-loss support group, and I left ten minutes in because nobody brought doughnuts? What if he's someone I hooked up with in the second month after my breakup, when I went from not leaving my bed to jumping into lots of other people's?

"Where do I know you from?" I ask.

He tilts his head to one side like he's trying to ascertain whether I actually am crazy. "I don't think we've met before."

I study his face, trying to place him, and then it hits me. He's the guy from Chloe Wellington's disastrous birthday party, the one who laughed his ass off while I dragged my golden throne and the last of my dignity away from Beth and Sarah.

"Oh yes, we have," I say tightly, walking past him without a backward glance. "Have a good night. Try not to choke on your drink."

Fuming, I take a deep breath and march past the indoor bar. Maisie said to meet her on the patio, so I push the door open a little harder than necessary and step outside. VASO's patio is like an oasis in the sky, and I take a deep breath and survey my surroundings in an attempt to calm down. Glass paneling surrounds the rooftop, and clusters of tables and fire pits line the path to the outdoor bar. Now that my nerves are amplified by anger, I'm ready for a drink.

The *nerve* of that awful man. To not even recognize me after he found my mortifying turn as Princess Sparkleheart so goddamn funny, so freaking hilarious, that he *doubled over* in laughter—

"Willa! Willa, we're over here!"

Maisie's voice interrupts my thought spiral, and I scan the patio to find her waving at me from a canopied set of couches.

I peek under my armpits for sweat marks as subtly as I can before returning her wave. I mentally scroll through what I've rehearsed—summer camp, coffee Mondays, a book about gorillas—and head toward her.

Long white curtains tied to wooden posts border the rooftop tables. I consider wrapping myself in one and hiding until the bar closes, but Maisie's practically jumping up and down with excitement as I approach.

"Willa!" she says when I reach her. "You're here!"

Dressed in a cherry-print romper and wearing her long hair in a loose braid, she loops an arm through mine and guides me the final feet toward her table.

"You remember Finn, right?" Maisie motions to her fiancé, who raises his hand in greeting and gives me a warm smile.

"Hiya, Willa. Thanks for coming out."

"Hi, Finn," I say, trying to remember how a normal person with adequate social skills behaves. "Happy birthday."

"He's thirty-one!" an olive-skinned woman in a crop top and well-fitting jeans declares. Her black hair is pulled into an adorable messy bun, a look I can't pull off no matter how many YouTube tutorials I watch on the subject. "Thirty-one is ancient. Do you feel ancient, Finn?"

From the next table, a woman who is definitely not thirty-one sends over a death glare.

"No, I don't feel ancient," Finn says good-naturedly. "But that joke does."

"Willa, this is Finn's cousin Rose," Willa explains. "Rose, this is Willa."

Rose squints at me. "You look really familiar. Do you practice at GoYoga? I feel like I've seen you at one of my Sunday candlelight flows."

The only Sunday flow I've been involved with lately is the flow of wine from the bottle to my glass, but I keep that to myself.

"Don't get Rose started on yoga," Finn says, rescuing me from having to participate in the conversation. "Or else we'll spend my whole birthday getting lectured about how our chakras aren't open enough."

Rose shrugs. "It's not my fault you can't touch your toes, old man." She stands on her tiptoes and scans the crowd. "Where's our waiter? My frozen mojito's gonna be melted by the time I get it. And where the heck is Liam?"

"Probably got stuck late at work," Finn says. "You know Liam. I don't think he's clocked out on time a day in his life. Chill out, Rose. You'll have plenty of time to scold us about how our chis are blocked and our posture sucks."

Rose pokes at a small plate of mushrooms and grins slyly. "Speak for yourself. Liam has excellent posture. Now come help me find our waiter, birthday boy." She grabs Finn by the arm and guides him toward the bar, promising to bring back a round of drinks for everyone.

"Don't mind Rose," Maisie says as they traipse off. "She's a little bit all over the place, but she's a sweetheart. Finn's right, though. Don't get her started on yoga."

"Maisie," I say when it's just the two of us. "I'm not sure I can do this." I wipe my clammy hands on my cardigan and try to tune out the din of the conversations around us. In my brief time as a hermit, I've forgotten how loud crowds of people can be. I long for the quiet comfort of my bedroom, where the only people I have to deal with are the fictional ones on my TV screen.

"What do you mean?"

"I'm not . . . I'm not good with people anymore. Or crowds. Or doing things that involve leaving the house." I wonder if everyone around us can read the anxiety on my face. I also wonder if I should start wearing prescription-strength deodorant.

"Well, you're not actually being you, are you?" Maisie smiles and brushes my arm with hers. "You're playing the role of Willa Callister, my long-lost summer camp friend. Hey, do you remember that time we snuck out of our cabin in the middle of the night and crept over to the boys' bunks?"

"Um, no. I do not."

Maisie nudges me with her elbow. "Come on. Just try, Willa. Our friendship is a story that we get to write. We can make it anything we want. So, do you remember? When we snuck into the boys' bunks?"

I sigh and try to play along, no matter how weird it feels. "Um, sort of. Vaguely."

"Well, I remember it like it was yesterday. Their bunks smelled like dirty shoes and sunscreen. We stole Twinkies and Hershey bars from their cabin while they slept, remember? We were so quiet. Like ninjas."

"Right," I say with uncertainty, wondering just how much thought Maisie has put into our official backstory. "Ninjas."

"See? Just go with it." She smiles and flips her braid over one shoulder. "You're my bridesmaid now, and you can be anyone you want."

I like the idea of being anyone I want. I like the idea of being new Willa somewhere far, far away from Max and Sarah and my Princess Sparkleheart ball gown. "Okay. I can try that."

Before Maisie can say anything else, Rose and Finn return from the bar with Rose's frozen mojito.

"Bottoms up!" Rose exclaims, sipping her mojito with gusto. "In honor of my older—wish I could say wiser—cousin." But before she lifts her drink for a toast, she lets out a little squeal of delight and bounces up and down like a cheerleader. "Liam's here!"

"Rude," Finn says, then lifts his beer to toast himself anyway.

I start to ask Finn what he's drinking, because even in my sorry social state, I know it's customary to buy the guest of honor a beverage. But I'm quickly distracted by the man sauntering toward our group, who Rose is so delighted to see that she almost knocks her long-awaited mojito off the table.

Damn that man with his thousand-watt smile and Roman numeral tattoo.

"Hey, man," Finn greets him, clapping the stupid man's stupid back. "Glad you made it."

"Wouldn't miss it for the world," the stupid man responds. He scans the group and lands, finally, on me. "Sorry I'm late. It's just been a crazy night so far."

"Well, we're happy you're here," Maisie says, apparently not aware that this guy is a complete and total douchecanoe.

She places a hand on my elbow and gives it a gentle squeeze. "Liam, this is my friend Willa Callister. Willa, this is Liam Rafferty."

I glance from Liam to Maisie and back to Liam. "You know Maisie and Finn?" I ask, my tone acidic.

"Know them?" He smiles, and his whole face lights up in a way that makes me want to punch it. "I'd say so. I'm Finn's best man."

10

"*Finn and Liam* have been friends since they were like, two years old," Maisie says, blissfully oblivious to the fact that I hate Liam with the fire of a thousand suns.

"Since we were one, actually. We grew up on the same street, and our moms used to walk us in our strollers together." Liam smiles at the fond memory, as if he's a completely normal person instead of a raging asshole.

"Charming." I cross my arms over my chest and wonder what happened to turn him from a cute baby in a stroller to a grown-up asshole who laughs at other people's misery.

"Wait, do you guys know each other?" Maisie asks, glancing from Liam to me.

"Yes," Liam answers.

"No," I say firmly.

"I'm sorry, I'm confused." Rose forms a T with her hands for time-out and focuses her gaze on me. "Do you or do you not come to my candlelight flows?"

"I don't. And I don't know Liam. We just ran into each other a moment ago in the lobby."

"We share a mutual dislike of elevators," Liam explains.

"Liam hates heights," Rose agrees, brushing her fingertips over his forearm tattoo. "Remember when we went to Cedar Point last summer and I got you to ride Millennium Force?"

"I've tried to block it out," Liam says.

Rose swats his chest playfully. "He literally burst into tears while we were going up the hill. It was amazing."

"Didn't he puke a dozen times on the ride home?" Finn remembers.

"It was the longest drive of my life," Maisie agrees. "He stuck his head out the window like he was a German shepherd."

"The airflow helped my stomach settle," Liam says tightly, crossing his arms over his chest. "But thanks for the stroll down memory lane."

"So," Rose says, studying me, "how do you know Finn and Maisie?"

"Well," I say, trying to remember Maisie's carefully devised backstory. "I . . . we . . ." I can feel Rose's gaze boring into me as sticky sweat trickles down my back and pools under my boobs. "We, you see . . ."

"Willa and I are friends from childhood, too," Maisie explains, jumping in to rescue me.

"We went to summer camp," I sputter. "We snuck into cabins. Boys' cabins. And we stole from them." I push my hair off my neck, where the strands have conglomerated into a sweaty tangle.

"You stole from other children?" Rose asks. She adjusts her sunglasses to rest on top of her head, where they perfectly complement her bun. "That's so un-Maisie-like."

"We stole Hershey bars," I continue, wondering how long I have until I pass out from the heat and the pressure of pretending. "And Twinkies. At summer camp."

Maisie, who's probably severely regretting her life choices at this point, gives me an encouraging smile. "That's right. We were just a couple of troublemakers, weren't we, Willa?"

"Yep. We were always making trouble. Trouble, trouble, trouble. And lanyards. We made a lot of lanyards."

"Sounds like a good time." Finn wraps an arm around Maisie's shoulders and kisses the top of her head.

She grins. "I mostly remember being sunburned and covered in mosquito bites. And meeting Willa, of course."

"What camp was it?" Rose asks. "I went to horseback riding camp in North Carolina when I was a kid."

"Oh, our camp was nothing fancy," I lie, scrambling to think of the name of one. The only summer camp I'd ever gone to was the free Bible school camp at the Methodist church down the road. My mom would drop Stacey and me off before her teller shift at the bank, and we'd spend eight long hours watching the clock and singing songs about Jesus.

"It was called . . . it was called Camp Anawanna," I say finally. "Good ol' Camp Anawanna, we hold it in our hearts."

"Isn't that the name of a camp from a Nickelodeon TV show?" Liam asks. *Salute Your Shorts?*"

"Yes, it is," Maisie says while I contemplate throwing myself off the rooftop. "We loved that show. And we loved to pretend we went there."

"So we called our camp Camp Anawanna," I add. "Its official title was Camp Wildwood. There were tons of woods there. Acres and acres of woods."

"Sounds like a lot of fun," Finn says. "Liam and I went to sailing camp in the summers, but we would have liked acres of woods much better."

I make a mental note to tell Stacey that sailing camp is a thing, in case she and Glory ever want to send the girls there.

"So are you new to Columbus, Willa?" Rose asks. "Why are we just getting to meet you now?"

"Willa and I lost touch for a long time, but we ran into each other last year at the library," Maisie explains. She touches my arm briefly, and the display of easy familiarity helps to sell her lie. "Luckily, Willa's work schedule has calmed down a lot, so we finally get to spend more time together."

"I was getting a book on interior design," I announce. "At the library." The words sound stiff and awkward to my ears, and I wish I could snatch them from the air and swallow them back down. Nobody cares what book I was supposedly searching for when I ran into Maisie, and sharing too much detail probably makes me look suspicious. Panic forms in my chest, making my heart pound. Am I making too much eye contact with the others? Too little? I glance at Maisie to see if she's sweating as much as I am, but she's brushing lint off Finn's shirt like she doesn't have a care in the world. I can't help but wonder how she's as cool as a cucumber while I'm practically crawling out of my skin with each lie.

"Cool," Rose says. "I'm really into interior design. Feng shui and all that. So anyway, you're coming to the wedding?"

"Oh, Willa's not just coming to the wedding," Maisie says, beaming. "She's going to be in it."

"When Maisie asked me to be a bridesmaid, I couldn't refuse," I lie. The drum in my chest beats faster, and I wipe my palms against my shorts. "It's such an honor."

"You'll like the dresses she picked out," Rose says. "Lavender will look good with your skin tone."

"Right? I think so, too," Maisie says. The two of them launch into a discussion about necklines and lace details, and I excuse myself from the conversation to make a trip to the bar. I need a moment to calm my nerves, and maybe a glass of iced water—plus a glass of something stronger—will help me stop sweating buckets.

I've only had a moment to scour the cocktail menu when I hear a deep voice behind me.

"Just a hunch, but I think we might have gotten off on the wrong foot."

I turn around to find Liam behind me in line for the bar, his hands shoved into his pockets.

"And what gives you that impression?"

"Oh, I don't know. Maybe the fact that you're glaring at me like you wish I were dead."

I shrug and stare at the cocktail menu as if my eyes are glued to it, refusing to look at him. "This is just how my face looks. I can't help it."

"If I've done something to offend you, I'd like to make amends. Can I buy you a drink?"

I roll my eyes. "I'm capable of buying my own drinks, thanks." Glory did slip me a twenty, after all.

"I'm sure you are. But clearly I've upset you in some way, and I'd like to know what that was."

"You really don't remember me?" I wave the menu in exasperation, and Liam takes a quick step left.

"I remember you getting off the elevator, which I took the stairs to avoid. I really don't like heights. I almost passed out on Millennium Force, as Rose kindly shared with the group."

"But you don't remember the first time we met. How surprising."
My voice drips with sarcasm. Of course Liam, with his childhood of
fancy summer sailing camps, doesn't remember me. He's probably
the type of moneyed douchebag who leaves crappy tips and doesn't
view service workers as people.

"Fill me in, then."

"Okay. Picture it: instead of this restaurant, we're at a tacky
child's birthday party—"

"Hang on. Is the party tacky, or is the child?"

"The party, obviously." I pause. "But also the child. Ring any bells?"

Liam looks at me with a blank expression. "I have no clue what
you're talking about."

"Seriously? How many children's birthday parties do you attend?
Okay, well, picture me in a ridiculously fluffy ball gown, dragging
my throne behind me while you laugh your ass off. Now do you
remember?"

Liam's mouth drops open. "Oh, shit. Chloe's birthday party.
You're the lady who called me an asshole and a liar."

"And I was right. I'm not sure what made you into the kind of
person who laughs at other people's misery, but you should be ashamed
of yourself."

"I'm sorry I didn't recognize you," Liam says. "You look really different when you're not wearing your fairy godmother costume."

"Uh, it's a *princess* costume, genius. There aren't any godmothers
involved."

"Right." Liam scratches his head. "I vaguely remember you lifting
a folding chair over your head and slamming it onto the ground. It
was like watching WWE."

"It was Princess Sparkleheart's *throne*," I correct him before realizing that I can probably exclude certain details. "And I didn't slam it into the ground. I sort of just tossed it."

"Oh, you slammed it. You slammed it good."

"I did not."

"Did too." Liam smiles at me, his brown eyes gleaming. "This is fun."

"It is most certainly not fun." I wave to the bartender, who's possibly the slowest-moving person in the world.

"If you let me explain why I was laughing so hard at Chloe's party," Liam says, "you'll realize I wasn't actually laughing at y—"

"I don't want to hear your lame excuse." His insistence that he did nothing wrong at the party grates on my already-fried nerves, and I can't even bear to let him finish his sentence. God forbid he just admit that he acted like an asshole and apologize for it.

"So what, you're just going to hate me forever? Because that's going to make for some really awkward bridal party pictures."

"I'll smile for the pictures, don't worry." I beam at Liam like he's my favorite person in the world. "See?"

"See what?" Finn asks, sidling up to us. "Don't mind me. I'm as excited about the wedding as Maisie is, but I can only listen to so many minutes of her and Rose talking about floral arrangements."

"Oh, nothing. Liam and I were just getting to know each other a little bit."

Finn nods as a waitress hurries past with a tray of colorful drinks. "I have to say, Willa, it's great to meet someone from Maisie's childhood. I've never met anyone who knew her when she was younger."

"No?"

Finn shakes his head. "It's hard for her parents to travel, with her dad's health issues and all. And they're not big on visitors. They're coming to the wedding, though, and I can't wait to meet them. Plus,

Maisie's so excited to see her sister. All she talks about is Clara this, Clara that. It's gonna be awesome to see them together."

"Right," I say. "Of course." I focus on keeping my expression neutral, but it's hard for me to fathom how Finn hasn't met Maisie's family after two years of dating. If her dad's ill, wouldn't she want to visit him as much as possible? And what does "not big on visitors" even mean? Was Maisie raised by a family of hermits? Is there something about her parents that she's hiding from Finn? Or maybe there's something about Finn that she's keeping from her parents.

Plus, she never mentioned anything to me about having a sister. I wonder why she didn't just ask *her* to be a bridesmaid. I know that sibling relationships can be difficult—Stacey and I don't always see eye-to-eye, as evidenced by the fact that she left a copy of *Who Moved My Cheese?* on my bed yesterday, and I gave it to Nala to use as a chew toy—but still. I'd assume that even a sister Maisie's not close with would make a better bridesmaid than me, a total stranger. Cheaper, too. And from the way Finn talks about it, Maisie's crazy about Clara, which makes her choice to hire me as a bridesmaid even more confusing. I glance in Maisie's direction, as if her body language might reveal a clue, but she's grinning and pointing at something on Rose's phone like she doesn't have a worry in the world.

"What was Maisie like as a kid?" Liam asks, drawing my attention away from her. "At Camp Anawanna?"

I side-eye him for the last comment but smile at Finn. I'm getting paid to do a job here, and I have to keep things professional. I can ponder the mysteries of Maisie's personal life and make voodoo dolls of Liam on my own time.

"She was amazing. I got really homesick, and Maisie took me under her wing. She taught me how to play tetherball and fish and make lizard keychains out of beads." I give myself a mental high five for quickly thinking of what sound like normal camp activities.

Finn grins. "That sounds like my Maisie. Always looking out for people. Always up for adventure."

The affection that his voice holds for her, paired with the crazy-in-love look on his face, make me like Finn. He might have gone to rich-kid summer camps and have the terrible luck of being friends with Liam, but he clearly adores his fiancée.

"Maisie's great," I say, wanting to earn the huge sum she's paying me. "You're really lucky." When I've finally reached the front of the bar line, I ask Finn what he'd like to drink. "And let me know what Maisie drinks, too. I'll bring one back for her."

"Oh, Maisie doesn't drink," Finn says. "I already got her a tonic water." When someone calls his name from the other side of the patio, he excuses himself and heads in that direction.

"Thanks for offering me a drink, Willa," Liam says dryly. "That was so kind of you."

I ignore him as the bartender hands me my order, a cocktail with tequila, apple cider, lime, and chile. I make my way back to the group, where Maisie, Finn, and Rose are clustered among a growing crowd. With tequila flowing through my bloodstream, the throng of people doesn't bother me quite as much, and the knot in my stomach loosens. I can almost imagine myself, or at least the old Willa, being real friends with Maisie and Finn.

"Tonight is going great," Maisie whispers when no one is looking. "You're doing great, Willa. Thank you." She squeezes my hand, and instead of yanking my hand away like instinct tells me to, I don't. I squeeze her hand back, her palm warm against mine, and in that moment I feel less alone than I have in months.

"Everybody squeeze in close," Rose instructs, motioning for the group to gather around her. "I need a picture for Instagram."

Liam, ever the charmer, groans in exasperation. "Seriously? Can't we have one outing where we all focus on each other instead of posing for your Facebook audience?"

"I said Instagram, not Facebook." Rose reaches toward him and ruffles his hair.

He shrugs. "Isn't it all the same?"

"It's not, actually," I say. Despite his attempt to make amends by offering to buy me a drink, Liam's already done plenty to make me dislike him, and his blatant dismissal of Rose's request only annoys me further. "I don't think one picture is gonna kill you."

He tries to fix his hair where Rose tousled it but gives up, thrusting his hands into the pockets of his jeans. "But it's never just one picture, is it? It's one for Instagram, and three for Snapchat, and oh look, we didn't get the angle right, and someone has a double chin, so let's take another and another and another. And before you know it, the night's over and we've spent the whole time focused on *looking* like we're having fun than actually having any."

"Really?" I ask, my tone sharp. "The whole time?"

Liam smirks. "That might be an exaggeration, but my point stands."

"Don't mind Liam," Rose says, motioning for Finn and Maisie and several of Finn's friends to come closer. "He's a grumpy Luddite who doesn't even know how to share a Snapchat story, but we love him anyway."

"I'm not a grumpy Luddite," he protests, his tone sounding grumpier by the second. "I just think social media is a pathetic substitute for actual human relationships. It's a waste of time and energy."

My hackles rise like Nala's do when she sees the neighbor's yappy Pomeranian. My blog and my Instagram account weren't a waste of time and energy; they were a career, and a way for me to connect with other people and let them feel connected to me. "Social media can be a supplement to relationships, not a replacement for them. You make it sound vapid."

Liam frees his hands from his pockets and crosses his arms over his chest. "It *is* vapid."

"Maybe it is the way you use it, but that's a *you* problem. Not a social media one." I grip my cocktail glass with such force that my knuckles turn pale, and I force myself to take a deep breath. I'm here to do a job for Maisie, not to argue with Liam. Even if he is acting like a judgmental moron.

Sensing the rising tension, Maisie squeezes in between Rose and me and wraps an arm around my shoulders. "Now, now, kids. Play nice. Liam has his reasons for hating social media, and Willa has her reasons for feeling the opposite. But it's Finn's birthday, and I want a picture of all of us together. Sorry, Liam."

"Sorry, buddy," Finn echoes, slapping his friend on the back. "You're outnumbered."

Liam grumbles but doesn't argue. Instead, he slides into the spot next to me as Rose holds her phone out in front of her, adjusting the angle of the camera. His closeness unnerves me, and despite my determination to ignore him entirely, I find myself sneaking a sideways glance at his wrist tattoo and the thick tendons of his forearms. I can't stand him, but he smells like pine and lemon-scented soap, and I don't entirely hate it.

"It's not cologne, in case you're wondering," Liam whispers as if he's read my mind. He grins at me. "It's my natural scent."

I roll my eyes and lean closer toward Maisie, forcing myself to breathe only through my mouth.

"I have to head out," Liam announces after the one-minute—not all-night—photo session. His announcement practically sends Rose into convulsions of disappointment, but I breathe a sigh of relief.

"So soon?" Rose asks. "We haven't even ordered Finn's birthday dessert yet. We're getting flan!"

"I wish I could stay, but duty calls," Liam replies, as if he's freaking Batman off to save the world. I let out an annoyed sigh before remembering that I'm supposed to be a professional.

"It was nice to meet you, Willa," he tells me after saying his goodbyes to the group. Then, before I can launch the ice cubes from my drink at him and tell him his opinions on social media are stupid, he leans toward me, so close that I accidentally inhale the balsam-and-pine-needle scent of his aftershave again. "Try not to throw any chairs tonight."

"I didn't throw anything," I whisper back, my teeth gritted. "I gently tossed it. And it's a *throne*, goddammit."

Liam winks at me. "Whatever you say, Princess Sparkleheart."

Before I can retort, he's already off, sauntering through the crowd like he owns the place.

"Isn't Liam great?" Maisie asks, twisting the cap off her tonic water. When I raise my eyebrows at her, she laughs. "Okay, so maybe he's a little weird about social media and won't be friending you on Facebook, but you guys are gonna get along. I promise."

"Oh, he's really something," I say, making a focused effort to unclench my fist. "One of a kind."

"So!" Rose says brightly, her voice strained with cheer. "How about that flan?"

I down the last of my cocktail and ask the waiter for another. Pretending to be Maisie's friend is one thing. But if I have to pretend to get along with Liam Rafferty, it's going to be one hell of a long summer.

⌒⌒⌒

A new blog post starts writing itself in my head before I've even left the party. I tell myself to ignore it and it will simply go away, but the words are still there when I get home, begging to be let out. Unable to resist them, I curl up in bed with my laptop. Instead of writing what I would have back in my blogging/functional adult days, like details about my outfit and VASO's menu and ambience, I write exactly what comes to mind. I don't intend to publish anything on my blog, and nobody wants to read about my denim shorts, anyway.

Dear Waywards, I type, Princess effing Sparkleheart here. Desperate times call for desperate measures, and I'm more desperate for money than Stacey is for me to read *The Secret*. So, I've made the insane decision to work as a hired bridesmaid. My boss, the Animal Whisperer, and her betrothed, the Friendly Lumberjack, seem like a match made in heaven. But Friendly Lumberjack's best man, who I shall henceforth refer to as the Worst Man, is anything but angelic. Sure, he smells like a sexy fireplace and has a face that some misguided souls might call handsome, but that's all ruined the instant he opens his mouth.

But I'm not worried about him. Here's what scares me about tonight, besides the fact that I somehow thought it was a good idea to wear denim shorts in public: I had fun. Before tonight, the thought of a night out on the town made me want to seek shelter in my nieces' ball pit. But this evening, surrounded by the Animal Whisperer and her friends, I started to remember how it feels not to be alone. When the Yoga Fairy pulled me in for a group selfie, I realized how long it's been since someone's wanted to take a picture with me—not with Princess Sparkleheart, but with me, Willa Callister. I didn't even have to force myself to smile for the selfie, because it felt natural. It felt good.

For a half second, I started to imagine myself as a real friend of the Animal Whisperer. I pictured myself strolling around the zoo with her, teasing her for wearing khaki. I pictured us going to the Sunday brunch buffet at Union Cafe, stuffing ourselves with breakfast pizza and laughter. I even imagined myself attending one of the Yoga Fairy's mindful breathing seminars, twisting myself into a human pretzel and trying not to fall over.

I let myself fantasize about being part of a group again, a community. About being loved and cared for and loving and caring in return. And that's more dangerous than trying to bring non-organic fruit into Stacey's house. Because the second I let myself want that, it's game over. And I won't play with fire again. I won't give anyone a piece of my heart, let alone the whole thing. I did that before, and it wrecked me.

And there's no self-growth book in the world that can help me with that.

11

The Wednesday after Finn's birthday party, I hold up a copy of Dr. Phil's *Love Smart: Find the One You Want—Fix the One You Got* and flail it in my sister's direction. "I am not, by any means, going to read this book. So please stop putting it in my purse."

Stacey looks up from the kitchen countertop, where she's assembling a pile of peanut butter and jelly sandwiches. In true Stacey fashion, the peanut butter is all-natural and organic, and the bread is whole wheat. I accidentally brought a white-bread loaf home from Kroger once, and you would have thought by her reaction that I'd shown up with a bomb.

"I know you think Dr. Phil is hokey, but he does offer some good advice. It's not like I gave you that Steve Harvey book about making guys wait three months for sex."

"Act Like a Lady, Think Like a Man?" Glory asks with a playful smile. "I would have loved to see you give Willa that one."

I roll my eyes and deposit the book on the counter. When Dr. Phil won't stop grinning at me from the cover, I place a bowl of fruit on top of it.

"Come on, Willa," Glory says, doing her best Dr. Phil impression. *"Today's gonna be a changing day in your life."*

"First of all, you do a terrible Southern drawl. And second, you guys are really showing your age right now. Besides, Stacey, I've told you a hundred times. The last thing I need right now is a relationship. Or did you forget how the last one turned out?"

"Well, sometimes the relationship you most need to strengthen is the one you have with yourself," Stacey says, neatly cutting the edges off Kaya's sandwich. "And that's a Stacey original."

"Oh my God. Do me a favor and stab me with that butter knife so I never have to hear you inspirational-quote me again."

Glory pours a layer of Cheerios onto Lucy's high chair tray. "She's right, Stace. I'm deeply in love with you, but even I want to vomit after that one."

My sister finishes making the last sandwich and tosses her hands up. "Fine. If you want to sit at home all day being miserable, go ahead. I'm just trying to help. And so is Dr. Phil."

"I'm not sitting at home all day being miserable," I argue, although that is a new-Willa type of thing to do. "I'm going to Maisie's dress fitting."

Maisie had picked out her wedding gown months ago and requested some alterations to the bodice. She'd invited me and the other bridesmaids to help her analyze the results today.

"We're going to White of Dublin," I add. The same place where I'd bought my dress when I was engaged to Max.

Stacey stops putting sandwiches in Ziploc bags. "Oh, Willa."

Not wanting her to make a big deal out of it, and certainly not wanting her to bring up Max or Sarah, I shrug. "I'm sure it'll be fine. It's just a fitting, anyway, and then we're getting tacos for lunch."

"Tell her to skip the gown and do a casual wedding, like we did,"

Glory suggests. "She'll save a fortune and won't be driven to the brink of insanity."

"She could save a fortune by not hiring me as a bridesmaid. I don't think pinching pennies is her priority. I mean, think of what she could do with the money she's paying me. Five grand could buy a really high-end bridal gown," I say. "Or a honeymoon to Hawaii. Or something quirky and Maisie-like, like a pet Bengal cat." I still haven't wrapped my head around her willingness to shell out so much money for a fake bridesmaid.

Stacey's phone buzzes, and she frowns when she studies the screen. "Ugh. My client wants to change the color scheme of her daughter's goldfish's burial ceremony. I swear to God, I should have picked a different career. Something nice and boring, like accounting."

"People host parties for dead goldfish?" I ask. "And those parties have color schemes?"

"It's a *burial ceremony*, Willa," Glory corrects me with a playful nudge. "Show some respect."

Stacey rests her forehead on the countertop for a long moment. "The color palette was going to be orange, given the circumstances, but my client just decided that's too on the nose."

Stacey raises her head an inch before knocking it against the granite, then straightens up and rubs her temple. "I've got to call the baker and deal with this. Can someone drop Kaya off at Lily's house and take the other two to daycare?"

Glory glances at her watch. "I start seeing patients in half an hour."

"I'll take them," I volunteer.

Stacey looks up from her phone, surprised. "Really?"

"Sure. I don't have to be at the bridal shop for an hour, so I've got time. It's a perk of being up before noon, right?"

"Right," Stacey agrees, relief crossing her face. "Thank you, Willa."

While Glory finishes her last cup of coffee and Stacey scrambles to handle the last-minute color-change situation, I finish packing the girls' lunches and load them into my sister's giant SUV.

"Can I put on Kidz Bop?" Kaya asks. She squeezes into the back middle seat as I double-check the restraints on Lucy's seat.

So we listen to headache-inducing versions of pop songs sung by overenthusiastic children as I navigate the car out of Stacey's development. Kaya's friend Lily lives off Riverside Drive, a winding, scenic road that takes us past the Columbus Zoo and follows the Scioto River.

"What are you and Lily going to play today?" I ask as I turn into the driveway.

"We're not playing. We're doing a project on frogs."

"Awesome. What's the project?" I glance in the rearview mirror, and the sight of my three nieces makes the Kidz Bop rendition of "Call Me Maybe" a thousand times more bearable.

"It's a secret frog project," Kaya says in a hushed tone.

I marvel at the fact that this amazing, secret-frog-project-doing child is related to me, and then I drop her off at Lily's and drive three miles to the daycare Maeve and Lucy attend. Maeve skips happily into the three-year-olds' classroom, but Lucy requires an extra ten minutes of cuddling before she stops crying.

By the time I reach Dublin's historic district, a stretch of the suburb known for its cute shops and cozy restaurants, I have just enough time to find parking. White of Dublin is tucked between an upscale spa and a sushi spot, and the aroma of pepperoni and melted cheese from the pizza shop down the street makes my stomach rumble. I tuck my keys into my purse and hurry across the road.

Inside the shop, a sparkling chandelier and a round table set with crystal wineglasses and a mixed bouquet of white flowers welcome customers. A stone fireplace and a white couch add a touch of elegant warmth. Rows of stunning dresses hang in wooden nooks, waiting to be chosen by a hopeful bride.

I find Maisie next to one of the nooks, deep in conversation with a pantsuit-wearing salesperson and a slim brunette woman.

"Willa!" Maisie says when she sees me. "Come join us. This is Farrah, who did the alterations for my gown. And this is Lorene, Finn's sister. She's my maid of honor."

Lorene, a tall, lithe woman wearing a cardigan over a white oxford, pinstripe slacks, and heels so pointy they could probably poke out my eyeballs, gives me a brief nod. "Nice to meet you. Anyway, Farrah, are you confident about those changes to the hemline? We're dying to see them, aren't we, Maisie?"

Maisie nods, her head bobbing up and down with each word out of Lorene's mouth.

"Let me go get your gown," Farrah says, heading toward the back of the shop.

"I'll help," Lorene says, trailing after her.

"So," Maisie says when they're gone, wringing her hands together nervously, "let's hope it fits. I've been stress-eating a lot of peanut-butter M&M's this summer."

"I'm sure it will fit perfectly. Besides, if worse comes to worst, you can just get married naked. Finn won't mind, and at the end of the day, a dress is just an outfit, right?"

As soon as the words leave my mouth, I realize it's the same thing Stacey said to me on the day she helped me pick out my wedding dress. I was so nervous about finding the perfect gown that I couldn't even touch the cinnamon rolls Glory baked for breakfast. *A dress is just an outfit, Willa,* my sister told me. *A wedding is just a party. All that matters is that you love the person you're marrying.*

"Don't make jokes about getting married naked in front of Mrs. Forsythe," Maisie whispers. "She doesn't really do humor."

"I'll remember that," I say as Farrah returns with a long white gown in her arms and beckons Maisie to the dressing area.

"Be right back," she says, crossing her fingers.

While Maisie changes from her khaki work uniform into her wedding dress, Lorene and I perch ourselves on the couch to wait.

"So," I say when Lorene makes no move to start a conversation, "guess we're in this together, huh?"

"Pardon me?"

"Because we're both bridesmaids," I explain. "Team Maisie, right? Bride tribe. The I Do crew. Et cetera."

"Oh. Right." Lorene's phone chimes, and she glances at it briefly before we sit in silence again.

"So you've known Maisie for a while?" I ask, making a second attempt. Since Maisie is paying me thousands of dollars to be in her wedding, the least I can do is try to get along with my fellow bridesmaids.

Lorene nods and crosses one leg over the other primly. Rose is probably a huge fan of her posture. "I've known her since she started dating Finn. So that's, what? Two years now."

"And you're Finn's older sister, right?"

"Yes."

"Cool, very cool," I say, praying that Maisie's almost done changing. "I have a sister, too."

Lorene nods and smiles politely as she uncrosses and recrosses her legs.

"I know Maisie from summer camp," I say after a full sixty seconds of silence pass by. "We snuck into boys' cabins and stole Hershey bars."

Lorene's eyes widen, but she doesn't have a chance to respond. Farrah slides open the curtains blocking off the dressing room so that Maisie can emerge.

"Oh, Maisie," Lorene whispers. "You're stunning."

"It's the Corfu dress by Rosa Clará," Farrah tells me. "It's like something you'd see in a fairy tale, isn't it?"

Lorene and Farrah are right. Maisie's dress, an A-line tulle gown, is jaw-dropping. The sleeves, which end just below her elbow, are made of delicate lace, and a small sash around her waist defines her curves.

"It's perfect," I agree.

"I love what the illusion overlay does for your torso," Lorene observes. "It's going to photograph beautifully."

Maisie beams at Lorene, then steps onto the round platform in front of a mirrored wall. She studies her reflection carefully and turns around to analyze the back of the gown, where a bow holds the sash in place.

"You're sure it's not too much?" she asks, facing front again. "Too overstated?"

"You're the bride," Lorene says. "It's impossible for you to be overstated."

I want to protest, because Stacey once planned a wedding where the bride's train was so ridiculously long that it got trapped in the doors of the church and ripped into pieces, but I stay quiet.

"It's just . . . will I be able to dance in it?" Maisie asks, trying to swivel in the dress. "Because if it gets in the way of the Cha Cha Slide, maybe I should—"

"It won't get in the way. Besides, you'll be so busy taking pictures and talking to your guests that you won't have much time for dancing," Lorene assures her.

Maisie tilts her head from one side to the other, studying the gown. "That's true. Besides, all that matters is I get to marry Finn. Do you think he'll like it?"

"Who wouldn't like it?" Farrah asks. "You look like a princess."

"Of course he will," Lorene says.

"He'll love it," I say with one hundred percent certainty. I may not have known Maisie or Finn as long as Lorene has, but the look on Finn's face when he talks about Maisie tells me everything I need to know. That man would marry her if she wore a clown costume and stilts to their wedding.

When Maisie spins around again, studying the dress from every angle, I'm reminded of the time I stood where she is, wearing my off-white mermaid wedding dress, dreaming of the moment I'd walk down the aisle to marry Max. I'd liked a fair number of dresses, but when I tried that one on, Stacey, Sarah, and even Glory had teared up. Looking back, I can't help but wonder if Sarah's tears weren't about the dress at all.

Suddenly struggling for air, I cough and try to think of happy things: Kaya's secret frog project. The little patch of white fur on Nala's chest. Sitting in Ruthie's kitchen with a slice of pie and a glass of wine.

"Willa? You okay?" Maisie watches me with a concerned expression. "You look a little faint."

I nod, trying not to think of the rows and rows of beautiful dresses and the happy brides who will actually get to wear the one they choose. The brides who won't lose both of their best friends in a single day.

"I'm fine," I insist. "Got a tickle in my throat." I cough again for emphasis as Lorene gives me some serious side-eye. "Restroom?"

Farrah points toward the back of the shop, and I clamber up from the couch while Lorene points out a minor detail on Maisie's gown. I rush past the neat rows of dresses, but it's impossible not to remember the day I took my time looking at each one, imagining myself in each layer of fabric and pondering whether I should wear a veil.

In the bathroom, I lean over the sink and take slow, deep breaths. I catch a glimpse of my reflection in the mirror and wish I hadn't. My bangs are stuck to my forehead with sweat, and my eyes are red from the effort of blinking back tears. I wet a paper towel and press it to my cheeks, trying to calm down. I'm on the job, and I can't afford an emotional breakdown. I need Maisie's money so I can get out of Columbus. So I can stop having moments like this one.

"Willa?" There's a knock on the door.

I shut off the faucet and quickly blot my face with a clean paper towel. "Coming!"

"Are you oka—" I open the door to find Maisie back in her khaki ensemble, her fist raised to knock again. "Oh. There you are. Are you okay? You look like you're sweating bullets."

"I'm fine. I just got really hot for a second. Aren't you just burning up in here?" I fan myself with my hand.

"No. I actually think it's kind of chilly. They have the AC going at full blast." Maisie bites her lip. "If you're not feeling well, it's okay. You can tell me. I get really bad IBS sometimes, so I've been there, done that. You have nothing to be embarrassed about."

"Oh, no. It's not . . ." I think of Maisie in her stunning gown, standing on the same platform where I stood, and tears spring to my eyes despite myself. "It's not IBS."

"Is it your period? Not to pry or anything. But I get super emotional when I'm on my period. Last week I burst into tears at a Geico commercial. Hormones are fun." She shrugs. "Anyway, I have Dove chocolates in my purse if you want them."

I can't understand how the woman in front of me, the one worried about being able to do the Cha Cha Slide at her wedding and caring enough about me to follow me to the bathroom, doesn't have real friends.

"Willa," Maisie says softly. "It's okay."

Her kindness makes the floodgates open. I try to think of pleasant things, like escaping Columbus, but I can't. My shoulders shake with little sobs as tears spill onto my cheeks.

"Oh my gosh. Come here." Maisie pulls me toward her before I can step backward and wraps both arms around me. "Shh, shh, it's okay."

When my tears have slowed enough that I can breathe again, I step out of the cocoon of Maisie's arms and wipe my face with my sleeves. Here we are at her gown fitting, which is supposed to be a joyous occasion, and I'm ruining it with waterworks.

"Sorry," I whisper. "I'm the worst professional bridesmaid of all time."

"Are you kidding? I'd rather be back here with you than standing in front of those awful mirrors, listening to Lorene go on and on about hem stitching. You gave me an escape."

I laugh, and a little snot bubble emerges from my nostril.

"Let's go get tacos," Maisie says, passing me a tissue. "Tacos can fix anything."

12

Condado Tacos is a five-minute walk from the bridal shop, a route that takes Maisie and me past the Dublin library—the site of our fictional reunion—and an Irish pub. Lorene had to leave after Maisie's fitting to pick her kids up from day camp, so it's just the two of us. The air is heavy with humidity, but I'm grateful for each step that gets me farther away from White. I catch a glimpse of our reflections as we stroll past the window of a steakhouse, and I'm horrified to see that my mascara has started to trail down one cheek, giving me the look of a pathetic raccoon.

"Here." Maisie removes a handkerchief from her purse and uses it to dab my cheek. "I'd use my thumb and a bit of saliva, but I'm not sure we're on that level yet."

I laugh despite my embarrassment. "Thank you." It's been months since I've let myself be vulnerable in front of anyone, and having Maisie see me like this is scarier than marching down the street naked. "I'm sorry for freaking out back there. It won't happen again, I promise."

Her lips curl up in amusement. "What do you think I'm gonna

do, dock your pay for being human? You're allowed to have feelings, Willa. And you're allowed to show them."

Her kindness helps to dull the ache in my chest, but I'm still mortified by my outburst of emotion. I scramble to think of a new topic of conversation—how gorgeous Maisie looked in her dress, what flowers she'll carry in her bouquet, the fact that Lorene probably thinks I'm insane. Anything to get my mind off the day I chose my dress with Sarah's help. Anything to get my mind off Sarah. "So," I say, tucking my fingernails into my palms. "Flowers."

Maisie laughs and opens the door to the taco joint, ushering me inside. "You're gonna feel much better with some queso in you. Just wait and see."

I take a deep breath and pray that she's right as the hostess guides us to a table. The eclectic, colorful murals that cover the interior of the restaurant are enough to distract me for a moment; the wall behind the bar features a series of mushrooms with faces, and another wall bears the giant image of a green-and-blue dragon.

Maisie and I sit at a table near the window and peruse the menu. Away from the bridal shop, back in the regular world, I start to feel less unhinged. The cool breeze of an overhead AC vent dries the sweat that's pooled under my arms, and the aroma of sizzling beef helps me relax. I consider ordering a margarita, but then I remember that Maisie doesn't drink and decide not to.

When our waitress arrives, we order a round of Diet Cokes and tortilla chips with black bean queso to share.

"Thanks again for coming to the fitting," Maisie says, acting like I didn't ruin the whole thing with my breakdown. "Rose had to work today, and Jenna, the only bridesmaid you haven't met yet, is in Chicago for work. It was nice to have the extra support."

"I'm glad I could make it," I say, as though Maisie's not paying me a shit-ton of money to attend events like that one. "You really did look gorgeous. Finn's gonna lose it when he sees you."

Maisie smiles and adjusts the blue-and-white striped headband in her hair. "I hope so. It's not the dress I imagined myself wearing, but the second Mrs. Forsythe saw me in it, her reaction convinced me it was the one. She loved it."

I wonder why Mrs. Forsythe's reaction carried more meaning for Maisie than her own. "Do you love it, too? Since you're the one who's actually going to wear it?"

Maisie bites a chip in half and shrugs. "I wanted to go with something shorter, like a rockabilly-style dress. But that doesn't exactly work for a black-tie affair."

"So skip the black-tie affair."

She smiles. "Wouldn't I love to. But weddings are like, a *thing* in Finn's family. When his parents got married, Mrs. Forsythe arrived at the church in a horse and carriage. She still raves about it. And when Lorene married her husband, their wedding was featured in *Columbus Weddings*. Mrs. Forsythe was very proud."

I'm not convinced that Maisie's easy-breezy, Mrs. Forsythe-is-wonderful-and-I-don't-mind-calling-her-Mrs.-Forsythe routine is entirely genuine—no sane person likes her in-laws *that* much—but I don't press further. Considering our arrangement, Maisie's true feelings about Finn's family are none of my business. Besides, I'm more interested in learning about her family, and why she didn't ask her sister Clara to be a bridesmaid. "Are weddings a big deal in your family?" I ask, sipping my Diet Coke.

Maisie shakes her head. "Trust me, there are no black-tie weddings in my family tree. My mom married my dad in a shotgun wedding at city hall in a tiny town in West Virginia. All thanks to little old me." She pats her belly and motions to make it appear rounder.

"My mom wore a dress from the clearance rack at JCPenney. She'll be so, so happy for me when she sees my gown." She tears her straw wrapper into little bits as she speaks, littering the table with tiny paper snowflakes. "Like, the happiest."

I watch as Maisie grabs my wrapper and starts to add to her little paper mountain. I pull my napkin toward me so she won't get any ideas about shredding it, too. "Has your mom been involved in planning the wedding?"

"No. My parents still live in West Virginia, and they're busy taking care of my grandparents. Plus, my dad has chronic health issues. My mom would love to help with the wedding, but she has a lot on her plate."

"Finn mentioned that he hasn't met your family yet. That must be hard, not seeing them very often." I take another sip of my drink, careful to keep my tone neutral.

Maisie picks up the salt and pepper shakers and spins them in little circles, their glass bottoms making a grinding noise against the tabletop. Her movements are so distracting that I'm tempted to reach out and rip the shakers from her grip. "It's not easy. I miss them a lot. More than you can imagine. There's a lot they're missing out on, you know? Being so busy. And so far away."

"West Virginia's only, like, a four-hour drive, right? Maybe you and Finn could visit for a weekend. I bet your mom would love that. Your sister, too."

Maisie spins the pepper shaker too fast, knocking it over and spilling its contents across her menu. "How'd you know I have a sister?"

"Finn mentioned her at VASO. He said you're really excited to see her at the wedding."

"Oh, right. Well, I am. I can't wait to see her." She turns her hand sideways and uses the edge of her pinky finger to push the spilled pepper flakes to the corner of the table. "What else did he say?"

I watch as she carefully returns the shakers to their holder and then folds her hands together like she's praying. "Nothing, really. Just that he's looking forward to meeting your family. I told him you were really sweet to me at summer camp, and he ate it up. He's crazy in love with you, Maisie."

A pink blush creeps up her cheeks, and she meets my gaze with hers. "Thank you for telling him that. I know it's not easy for you to make up stories."

I want to ask the obvious question that springs to mind: how is it so easy for *her* to make up stories? And why are we making them up in the first place? But I bite my tongue and remember what five thousand dollars will do for me. "It's my job," I say with a shrug.

Maisie nods. "Anyway, I do wish we could get away to West Virginia for a weekend, but there's so much to do before the wedding. We have my bridal shower, our bachelor and bachelorette parties, meetings with the caterer and the florist and the band. I could go on and on. There's just no time for anything else. Plus, it's Pippa's birthday in August."

A dog's birthday sounds like a pretty lame reason not to visit, but I have no right to judge. I'm not close to either of my parents, and I would have used a pet parakeet's birthday as an excuse to get out of some family commitments. Besides, I hate when Glory and Stacey pry into my private life, and I'm not about to do the same to Maisie just to satisfy my curiosity—even if I am dying to ask her a thousand questions.

"But my parents and Clara are going to love the wedding," she continues. "Finn and I are having a roast turkey carving station at the reception because that's Clara's favorite."

"Well, I look forward to meeting them."

"It's going to be the best day." Maisie checks a box on the form we use to select our tacos, and the waiter stops by to grab our orders.

"I promise not to ruin it with a nervous breakdown," I joke, still feeling humiliated by my tears. "That's a money-back guarantee."

"It's really okay," she says kindly. "If it makes you feel better, I've burst into tears at all kinds of public places: Nordstrom Rack, Barnes and Noble, even that little Somali restaurant over on Cleveland Avenue. Sometimes you just can't help it." She dunks a chip in the bowl of queso. "Was there something in particular that bothered you?"

"Allergies," I lie at first. But as I'm about to change the topic to the wall murals—anything to get off the subject of my emotional turmoil—I remember the kindness Maisie showed me at the bridal shop. Maybe it's okay to admit to having feelings once in a while. After all, once her wedding is over, we'll never see each other again. I'll be far away, living in a different town, and our business partnership will just be a memory. Maybe it's okay to pretend *for* her instead of *with* her.

"Actually, it wasn't allergies. I . . . I've been to that shop before. When I picked out my own wedding dress. The wedding never happened, and being back there brought up some memories I wish I could forget."

"Oh, Willa. I'm sorry. I wish you'd told me before we went. I wouldn't have asked you to come if I'd known."

I shake my head sharply. "No, I wanted to come. It's what a real bridesmaid would do."

"You *are* a real bridesmaid." She brushes her lips with her napkin and sets it in her lap. "Do you wish it had happened? The wedding?"

I pause. No one's asked me questions about my broken engagement in a long time. The therapist did until I stopped going, and Kaya asked a few times in the months afterward about why she wouldn't get to wear a flower girl dress anymore, but that was it. Stacey was so focused on helping me move forward, and I was so insistent on not looking back, that I'm not sure I've actually processed what happened.

"No," I say finally. "I don't. He wasn't the right guy for me to marry."

Maisie nods. "Silver lining."

"Something like that."

The way Maisie doesn't pry further, doesn't ask me a zillion questions about how I feel or what my dress looked like or if I've read *It's Called a Break-Up Because It's Broken: The Smart Girl's Breakup Buddy*, makes me feel safe telling her more.

"He had an affair with my best-friend-slash-maid-of-honor," I say in a half whisper. "I found out about it six weeks before our ceremony date. The cherry on top is that they're still together."

"Holy crap," Maisie says, covering her mouth with her hand. Our waiter drops off our food, and she grabs her beef brisket taco and takes a bite. "Those little motherfuckers."

Hearing sweet-faced Maisie drop an expletive like that catches me off-guard, and I can't help but laugh. "Little motherfuckers is right."

"See, that crap is part of the reason I chose to work with animals. They're so much better than people, you know?"

I nod and sample my portobello mushroom taco. "After everything happened, I didn't know what to do with myself. My blog was focused on the things I did in Columbus, but everything I did in Columbus, I did with Sar—" I bite my lip, remembering my vow not to say their names. "I did with them. They were so intertwined with my blog that I didn't know how to keep it going without them. I've tried, but I just can't find the words."

"What do you mean?"

I sigh and set my taco down on its foil wrapper. How can I explain to Maisie what it's like to be a writer who can't write anymore? "I mean, I sit at my computer and I stare at the screen, and that's it," I tell her. *Or I write scathing posts and delete them.* "My readers were used to aspirational content: posts about how I found the best florist in Columbus for my wedding, or a guide to my top outfit picks for the Memorial golf tournament. They don't want to read about how the image of my best friend fucking my fiancé haunts me when I close my eyes."

I don't mention how my failure to keep my blog going led me to stop trying in other areas of my life, too: how I'd stopped showing up to the office for my lifestyle reporter gig and eventually got fired; how I stopped going for runs along the Olentangy Trail; how I stopped painting my nails and paying my bills and returning my friends' text messages. And I don't tell Maisie about the post I drafted, then deleted, the night I visited Sarah's Facebook page. I don't think my venom-filled references to asshole children and Max's distaste for cunnilingus will inspire confidence in my ability to be a great bridesmaid.

"I understand," Maisie says. "I haven't been in your exact situation, but I get it, what it's like to have memories you wish you could forget. I get it more than you know." She balls her napkin up and gets up from her seat. "I drank way too much Diet Coke. I'll be right back."

I nod and swallow another bite of mushroom, but inside I'm wondering what it is that Maisie's trying to forget.

"Hey, Willa?" Maisie stops en route to the bathroom. "I'm really glad you're in my wedding."

"Thanks, Maisie. Me too." And even though she's paying me a lot of money to pretend, in that moment, I don't have to.

13

Six days after Maisie's dress fitting, I find myself knee-deep in wool sweaters in Ruthie's bedroom. At Ruthie's Monday game night, her least favorite attendee, seventy-seven-year-old Edna Rogers, spent an entire game of Egyptian War bragging about her recent dating exploits. Edna's granddaughter had helped her create a profile on Silver Singles, a dating site for the over-fifty crowd, and apparently Edna was a hot commodity. Or so she claimed. Not to be outdone, Ruthie invited me over the next day for chicken salad sandwiches and a fun afternoon of profile creating. But she insisted on finding the perfect outfit for her profile picture, so we've spent the better part of the morning riffling through her multiple walk-in closets. The woman owns more sweaters than an Ann Taylor outlet.

"Ruthie," I say, watching as she holds up a white chiffon blouse, frowns, and returns it to the closet. "Have you heard of the KonMari method?"

She holds up a pair of red high heels. "Too stripperish?"

"Depends. Are you wearing them with a sequined bodysuit?"

Ruthie sets the heels down and picks up a pair of wedge sandals.

"Anyway," I continue, "the KonMari method—"

"Are you about to tell me about one of those new millennial sex tricks?" Ruthie asks, digging a cardboard box full of hosiery out from the back of the closet. "Because let me remind you, most of those new things aren't actually new. I'm in my seventies, Wilhelmina. I've tried everything under the sun."

"Okay, first of all, that's oversharing. Secondly, aren't you eighty-three?"

Ruthie scowls at me. "Do you or do you not want my old Cartier earrings?"

"Seventy-three it is."

"Are you sure about this whole dating thing?" I ask as Ruthie wraps a cashmere scarf around her neck and rifles through a pile of blouses. "Because you told me that men are boring and that Herman was the exception."

"Herman *was* the exception. And men *are* boring, as a rule. But I'm not looking for a life partner here. As distasteful as I sometimes find Edna to be, this isn't all about getting more matches than her. I'll never find another Herman, but maybe I can find someone to go to the movies with. Although not in this outfit." She shudders as she tosses a neon-yellow pair of pants onto her bedroom floor.

I grab the pants and put them in the discard pile I'm creating. "If you dislike Edna so much, why do you keep inviting her to game nights?"

Ruthie shrugs. "She makes excellent crab dip."

Before I can steer the conversation back to the Marie Kondo method of organization—*The Life-Changing Magic of Tidying Up* is one of the few books Stacey gave me that I actually read—my phone chimes from underneath a pile of sweaters. The only calls I get in the middle of the day are from very persistent student-loan creditors, but I fish my phone out anyway. It could be Stacey or Glory asking me to run an errand or help with the girls.

When I see Maisie's name on the screen, I answer immediately. "Hello?"

"Willa, thank God you picked up." Maisie's voice is strained, as if she just ran a mile and is out of breath as a result. "Please tell me that you're free right now, because I really need your help. We have a serious cake emergency. And yes, I do realize how stupid that sounds."

"It doesn't sound stupid," I say as Ruthie holds up a leopard-print bra and gives me a thumbs-up. "What's up?"

"Finn and I have been waiting for months for Mrs. Yummy's to announce that she's taking new orders," Maisie explains. "You know how exclusive Mrs. Yummy's is. She only takes orders a few times a year. Well, I checked the bakery Facebook page like I do every morning, and today's the day!"

"You're getting your wedding cake from Mrs. Yummy's?" I ask. Mrs. Yummy's is the most exclusive, high-end bakery in all of central Ohio, and like Maisie said, Mrs. Yummy only bakes a limited number of cakes each season. I tried to order one for my wedding to Max, but I couldn't get on her list.

"Well, I'm trying to. But if we don't get the deposit in today, we won't get one of her cakes. And we *need* to have one. Lorene had one at her wedding, and Mr. and Mrs. Forsythe had one at theirs. It's a family tradition."

"And it's happening today?" I ask, as if Maisie and I are discussing a strategic military operation. "The bakery's opening again?"

"Yes. But Finn had to fly to San Francisco for work this morning.

And Glen got out of his exhibit, so I can't leave the zoo to drop off a deposit."

"Who's Glen?"

"He's a southern hairy-nosed wombat," Maisie explains. "A marsupial."

"What's happening?" Ruthie asks, modeling a pair of knee-high boots.

"The wombat got out of his exhibit, and Maisie needs a cake from Mrs. Yummy's," I whisper.

Ruthie stares at me like I'm speaking Japanese, shrugs, and returns to her shoe collection.

"Sorry, Willa, are you still there?" Maisie asks. I hear garbled voices over a walkie-talkie in the background, paired with the sound of carousel music. "I was at the polar bear exhibit, which is across the zoo from Glen, so sorry that I'm out of breath. Anyway, is there any way you can drop the deposit off for us? I can't reach Lorene or Mrs. Forsythe, and Finn tried to call Liam to see if he could do it, but he's not answering his phone."

"Sure. Just tell me what to do."

Thanking me profusely, Maisie lays out my mission: I need to drive to her and Finn's place, get their house key from under a ceramic frog on the front porch, and then grab cash from the emergency stash they keep in the study. After that, I'll have to hurry to Mrs. Yummy's bakery in Hilliard and drop off a deposit for the cake.

"The bakery's Facebook announcement just went live ten minutes ago, but don't be surprised if there's a rush of people," Maisie continues. "Be careful, but be aggressive."

"Okay. If another bride tries to jump the line, I will absolutely drop-kick her."

Maisie doesn't laugh, and it occurs to me that a rumble of

drop-kicking brides might not be outside the realm of possibility. Mrs. Yummy's wedding cakes are the holy grail of Columbus baked goods.

"Good luck," Maisie says before she hangs up, like I'm about to board a rocket ship aimed for Mars. "And Godspeed."

14

Ruthie doesn't mind postponing our Silver Singles photography session, so I rush home and grab my car keys. Maisie texted me her address, and I plug it into my Waze app as I slip on my seat belt. She and Finn live in the small, eclectic neighborhood of Clintonville, a stretch of High Street that encompasses the Park of Roses and a cluster of quirky shops and delicious gastropubs.

I merge onto the highway and weave through traffic like I'm auditioning for a role in the next *The Fast and the Furious* movie. I haven't been on a deadline since I lost my job at *Buckeye Buzz*, and my race against the clock exhilarates me. I *need* to get this deposit made—not only because Maisie's paying me to do a job, but because despite my best efforts, I'm actually starting to like her. I've spent the last few months determined not to get attached to anyone, but Maisie's genuine concern for me at the bridal shop touched me in a way I didn't expect. I know how important it is to her that everything in her wedding go according to plan, and I'm determined to make this cake happen. I may be a terrible Princess Sparkleheart, but I want to prove that I'm not a total screw-up. That I can be a good bridesmaid.

I follow the app's directions until I reach Maisie's address on Garden Road. The home she shares with Finn is a charming yellow Colonial with a neat lawn and a row of tulips lining the mailbox. I park in the driveway and clamber up the front steps and onto the porch, where I find a cluster of ceramic animals and an adorable fairy garden. It's all very Maisie, especially the welcome mat shaped like a hedgehog. I lift up a green ceramic bullfrog to find a key underneath. As soon as I open the screen door, a loud barking sounds from the other side.

I unlock the door to find Pippa, a black-and-white border collie with a set of paws that seem too large for her body, greeting me with a wagging tail and an enthusiastic jump.

"Hi, girl," I say as she barks a few more times. When I hold out my hand for her to sniff, she licks the back of my palm and sits expectantly. I pet her head and survey the layout of the house. Maisie's living room is a bright, open space, with plenty of natural light that shines on cheerful blue walls. Framed photographs of Maisie and Finn rest on the fireplace mantel, along with a family of purple elephant figurines.

Maisie's text said the study is through the kitchen and on the right, so I follow her directions to the office at the end of the hall. A sleek Mac with a giant screen sits on a glass tabletop, along with a book about the changing structure of the IT world (probably Finn's) and a journal article on the mating mechanisms of mangrove hummingbirds (definitely Maisie's). Per Maisie's instructions, I open the top drawer of the cabinet near the desk and look for a money pouch. Instead, I find a rubber-band ball, a package of printer paper, and a pile of loose paper clips. In the bottom drawer, I discover a few shiny travel brochures and a large manila envelope. Thinking the cash might be stuffed inside the envelope, I empty its contents onto the desk, but it's just a stack of papers. Panic starts to rush over me. While I glance under the books on the desktop, Pippa watches from the doorway, as if I might stop what I'm doing to come into the kitchen and get her a treat.

"Where's the money, Pippa?" I ask, like she might launch into full Lassie mode and go fetch it.

Sighing, I start to dial Maisie's number, but then I spot a small cabinet in the corner of the office. Relief floods me when I open the top drawer to find a slim blue pouch with cash inside, and I'm so happy I could kiss it.

I hurry out of the study, stopping only to pet Pippa behind her ears. When I do, I notice the collection of papers magnet-stuck to Maisie and Finn's refrigerator: save-the-dates, Christmas cards, a roll of photo booth pictures showing Maisie and Rose making silly faces. Almost every inch of the refrigerator is covered with invitations to some type of party or fund-raiser. How is it, I wonder as I marvel at their wall of social obligations, that Maisie doesn't have enough friends to make four bridesmaids? What happened to make someone who's kind enough to comfort me at her own dress fitting, and treat me to tacos afterward, be willing to pay a stranger five grand to stand beside her on her wedding day? And why does she lie to her completely besotted fiancé about where she goes on Mondays at noon?

My phone chimes with a text from Maisie: Columbus Weddings magazine just tweeted that there's already a line around the block. Please hurry!

I slip my phone into my pocket and leave my questions for another time. I've got a goddamn wedding cake to order.

15

Mrs. Yummy's bakery is a small red-brick building that sits half a mile from the Hilliard library. My jaw drops when I get close enough to see a line of hopeful brides that starts at the bakery door and snakes all the way to the ice cream shop at the end of the street. I find a parking spot on the street and hustle to the end of the line, trying to count the number of people in front of me.

In line, I text Maisie. Ready to drop-kick if necessary. She immediately sends back an emoji of two hands raised in celebration, and I tuck my phone in my pocket and clutch my purse to my chest, the cash pouch hidden safely inside it.

"I can't believe Mrs. Yummy's is taking orders again," the woman in front of me says to me, her tone downright chipper. "My cousin's girlfriend's best friend had a Mrs. Yummy cake at her wedding, and people *still* talk about it. They also talk about the fact that her maid of honor hooked up with the groom's dad in the men's bathroom, but that's neither here nor there."

"Oh," I say. "Wow."

"My fiancé and I considered so many different cake flavors. We were gonna go with mango because we love mango, but that's a little crazy for a September wedding, don't you think? And we weren't sure that our guests are mango people."

"Sure," I agree as another rush of brides gets in line behind me, one of them accidentally elbowing me in the back. "Some people just aren't the mango type."

"Exactly. Which is why we decided to go in the strawberry direction. It's still a playful fruit, but it's more mainstream."

I wonder how long I'll have to listen to this woman assign personalities to fruit before Mrs. Yummy opens her doors.

"What type of cake are you ordering?" she asks, fingering one of her dreadlocks.

I consider sending her into convulsions by announcing that my wedding cake will be a matcha/brambleberry fusion, but instead I tell her the flavor Maisie texted me to order. "Belgian chocolate."

"Oooh, classic with a touch of grandeur," she says, nodding. "Excellent. Have you decided which cake topper option you're going to pursue?"

Before I'm forced to respond, her phone rings with a call from her mother. I know this because she keeps repeating, "I said the boutonnieres should be orange-infused coral, *Mom!*" in an increasingly higher pitch.

As the minutes pass, the line behind me doubles in size. I don't have much phone battery, so I'm forced to people-watch.

"What in the world," the woman behind me mutters. "Damn crazy person."

I glance in the direction she's pointing to see a grown man dressed in navy-blue slacks and a charcoal dress shirt sprinting down the block toward Mrs. Yummy's. He runs at full force, with no regard for the lady walking her Cavalier King Charles spaniel in his path. Not slowing his pace, he leaps over the dog like an Olympic hurdler and continues sprinting, doing an excellent impression of Forrest Gump after he broke free of his leg braces.

As the man gets closer, not appearing to care or notice that a hundred women are staring openmouthed at him, I inhale sharply. The crazy man running like he's being chased by a bear is Liam Rafferty.

He runs right past me before stopping dead in his tracks. "Willa?" he asks, bending over on the sidewalk to put his hands on his knees. "Is that you?"

Or at least that's what I think he says. He's so out of breath that he's wheezing for air, and I almost feel bad for him. Then I remember how he laughed at me during Chloe Wellington's party and called social media vapid, and I hope he drops dead on the sidewalk. I glance at my phone and pretend like I'm too busy texting to hear him.

"Willa?" he repeats. "Willa, it's me. Liam." Finally recovered enough to stand upright, he adjusts his tie and puts his hands on his hips, revealing a gnarly set of sweat stains underneath his arms.

"Oh," I say when it's clear I can no longer ignore him. "Liam. Hello."

He walks over to join me in line, setting off a loud series of protests from the fifty brides behind me. "It's okay, ladies," he assures them, giving his best thousand-watt smile. "I'm with her. We're on the same cake order, so I'm not cutting anyone."

"I've been in line for forty-five minutes!" a red-faced woman argues, holding her purse in front of her like she might hit Liam over the head with it.

"I understand, but I'm just joining my fiancée in line here," Liam says, sidling up next to me. "I'm not cutting, I swear."

The purse-clutching woman mutters something under her breath as Liam, apparently still not fully recovered, puts his hands over his head and tries to catch his breath. "Hey."

I glare at him. "I am *not* your fiancée."

"Shh!" Liam looks over his shoulder like he's frightened for his life. "Are you trying to get me killed by a mob of bridezillas?"

"It wouldn't be the worst outcome." I watch with distaste as he pats his chest and makes a series of annoying grunting noises. "What are you even doing here?"

He shoots me a dark look. "Finn left me three voice mails about a freaking cake emergency. Told me I had to get to Mrs. Yummy's to put their order in or Maisie was gonna lose her mind." He squints at the red-brick building in the distance. "Seriously, Mrs. Yummy's? What a ridiculous name."

The strawberry-cake lady in front of us, still deep in conversation with her mother, whips around to glare at him. "Mrs. Yummy's is an *institution*. Show some respect or shut your damn mouth. No, not you, Mom."

Liam takes a step backward from the strawberry-cake lady. After he's confident she's not going to punch him, he nudges me with his arm. "What are you doing here, Sparkles?"

I pull away as if he's burned me. "First of all, do *not* call me Sparkles. Second of all, what other reason could I possibly have for being here besides the same one you are?"

He smiles. "Calm down, Sparks. I don't know your life."

I roll my eyes and decide not to comment on the nickname again. He clearly has the emotional maturity of a fifth-grader, so getting mad about it will only make him use it more. "Maisie called me about the cake emergency, too. *I* actually picked up her call."

"Two points for Sparkles," Liam says dryly. "Some of us can't answer our phones at work."

"Right. Because you're too busy—let me guess—being a corporate attorney who sues little old ladies?"

"I'm not an attorney. But in your little fantasy, what am I suing these little old ladies for, exactly? Just curious."

I shudder. "You're more of a nightmare than a fantasy. And I don't know why you're suing them. This may surprise you, but I don't actually think about you very much."

"But you think about me a little bit, huh?" Liam grins.

"Scratch the attorney guess. I bet you're, like, a pharmaceutical sales rep. Or a used-car salesman. Or one of those Wall Street traders who helped cause the Great Recession and then got off scot-free."

"What about me screams drug rep?" he asks. "I mean, besides my obvious good looks and charming personality?"

"The fact that you never shut up, for one." I cross my arms over my chest and pray for Mrs. Yummy to open the doors of her stupid bakery. "You know, it's not really necessary for both of us to wait in line. I've got the cake situation handled. Feel free to go home and shower."

"And let Maisie and Finn think *you're* the most dedicated member of the wedding party? I think not."

I narrow my eyes at him. "Don't act like you care about the cake."

"Oh, I care about the cake. I care about the cake very, very deeply." He rolls up the sleeves of his dress shirt just enough that I can see the edges of his tattoo. "Just so you know, I'm not a Wall Street trader. I'm a pediatrician."

I freeze. There is no way that Liam Rafferty, supreme asshole, has a career as noble as that one. "You mean you're a doctor for *children?*"

"No, Willa, I'm a doctor for dinosaurs," he says pointedly. "Yes, a doctor for children. What other kind of pediatrician is there?"

I blush. "I just meant, it doesn't seem very . . . you." But it also doesn't seem very Liam-like to drop everything in the middle of a workday and wait in line for a cake just because his best friend asked him to. It occurs to me that maybe I've judged him too harshly, but I mentally swat the thought away like a gnat. I've given people the benefit of the doubt before, and look where that got me.

"And you feel qualified to assess that based on what, exactly? The twenty minutes of your life you've spent with me?"

He has a point, but I shrug. "I would have pegged you for a plastic surgeon or something. The kind that spends all day doing boob jobs and lipo."

"Well, you're wrong. But I'm sure that's a common occurrence for you."

"You're such a jerk," I mutter.

"Well, you're not exactly a ray of sunshine either, Sparks."

"At least *I* don't laugh at people who are clearly having a hard time." My skin grows hot as I remember the sight of him doubled over in hilarity at Chloe's party. "At least *I* have a shred of empathy."

"Has anyone ever told you that you're great at holding a grudge?"

"Has anyone ever told you you're a dumb butthead?" The insult pops out of my mouth before my brain has time to come up with anything better.

Liam stares at me. "Did you seriously just call me a butthead? What are you, nine?"

"Willa!" Someone behind us in line calls my name before I have time to respond to Liam's comment. "Willa Callister!"

"Don't move," Liam says as a blond woman a few meters back waves at me. "It's a trick to steal our spot in line."

But it's not a trick. It's worse—my former colleague Jennifer from

Buckeye Buzz. She covered the fashion beat and frequently joined Sarah and me for Sunday brunch at Union Cafe.

"Willa," she repeats, entreating the woman behind her to hold her place in line. She sidles up to Liam and me and reaches out to wrap me in a hug. I stiffen at her touch and pull away from the embrace as quickly as I can without appearing rude. "I can't believe it's you! Nobody's heard from you in ages."

"Yeah, I've been pretty busy," I say awkwardly, wishing the sidewalk would open up and swallow me whole. Jennifer is as gossipy as they come, and I could do without the fun stroll down old-Willa memory lane. Especially with Liam right next to me.

"We thought you moved to Siberia or something," Jennifer continues. "I couldn't find you on Facebook or Insta or anywhere. It's like you up and disappeared."

I would trade my right boob to be in Siberia right now instead of standing on a sidewalk with Jennifer and Liam in the ninety-degree heat, but I don't say that. I stay quiet, hoping Jennifer will get the hint.

"I was so, so sad to hear about your engagement ending," she says, taking my hand into hers. "Max seemed like such a great guy, but you never really know about people, I guess. And the fact that it was with Sarah . . . I just can't imagine what you went through."

I want to kick Jennifer across the sidewalk more than I've ever wanted anything. I glance at Liam to see if he's listening, and sure enough, he's watching my interaction with Jennifer like it's a particularly interesting tennis match. Liam learning about my broken engagement makes me die a little on the inside, and I tug my purse closer to my chest like I'm suddenly naked, exposed, and it's the only thing covering me.

"Yep," I say to Jennifer, wanting this conversation to end more desperately than I want world peace. "Anyway, I think the line is going to start mov—"

"Have you talked to her since? I saw her and Max a few weeks ago at Bigelow's, and did you know that sh—"

"I haven't talked to her." My tone is razor-sharp, and Jennifer steps back like I've cut her. Good. She hadn't bothered to call me after I lost my job at *Buckeye Buzz*, but she has plenty to say now. I don't want to hear another word from her stupid mouth. I don't want to hear a single thing about Sarah or Max or their adorable little outing to Bigelow's, where they probably snuggled in the corner booth and shared Max's favorite dish, the cannoli pancakes the diner's known for. I was so focused on Maisie's cake errand that I hadn't thought about Sarah or Max today until Jennifer appeared, and I'm furious that she's marred the day with a mention of them.

"Oh," Jennifer says, her voice hesitant. "Okay."

There's a long pause where neither Jennifer nor I speak, and all I hear is the bride in front of us screeching into her phone at full volume, scolding her mother about the size of her bridesmaids' corsages. I glance at Liam, who's looking from me to Jennifer and back again like he's not sure what the hell's going on.

"I don't like Bigelow's," he says finally. "I think the cannoli pancakes are overrated. Way too much orange zest."

A surge of affection for him blooms in my chest, and I loosen my death grip on the strap of my purse. "I agree."

"If you're really looking for good pancakes, I'd recommend Jack and Benny's," he continues. "They do a killer buckeye pancake. The apple cinnamon is also great if you're searching for something a little lighter."

"Oh," Jennifer says, looking deflated now that the conversation is centered on breakfast food instead of my blown-up love life.

"Awesome." She starts to turn back toward the end of the line, but Liam keeps going.

"Now, if you're okay with a modern twist on a classic dish, might I recommend Katalina's? They make these incredible pancake balls, and you get to choose the filling. I like Nutella, but there's also dulce de leche, and pumpkin-apple butter, and bacon—"

"Sounds yummy," Jennifer interrupts, her eyes glazing over. "You know, I really should get back to my spot. The line could move at any second." She gives Liam a polite smile and places her hand on my arm. "Take care, Willa. And know that we're all rooting for you, okay? I'll call to set up a lunch date."

I resist the urge to tell her to go fuck herself. I know she won't call, and I wouldn't answer even if she did. "Sure. Thanks."

"Wait!" Liam calls as Jennifer walks away, her departure filling me with relief. "I didn't get a chance to tell you about the bacon alternative! They can use veggie sausage instead!"

Jennifer glances over her shoulder but continues hurrying toward the back of the line. Her absence brings me such joy that I could hug Liam, smug smile and all.

"Thank you," I tell him.

He tilts his head as if he has no clue what I'm talking about. "For what? I'm just really passionate about pancakes."

I laugh, and it pushes away some of the nausea that took root in my stomach. I'm not sure what to say next, so I just wipe away the trail of sweat on my forehead and shrug. "That was Jennifer."

Liam nods and thrusts his hands into the pockets of his slacks. "I don't think she was very interested in what I had to say."

"To be fair, I don't think she's interested in what most people have to say." I shift my weight from side to side, wondering if he'll ask about Max or Sarah or why people thought I moved to Siberia. "What Jennifer said about . . . well, I was engaged once." I run my thumb over my bare ring finger and stuff my hand in my pocket to stop myself. "It didn't work out, obviously. It was kind of a messy situation, and it's not something I like to talk about."

Liam glances at me, and he's not smirking anymore. "I get it. I have more experience with messy situations than I'd care to. And I work with patients in diapers all day."

The warmth in his voice makes me think that he might be telling the truth—that he just might actually understand. Maybe there's more to Liam than laughing at party princesses and getting all high and mighty about Instagram. Maybe Maisie was right, and we will get along after all.

Maybe. But now isn't the time to find out, because Mrs. Yummy, a gray-haired, round-bellied woman, emerges from her bakery. "Welcome!" she says. A hush falls over the line as everyone strains to hear her words. "I wanted to thank you all for your business and remind you that I'll only be able to take orders from the first fifty brides. Please be patient and respectful of each other."

She disappears back into the bakery, and the throng of waiting brides grows instantly restless.

"Fifty orders!" a disgruntled voice behind us calls out. "There's at least a hundred of us out here!"

Startled by Mrs. Yummy's revelation, the brides don't obey her instructions to be patient and respectful. Instead, a scuffle begins at the front of the line as two brides get into a loud disagreement over who's next. The commotion spreads down the line like wildfire, and soon people are pushing forward toward the bakery, completely ignoring the proper order.

"Listen, Willa," Liam says as the brides behind us shuffle closer and someone accidentally—or perhaps not accidentally—smacks him in the back of the head with a handbag. "You've gotta make a run for it."

"What?" Someone jostles me from behind, and I clutch my purse tighter.

"The line's falling apart. It's gonna be pure chaos in a matter of seconds. You gotta make a run for the bakery."

I glance at Liam, who's looking at me with a grave expression on his face. "Are you kidding?"

He shakes his head. "Do you or do you not want Maisie to have the cake of her dreams?"

"I do."

"Then listen to me." He reaches out and pulls me toward him to whisper into my ear. Unlike when we took the group photo at Finn's birthday, his closeness doesn't make me want to gag this time. "When I say go, you run like the wind, okay?"

"What about you?"

"Don't worry about me. I'll stay back to hold the line as long as I can." He takes a deep, bracing breath, like we're about to storm the beaches of Normandy. "Whatever happens, don't look back."

"I don't know about this," I say as the strawberry-cake lady gives the bride in front of her a not-so-gentle push. "It really is just cake—"

The scuffle toward the front of the line worsens, and all hell breaks loose. Strawberry-cake lady abandons her place in line and charges toward Mrs. Yummy's.

"Willa, go!" Liam shouts, steeling himself to form a human barrier between me and the line behind us. "Run like the wind!"

"But—"

"RUN!" he shouts, and I do as instructed. I run full-force toward the bakery, weaving through throngs of brides.

It's the first time I've run in months, and the sensation of my limbs in motion sends a thrill through me.

"For Maisie!" Liam cries as if he's the hero in the battle scene of a movie, ready to meet his death for greater glory.

I pump my legs and arms harder, the sidewalk disappearing beneath my feet. For Maisie.

16

"*I still can't* believe you did it," Maisie says the next week. It's the day of her bridal shower, and she invited me to join her in getting her hair done before the event.

We sit next to each other in comfy chairs as stylists work on our hair at the Blowout Bar, a chic blow-dry salon in Dublin. The salon is sparkling white with shiny maple-wood floors. *Clueless* plays on large TV screens in front of us.

Maisie takes a sip of orange juice and continues praising me for the cake-deposit success. "*Columbus Weddings* tweeted that most of the brides were turned away. You really are a freaking hero."

"To be fair, I had help."

Maisie nods. "Liam told Finn it was a bloodbath. He also said you're a really fast runner. He was impressed."

I shrug. I still don't like the way Liam treated me when I was Princess Sparkleheart, but I wouldn't have been able to laugh off Jennifer's faux concern if it weren't for him. And I probably wouldn't have made it inside Mrs. Yummy's, either. "I had a good reason to run fast."

Maisie grins at me. "I'm so happy you did. And I really, really hope today goes well."

"It's your bridal shower. Of course it'll go well."

"I hope so. Mrs. Forsythe put a lot of work into organizing it." She taps her foot against the chair and bites her lip, like she's thinking about something else. I wonder if mentioning Mrs. Forsythe makes her think of her own mom, and my heart goes out to her.

"You know, I can take a bunch of pictures for you at the shower. I used to take tons for my blog, so I have a pretty decent camera. And this way, you'll have so many to send to your family, it'll almost be like they were there." As soon as the words leave my mouth, I realize I'm not extending my offer just because Maisie's paying me. I'm offering because I want to make her happy—as if she's my friend. The realization that I'm starting to regard her as a friend plants a seed of anxiety in my chest. I used to feel that way about Sarah, like I'd do anything to help ease her pain. Because I thought she'd do the same for me. Because I thought we could rely on each other no matter what. But I was wrong, and the last thing I want is to risk letting a new version of Sarah wreck me again.

Maisie's my boss, not my friend, and I will myself to remember it.

Maisie's expression brightens at my offer. "You're sweet, Willa. But Mrs. Forsythe hired a professional photographer, so all you need to do is enjoy yourself. And field any questions about how we know each other, of course."

"What do you think?" Maisie's stylist asks, arranging one last perfect wave on Maisie's head. She chose a style called the Flirtini, and her smooth curls are bouncy and voluminous. My choice, the Cosmo, has just a bit less volume.

"I love it," Maisie says, studying her reflection in the mirror. It's almost comical to see Maisie so intent on her hair, because she's usually wearing it in a loose bun or a haphazard braid. "Do you mind fixing that tiny section in the back? Sorry to be annoying. I just need my hair to look good from every angle. Mrs. Forysthe is really particular."

"This Mrs. Forsythe sounds like a piece of work," I say as the stylist makes sure every strand on Maisie's head is impeccable.

Maisie shrugs. "She just wants things to be perfect for Finn."

"And for you, I hope."

Maisie smiles and downs the last of her orange juice. "Let's go get showered."

17

Finn's parents live in a massive English Tudor–style home on a quiet street filled with other massive English Tudor–style homes.

"Holy shit," I say when Maisie parks her Prius on the street. "This place is like its own small village. How many bedrooms?"

"Five bedrooms, five bathrooms." Maisie smiles. "Quite a difference from my parents' three-bedroom place in West Virginia. We had one bathroom for me, my parents, Clara, *and* my grandma."

I grab my shower present from Maisie's trunk: a suitcase from her registry, along with a set of monogrammed his-and-hers spoons that I thought was dumb but Stacey insisted was adorable.

Maisie sets her shoulders back like she's about to strut down a runway. "Let's do this."

We walk the considerable distance from the street to the house, strolling past a pair of marble lion statues that mark the end of the driveway and the greenest lawn I've ever seen. The front door, which features an actual brass knocker in the shape of a lion's face, is already open.

"Who are these people, the Lannisters?" I mutter as we step across the threshold. I avoid eye contact with the creepy lion knocker.

The interior of the home is all polished wood and thick rugs. A grandfather clock ticks in one corner of the foyer, and in the front room, a large oil painting of an elderly woman hangs over the fireplace.

"Grandmother Forsythe," Maisie whispers as we tiptoe through the front room like we're in a museum. "May she rest in peace."

In a large, gleaming kitchen that puts Stacey's to shame, we find Lorene and an older, taller version of her arranging neat trays of fruit, veggies, and cheeses.

"Hi, Lorene," Maisie says. "Hi, Mrs. Forsythe. We were just admiring the painting of Grandmother Forsythe in the sitting room."

Lorene and Mrs. Forsythe, who wears a plum sheath dress with nude heels, both greet Maisie with a hug.

"I'm Willa," I say when Mrs. Forsythe's gaze turns toward me. "I've never been in a house with a sitting room before."

Finn's mom smiles politely while I realize how stupid my comment sounded. "It's lovely to meet you, Willa. Welcome."

She pours two glasses of champagne and hands one to me. The other she tries to pass to Maisie.

"Mom!" Lorene says sharply, and it's the first time I've heard intonation in her voice. "Maisie doesn't drink. Here, Mais, let me grab you a Sprite."

She shoots her mother a dark look and grabs the glass from her hand before fetching Maisie a can of Sprite from the refrigerator.

"Thanks," Maisie says, her voice quieter than before. "And thanks for the offer, Mrs. Forsythe."

Someone calls for Mrs. Forsythe from the foyer. "Oh, that's Himari, the photographer," she says, smoothing the front of her dress. She touches the ends of Maisie's hair as she passes her in the hallway. "Why don't you touch up your hair a bit before we get started? You can use the master bathroom upstairs. Lorene will help you." She struts out of the kitchen, leaving Maisie looking like someone just kicked her puppy.

"Whatever," I say after a long pause. "I think your hair looks fucking amazing." It occurs to me that if Maisie decided to murder her future mother-in-law, I'd help her hide the body. No questions asked.

"It's fine." Maisie's smile bounces back, and she grabs a clump of hair and studies the ends. "It is a little flippy. I'll be right back."

She ascends the stairwell while Lorene downs the glass of champagne that was intended for Maisie and pours herself another.

"You drink, don't you, Willa?" Lorene asks.

"Um, yes. I do."

"Good." She pours another glass and slides it across the kitchen counter toward me, even though I haven't started to sip the first one. "I give Maisie all the credit in the world. You have to be tough as hell to put up with my mom, let alone do it sober."

I decide that I like the tipsy version of Lorene more than the tense one I met at the bridal shop. "Maisie's very tough," I agree, like I have any clue what I'm talking about.

Lorene nods. "We went to lunch for my mom's birthday last week, and when Maisie ordered fettuccine Alfredo, Mom warned her that she should watch her calories before the wedding. She actually used the phrase 'a moment on the lips, forever on the hips,' and Maisie didn't even try to stab her with the butter knife. That takes a serious level of Zen."

God, Mrs. Forsythe sounds even worse than I thought. A woman like that doesn't even deserve to *look* at a plate of fettuccine Alfredo, let alone tell someone else what to eat. "Maisie can be really stoic when she needs to," I tell Lorene, as if I really have known Maisie for years. I figure that dropping an occasional, made-up anecdote from our childhood together will really help to sell our story. "This one time at camp, we were playing Frisbee, and the Frisbee got stuck in a tree. One of the boys dared Maisie to climb up and get it." If I imagine hard enough, I can almost picture a younger Maisie with grass stains on her shorts and her hair in a long, messy braid. I can almost believe my own story. "He thought she'd be too scared, but nothing stops her. You know how she is. She convinced me to hoist her up, and she climbed so high up the tree that she definitely would have broken her legs if she fell. The Frisbee was lodged right next to a beehive, but Maisie didn't care. She climbed down from that tree with the Frisbee and the biggest smile you ever saw. And about six bee stings."

Lorene coughs up a sip of champagne. "Six bee stings?"

"Yep. And she acted like it was nothing. Tossed the Frisbee right at the boy's feet, and then she marched off to the mess hall to get a Popsicle like the badass she is." I'm surprised by my own ability to think so quickly on my feet, and I give myself a mental pat on the back.

Lorene's eyes widen in horror, which is not the reaction I was going for. At all. "Where were the counselors when this was happening?"

"I mean, our counselors were really just a bunch of underpaid teenagers," I answer, wondering why Lorene is taking the story so seriously. It was supposed to be about Maisie's toughness, not the glaring lack of supervision at the fictional Camp Wildwood. "They spent most of their time making out with each other."

"So who gave Maisie the EpiPen?" Lorene asks, abandoning her drink on the countertop. "I mean, she could have *died*."

"What?" I ask, suddenly not so quick on my feet anymore. My heart thuds in my chest as I scramble to make sense of where I went wrong—probably the instant I opened my stupid mouth.

"Maisie is severely allergic to bee stings," Lorene says, narrowing her eyes at me. "Last summer, at our Labor Day cookout, she stepped on a bee and broke out in hives immediately. Her face swelled up like a balloon, and she could barely swallow. If Finn hadn't used an EpiPen on her, we would have had to call 911." She crosses her arms over her chest. "You're telling me she got stung by six bees and skipped right off for a Popsicle?"

"Oh," I say, my stomach sinking. I rush to think of something, anything to say that will help me undo the damage I've just done. "Of course. I must have been confused—"

"What's this about six bees?" Maisie asks, strolling back into the kitchen. Her hair looks just as glorious as it did before, but I'm sweating so profusely that my blowout is mere seconds away from getting ruined.

"Willa was telling me about the time you climbed a tree to get a Frisbee back at camp," Lorene says. "She said you were stung by six bees."

Maisie's gaze flickers toward me for the briefest of moments, but it's long enough for her to read the panic on my face. I've somehow managed to poke holes in our own cover story in the two minutes she left me alone with Lorene, and if our whole partnership comes crashing down because of it, I'll only have myself to blame.

Maisie lets out a breezy laugh, as if I haven't single-handedly destroyed everything. "Oh my gosh, Willa, no. Those were wasps, not bees, thank God." She grabs two chocolate-covered strawberries from a tray on the countertop and passes one to Lorene. "Wasp and bee venom are made of different antigens. Fun little insect fact."

"Huh," Lorene says, taking a small bite of her strawberry.

"I had no idea," I say, forcing myself to speak above a whisper.

Maisie licks chocolate off her fingertip like she doesn't have a care in the world. "A few wasp stings can't slow me down. But bee stings? That would have been a different story." She winks at me and lifts her Sprite can. "How about a toast to get this shower started? For good luck."

"It's your bridal shower, Mais," Lorene says. "You don't need any luck."

The sound of Mrs. Forsythe's voice floats in from the living room, where she's scolding a catering attendant for spilling a tray of coconut shrimp.

"On second thought," Lorene says, raising her glass, "here's to Maisie. Good luck."

She glances at me, and I swear she can see right through me and my ridiculous lies, but then I realize she's just waiting for me to join in on the toast.

I was planning to follow Maisie's lead and abstain from alcohol today, but Lorene nods toward my glass. What the hell, I think as I watch the little bubbles float to the top of the liquid.

"To Maisie," I echo. Then I tilt my glass toward Lorene's and take a long sip of champagne. Something tells me I'm really gonna need it.

18

Its a good thing the Forsythes live in such a large house, because Maisie's bridal shower is the biggest I've ever been to. I try to count how many women are in attendance, just so I can tell Ruthie about it later, but I lose track before I get to a hundred. There are cousins from every part of the Midwest, friends from the neighborhood, and even a math teacher who taught Finn in elementary school. I drink champagne and snack on finger foods carted around on trays by catering staff while I try to forget about the near-disaster I caused in the kitchen. Mrs. Forsythe acts as Maisie's personal attendant, guiding her from one group of ladies to another and intervening if anyone tries to corner her for too long.

What strikes me as I stand near the dessert table with Rose, downing M&M's while she tells me about a yoga retreat in Costa Rica, is that hardly any of the guests are here on behalf of Maisie. The realization plants a seed of empathy in me—I know exactly how crushing it is to feel alone in the world—but also deepens the mystery of Maisie. Sure, maybe her family from West Virginia can't attend, but what about her friends? Her closest work buddies? The women she gets bagels with after yoga? Where are *they*? Did Mrs. Forsythe simply not invite them, or are they not here because they don't exist?

"It was all about soulful breathwork," Rose says, drawing me out of my thoughts. "Which isn't something I think about on a daily basis, you know?"

"Yes," I reply, trying not to sound like a dumbass who knows nothing about yoga. "I also struggle with maintaining soulful breathwork."

"See? It's such a common issue. Which reminds me of this upcoming workshop I'm going to in the Mojave Desert . . ."

I half listen to Rose as I glance around the Forsythes' house. Women flow in and out of the living room and the dining room, and I try to count how many of them have a connection to Maisie. There's me, obviously, and an engineer bridesmaid named Jenna who befriended Maisie at barre class. Maisie also introduced me to two of her co-workers and an elderly neighbor who lives next door to her and Finn, but that's it. Everyone else is related to Finn, either familially or socially. Even Rose and Lorene, who adore Maisie and are in her bridal party, are technically Finn's relatives.

There's no one from Maisie's past in attendance. No distant cousins from Pittsburgh or friends from high school. No great-aunts or a grandmother or bored young cousins who would actually know about Maisie's deathly bee allergy. There's just me, Maisie's childhood summer-camp friend. And even our history is fake.

". . . and that's how I started leading the chaturanga clinic," Rose says.

"That's awesome." I tune back in as fast as I can and hear something about chaturangas. "You know what's funny about chaturangas? They always make me think of chimichangas. And that always makes me hungry."

I mentally kick myself for saying that shit out loud, but Rose only nods in total agreement. "Yeah, totally. It's that whole body-mind connection, you know? We should definitely get chimichangas sometime."

Lorene, looking drop-dead gorgeous in a sleeveless red dress, joins us near the candy table. "Poor Maisie," she says, watching as Mrs. Forsythe takes the bride's hand to lead her toward a group of white-haired women. "Mom's trotting her around like a show pony, and she's not even buzzed to deal with it."

"Are you buzzed?" Rose asks her.

Lorene smirks. "What do you think? I drank a ton of champagne, plus I have a flask in my purse. You guys want any?"

When Rose and I both decline, Lorene shrugs. "Fine, Little Miss Summer Camp. But it's the only way I can survive a Forsythe family function."

Rose watches with an arched eyebrow as Lorene sneaks a sip from a silver flask. "I prefer soulful breathing."

"Fuck soulful breathing," Lorene mutters before heading toward the kitchen.

She doesn't give me any weird looks or ask any pressing questions, which leads me to believe that she accepted Maisie's correction to my story. Still, I need to be more careful. One more misstep like the one I took earlier, and I could be out of a job—not to mention how humiliated Maisie would be if anyone found out the truth.

"Don't mind Lorene," Rose says when her cousin's gone. "She's going through a really rough time."

I nod and grab another handful of pretzel M&M's bearing Finn and Maisie's initials.

"Her husband is a total scumbag," Rose continues, crossing her toned arms over her chest. "He's this super successful investment banker, so Lorene's parents love him, but he travels all the time for work, and he's a girl-in-every-port type. Lorene's finally had enough, but she's terrified to file for divorce. She thinks her parents will disown her."

"Over a divorce?" I ask. "What is this, the 1950s?"

"Try the 1800s," Rose replies. "Have you seen the oil painting in the sitting room?"

"Yes. It's creepy."

"Nobody in the Forsythe family gets divorced. They're like the fucking Kennedys without all the tragedy. Or the political power."

"Aren't you a Forsythe?"

Rose smiles. "My mom's a Forsythe. My dad's a Jackson. So yes and no."

I watch as Mrs. Forsythe leads Maisie to the living room while the photographer trails behind, snapping pictures of Maisie like she's Kate Middleton.

"Oh, good," Rose says dryly as Mrs. Forsythe motions for Lorene to approach the gift table. "It's time to watch Maisie open presents for two hours. Do you think she'll get a blender?"

"Rose," I whisper, watching as Lorene hands Maisie a wrapped gift and the beaming bride opens it. "What about Finn? He's good to her, right?" It occurred to me that maybe Finn, as charming and good-natured as he seems, could be the reason for Maisie's lack of friends. I don't know him well enough to eliminate the possibility that he's secretly a power-tripping control freak. It seems unlikely, but you never know, and despite my attempts to stay strictly professional, I'm concerned for Maisie. I'm surprised by the protectiveness I feel toward her; I thought the part of my heart that bonded with other people, the part that loved and looked out for them, was scarred over for good. I chomp on another M&M and force myself to push any sentimental thoughts away. I'm just doing my job, after all. I'm being a good bridesmaid and looking out for Maisie. That's what she's paying me to do.

"Finn's the best," Rose whispers back. "And so is Maisie. You don't have to worry about that."

When a tipsy Lorene almost loses her balance while handing Maisie another present, Rose whispers an expletive and hurries over to join them, a smile glued to her face. She's clearly survived her fair share of Forsythe parties.

A woozy lightness takes root in my head, and I put down my glass of champagne. I'm technically on the job, so I need to watch my alcohol intake. I head for the bowl of punch in the kitchen, but I stop when I hear hushed voices in the hallway.

". . . says she's from West Virginia or Kentucky or someplace down South," a high-pitched voice whispers. "No one's met her parents. Not even Finn. Victoria thinks her father might be incarcerated."

"She's not Catholic," another woman, one with a smoker's deep voice, chimes in. "Victoria said the first time Finn brought her to Easter Mass at St. Agatha's, she referred to Father Ochs as 'Your Honor.' And during the sign of peace, when the man in the pew behind her shook her hand and said, 'Peace be with you', she didn't say, 'And also with your spirit.' She gave him a big smile and said, 'Hey, thanks!'"

Laughter rings out from the group, and I contemplate peeking around the corner and launching a handful of M&M's at their heads.

"Well, I heard she has a drinking problem," the first speaker states. "Victoria says the girl never drinks, and who ever heard of a nonreligious teetotaler who didn't have trouble with the bottle?"

"Alcoholism has a lot to do with genetics," a third woman whispers. "You have to wonder if she'll pass it along to her kids."

I almost choke on a chunk of pretzel, and I put my hand over my mouth to stay quiet. The callous way they talk about Maisie makes my skin crawl, and I want to pop around the corner and shame them into silence, but I don't. Because I want to hear what they have to say. I want to find out if they know something about Maisie that I don't—something that explains why she only has a handful of acquaintances at her own bridal shower. Something that explains why she hired me in the first place.

"And you heard how she refuses to drive at night, right? Victoria says she's really strange about it."

"Maybe she has poor vision," the gravelly voice suggests. "That's not good for a child's genetics, either."

"Victoria thinks Finn will come to his senses by the wedding date. That's why she offered to host the wedding here, you know. So they won't lose the deposit on a venue if he decides not to go through with it."

"Hey, what are you doing in the corner?" Lorene asks, speaking directly into my ear.

I'm so surprised that I jump and let out a little screech, then clap a hand over my mouth. "Nothing."

"Who are you eavesdropping on?" she whispers entirely too loudly, peeking around the corner and almost falling sideways.

"I'm not sure," I say, ashamed that I was just waiting for them to get to the good stuff. "Some people gossiping about Maisie."

"Oh, for the love of God." Lorene rolls her eyes and grabs the glass of champagne I'd set down. She downs it in a single swig and straightens her shoulders. "Those miserable bitches." She strides around the corner into the kitchen, and I trail behind her.

"Hello, ladies," she says when we meet the gossipers in the kitchen. "Have you met Willa? She's another one of Maisie's bridesmaids."

The women, all around Mrs. Forsythe's age, smile at Lorene and me politely. "I don't think we have."

"Oh." Lorene shrugs. "Well, that's probably because you're hiding in the kitchen talking shit like a bunch of twelve-year-olds. If you'd mingled, like you're *supposed* to do at a bridal shower, you would have met Willa."

"Lorene," the gravelly-voiced woman protests, "we certainly didn't mean to offend—"

Lorene holds up a hand to quiet her, loses her balance, and regains it slowly. "The bride—you know, the person we're all here to celebrate—is opening her gifts in the living room. You should probably go watch. You wouldn't want to appear rude, would you?"

"Well, of course we're going to go watch," one of the women says, sounding affronted. She ducks her head and leads the others into the living room. "Nice to meet you, Julia."

"It's *Willa*," Lorene shouts after them, causing a very displeased-looking Mrs. Forsythe to glance over.

"I'm definitely gonna hear about that later," Lorene mutters, leaning against the kitchen counter. "Willa, get me another drink, will you?"

I fill both of us cups of alcohol-free punch and pass one to Lorene. "Yummy," she says, taking a long swig. "I love bridal showers."

"At least Maisie's having a good time, right?" I ask.

I stand in the entryway to the living room, watching as Maisie unwraps my suitcase and holds it up for Mrs. Forsythe to admire while Himari the photographer captures all of it. I bought myself an identical suitcase with some of the money Maisie paid me up front. Someday, someday soon, I'll pack what I need in it and get the hell away from this town.

"Yeah," Lorene says softly. "At least she is."

She holds her cup of punch out for a toast. "Welcome to the bride tribe, Willa. And welcome to the jungle."

I clink my glass to her cup and wish I could ask her about Maisie's friends and family. Lorene seems to care about her a great deal, so maybe she could shed some light on the situation and help me understand Maisie better. But I can't risk raising any more suspicion. I've already put my foot in my mouth with my genius little tree-climbing tale, and the last thing I need is to give anyone reason to doubt my friendship with Maisie. As her supposed childhood friend, I should know just as much as Maisie's future sister-in-law—I should know *more*—about her background. I sip my drink and try to shake off the questions buzzing through my mind. Maisie's social life shouldn't matter to me. Her happiness shouldn't, either. All that matters is that I perform my duties well and get the paycheck I need to move away from the city that holds all of my worst memories. Worrying about her is something I'd do for a friend, not a boss.

And a friend is the last thing I need.

19

I may have a strict no-friends policy—I wouldn't survive a Sarah 2.0 working her way into my heart and breaking it all over again—but family is different. And nothing makes my protective instincts come out like one of my nieces in pain.

Kaya has been up half the night with an aching belly. I sit on the edge of her bed, holding a cold washcloth to her face and wishing whatever virus is rumbling around in her stomach would come for me instead.

The thermometer in her mouth beeps, and Stacey removes it, her forehead wrinkling as she studies it. "You have a fever, baby."

Kaya pushes the washcloth off her forehead. "I just want to sleep."

With Glory in Nashville for the annual American Academy of Pediatric Dentistry conference, I've been upgraded from aunt to co-parent. I cuddle baby Lucy against my chest and stroke Kaya's hair while Maeve vrooms a toy fire truck on the floor beside the bed.

"Shh, Maeve," I whisper. "Play quieter, okay?"

"Try to get some rest, sweetie," Stacey tells Kaya, who makes a small whimpering noise and closes her eyes obediently. After a quick kiss to Kaya's forehead, Stacey steps into the hallway. I follow her, trying to extract a clump of my hair from Lucy's fingers.

"I should stay home with her," my sister whispers, rubbing her eyes. "I can't move my meeting with Chelsea Rickenbacker's florist, but maybe I could cancel on touring that new venue in Grandview. But then I'm supposed to meet a vendor right near there. Shit."

"Stace, what time's your meeting with the florist? And how many hours of sleep did you get?"

Sighing, she runs a hand through her hair, which smells of sweat and vomit. "Meeting at nine. As for sleep, I don't know, three hours? Maybe four."

My only plans today are to help Ruthie get ready for a date. My lack of nine-to-five employment and a typical social life leaves plenty of free time to take care of my nieces. I might have been the world's worst Princess Sparkleheart, but I can be a damn good aunt.

"I'll take care of the girls," I tell my sister. "You take a shower and go to your meetings. We'll be fine, I promise."

Stacey's eyes well with actual tears of relief—or maybe exhaustion—and she squeezes my hand like I've just announced that I'm giving her a billion dollars. "Are you sure? Because that's your whole day, Willa. I could drop Luce and Maeve off at daycare if I hurry."

The fact that the small favor of me handling the girls for a day provokes such emotion in her fills with me guilt. Before The Incident, I was so busy with wedding planning and blog posting and spending time with Max that I didn't have much time for my nieces. I took them out for ice cream every so often, sure, but that was about it, and I never really considered how it might have impacted Stacey.

I clutch Lucy tighter to my chest, eager to show my sister that I can be there for her.

I shake my head. "No need for daycare. Aunt Willa's got it covered. We'll eat microwaved chicken noodle soup and watch *Frozen*. I can do this."

Stacey nods. "I know you can. Thank you, Willa." She leans forward to hug me, but I jump back.

"Ugh, go wash your vomit hair, please. I'll make you a PB&J for lunch."

I carry Lucy to the kitchen and get Maeve to follow us by promising that she can have dinosaur-shaped chicken nuggets for lunch. I set Lucy in her high chair and give her a pile of Cheerios while Maeve darts around the kitchen, pretending that a giant pterodactyl is chasing her.

I make a sandwich for Stacey and one for myself for lunch later, then slice up some strawberries for Maeve and Lucy. My phone chimes with a text from Nate: Thanks for taking care of Kaya today. Aunt Willa to the rescue! I don't get off until six, but text me if you need anything.

I respond with a thumbs-up and get to work loading the dishwasher. When Stacey comes downstairs, freshly showered and smelling a whole lot better, I hand her a brown lunch bag.

"It's a sandwich and Goldfish crackers. Don't get too excited."

"Remember," my sister says, slipping her high heels on, "the mowers are coming to cut the grass. And Maeve shouldn't have any chocolate, despite what she tells you. And you need to check on Kaya regularly. Make sure she gets something in her stomach, even if it's just Gatorade and saltines. And keep track of her fever."

"Stacey," I say patiently, handing her a cup of coffee. "Go to work. I've got this."

❦

I don't have this. By noon, I'm exhausted. Lucy's been fussy all morning, and Maeve is a bundle of energy who accidentally knocked over her plate of dino nuggets twice, giving Nala an extra-large lunch. Nobody wants to take a nap except for me, and I practically have to wrestle Maeve and Lucy upstairs to check on Kaya every half hour.

"I'm bored," Maeve whines as we clamber up the stairs, Lucy pinching my arms and Nala trudging along behind us. "I wanna watch *Daniel Tiger.*"

"You just said you didn't want to watch it, Maeve."

"Yeah, well, now I do!" She flings her dinosaur-hunting Nerf gun onto the carpet, and I'm too overwhelmed to even bother reprimanding her.

"Kaya," I whisper, flicking on the bedside lamp. "I need to check your temperature, sweetheart."

I hold the thermometer under Kaya's tongue while Lucy tries to rip my earrings out. When it beeps, I have to hold it with two hands to keep it from shaking. Kaya's fever has jumped to 102 degrees. Hoping that getting a little food in her belly will help, I hold a cracker to her lips.

"Aunt Willa," Kaya says after refusing to try the saltine, "it hurts really bad."

"What hurts, baby girl?"

"My tummy. It hurts so bad." Without further ceremony, she leans over and pukes into the bowl Stacey set out, and Lucy starts to wail.

"It's okay, babies," I say, rubbing Kaya's back and trying to bounce Lucy on my hip.

I turn on *Daniel Tiger's Neighborhood* in the playroom to keep Maeve quiet while I clean up after Kaya. When she moans in pain when I feel around on her belly, rational thought goes out the window. It's probably just the stomach flu, but what if she's contracted some bizarre, flesh-eating bacteria? What if she needs medical attention? I'm so not qualified for this.

Unable to bear the sight of Kaya in pain, I sing her a lullaby while I call Stacey, Nate, Glory, and even Ruthie. When none of them pick up, I give in and call the doctor. Stacey made me save Happy Faces Pediatrics' number in my phone as soon as Kaya was born just in case. Apparently that was a smart move on her part. I explain Kaya's symptoms to the receptionist, and she tells me they can squeeze her in within the hour. After sending a group text to the girls' parents to notify them, I launch into super-aunt mode, fastening Lucy and a very displeased Maeve into their car seats before coming back into the house for Kaya.

"Come on, sweetheart," I whisper, encouraging her to sit up. She's wearing a blue set of cotton pajamas with little elephants on them, and I help her slip on socks and tennis shoes.

"I don't want to get up," Kaya moans. "It hurts."

"I know. That's why we're going to see Dr. Hickman." I heft her out of bed, and heat radiates off her like an oven. Her stomach hurts so bad that she can't stand up straight, and she leans on me as we make our way to the car.

"Aunt Willa!" Maeve shouts at the top of her lungs while I fasten Kaya's seat belt. "I want to watch *Daniel Tiger*! And I want my dino nuggets!"

"You had your dino nuggets and you watched your show. Your sister needs us now, Maeve. I need you to be a big girl."

She flings a tiny toy dinosaur at the back of my seat, and it lands on the floor with a thump. I leave it there, refusing to give in to her tantrum, and climb in the driver's seat. One niece crisis is my limit. And Kaya has dibs.

"It hurts," Kaya repeats, pressing her hands to her stomach. "Oww."

I drive the few miles to the doctor's office with my knuckles white against the steering wheel. Happy Faces is a group practice tucked inside a large block of gray-walled medical offices, and once I wrangle the girls out of the car, we have to take an elevator to the third floor.

"Come on, come on," I mutter, willing the elevator to move faster. When we finally reach the waiting room, a bright space with a Peter Rabbit mural and a tropical fish tank that Maeve immediately tries to shoot at with her Nerf gun, I breathe a sigh of relief.

"Sit here, honey." I help Kaya settle onto a couch near a shelf of children's books, and the grimace on her face makes me want to cry. Once I've signed her in at the reception desk, I check my phone and see that Nate responded to my text: Okay. Leaving work now. I'll meet you at Dr. Hickman's.

"Kaya?" A nurse in a pair of purple scrubs with smiling teddy bears pops her head into the waiting room. "Come this way, honey."

I wrestle Maeve away from the fish tank and balance Lucy on one hip and Kaya's weight on the other. At a painstakingly slow speed, we follow the nurse down a hallway and into an exam room that smells of disinfectant and hand sanitizer. The nurse checks Kaya's height, weight, and vital signs while I list off her symptoms and try to keep Maeve from damaging any very expensive medical equipment.

"Okay, honey," the nurse says while she enters information into the computer. "Dr. Rafferty will be right in to help you."

I almost drop Lucy in my shock. Surely she can't mean *Liam* Rafferty, lover of pancakes and hater of Instagram? The guy grew on me a little when he helped me out at the bakery, but still. I want Kaya to be examined by a different doctor. Someone older. Someone wiser. Someone who doesn't laugh his head off at people in misery.

"What?" I ask. "No. The girls see Dr. Hickman. He's been taking care of Kaya since she was born."

The nurse smiles and tucks a pen into the pocket of her scrubs. "Dr. Hickman is on vacation this week. But don't worry, Dr. Rafferty is excellent. You'll like him. He's a real charmer." She hands Maeve and Lucy a sticker each before shutting the door behind her.

It can't be. There's no way that out of all the pediatricians in Columbus, Kaya's stuck with Liam Rafferty. Maybe he has a family member with the same last name who's a pediatrician, too—a parent or a sibling. Doctors always come from doctor families, right? Or maybe it's just a coincidence, and the pediatrician responsible for assessing my precious niece just happens to share a surname with the guy who witnessed my most humiliating moment of all time.

"Aunt Willa, I want Mommy and Daddy," Kaya whispers.

"I know, baby. I know. They'll see you real soon, okay?" I wrap my arms around Kaya and grab Lucy's chubby fingers before she can wrap them around her sister's hair.

When ten minutes pass with no sign of anyone, I wonder what the hell is taking so long. Kaya whimpers next to me, clutching her stomach and turning even paler. After double-checking that Maeve is busy playing with her dinosaur figurines, I grab Lucy and open the door to the hallway. I find the teddy-bear-scrubs nurse jotting something on a clipboard, and I flag her down.

"Hi, hello there. Not to be rude or anything, but do you know where our doctor is? Because my niece is in a lot of pain, and it seems like it's getting worse."

"The doctor should be with you shortly."

"Right," I say as she starts to walk away, "but how shortly are we talking? Because like I said, my niece seems really uncomfortable—"

"I can't tell you exactly how many minutes. It's a busy day, and the doctor will be with you as soon as possible."

"Aunt Willa," Kaya calls from the exam room, her voice trembling, "it hurts so bad."

Lucy pinches a tiny fold of skin on the back of my arm as hard as she can, and the pain sends me over the edge.

"Where. Is. The. Doctor?" I ask the nurse while Kaya cries softly. "We need a goddamn doctor, and we need one *now*."

"Willa?"

I turn around to see Liam standing behind us, dressed in slacks and a blue button-up underneath a long white coat.

"Oh, look," the nurse says dryly. "It's the goddamn doctor."

"What are you doing here?" Liam asks, as if I'm standing in the hallway with a pinching baby for my own amusement.

Any lingering hostility I hold toward him goes out the window when Kaya lets out another wail. This isn't the moment for me to dwell on grievances. There will be plenty of time for that later.

"It's my niece Kaya. She's really sick. Something with her stomach. She keeps throwing up and her fever's climbing, and she's supposed to see Dr. Hickman but—"

"Do you have Kaya's chart, Brianna?" Liam asks the nurse, and he thanks her when she hands it over. "Okay, let's go."

He ushers Lucy and me back into the exam room, where Maeve promptly launches a three-inch rubber T. rex at him.

"Maeve!" I hiss. "Stop it."

"No problem," Liam says. He picks up the little T. rex and trots it back toward Maeve, making little growling sounds. "I love dinosaurs."

He turns his attention to Kaya while I describe her symptoms again, listing every temperature measurement and vomiting episode I can think of.

"Hi, Kaya." Liam bends down so that he's eye level with her. "I'm Dr. Rafferty. I'm going to help you feel better, okay?"

Kaya doesn't say anything in response. Instead, she leans forward, opens her mouth, and unleashes a torrent of vomit directly onto Liam's white coat.

"Ew," Maeve says while I sit in stunned silence. "Yucky."

Any other time, I'd be at least somewhat amused by the thought of Liam getting vomited on. But watching Kaya suffer is almost unbearable. I jump up and grab a handful of paper towels from a dispenser on the wall.

Once I've cleaned Kaya up a little bit and Liam's taken his white coat off, he asks me to help her onto the examination table. He listens to her heart and lungs and peeks at her eyes and into her ears. Then, while I hold her hand, he presses his stethoscope against her abdomen.

"Ow," Kaya cries when he uses his hands to examine her tummy. "Stop."

Liam does as instructed, looping his stethoscope around his neck. "Be right back." He steps out of the exam room and closes the door behind him.

When he returns a moment later, I'm so anxious that I think I might vomit, too. "What the hell? Where'd you go? Are you gonna tell me what's wrong with Kaya? And can you get the teddy-bear nurse to bring her some medicine or something?"

Liam looks at me intently. "Willa, I need you to stay calm, okay?" He speaks in the soothing tone one might use to comfort a small child.

My heart pounds. "Calm? Why wouldn't I stay calm? You think I'm gonna freak out or something? I'm not. I'm gonna stay calm. Calm, calm, calm. Calm like Donkey Kong."

Liam nods. "Okay. Because of Kaya's symptoms and her elevated heart rate, I'm concerned about appendicitis."

"Appendicitis," I say, blinking. "Okay. That's when your appendix is inflamed. I had that when I was little."

"Kaya's pain level seems very high, and it worsens with even the smallest of movements," Liam continues. "Which makes me worry that her appendix could be ruptured. It only happens in a small percentage of cases, but if it does, it's an emergency."

"An emergency," I repeat, to drown out the ringing in my ears.

"Yes. So Brianna called for an ambulance to transport Kaya to the hospital."

"An ambulance. Okay. I'm calm. Calm, calm, calm." I wrap my hand around Kaya's sweaty one, praying that I don't pass out.

"I'm going to stay with Kaya and monitor her until the ambulance arrives. If you need to call her parents, go right ahead. I have every-thing under control here."

"Right. Okay. Calm." I step into the hallway so the girls don't witness me losing my shit. Just as I start to call Stacey, the nurse opens the door to the waiting room to let Nate charge through.

"Nate!"

"Willa, what's going on?" Still wearing his firefighter's uniform, Nate looks like he's on the verge of tears. "Where is she?"

"Here." I show him to the exam room, where Kaya is so relieved to see her dad that she bursts into tears.

"I'm Dr. Rafferty," Liam says, extending his hand to shake Nate's. "Let me tell you what we're going to do."

While Liam—Dr. Rafferty—explains Kaya's case to Nate, I text Stacey the details and instruct her to head to the children's hospital. Less than three minutes later, the ambulance arrives at the clinic, and a pair of EMTs lift Kaya onto a gurney.

"I'll ride with Kaya. You take Maeve and Lucy home," Nate instructs, hurrying after the EMTs. "I'll call you when I know anything. And Willa? Thank you."

The sight of Kaya's little body on the gurney makes me lose whatever shred of calm I was clinging to, and I blink back tears, trying to stay strong for Maeve and Lucy.

After Liam gets off the phone with the ER doctors at Nationwide Children's, he places a comforting hand on my shoulder. It's strange to see this side of him—the professional, mature side—and it's bizarre to me that he probably spends every day getting thrown up on and placing a comforting hand on the shoulders of worried parents and aunts. This Liam is so unlike the man who laughed at me at Chloe's party that I can't put the pieces together.

"They're going to do a CT scan as soon as Kaya gets there," Liam says. "She's in good hands, Willa."

He motions to Maeve, who huddled against my leg amid all the commotion. "Can I help you get them to the car?"

I'm so tired and stressed that I only nod in response. Liam scoops up Maeve in his arms and grabs the gigantic diaper bag I carried in, then marches into the parking lot while Lucy and I follow along. He holds Maeve while I strap Lucy in, and then I take Maeve from his arms and buckle her in, too.

"Are you okay?" he asks when the girls are safely inside the car.

I'm so terrified for Kaya that *okay* isn't even a blip on the horizon right now. "I . . . I don't know. Yes. Maybe. That scared the shit out of me. I mean, I'm still scared."

He nods. "I know you are. Just remember to breathe."

"Yeah. Okay. Breathe. I can do that."

"It is necessary for survival," Liam says, giving me a small smile. "So I don't think you have much of a choice."

"Good point."

He removes a folded paper from his pocket. "That's my cell number. I have more patients to see, but Kaya's doctors at Nationwide will keep me posted on her. Reach out if you need anything at all." He waves good-bye to Lucy and Maeve, neither of whom pay him any attention.

"Liam," I say when he turns to head back to the clinic. "I mean, Dr. Rafferty."

He smiles. "Liam is fine."

"I just . . ." I pause. Anxiety has scrambled my brain, making it impossible to find the words I'm looking for. "I . . . thank you."

"You're welcome, Willa. Drive safe."

As I peek into the back seat to check on the girls, where Lucy has already fallen asleep and Maeve is resting her head on the side of her car seat, I do as Liam instructed and take a breath.

I'm a jumble of emotions—fear, mostly, and worry for Kaya. But there's something else, too: a little wave of tingling that starts in my toes and spreads to my pounding heart. It's laser-focused on Liam, and this time I'm not so sure it's hate.

20

It's a first. Dr. Liam Rafferty was right. Kaya's appendix ruptured, and the surgeons at Nationwide Children's Hospital took her
into the operating room to remove it as soon as they saw the results
of her CT scan. Stacey texts me that the surgery went well, and that
Kaya should be waking up from the anesthesia sometime soon.

Ruthie agrees to watch Lucy and Maeve so that I can join Stacey,
Nate, and Glory, who caught the first flight home from Nashville, at
the hospital. Once Ruthie and the girls are settled in with snacks
and *Frozen*, I break the speed limit all the way to the hospital.

When I reach Kaya's room, I tiptoe inside to find everyone clustered around Kaya's bed. They're so deep in conversation with someone, they don't notice me enter. But I notice Liam immediately.

". . . day after tomorrow, most likely," Liam says. "And then oral
antibiotics from there."

"Knock knock." I don't want to interrupt their conversation, but
I want the latest news on Kaya. And to find out why Liam's here.

Liam, still in his work clothes (and probably still wearing my niece's vomit), lifts a hand in greeting. "Hi, Willa. I just stopped by to check on my patient."

"Dr. Rafferty's been explaining what they did during the surgery," Nate says. "And explaining the medicine Kaya's getting." He holds up the pad of paper on which he's scribbled notes.

"Didn't the surgeon go over that?" I ask, causing Liam to raise his eyebrows at me.

"The surgeon talked a hundred miles an hour," says Nate. "Dr. Rafferty's giving us the slowed-down version for dummies. Way slowed down."

"We were just discussing her meds," Liam tells me. "She'll get her antibiotics through an IV line for the first forty-eight hours or so. After that, if she's eating and drinking well and her vitals look good, she'll likely be discharged."

"But she's okay?" I ask, watching as my beautiful niece stirs slightly in her sleep. "She's gonna be okay?"

Liam smiles. "She's going to be fine, Willa."

"Yeah, super aunt." Stacey slings an arm around my shoulders. "If it weren't for you and Dr. Rafferty here . . ." She shudders. "I am so, so thankful you were there for Kaya today."

Praise from Stacey is as rare as snow in July, and I don't know how to process it. "All that matters is she's okay."

"We should probably give her some peace and quiet," Liam suggests. "Her body needs rest."

I tiptoe over to Kaya's bed and place my lips gently against her forehead. Her skin, so hot to the touch earlier, has returned to a normal temperature, and relief floods me. Stacey, in full mama-bear mode, ushers everyone out of the room and into the hallway.

"If you have more questions, or if you need anything, just give me a call," Liam says to Nate and Stacey.

Nate shakes Liam's hand repeatedly, and Stacey throws her arms around him like he's the second coming of Jesus Christ. When Liam heads toward the stairwell—he really must not like elevators—I realize I should probably say something, too. He quite possibly saved my niece's life, after all.

"Liam!" I jog to catch up with him, but I haven't run since our bakery adventure, so I end up out of breath quickly.

He stops to let me catch up. "Hey, Sparkles. How are you feeling?"

Apparently we still aren't done with that ridiculous nickname, but I've forfeited the right to call him a stupid butthead in retaliation. He's done too much for my family for me to get annoyed by a silly name. At least, that's what I try to remind myself.

"I'm going to ignore that, because you actually did something really amazing today."

He shrugs. "I just did my job."

"Is it your job to drive to the hospital after work and personally check on your patients?"

"Just the ones who vomit on me." He laughs, but then his smile fades. "I'm sorry if I overstepped my bounds here, coming to the hospital and all. I know you're not my biggest fan, and I don't mean to get in your family's way. But Maisie would have had my head on a platter if I didn't check up on your niece."

His loyalty to Maisie and the care he's shown for Kaya make me do a double take, and I'm tempted to pinch myself and make sure I'm not dreaming. Surely this can't be the same guy who rolled his eyes at the mere mention of Instagram and laughed so hard at my Princess Sparkleheart debacle that he almost broke a rib. I can't loathe him anymore, regardless of how hard I try. The way he took care of my niece makes it impossible to hold on to my grudge, no matter how badly I want to.

"Overstepped your bounds? Are you kidding? Nate's so grateful for you that he almost shook your hand off. And my sister thinks you practically walk on water, so you can expect a fruit basket to get delivered to your clinic every week for the next six months."

Liam smiles, the folds around his eyes crinkling. "I don't want a fruit basket, Sparkles. I'm just glad everything turned out okay."

His statement makes my mind jump to an alternate reality where everything *didn't* turn out okay. What if the worst had happened to Kaya? What if I hadn't brought her to the doctor in time, or the ambulance hadn't reached the hospital fast enough? What if the surgeons hadn't—

"Willa? What's wrong?" Liam's forehead is wrinkled with concern, and he's almost unrecognizable without his characteristic smirk. "What is it?"

My eyes burn with the threat of tears, and I try to blink them away. I've already lost my shit in front of Maisie; I can't do it in front of Liam, too. I won't let myself. But the thought of today turning out differently causes my chest to constrict, as if trying to squeeze out the pain. I try to take a deep breath, but the air gets caught in my throat. What if I'd lost Kaya? What if I never got to learn more about her secret frog project, or have her slam another soccer ball into my stomach, or help her search Ruthie's backyard for dinosaurs with her gigantic magnifying glass? I let out a little hiccup of terror and wipe my eyes with the back of my hand.

"What if," I say to Liam. "What if—" But I can't even bring myself to finish the sentence, because it would make that unimaginable possibility imaginable.

"Willa, hey. It's okay. Come here." Liam moves forward to wrap me in a hug, and his gesture is so compassionate, so non-jerkfacey, that it catches me off guard. "I know what you're thinking," he says, his voice muffled against my hair. "But there's no 'what if' here. She's fine. We all got lucky. It really is okay."

His tone is the same gentle one Stacey used when Maeve sobbed over the death of her pet goldfish, and embarrassment floods me. Praying that I didn't get snot on Liam's shirt, I jump back from his embrace. I don't need his pity, and I refuse to let anyone get close to me. I've already crossed lines with Maisie. I can't do the same with him. Especially considering the fact that the feel of his arms around me made me wish I'd washed my hair.

"Thanks," I say tightly, taking another step back and doubling the space between us.

"You sure you're okay?"

"Yes. I'm fine." My voice is strained, and I force myself to give Liam a little smile so he won't try to hug me again.

"You don't exactly look fine."

I narrow my eyes at him. "Pardon me for not wearing makeup today. I've been a little busy."

"I wasn't talking about your makeup, Willa. I meant that you look like you're about to burst into tears. And you have food in your hair."

I run a hand through the ends of my hair, where I find bits of wet Cheerios clinging to the strands. My cheeks burn as I do my best to finger-comb the cereal out. "Lucy's a very messy eater."

"Have *you* eaten today?"

"Yes. I think so." I was too sick with worry to eat for most of the day, but I stole a few bites from the girls during snack time. "I ate strawberries and Goldfish. You know, the snack that smiles back." I stop talking before I can embarrass myself further.

"I think some real food would do you a lot of good. Are you hungry?" Without waiting for an answer, he motions for me to follow him downstairs. "Come on, let me get you some dinner."

"Dinner?"

He grins. "Yes. It's the customary meal that people eat at the end of the day."

"I know what dinner is. I meant, you want to get dinner *together*?"

His forehead wrinkles. "Is it that crazy of an idea? I mean, I know we got off on the wrong foot—"

"Feet," I correct him, remembering our initial meeting at Chloe's party and our argument on Finn's birthday. "Because we got off on the wrong foot twice."

"Thanks for clarifying, Sparkles. Anyway, as I was saying, I know we got off on the wrong *feet*, but there's no reason we can't sit down for a nice, peaceful meal together. We've both had a stressful day, and it would be nice if we're not at each other's throats at Finn and Maisie's wedding."

The fact that Liam saved Kaya makes it impossible for me to ever go at his throat again, regardless of how many times he calls me Sparkles. And I *am* hungry; now that the adrenaline of the day is wearing off, I'm realizing that a handful of Goldfish crackers didn't get the job done.

"You promise it will be peaceful and nice?" I ask, wary that Liam will laugh at me again or go off on a rant about how vapid and mindless Instagram is.

"Peaceful. And nice." He holds up two fingers in a scout's honor gesture.

"Okay," I agree. "But you saved my niece, so I'm buying." I'm still broke, but Maisie's money sure is coming in handy. "Let me see if my sister needs anything before we leave."

I head back toward Kaya's room, telling myself that I only agreed to dinner with Liam as a thank-you for helping my family. There's no way I could have turned him down without appearing rude. Plus, Stacey loves him so much now that she'd have evicted me from my bedroom and made me move into Kaya's playhouse. And I owe it to Maisie to at least try to get along with her fiancé's best man.

I'm definitely not going to dinner with Liam because he smelled so good when he hugged me that I wanted to bottle his scent up and save it for later. Or because the feel of his arms around me tempted me to lay my head on his chest and hang out there for a while. Definitely, definitely not.

"Go home," Stacey says when I reach her, Glory, and Nate in the hallway. "You've done more than enough for one day."

"You sure you don't need anything?"

"Maybe a week's worth of sleep. But I'll be able to rest once Kaya's home."

"Okay. Well, I'm going to dinner with Liam—I mean, Dr. Rafferty—and I'll be home after that."

Glory holds her hands up for time-out. "Hold up. What?"

"It's a long story," I say, not wanting to get into the details of how we met and remind Stacey of my epic screw-up at Chloe Wellington's party. "Liam is Maisie's fiancé's best man."

"Small world," Stacey says.

"No kidding," I agree.

"Wait a sec." Glory eyes me up and down. "You're telling me that you're getting dinner with the dreamboat pediatrician who saved your niece's life, and you're going in *that* outfit?"

"'Dreamboat' is a little much. And it was technically the surgeons who saved her life."

"Really, Willa?" Glory asks, her eyes wide in disbelief. "That's how you're gonna play this?"

I groan. "Fine, yes, he did help to save her life. But it's not, like, a date. It's a dinner between—" I'm about to say *friends*, but that's not the right term for our situation. "Co-wedding-party people. Plus, my outfit's fine."

Stacey and Glory look at my outfit, a pair of black leggings and a gray T-shirt that are definitely not fine.

"Well," Stacey says after a moment, "you've had a long day."

"Excuse me for not dressing up for the hospital," I mutter. "Anyway, we're both in Maisie's wedding, and we're both hungry. That's all."

"Here, take this." My sister removes her olive-green jacket and hands it to me. "It'll at least cover your armpit stains."

"I sweated a lot today because I was worried about *your daughter*," I protest. "I don't need your jacket."

"For fuck's sake, Willa, that man is a regular McDreamy!" Glory hisses. "Take the fucking jacket."

"He does seem like a great guy," Nate chimes in. "Not that there's anything wrong with your outfit."

I realize I'm fighting a losing battle. Liam Rafferty, hater of Facebook and enemy of Princess Sparkleheart, is a real-life American hero.

"Fine," I say, and I take the fucking jacket.

21

"*Do you like* tacos?" Liam asks when I climb into the passenger seat of his car. It's a Ford Fusion, trusty and practical, and I'm surprised he doesn't drive something flashier.

"Of course I like tacos. That's like asking someone if they enjoy sleeping or breathing oxygen."

"A simple *yes* would have sufficed."

"Fair enough." I buckle up as Liam eases the car onto Children's Drive and accelerates. I tap my fingers against the buckle, trying to think of topics for conversation.

But Liam seems to have that covered. "Your sister and sister-in-law seem really great. And Kaya's dad seems awesome, too."

"They are, actually," I say, choosing to overlook Stacey's penchant for cramming self-help books down my throat. "I've never seen a blended family get along like they do."

"My parents split up when I was eight, and they still hate each other. It's nice to see people who can put their differences aside for their kids."

This mature, let's-think-of-the-children side of Liam is still un-nerving to me, and I'm tempted to sneak a peek at his wrist tattoo and check that he's the same guy who spit up his beer at Chloe's.

I nod. "I think it helps that Stacey and Nate didn't divorce for a dramatic reason. Nobody cheated or anything like that. They'd been together since high school when they got married, and I think they just kind of grew in different directions, you know? Stacey wanted to build her business, Nate just wanted a simple life. So they broke up a few years after Kaya was born, and then Stacey met Glory. And Nate has a girlfriend he's been seeing for a while now."

"And what about you?" Liam asks as we switch lanes. "Where do you fit into the whole *Modern Family* setup?"

I shrug, not wanting to divulge to him that I don't quite fit in anywhere. Not anymore. "I don't, really. I'm staying with Stacey and Glory temporarily, but it's not like they need me or anything. Their lives are well-oiled machines."

Liam glances sideways at me. "Seems like they needed your help today."

"I guess that's true. But this day might go down in infamy, be-cause it's the first time Stacey's ever needed my help. Usually it's the opposite. She's the successful one. Happy marriage, beautiful kids, big house, thriving business. She's got it all."

"Nobody's got it all, Sparks."

I shrug, because I know better. Some people do have it all. I used to be one of them.

⌒⌒⌒

Liam takes us to Tio's Tacos & Tequila, a little place on High Street with a bright yellow exterior. My stomach growls when I inhale the scent of sizzling meat. Inside, dim mood lighting and exposed brick walls give the restaurant a cozy vibe. Colorful chairs hung upside down serve as wall art, adding a touch of quirkiness.

We sit in a booth toward the middle of the restaurant, and I'm so worn out from the day's events that I could lie down and take a nap on it. It's a good thing this isn't a real date.

We each order a house margarita, and Liam orders Texas dip for us to share. It's a lot like my meal at Condado Tacos with Maisie, except I don't have such a fraught history with Maisie, nor does her smile send a tingle down my spine.

"So," Liam says, leaning back in the booth, "I think we should start this dinner off by calling a truce."

"A truce?"

"Yes, Sparks. A truce. That's when two parties in a conflict agree to set aside their grievances for a certain length of time."

His penchant for acting like a human dictionary grates on me, but I've resolved to be on my best behavior during this dinner. Nice and peaceful, I remind myself. Nice and peaceful.

"I know what a truce is, thank you very much. But even though you did a wonderful job treating my niece, I'm not very good at setting aside my grievances. That's not one of my strong suits."

"You don't say," Liam responds, ducking when I toss a chip fragment at him. "Look, I think we have a lot more in common than you think."

"Like what?" I ask. "We both really want our food to come out soon?"

He gives me an easy smile, and I do my best to ignore the little firework that erupts in my chest. "I was going to say that we both want Kaya to be healthy and happy, and we both want Finn and

Maisie's wedding to go off without a hitch. But yes, I think we both really, really want our food to come out soon."

As if on cue, our waiter drops two steaming plates of tacos off at the table. I'm so hungry that I bite into my pork belly taco immediately, and juice drips onto my chin and my lap.

"You have beautiful table manners, Willa. You eat with such class."

I give him the finger, and Liam lets out a throaty laugh. The sound of it makes my stomach flutter, and I send a mental note to my vagina not to get any ideas.

"So, the truce," Liam continues. "It should include some kind of peace offering."

"I'm not slaughtering any animals, weirdo."

He ignores my comment. "These tacos and margaritas, for example, and this delicious Texas dip, they're a peace offering from me unto you."

"*Unto?* Who are you, Abraham Lincoln? Besides, I said I was buying."

Liam narrows his eyes at me. "Did Abraham Lincoln say *unto* a lot?"

Heat creeps up my cheeks. "I'm not sure, honestly. He's just old."

"Anyway, I invited you to dinner, so I'm going to pay. It's a peace offering I'm extending to you. In exchange, if you agree to the truce, you should extend one to me."

I'm not sure what this truce entails, but I don't want to get tangled up in any agreements. I need to keep things with Liam—and with Maisie—as clear-cut and professional as possible. "Can't we both just pay for our own food?"

Liam swallows a bite of his shrimp taco and takes a deep breath, as if preparing to engage in an argument with a kindergartener. "Would it help if I cleared up your misconception that I'm a total asshole?"

"I don't think you're a total asshole." A total asshole wouldn't have dropped everything in the middle of the day to secure a wedding cake for his best friend. Nor would a total asshole have reacted so well to Kaya vomiting on him, or visited her at the hospital after his shift. But an *occasional* asshole might have done those things, and an occasional asshole would definitely laugh at a woman just trying to do her job. For the sake of keeping things nice and peaceful, I don't try to define what grade of asshole Liam is out loud.

"Well, I know I can be. At times. Very occasionally. Like one time last winter, I forgot to bring a bag when I walked my dog. He did his business, and instead of walking all the way back to my apartment for a bag, I just covered the evidence with snow. In my defense, it was negative three degrees out."

Liam continues to surprise me. I imagined him living alone in a sterile apartment with chrome everything, where he spent his days judging the neighbors and waxing poetic about the days before big, bad social media ruined the world. I never imagined a dog.

Maybe Liam isn't the judgmental one here. "You have a dog?"

"Yes. His name is Frodo."

"Like the hobbit?"

"No, like the president. Of course like the hobbit."

I take another bite of my taco. "Sarcasm doesn't help your claim that you're not an asshole, you know."

Liam nods. "Good point. What I'm saying is, I can have asshole-ish moments, but I like to think they're rare and human. All in all, I think I'm a pretty good guy. At least I try to be."

"How old is Frodo? And what breed?"

"He's four. Chocolate lab. What's that have to do with anything?"

I shrug. "Nothing. I just like dogs."

"Me too. Anyway, will you give me a chance to explain why I laughed at you at Chloe Wellington's birthday party?"

I ponder the question. Delving into a conversation about that party runs the risk of stirring up my initial hatred of Liam, but I'm curious to hear the explanation he's come up with. "If I say yes, will you buy me more tacos and another margarita?"

"Yes, Willa. I'll buy you more tacos and another margarita."

"Okay." I take a long sip of my drink and cross my arms over my chest. This should be good. "Go ahead."

"So, Beth Wellington's mom is married to my dad," Liam explains. "And—"

That is not at all what I expected him to say, and I'm so surprised that I drop my taco. It lands on its side near the edge of the table, and I waste no time in rescuing it. "Wait a second. Chloe's mom is your stepsister?"

Liam's jaw tenses. "'Stepsister' implies that her mom is my stepmom. Which she is not."

"But Chloe's mom's mom *is* married to your dad."

"This is giving me a headache, but yes. Beth's mom is married to my dad, which means she could technically be referred to as my stepmother. But I would never refer to her as such." He bites into his taco as if he's trying to kill it.

"Oh. So she's a bitch like Beth."

"Beth's mom is my dad's fourth wife. They got married when I was fifteen, I think? Beth was a few years older than me, probably seventeen or so, and we never get along."

I nod in understanding. If there's one thing that will make me warm up to Liam—besides the expert medical care he provided to

Kaya, of course—it's a shared dislike of Beth Wellington. "Did you hate her because she gave Disney World a one-star Yelp review? Because that's a totally understandable reason."

"No, although I have seen that review, and it's the most Beth thing of all time." A half smile crosses his face for an instant, then disappears. "I never liked Beth because she picked on me a lot. I was chubby when I was a kid, with acne and the works. She didn't let me forget about it for a second."

"That sucks," I say softly.

"Yeah. To be fair, she was going through her own shit, too, and I was just a convenient outlet for her anger. Neither of our parents are delightful people to be around, and we both had it rough." He pauses to take a long sip of his margarita. "I was only at the house every other weekend, but still. I dreaded seeing Beth."

"Did she get better when you got older?"

He shrugs. "Somewhat. She doesn't make fun of me for being fat anymore, I'll tell you that much."

I imagine the handsome, confident man in front of me as an unhappy, unfortunate-looking teenager, and my cold, dead heart cracks open a little bit. "Well, there's nothing wrong with being fat. She was just dumping her own insecurities on you."

"Yeah. And we're civil to each other now. My dad gives me a hard time if I don't show up to family events, so I make an appearance here and there. And I like Chloe, even if she does turn out to be a miniature version of her mother."

I remember Chloe forcing her party guests to let her ride them like horses. "I think that's likely."

"Everything is about perfection with Beth, you know? At every holiday, we have to spend thirty minutes taking 'candid' pictures until everyone hits their best angles. One year, she edited her great-uncle out of the Thanksgiving picture because his bald spot caught the light too much."

His distaste for Rose's desire to take a picture at VASO makes more sense to me now. "That's just evil."

"So anyway, Chloe's birthday party was the typical Beth event. Simultaneously over the top and underwhelming. Do you know that Chloe wasn't even allowed to play in that bounce house because Beth worried she'd get her dress dirty?"

"Jesus Christ."

He nods, scooping up a fallen piece of chicken and popping it into his mouth. "Everything was set up to look perfect. The decorations, the bounce house, the ponies. And then you, Willa Callister, came along and turned her world upside down."

I sit up straighter, remembering how humiliated I felt that day. How I wanted to crawl into a hole in Chloe's backyard and never crawl back out. "Not on purpose."

Liam leans forward, pressing his elbows against the tabletop. "When I laughed at you, I wasn't laughing at *you*. Although I shouldn't have done it. And I should have offered to help you carry that chair."

"Throne," I say tightly.

"Right. Throne. But I wasn't trying to be cruel, even if it came across that way. I'd had more beers than I probably should have, because that's how I survive family events, and the look on Beth's face when you offered to get a cake from Costco, oh my God." Liam laughs so hard that tears spring to his eyes. "You gave me a greater gift than you can ever imagine, and I'll never be able to properly thank you for it."

"That's me, a regular hero." I finish off one taco and pick up another, considering Liam's story. His complicated relationship with Beth does make his actions at the party more understandable, and he seems genuinely remorseful. "I guess when I consider the context, you're not such an asshole after all."

He beams. "Thanks, Sparks."

"I said *such*. Don't get too excited."

My phone pings with a text, and I fish it out of my purse in case Stacey needs something for Kaya. The message is from Maisie: Just got your text. I'm so glad your niece is okay. That's so scary! I'm bringing a casserole over to your house tomorrow. Does anyone have food allergies?

I grin when I read the message. Maisie may be my boss, but the fact that she goes to the trouble of acting like a real friend says a lot about her. Then, realizing that my brain decided to pair *Maisie* and *friend* in the same thought again, I frown and stuff my phone back into my purse.

"Boyfriend?" Liam asks when he sees how hastily I put my phone away.

I smirk. "Yes. One of many. Princess Sparkleheart is a real heartbreaker."

"I can imagine," he says, resting one arm on the back of the booth. The memory of that arm around me at the hospital jumps to the front of my mind, and I wolf down a giant bite of taco to distract myself.

My phone chimes a second time, and I fish it out of my purse again. It's another text from Maisie: I'm bringing a get-well cheesecake, too. But don't be surprised if I eat half of it beforehand.

"Second boyfriend?" Liam asks, smiling.

"No. Maisie." I set my phone on the table and pick at my taco. I should be focused on my budding truce with Liam right now, but Maisie's sweet texts make me wonder even more about her. There's a missing piece to the Maisie puzzle, and all the tacos and margaritas in the world won't solve it for me.

"Hey, Liam," I ask, starting to feel the effects of the margaritas. "Finn's a good guy, right?"

Liam's eyes widen like he's surprised by the question. Which, of course, he is. "Finn's a great guy. He wouldn't be my best friend if he weren't. Why do you ask?"

I freeze, realizing I've said too much. I already asked Rose the same question, and if news gets around that I'm asking Finn's friends and family whether he's secretly a psycho killer or not, people will start raising eyebrows. "I just don't know him as well as I know Maisie, that's all. And she's . . . she's a really great person. She deserves to be happy."

Liam nods. "I think she is happy. I think she and Finn make each other happy. That's the dream, isn't it?"

It's some people's dream. It's not mine anymore.

"What about you?" I ask, eager to turn the conversation away from Maisie and Finn. I don't want to accidentally reveal anything about my relationship with her.

"What about me?"

I shrug. "We've established that you're not an asshole one hundred percent of the time. And you're a doctor. A doctor who's good with kids, no less. That's like catnip to a lot of women. So why aren't you married?"

"I was." Liam sips his margarita and runs a hand through his hair.

"You were married?" My tone holds more surprise than I intend, but I can't help it. The thought of Liam Rafferty as somebody's husband catches me off guard.

"For four years."

"Oh. Wow. Well, I'm sorry it ended."

"Don't be." Liam's voice is free of bitterness. "It wasn't a good marriage. She had an affair, and I tried to work it out because I thought that's what I was supposed to do. I took my vows seriously. We stuck it out for a while, but I should have called it earlier and saved myself a lot of trouble."

This information clashes completely with the image I previously held of him as a handsome, freewheeling bachelor who wins women over with his smirks and sandalwood scent. And the fact that he's been cheated on, that he knows the agony of that betrayal like I do, shocks me. We have more in common than I ever imagined. I try to picture him as a married man, and I wonder what kind of person would cause him the pain that Max caused me.

"What was your ex like? Was she a doctor, too?"

Liam smiles. "She's a plastic surgeon. The kind that spends all day doing boob jobs and lipo."

"Figures."

He rolls up his shirt sleeve to show me his Roman numeral tattoo. "The day after the divorce was finalized, I got the date tattooed on my wrist. It was kind of stupid, in retrospect."

I can relate. After I found out about Max and Sarah, I didn't just put some ink into my skin. I blew up my whole life. "Like a post-breakup haircut, but permanent."

"Exactly. But it's a symbol of the fact that I chose to start over, to move on from all the lies and the bullshit. I don't pretend anymore. I am who I am, and I value honesty and integrity. And a good margarita."

The fact that Liam was able to start over gives me hope. Once Maisie's wedding is over and I have the rest of my paycheck, I'll be able to leave Columbus. I'll have a chance to start over, too. The thought fills me with optimism, and when Liam lifts his glass toward mine, we tap them together in cheers.

"I made a lot of changes in my life after my marriage ended," Liam continues. "The tattoo was one. Getting Frodo was another. And I quit social media. All good decisions, in retrospect."

I remember his snooty reluctance to pose for Rose's picture at VASO, and how adamant he was that sharing stuff online was nothing but a waste of time. "It doesn't seem like you just *quit* social media. It seems like you have a personal vendetta against it."

"Why, because I called it vapid?" Liam scowls at me over his margarita glass.

"Yes. You also called it pathetic. 'A pathetic substitute for actual human relationships,' you said."

He smirks. "My, my, Sparks. You sure do pay close attention to what I say."

A warm blush spreads over my cheeks. "Don't flatter yourself. I remember the comment because it struck me as particularly idiotic." I remember that this dinner is supposed to be peaceful and nice, and I try to tone it down a little. "I mean, sure, social media has its flaws, but it's revolutionized communication. People are more connected than ever before."

"Well, after my divorce, I didn't want to be connected."

"How do you mean?"

Liam wipes his hands with a napkin and leans forward, his elbows on the table. "I lost a lot of friends when my marriage ended. People I thought were friends, I mean. Who knew about the affair and didn't tell me. I didn't want them in my life anymore. And I certainly didn't want them on my news feed."

His admission that he's known the same pain I have almost knocks the breath out of me. "I deleted my accounts after my breakup, too.

And I also . . . I also lost friends. I lost my best friend." My voice is quiet, somber, like I'm telling him about the death of a loved one. And in a lot of ways, I am.

Liam's face softens. "What happened?"

"I found her in bed with my fiancé six weeks before my wedding," I tell him. My throat starts to swell, as if I'm having an allergic reaction to the memory, but I cough and force myself to keep talking. "She—Sarah—was my best friend in the whole world for twenty-two years, and then suddenly she wasn't."

It's the first time I've said her name aloud in months, and I feel like a character in *Harry Potter* uttering Voldemort's name. Maybe being okay with saying it means I'm taking some of my power back. Maybe it means I'm on my way to starting over, like Liam did. Or maybe it just means I should slow down on the margaritas.

"She's the one who chased me around the yard at Chloe's party," I continue. "That's why I was such a wreck that day, and why I dropped the cake. I hadn't seen her since . . . well, I didn't expect to see her again. Ever."

"Jesus, Willa." Liam's tone is hushed, stunned, like he can't think of what to say next. "I'm sorry. Finn was a huge part of how I got through everything. If I'd lost him, too, if I'd lost everything *because* of him . . ." He trails off, his eyes on mine. "I don't know how you survived that. You must be incredibly strong."

His compliment couldn't be further from the truth. I remember how I assumed the fetal position for weeks after The Incident, how I only ate and showered because Stacey forced me to. "Strong? No. I fell apart. Completely."

"People fall apart sometimes. And that's okay. But you didn't stay apart."

"What do you mean?"

Liam smiles. "I mean, you were Super Aunt today. And you have an amazing friend in Maisie. And you're here having dinner with the coolest guy of all time." He winks at me, and the private, intimate nature of the gesture makes my chest thud. "What Sarah did could have torn you apart forever, but here you are. Rebuilding. Surviving."

No one's called me strong in a very long time, and his words are like a salve to the aching wound of my heart. Sure, I'm leaving out a piece of critical information—that Maisie's my boss, not my amazing friend, and that we're lying to everyone about how we met—but still. The fact that someone thinks I'm doing okay, even without reading Stacey's entire library of self-help books, makes me feel almost proud of myself. And that's a nice break from the shame I'm used to.

"I think it's worth noting that Sarah, like, really fucking sucks," Liam says, crossing his arms over his chest. "Let it be known."

I let out an amused snort, and being able to laugh about the whole disaster makes me feel better than any margarita ever could. "Sarah totally fucking sucks. And so does Max, my ex."

Liam nods. "Well, look at it this way. At least you didn't spend four years married to a liar who didn't love you and then get evidence of it inked onto your body."

"Yeah," I say with a giggle. "At least I didn't do that."

"And, instead of spending the evening watching Netflix on your couch with your boring husband Dex—"

"Max," I correct him.

"—you're here, eating tacos, with me. So I think you're doing just fine." He holds my gaze for a moment longer than necessary, causing my stomach to do a cartwheel.

"Hey, I like Netflix."

Liam grins. "Me too. How do you think Frodo and I spend our weekends? I've got a cabin in the Hocking Hills, and I'm there watching movies every weekend I'm not moonlighting. Frodo and I are big fans of westerns. And hiking."

He reaches for a tortilla chip at the same time I do, and his hand brushes against mine. Our hands linger there, touching, before I finally pull mine away. A jolt of excitement runs through me, and I stuff my entire chip into my mouth to quash it. I can't cross any lines with Liam. As Finn's best man, he's basically my co-worker, even if he doesn't know it. The last thing I need is any sexual tension—or worse, emotional attachments—making me lose focus on my goal: performing the role of Maisie's bridesmaid perfectly, and then getting the hell out of town. So I can start over, preferably without a tattoo.

Liam coughs and glances at his watch. "Do you want any more tacos before we head out? I've got an early start time tomorrow."

Relieved that our dinner is coming to an end before my hormones can get any more ideas about Liam, I pat my stomach. "I think four is enough. Thank you for the tasty peace offering."

After Liam pays the bill, we return to the car and head back toward the hospital. The atmosphere during the ride is charged somehow, as if our hands meeting over that bowl of Texas dip altered the electricity between us. Liam and I are both silent, and I consider making an observation about the August humidity just to ease the tension. But despite my firm commitment to not fucking this whole gig up, I don't want to talk to Liam Rafferty about the weather.

I want to do other things with him. The way he opened up to me about his childhood and his marriage, and the way he listened to me talk about my failed engagement and took it in stride, has me seeing him in a whole new light. A sexy light. Worse, a romantic one. I tap my foot against the floor mat, as if moving some part of my body will help to release the yearning that's brewing inside me.

"My car's in the blue garage," I tell him, clearing my throat. "You can let me out right in front of it, please."

Liam shakes his head. "Parking garages are dangerous, Willa. I'll drive you to your car."

"If you drive me to my car, you'll have to pay to get back out of the garage. Which is just silly."

"What's silly is your refusal to let me—"

A car lingering behind us beeps its horn, leaving Liam no choice but to pull into the garage.

"Fine," I say with a huff. "It's your money."

"I win this round, Sparks." Smiling like the damn cat that got the cream, Liam follows my directions to my parking spot on the third floor of the garage.

"Well, thank you for dinner," I say when he parks next to my Corolla. "I had a surprisingly non-terrible time."

He laughs, and the sound of it does nothing to help the tension in my belly. "I also had a surprisingly non-terrible time. Lucky us."

I move to unbuckle my seat belt, but the latch sticks. I wrestle with the belt a little, growing frustrated in more ways than one.

"Here," Liam says, reaching over to help me. "You just have to—"

"I have it," I insist, but I don't have it, and my hand gets tangled up with Liam's as he finally unlocks the belt.

I don't pull my hand away. I can't. Instead, I open it, and Liam runs his fingers over my palm. I let our fingers intertwine for a moment, and then I run my index finger over the tattoo on his forearm.

"I've thought about having it removed," he says quietly. "Getting it was a spur-of-the-moment decision. But I like looking at it and knowing that I survived starting over."

"I like it," I say, tracing the black lines with my hand. "I like that you survived, and that you started over."

Liam nods and reaches up to push a stray strand of hair away from my face. He traces the outline of my jaw and then runs a finger along my collarbone, sending shivers down my spine.

I have no idea what I'm doing. I know I haven't been touched like this in a very long time, and that this moment with Liam is fleeting. I know I want nothing more than to escape, and that once Maisie's wedding is over, I'll be hundreds of miles away from here, starting over in a different city.

But I want something else, too, in this moment. I want Liam's soft, strong hands to keep touching me. I want to feel his breath warm against my ear and his arms wrapped around me. I want to feel.

"Willa," he says.

In response, I lean toward him and close the distance between us. I press a hand to his cheek and run my fingers through his hair. And then, I raise my lips to his.

His lips are warm and soft against mine, and his arm snakes around my waist to draw me closer. It's a gentle, curious kiss at first, and then it turns passionate, wanting, and the taste of his tongue makes me want more.

When our lips part, Liam nuzzles my cheek with his. "Damn, Sparkles. What was that?"

I smile as he presses his forehead to mine. "My peace offering."

22

Plot twist, Waywards: The Worst Man isn't actually the worst after all. In fact, he's pretty great. So great that I can't call him the Worst Man anymore. If Stacey knew I'd deemed him that in the first place, she'd knock me over the head with my niece's plastic T-ball bat. And my sister's got quite the swing.

From now on, I'll refer to him as Dr. Dreamboat. He diagnosed my niece's medical emergency and gave me the best kiss of my life all in the same day, so I think it's an appropriate moniker. Sure, he still calls me by an annoying nickname and gets under my skin from time to time, but nobody's perfect. Even though his forearms come close.

But when it comes to Dr. Dreamboat, I've screwed up big-time. I can't get him off my mind, and that's a huge no-no. Because I'm supposed to be laser-focused on the Animal Whisperer and her big day—not the way his tongue tasted. Not the heavy, welcome pressure of his hand on the back of my head, pulling me closer. Not the fact that one kiss with him gave me more to fantasize about than eight years' worth of hookups with my ex.

When I'm with Dr. Dreamboat, I feel like I can be myself. Not old Willa, with her busy social schedule and cute wardrobe, or new Willa, with her fierce independence and no-friends boundaries. I feel like I can be now-Willa. Like he'll accept me for who I am right at this very moment, whether I'm wearing denim shorts or a silly ball gown or my sister's olive-green jacket.

But he can't. Because he doesn't know who I truly am. He has no idea that I'm only in his life because of the Animal Whisperer's wallet. If he did, if he had any clue that she and I are lying to him about our friendship—and more importantly, to his best friend—everything would be ruined. And he'd hate me more than he hates Facebook and Snapchat combined.

So I'm making a promise to you, Waywards, even though I'll never publish this post. I vow to never kiss Dr. Dreamboat again. Because another kiss with him could destroy everything, including the Animal Whisperer's wedding to the Friendly Lumberjack. And I need that wedding to go off without a hitch. It's my ticket out of here, to a place where the Animal Whisperer and the way she hands me a hanky when I'm crying don't make me second-guess my friendship moratorium.

I'm nearly free, Waywards. I'm nearly out of here. And I can't let anything stop me now.

ꙮ

"Holy crap. You did *what?*" Maisie sits next to me at Ruthie's kitchen table, helping me slice vegetables.

When she stopped over at Stacey's to drop off six varieties of casserole, I was just about to head to Ruthie's, and Maisie decided to tag along. We weren't at my next-door-neighbor's for five minutes before I dropped the I-kissed-Liam bomb on her.

I sigh and grab a red bell pepper, praying that she doesn't go into full Hulk mode. I can hardly believe I let my newfound desire for Liam get the best of me last night. In doing so, I've made my role as Maisie's bridesmaid infinitely more complicated, and I've put my job at risk.

"I know," I say, bracing for Maisie's reaction. "It's not good. I understand if you're mad about it, but I thought you should know what happened last night." As much as I don't want to upset Maisie, I knew I had to tell her the truth. She's the one person in the wedding party I'm not lying to, and the fact that I crossed a ton of professional boundaries by kissing Liam is something she deserves to know. Besides, if Liam tells Finn that we kissed, word will get back to her anyway, and it's better coming from me.

There's another reason I'm telling Maisie about the kiss, even if I don't want to admit it to myself: it feels good to tell someone the juicy details of a date—or whatever my dinner with Liam was. I haven't had a friend in so long that engaging in girl talk with Maisie is like stretching my legs after an impossibly long car ride. I didn't realize how much I missed having someone besides Stacey to talk to. Sitting beside Maisie in Ruthie's sunny kitchen with a cup of tea in front of me, I'm the happiest I've been since The Incident.

But that happiness might disappear if Maisie loses her shit over my news.

Before Maisie can respond, Ruthie struts into the kitchen to model a black sleeveless dress. She has her third date with a gentleman named Albert tonight, and her struggles to choose an outfit prompted her to invite me over to help. Albert, who she met through the Silver Singles site, is apparently a retired accountant with a penchant for line dancing.

"What do you think?" she asks, performing an impeccable pirouette.

"You know there are zero pirouettes involved in line dancing, right?" I ask, smiling at her. "And wear whatever you want. The third date is when the clothes come off, anyway."

"I think I liked the blue dress better," Maisie says. "It made your eyes pop."

"At least one of you is helpful." Ruthie beams at Maisie before glaring at me. "I'll try the blue one again."

"Okay, so let me get this straight," Maisie says once Ruthie has traipsed back to her bedroom. "You brought Kaya to the doctor's office, and the doctor turned out to be Liam. And then Liam saved her life. And then he carried your other niece to your car. And then he visited you at the hospital and took you out to dinner. And *then* you guys kissed. Do I have that right?"

"Technically, it was the surgeon who saved Kaya's life," I say, wondering how many more times I'll need to clarify that for people. "But Liam did help. And he visited Kaya at the hospital, not me."

Maisie raises an eyebrow. "It wasn't the surgeon you were making out with last night, was it?"

I'm trying very hard not to relive the kiss over and over in my mind, and Maisie isn't making it any easier. I resume slicing the pepper, focusing as hard as I can on my knife technique instead of the softness of Liam's lips. "We didn't make out. It was one kiss!"

Maisie, who's paying no attention whatsoever to the vegetables we're supposed to be chopping, wrinkles her forehead in doubt. "Was there tongue?"

I squirm in my seat, slicing the pepper into even tinier pieces. "There was a small amount of tongue."

I was worried Maisie would be angry, but instead she looks positively enthralled, as if I'm giving her a play-by-play of the most exciting news story of all time. "Tongue from you or from him?"

"What is this, fifth grade?" When Maisie just stares at me blankly, I sigh. "From him. At first. And then from both of us."

She smacks the table with her palm. "If there was tongue, you made out. Those are just the rules."

"According to who?" I ask, coming very close to slicing off the tip of my finger.

"According to, like, everyone in the world. Hey, Ruthie!"

Ruthie returns to the kitchen wearing a blue sundress that proves Maisie right. It really does make her eyes pop.

"That dress is perfect," Maisie says, clapping her hands in approval. "Ruthie, it's none of my business, but have you made out with Albert yet?"

"Oh, yes," Ruthie says without a hint of shyness. "He's very good at it."

"And in your opinion, what distinguishes kissing from making out?"

"Tongue," Ruthie answers. "Obviously." She scratches the back of her neck. "This one's itchy. I'll try the yellow again. And Willa, I asked you to slice the peppers, not dice them. I'm making salad for a man, not a hamster."

I grumble and set the knife down.

"See?" Maisie grins. "You made out with Liam."

"You aren't upset?" She's smiling like Glen the southern hairy-nosed wombat just announced he's having babies.

"Why would I be upset?"

"Well, Liam is Finn's best man. So that makes things inherently complicated. And there's also the fact that I'm not, you know, a real bridesmaid."

"Willa, you're gonna stand up with me on the biggest day of my life, in a real bridesmaid's dress, with real bridesmaid's hair and makeup. You're as real as the rest of them."

I'm quiet as I pick up a cucumber to chop. I don't tell Maisie that I woke up with my stomach in knots. As much as I'm trying not to obsess over the kiss, I can't escape the fact that I like Liam. Just thinking about the kiss, about the way his voice sounds when he says my name, makes my stomach flutter. But I have too much at stake to pursue anything with him. I can't jeopardize my position in Maisie's bridal party over a guy. After all, if I started something with Liam and it went south before the wedding, it could ruin my relationship with Maisie, and I could even get kicked out of my role.

And I need the rest of that wedding money. It's my ticket out of here. It's the only way I can start over without constantly being reminded of Sarah and Max and the fact that I spent months of my adult life dressing as a children's birthday party character. It's the only way I can heal.

There's that other thing, too: the fact that if Liam knew who I really am, a broken woman who can't seem to get over The Incident, he'd regret ever kissing me in the first place. If he finds out that I've been lying to him—that Maisie and I are lying to everyone—he'll hate me forever. And he might hate Maisie, too.

"Do you think you really like Liam?" Maisie asks. "Or do you think what you really feel for him is gratitude for helping Kaya? 'Cause I listened to an interview on NPR the other day about a woman who thought she was in love with her therapist, but turns out it was just transference. She needed even more therapy after that."

I focus on cutting the cucumber into symmetrical slices. Is what I feel for Liam simply transference, or whatever Maisie described? I *am* grateful to him for how he helped Kaya. Eternally grateful. If he hadn't rushed her to the hospital . . . I can't even bring myself to finish the thought. But is gratitude the extent of my emotion toward him? I think of the pure fury I felt the first time we met, and how that fury changed to annoyance, and then affection. I consider the way he opened up to me about Beth and his childhood and even his divorce. I remember how I felt when I ran my fingers over his tattoo.

I remember the way his lips felt against mine.

"No," I say. "It's not just gratitude."

"So there you go." Maisie tosses carrot slices into the salad bowl and flips her braid over her shoulder. "Maybe one day I'll be standing beside you at your wedding to Liam. Stranger things have happened. Besides, you guys would make super cute babies."

I try not to pass out at the thought. After The Incident, I promised myself that I'd never go through the whole wedding drama again. There will be no poufy white dress for me, no bridesmaids or Mrs. Yummy's Belgian chocolate cake. There will only be freedom from those awful, aching memories.

"I think this is the outfit. What do you think?" Ruthie returns to the kitchen in a pair of white linen pants and a salmon-colored tunic, a look topped off with pearl earrings and a gold hairpin clasping her silver waves.

"It's perfect," Maisie says in a breathless voice, as if Ruthie's about to trot off to prom.

"I love it," I agree. "And Albert will, too."

"I think Herman would have liked it also," Ruthie says. "He always had a sense for fashion, unlike most men. He was the exception."

My eyes dart over to a framed photograph of Herman on the kitchen counter, in which he's sporting a white T-shirt with khakis, tube socks, and a camo hat. Maybe love really is blind.

"Hopefully Albert likes salad, because we made a ton of it," I say.

"Looks delicious." Ruthie pats my hand and surveys our work.

"What else are you making for dinner?" Maisie asks.

"Shrimp ravioli, blistered tomatoes and capers, and peach pie for dessert."

My stomach growls. "What if you blow off Albert and we just do a girls' dinner instead?"

"And not have any good stories to shut Edna up when she brags about her rotating lineup of suitors? I think not."

"I better head home. Pippa needs dinner, too." Maisie gets up from the table, brushing a stray piece of lettuce from her lap.

"Thanks again for the casseroles," I say, walking Maisie to Ruthie's front door. "And for those animal books for Kaya. You really didn't have to."

Maisie taps her foot against the hardwood. "Sure I did, Willa. We're friends. Though not quite as friendly as you are with Liam, I'd say." Grinning, she waves good-bye to Ruthie and me and closes the front door behind her.

I'm quiet as I finish chopping tomatoes for Ruthie's salad. Maisie might be okay with the idea of Liam and me together, but I'm not. Because while Liam might think he likes me, he doesn't know the real Willa.

He doesn't know I'm pretending to be someone I'm not.

23

Even though I can't stop thinking about my kiss with Liam, I don't text him at all during the next week. For one thing, I'm not certain he wants me to. He gave me his number in case I needed anything related to Kaya's health, but she's home from the hospital and back to work on her secret frog project, thank God. I considered making up a question just to have an excuse to talk to him—*hey, hot doctor who I pounced on last week, what's the point of an appendix, anyway?*—but there's nothing I could feasibly ask him that I couldn't just Google.

Plus, I'm not sure how he feels about our kiss, and I don't want to risk reading more into it than I should. Our emotions were running high that night, thanks to Kaya's emergency, and adrenaline has a way of amplifying things to make them seem like more than they are. He bought me dinner as a peace offering, and I told him the kiss was a peace offering, too. Maybe he just wants to leave things like that—nice and peaceful.

But maybe the real reason I haven't texted Liam is that I'd be tempted to kiss him again. Our kiss was electric, and my body still tingles when I think about it. Which is exactly my problem—I need to stop thinking about it.

Luckily, I have plenty to keep me busy. Lorene, who takes her maid of honor duties very seriously, has filled my inbox with email after email about Maisie's bachelorette party, a weekend getaway in the Hocking Hills. Subject lines ranged from Ziplining: yay or nay? to Bear spray: BRING IT! We'll be staying in a cabin, and I'm pretty sure there hasn't been a bear sighting in Ohio in decades, but I send enthusiastic responses to every message about Lorene's carefully arranged carpool assignments and how many chocolate bars we should bring for s'mores. I know she wants Maisie to have the time of her life, and so do I. Besides, running out of chocolate with a group of tipsy women is not a situation anyone wants to be in.

In addition to endless discussions about the bachelorette party and how we're going to handle hair and makeup for the wedding, I'm busy at home, too. Unlike before I met Maisie, when I slept until two in the afternoon and the only meals I cooked were toast and frozen pizza, I now keep a semibusy schedule. I get up early to help get my nieces ready for the day, and I spend the bulk of my afternoons helping Stacey with Celebration! Events duties. And a few nights a week, I've started cooking dinner. They're not the super healthy meals Stacey and Glory usually prepare, but they're edible enough that even Ruthie, who's never met an opinion she wouldn't share, doesn't complain when she joins us.

I'm even making progress on my student loans, thank God. I'm not all the way caught up, but thanks to Maisie, I've paid enough toward them in the last month and a half that intimidating debt collectors are no longer blowing up my phone. I even started making my bed and shaving my legs again. If my life were a movie, the past six weeks would make for a very inspirational comeback montage.

I've also started to research where I want to move once Maisie's wedding is over. I like the idea of a quiet little beach town somewhere, a place where I can rent a tiny cottage and listen to the ocean waves and start publishing my blog posts again. I imagine myself sprawled out on the sand with a blanket underneath me and a notebook on my lap, someplace where I don't have to pretend to be a fairy princess or a dedicated alumna of Camp Wildwood. Where I don't have to lie to anyone, including myself.

"Hey." Stacey pops her head into my bedroom, a basket of laundry balanced on one hip.

I shut my laptop at a lightning-quick speed, as if I've been browsing something embarrassing, like porn or sex toy reviews.

Stacey notices. "Do I want to know?" she asks, arching an eyebrow.

"Not really." The truth is, I've spent all morning preparing to send my résumé to a host of small publications in beach towns across the country—local newspapers, county tourism offices, the works. I don't have great references, considering my five-year career at *Buckeye Buzz* ended with me not showing up for work nine days straight, and I don't think prospective employers will be blown away by my brief stint as Princess Sparkleheart. But I'm armed with strong writing samples and low expectations, and I'd scrub toilets at a Six Flags if it meant never running into Sarah again. Besides, if nobody wants to hire me, I can always freelance as a professional bridesmaid.

"It's a few minutes to ten, so you should probably leave for Maisie's soon. And Glory made sweet potato waffles, so grab some before you go."

I can't help but smile at my sister. She can be annoying as hell— she left a copy of Oprah's *What I Know for Sure* on my bed yesterday, and I was tempted to smack her over the head with it—but she looks out for me in a way no one else does.

"Thanks, Stace. And before you ask, yes, I packed my bug spray, two tubes of sunscreen, and a sweatshirt. And I won't forget the first aid kit."

Stacey, who reminded me eight times not to forget Band-Aids, gives me a salute and heads down the hallway with her laundry basket.

I unzip my weekender bag and double-check that I've packed everything I need for the trip. It's a gingham tote that I carried with me all the time back in my blogging days, when Max and I traveled to bed-and-breakfasts all over the state to generate new posting content. It sat untouched in my closet for the last six and a half months, and it feels good to be taking it on a new adventure.

My phone pings with a text from Lorene: DON'T FORGET YOUR LINGERIE, LADIES! VERY IMPORTANT!!! It's only a matter of seconds before the other members of the bachelorette trip send back affirmative responses. In classic bachelorette party fashion, Lorene planned a full day's worth of silly games, including one in which we each bring a gift of lingerie for the bride, and Maisie has to guess who each piece is from. I bought her a black silk teddy, which I still consider a ridiculous name for an article of clothing.

Flinging my bag over my shoulder, I hightail it downstairs to the kitchen. Lucy's making art out of yogurt on her high chair tray, and Maeve and Kaya are in deep discussion over whether to watch *Frozen* or *Moana* for family movie night.

"Happy Saturday," Glory says as I douse a sweet potato waffle with syrup and destroy it in a few swift bites. "Sure you don't wanna bail on the bachelorette party and watch *Frozen* for the eight thousandth time?"

"I'm good." I sing a note from "Let It Go," causing the girls to join in and Glory to scowl at me like she hopes I choke on my breakfast.

"Have fun with Elsa and Anna!" I blow Glory a kiss and stop to hug each one of my nieces before hurrying out the door. According to Lorene's military-grade car pool plan, her SUV will be too stuffed with alcohol and Target bags to accommodate anyone but her and Rose, so I get the important duty of picking up Maisie.

I find an upbeat Spotify playlist and try to get myself in a positive mind-set on the drive to Maisie and Finn's. I'm determined not to have another woe-is-Willa moment this weekend like I did at the bridal shop. The weekend is all about celebrating Maisie, and I refuse to let the shadow of my own would-be wedding hang over it. Even so, it's impossible not to think about my own bachelorette party, which took place a mere week before The Incident. I'd wanted something local that I could post about on the blog, so Sarah planned a staycation in the Short North, a clustered neighborhood of shops, bars, and restaurants near downtown Columbus. Ten of us got mani-pedis at the W Nail Bar, followed by a candle-making session at the Candle Lab and dinner at Hyde Park, a fancy steak house. After dinner, we partied at the Big Bang, a dueling piano bar, and ended the night at my favorite dive, Char Bar. Nate had watched all three of the girls, so Stacey and Glory attended, and Sarah booked everyone rooms at the upscale hotel Le Méridien Columbus, The Joseph.

It was one of the best days of my life, followed by the very worst. Since The Incident, I've often wondered where Sarah and Max's relationship was at that point. On the night of my bachelorette party, had they already been sleeping together for months? Had Sarah, the same woman who held my hand while I peed on a stick during a pregnancy scare in college, the woman who cried with me over every breakup or failed exam or gut-wrenching episode of *This Is Us*, been in love with Max all along? Maybe the reason she was quieter than usual in the weeks leading up to The Incident was that she was trying to work up the courage to tell me the truth. Or maybe the reason she broke down in tears during my bachelorette party toast, telling me how much she loved me, was that she knew heartbreak was coming for me.

For both of us.

24

When I pull into Maisie's driveway, Finn is outside mowing the grass while Pippa watches from the front porch. I wave to him as I get out of the car, inhaling the lovely scent of grass clippings, and he turns off the motor and abandons his chore.

"Hiya, Willa." He lifts up his Columbus Blue Jackets T-shirt to wipe sweat from his brow and points toward the house. "C'mon. Knowing Maisie, I bet she's got four suitcases packed."

We go inside, Pippa trailing behind us with an eager bark and a wagging tail. The house smells of chocolate chip cookies, and Maisie is already halfway down the stairs, wrestling an oversized suitcase alongside her.

"I didn't know you guys were going to Hocking Hills for two months," Finn says brightly. "I'll have to send you both a postcard."

Maisie scowls at him, and Finn laughs and helps her wrestle her suitcase the rest of the way down the stairs.

"Guys will never understand why travel is more complicated for women," I say. "We need so much more. Hair stuff, accessories, layers for all possible weather."

"Exactly. Oh, and tampons!" Maisie jogs upstairs, leaving Finn to tackle the suitcase alone. "I almost forgot tampons!"

"Can't forget the tampons," Finn says, leaning down to pet Pippa. "She also packed enough snacks to feed an entire NFL team for a week, so I think you guys are in good shape."

"Lorene had a spreadsheet for how much food and alcohol to bring. And she insisted that everyone pack bear spray."

"Sounds like my sister. When we were kids, she's the one who masterminded our family vacations. You don't know what tired is until you've followed Lorene Forsythe's Disney World itinerary." Finn grins. "Good luck this weekend."

"When's your bachelor party?"

"Two weeks before the wedding. Liam and my brothers and I are taking my dad's sailboat out on Lake Erie. It'll be nothing but fishing, drinking beer, and eating what we catch."

My heart leaps at Liam's name, but I do my best to keep a straight face. I don't know if he told Finn about our kiss or not, and Finn's tone and body language don't offer any clues.

"My handsome sailor," Maisie says, traipsing back downstairs with a box of tampons in hand. She tosses it into her suitcase and loops an arm around Finn's waist. "Watch out for that famous Lake Erie toxic algae."

"And you ladies watch out for ticks and mosquitoes," he says, pressing a kiss to her cheek. "And, apparently, bears."

"Bear spray!" Maisie cries, and sprints back upstairs to retrieve another forgotten item.

By the time Finn loads Maisie's giant suitcase into my trunk, along with two smaller ones and a freshly made batch of chocolate chip cookies for the road, it's almost noon.

"You two should probably take off," Finn says when Maisie stops to give Pippa a kiss for the tenth time. "Remember when we showed up late to the family reunion? I thought Lorene was gonna explode."

"She broke out in literal hives," Maisie adds. "It was horrifying." She pets Pippa one last time and then nestles into Finn's chest, nuzzling his neck with her head.

"I love you," he whispers, brushing her hair from her face, and she whispers it back. The warmth of their affection for each other is almost enough to make me believe that love is real, and I bend down to pet Pippa to keep myself from getting too sentimental.

"Okay, Willa Callister," Maisie says once we're settled in the car. She flips her hair over her shoulder and slides on her sunglasses. "Let's do this."

⟡

Hocking Hills State Park is just over an hour from Columbus, and Maisie and I spend the drive rocking out to the Backstreet Boys and old-school Britney Spears, with a little Rolling Stones mixed in. We open her Tupperware container full of cookies before we even reach the highway.

"So," Maisie says, giving me a sly look, "what's the latest with you and Liam?"

What's the latest? What are you, a celebrity gossip columnist?"

She shrugs. "You can't blame a girl for being curious. And before you ask, no, I didn't say anything to Finn about your kiss. I keep my friends' secrets private."

"Good to know." A little wave of happiness surges in my chest when she calls me her friend, but I push the feeling away.

"Liam came over to watch a ball game with Finn on Tuesday, and I swear his ears perked up when I mentioned your name."

"You mentioned my name? Why? What did you say?" Despite myself, I get the same tingly sensation I do whenever I think of Liam's lips on mine.

"Well, well, well, look who's the curious one now." Maisie beams. "They were talking about some baseball blogger, and I mentioned that you used to write a super popular blog."

The wave of happiness evaporates a little at the mention of my blog. I think of the recent posts I've written and stashed on a thumb drive. Posts no one will ever see. "It wasn't super popular, really."

"Well, it was Columbus popular. Just because it wasn't the *Huffington Post* doesn't mean it wasn't awesome. I told you before, I loved your blog. I used to read it every day." She hands me another cookie, perhaps to prevent me from arguing. "Anyway, I hung out with them for a while to watch the game, and I swear I saw Liam looking at your blog on his phone."

A wave of nausea sweeps over me. The thought of Liam scrolling through my old posts—reviews of restaurants Max and I visited, updates on my half marathon training, detailed posts on my bachelorette party and wedding dress shopping and how I chose my florist—gives me the urge to vomit. I don't want Liam to know the old Willa. I don't want him to compare me to her and end up disappointed.

I can't let him know the new Willa, either. Not without endangering the secret I share with Maisie. I eat the chocolate chip cookie without tasting it and decide to change the subject.

"So," I say as Maisie switches up the playlist for some Spice Girls. "It's less than a month until the big day. How are you feeling? Excited? Nervous? Got cold feet?"

Maisie smiles. "No cold feet. But I am nervous, because I want everything to be perfect. For Finn, and for the Forsythes."

"And for you," I add, glancing at her as I switch lanes. "Right?"

Maisie takes a bite of cookie and looks out the window, where endless green fields roll by. "Of course."

"Speaking of the Forsythes, doesn't Mrs. Forsythe strike you as a tad . . ."

"Bitchy?" Maisie smiles. "You bet. The first time I met her, I told her how excited I was to meet the woman who raised Finn, and she said, 'Bless your heart, Maisie.' I thought it was a compliment. It took me a few minutes to realize it wasn't." She tears another cookie in two and passes me half. "She was pretty standoffish for the first year I dated Finn. I don't think she believed it would last. And I can kind of understand where she was coming from. The Forsythes have a pretty large family fortune."

"And she thought you were what, some kind of gold digger? Ugh. Internalized misogyny at its finest."

"Maybe. Or maybe she just thought I wasn't a good match for Finn. I think she expected him to end up with someone like Lorene. You know, someone super Type A who wanted to be a stay-at-home mom. I love Lorene, but that's just not my style." Maisie glances at me sideways. "I don't think Mrs. Forsythe imagined her oldest son marrying a khaki-wearing girl from West Virginia who prefers animals to people."

"Well, maybe she doesn't know Finn very well." I pause, remembering what Rose told me at the bridal shower about Lorene's dissolving marriage. "Maybe she doesn't know her daughter too well, either."

Maisie shrugs. "Well, I just decided to kill her with kindness, and look at us now. She helped me pick out my wedding dress. She hosted my bridal shower. And she's letting Finn and me get married at her home, which is amazing, because it involves a ton of planning on her part and it's super special to Finn."

I remember the conversation between Mrs. Forsythe's friends that I overheard at her bridal shower: the rumors about Maisie being an alcoholic, and the assertion that Finn's mom only offered to host the wedding because she thought he would bail on it. I want to tell Maisie so that she can protect herself from Mrs. Forsythe, who certainly doesn't have her best interests at heart. There's no worse feeling than realizing you put your trust in someone you shouldn't have. I learned that the hard way, but Maisie shouldn't have to.

"Plus, weddings have a way of bringing people together," she continues, her optimism undeterred. "Bringing families together. Don't you think?"

I remember a wedding Stacey planned where the bride stopped speaking to everyone in her family—including her groom—over a disagreement about terrarium centerpieces, but I don't say that to Maisie. She's looking at me with such a hopeful expression that I can't bear to rain on her parade. "That's true. Weddings and babies are really good for that."

"I really, really hope so."

"Because of Mrs. Forsythe?" I ask, reaching for another cookie.

Maisie fidgets with her sunglasses. "Yes. And also because, well, things between my family and me aren't, you know, ideal."

It's the first time Maisie's admitted to something being less than perfect, and I almost choke on a chocolate chip. I'm not shocked by the fact that her relationship with her family isn't one thousand percent splendid; no one's is. But Maisie opening up to me about it seems like a big step for our friendship. Or it would be, if she weren't my employer.

"How so?" I pass her another cookie, determined to keep the mood in the car relaxed. I don't want her to clam up or think I'm prying for information—even if I have wondered over and over why Finn hasn't met her parents and why she had no family at her shower.

She fiddles with the sun visor, pulling it down and then popping it back up again. "It's just . . . my parents and I don't see eye to eye on a lot of things. They're not huge fans of some of my choices."

I watch as she quits messing with the sun visor and moves onto adjusting and re-adjusting her seat belt. What kind of parent wouldn't be overjoyed to have bright, kind Maisie as a daughter?

"I can't imagine anyone disapproving of your choices, Maisie. You're one of the best people I've ever met."

She blushes. "Thank you. But I wasn't always . . . I'm not . . . I just really hope the wedding goes perfectly. If it does, it'll help heal some old wounds, you know?"

I don't know what Maisie's old wounds are, exactly, but I know how badly they can hurt. I know how they can scab over and tear open again and again, paralyzing you long after they were inflicted.

"Anyway," she says, wiping a crumb off her lip, "enough about that. This weekend is all about having fun." She turns up the volume in the car, and "Wannabe" blares from the speakers.

I want to ask her more about her family, but the full-blast volume seems like a clear indication that she's done talking for now. "Maisie," I say, half shouting so that she can hear me, "I think you should know that any—"

"What?"

"Any family with you in it is really fucking lucky." I finish my sentence just as she turns down the volume, so that "fucking lucky" comes out like a yell in the now-silent car.

Maisie and I burst into laughter, and it takes a moment for her giggles to die down enough that she can speak. "Thanks, Willa."

She turns the music back up, and we nod along to the beat as we continue down the highway. I'm not just pumping Maisie up because she's paying me to be a bridesmaid. I mean what I've told her. I've only known her for a brief time, but something tells me that she'd poke her own eye out before betraying a best friend.

And if I were still the kind of person who needs friends, I'd pick Maisie to be mine in a heartbeat.

25

The cabin Lorene rented for the weekend sits at the top of a steep hill, and by the time I've driven my Corolla up the long drive-way, my knuckles are white against the steering wheel.

"Whew," Maisie says when we're parked. "At the pace you were going, I thought we might roll backward all the way down."

I toss a piece of cookie at her, laughing as she dodges it. When I climb out of the car, I stretch my legs and inhale the fresh air. It's not exactly the Le Méridien Columbus, The Joseph, but maybe it's even better.

"Maisie Mitchell, get your pretty butt in here!" Rose, standing on the front porch of the cabin with a bottle of wine in her hand, waves to us. "You too, Willa! It's time to party!"

"Oh, lord," Maisie says when a loud cheer rings out from inside the cabin. "Here we go."

We carry as much as we can from the trunk and trudge toward the cabin. It's nothing like the small, wooden building I imagined when I heard we were staying in a cabin. Well, it is made of wood, but it's certainly not small. Our cabin is a giant log structure with huge windows and a cobblestone path that leads from the driveway to the porch. My weekender bag nearly crushes my shoulder, and Maisie and I are panting from exertion by the time we step inside.

The interior is even more breathtaking. A chandelier hangs from the ceiling of the main room—what kind of cabin has a *chandelier?*—and thick rugs and leather couches give off a vibe of sophistication. A banner that reads *BACH SHIT CRAZY!* hangs from the ceiling, right next to a four-foot-tall inflatable penis. Never mind about the vibe of sophistication.

"Holy crap," Maisie says, dumping her bags in the middle of the entryway. "This place is amazing."

"It got excellent reviews on Airbnb," Lorene says, emerging from the kitchen. "Only the best for our bride."

While Rose goes out to the car to help Maisie with the rest of her luggage, Lorene grabs me by the arm and points to a blanket hanging from the wall. "There's a deer head under there," she whispers. "Whatever you do, do *not* mention it to Maisie. She's very sensitive about animal rights."

In addition to Rose and Jenna, Maisie's curly-haired friend who I met at the bridal shower, a half-dozen more women stand in the large, open kitchen drinking wine and snacking on a cheese tray. I recognize a few of them from Maisie's shower, including three brunette Forsythe cousins and Maisie's friend Angela, a gray-eyed herpetologist at the Columbus Zoo.

"Herpetology means I specialize in reptiles," Angela says. "Not that I study herpes. In case you were going to ask."

"I wasn't, but good to know," I reply, wondering just how many times in her life poor Angela has faced that question.

"Angela was an original member of the bridal party, but she won a grant to work in the Galápagos," Lorene explains. "Smarty pants."

"Willa's your replacement," Rose explains, looping an arm through mine.

Meeting Angela feels a bit like meeting a boyfriend's super cool ex-girlfriend who just happens to have an awesome job studying lizards. Self-consciousness sweeps over me.

"I used to be a children's party performer," I announce. Angela looks at me the way I look at Maeve whenever she tries to stick crayons up her nose, and Rose pats my arm affectionately.

When everyone's toted their luggage inside, Lorene gives us a tour of the cabin. In addition to the standard bedrooms and bathrooms, there's a small library full of leather-bound books that smells like heaven. There's also a billiards room, a home theater with DreamLounger recliners, and a hot tub in the backyard. The cabin overlooks a wooded area bordering the state forest, and when Lorene takes us out onto the back deck, we pause to listen to the soothing sounds of chirping birds and buzzing cicadas.

"Nature is the greatest antidepressant," Rose says, opening her arms wide for mountain pose.

Personally, I've found citalopram to be the best antidepressant, but nature probably helps, too. Nobody complains when Rose leads us in a ten-minute impromptu yoga session, and by the end of it, I'm more relaxed than I have been in months.

"So," Maisie says when we head inside, everyone eager to get back to the cheese tray. "What's on our agenda?"

Lorene has a carefully planned itinerary, which she emailed to everyone except Maisie in the week leading up to the trip. First, we're going to have light refreshments while everyone mingles. Then we'll head to a local stable for a horseback-riding expedition, followed by dinner at the cabin. After dinner, we'll play a round of games, including the lingerie-guessing game and Adult Pictionary—if people are still sober enough to draw by then. Finally, we'll head outside to the fire pit to make s'mores and hang out by the campfire. Tomorrow morning, Rose will lead us in a yoga class, followed by a hearty breakfast at the cabin and a nature walk in the woods.

"Oh my gosh," Maisie says when Lorene hands each of us a copy of the official itinerary. "This is perfect, Lorene." I'm not sure why we all need one, since we're not splitting up or anything, but the sheer joy on Lorene's face as she passes out the laminated copies is enough for me to keep my mouth shut.

Maisie literally jumps up and down when she sees horseback riding on the list of activities, and I feel a rush of affection for her. She and Finn clearly make good money, but she didn't want a luxurious trip to Vegas or Miami or Napa Valley—not that there's anything wrong with that—for her bachelorette party. She wanted a simple, relaxing weekend with the women she cares about, and I can't help but feel honored to be there.

In the kitchen, I load a plate with pecan-stuffed mushrooms and crackers with artichoke dip, then pass a plate to Maisie.

She accepts it without looking up from her itinerary, and I notice that she's biting her lip as her gaze skims the page.

"You okay?" I ask.

Maisie sets the itinerary down, tapping her foot quickly. The smack of her flip-flop against the hardwood makes a loud clapping sound. "I'm fine. Just excited. Overwhelmed."

My skepticism grows as she taps her foot faster, in the same rabbity motion she made when I first met her at Espresso 22. "Are you sure?"

She taps the countertop with her index finger. "I just wish . . . well, I wish my sister were here to enjoy this."

"Clara?"

Maisie nods. "She'd enjoy the horseback riding so much. She loves horses more than anything."

"Did you guys ride when you were kids?"

She laughs like I've asked her if unicorns are real. "God, no. We didn't get to do stuff like that growing up. But when she was little, we'd watch *Black Beauty* every day, and she'd pretend our dog was an Appaloosa. Or sometimes *I* was the Appaloosa." She twists her mouth into a half-smile. "She always got to be the rider. One of the perks of being the little sister."

"There are a lot of perks for little sisters," I say, thinking of how Stacey gave me a job and a place to live when I was in my darkest moments. "How old is Clara?"

"Not so little anymore. She's seventeen. A party with alcohol wouldn't be appropriate for her."

I consider what Maisie said in the car about not seeing eye to eye with her parents, and I wonder if alcohol is the real reason Clara's not here. Maisie doesn't drink anyway, so we could have easily made it a dry occasion.

"Maisie—" I start to say, but Rose interrupts me when she bounds into the kitchen.

"Picture time!" she announces, holding up her phone. "I want to get some good ones for Instagram before everyone gets trashed. Come into the living room. And Maisie, grab the penis balloon."

I sigh, wishing I could have had a longer moment with Maisie. Damn Rose and her phone. Maybe Liam wasn't entirely wrong about his distaste for social media.

"Duty calls." Maisie grabs a cracker from my plate, pops it into her mouth, and trails after Rose to take pictures.

And boy, do we take a ton of pictures. Before we leave for the stables, Rose makes everyone participate in her thirty-minute photo session. She takes so long making sure we get enough Instagrammable shots that we're almost late for our riding appointment. When we finally get to Blue Moon Acres stables, I ride a black-and-white Tennessee Walker horse named Penny, who seems to enjoy eating leaves off trees more than actually walking. By the end of our scenic two-hour ride, my ass feels like it's about to fall off, and my stomach rumbles when we return to the cabin for dinner.

We feast on baked stuffed shells and sun-dried tomato risotto, with cherry pie, banana cake, and chocolate ice cream for dessert. We drink wine, White Claws, and pineapple mango rum punch, and we howl with laughter during the lingerie game. Maisie's face burns red when she sees the crotchless panties Rose gifted her, and her feeble attempt at drawing "phone sex" during Adult Pictionary has Jenna and two of the Forsythe cousins laughing so hard they cry. By the time night falls and we venture outside for a campfire, I can feel the effects of the alcohol swing into high gear.

"Someone should tell a scary story," Jenna says as Lorene and Maisie work to get the fire going.

"Let Maisie tell you about the time Finn wore assless chaps to my Halloween party," Lorene laments, pouring lighter fluid directly onto the firewood. "I still have nightmares about that one."

"Finn has the cutest butt," Maisie says lovingly, causing her future sister-in-law to shudder with disgust. "We still bring out those chaps from time to time."

Lorene tosses a marshmallow at her, and Maisie ducks and slides her camping chair next to mine.

"Thanks for being here, Willa," she says, holding her hands out toward the fire. "I'm not sure that I could have done any of this without you."

I'm surprised by the ball of emotion that swells in my throat. "I'm happy to be here. You deserve to have the best night, Maisie. You deserve to have the best life."

"Hey, Mais," Jenna says, selecting a pristine campfire fork from the set of twelve Lorene purchased from Crate & Barrel. "Tell us, what's the best thing and the worst thing about your future husband, Finnaeus Ulysses Forsythe?"

"Finnaeus Ulysses?" I mutter. The Forsythes really are a strange breed.

"It's a family name," Rose whispers to me. "We have great-uncles named Chester and Barney, so it could have been worse."

Maisie tucks her hands into the sleeves of her Columbus Zoo hoodie, and the glow of the campfire makes her look radiant. "Gosh, there are so many good things. But the best thing about Finn is how good he is, right down to his core. No one's ever treated me with more kindness than he does."

"He's always been a gentle soul," Lorene agrees. "Even as a kid, he refused to kill any spiders we found inside the house. He'd set them free outside, or worse, keep them as pets." She shivers at the memory.

"Remember the night he proposed?" Rose asks. She tips back a mango-flavored White Claw and glances at me and the others. "He acted so weird in the week leading up to his proposal that Maisie thought he was breaking up with her."

"We went to the movies the day before, and he asked for Reese's *Pieces* instead of Reese's Pee-sees at the concession stand," Maisie explains. "I knew something was way off."

"You didn't say the worst thing about him," Jenna teases.

"We already discussed the assless chaps," Lorene answers for Maisie. "And I'm pretty sure it doesn't get much worse than that."

"In Finn's defense, he looked great." Maisie beams as she reaches for a marshmallow. "And Liam put him up to it."

At the mention of Liam, I take a long swig of pineapple mango rum punch, and then another. As much as I wish I could contact him, I don't dare to. I can't risk anything developing between us while I'm working for Maisie. Even if she wouldn't mind—in fact, she seemed downright thrilled at the idea when I told her about our kiss—I can't escape the fact that I'm lying to Liam about who I am. And he hates liars; he has a whole tattoo dedicated to starting over and living life honestly. Whatever he felt for me during our kiss will disappear the instant he learns that I'm capable of deceit, even if it is for a job.

And even if he was able to get past the lying, I'm in no position to open my heart to anyone. I know what happens when you let yourself love someone, and that's not something I'm prepared to do again. Having my soul crushed once in my lifetime is enough for me, thank you very much. Besides, in a few short weeks I'll be long gone from Ohio, and my kiss with Liam will be nothing but a distant memory.

I nibble on a marshmallow and try to pretend I'm not bothered by the fact that Liam hasn't texted me either. Sure, I never gave him my number, but if he really wanted to talk to me after our kiss, he could have gotten it from Maisie. I have to remind myself that the kiss might have been a bigger deal to me than it was to him. For me, it was the first night since The Incident that I let myself say Sarah's and Max's names out loud. Listening to Liam talk about his divorce, about how he'd been cheated on and somehow managed to build a new life for himself afterward, made me feel hopeful for the first time in months. Our kiss was the first time since The Incident that I let someone wrap his arms around me and whisper my name into my hair and make my heart threaten to pound out of my chest. Our kiss was more than just a kiss to me, despite my efforts to deny it. It was a possibility. A possibility that things can be good again, someday, if I keep holding on. That I might be down, but I'm not out. That I'm still Willa, and I can survive all of it. That I can heal.

But it's very possible that for Liam, our dinner was a peace offering and nothing more. And because I can't text him to find out, that's what I'm choosing to tell myself. If the kiss wasn't as world-altering for him as it was for me, then the Liam Problem is solved before it got any bigger, and I can go back to swearing off men forever.

"Earth to Willa," Rose says, holding a box of graham crackers toward me. She must have had quite a bit of punch, because she nearly drops the box into the campfire. "Are you making s'mores, or just demolishing marshmallows?"

My answer is cut off by a series of yells and hoots in the distance, followed by an outbreak of raucous laughter.

"What was that?" I ask, craning my neck toward the woods.

"There's a bunch of guys having some kind of party there." Lorene points to a neighboring cabin, which sits half a football field away. "We drove by their cabin on the way here. Let me just say that their balloons aren't nearly as classy as ours."

I consider the inflatable penis that's almost as tall as Maisie and bite my tongue.

"I bet it's a bachelor party. They had a game of giant beer pong set up in the yard," Rose says. "With red trash cans instead of Solo cups."

As if on cue, the guys release another series of yells.

"We should play a game, too," Jenna suggests. "How about Truth or Dare? It's a classic."

I sigh. I'd rather hide in a giant red trash can than play that game. Sarah and I played it at countless sleepovers when we were kids, always trying to one-up each other with the outrageousness of our dares. It's not an activity I want to revisit.

"Maisie," Rose says, taking another sip of punch. "Truth or dare?"

Maisie hasn't even agreed to play, but ever the good sport, she blows on her marshmallow to cool it off and nods at Finn's cousin. "Truth."

"I knew you were a truth person," Rose says. "Okay. How does it feel to know that you're only going to sleep with one man for the rest of your life? I know you love Finn like crazy, but still. Doesn't the idea of one penis forever make you want to curl up in a ball and die?"

Jenna, who's had more White Claws than I can count, snorts with laughter, but Maisie only smiles. "It doesn't, actually. You make it sound like it's some random, detached penis. But it's not. It's Finn for the rest of my life. And that's an amazing feeling."

"Cheers to that," Rose says, lifting her bottle and taking a long swig. I raise my graham cracker square in solidarity but don't take a sip of my drink. It's getting late, and I don't want a raging headache when I try to survive Rose's yoga class in the morning.

"Okay, Mais, it's your turn to challenge someone," Lorene says.

"I'll pass. I'm too busy with my s'mores." Maisie shakes her head, and it's clear that she's about ready to call it a night, too.

"Chug it!" one of the guys from the bachelor party shouts. The sound of his voice carries through the trees, disrupting the quiet of the night.

"Okay, I'll go," Jenna says. "Rose: truth or dare?"

Rose twirls her bottle, swishing the liquid inside around. "Dare, definitely."

Jenna, who's evidently also a dare person, grins. "I dare you to go crash the bachelor party."

The guys' group erupts into laughter, and I find myself wishing they'd go back inside their cabin and let us enjoy our campfire in peace. "I don't know," I say. "Giant beer pong sounds less fun than stuffing our faces with chocolate. Besides, we're here to focus on Maisie."

The bride-to-be gives me a small smile. "Yeah, let's go inside and finish off the artichoke dip. We can play more Pictionary."

Rose juts her chin out in a pout. "I've never backed down from a dare. Ever. And I'm not about to start now."

Lorene grumbles in annoyance. "We're not fourteen anymore, Rose. It's okay to turn down a dare. And Maisie doesn't want to play."

Rose rolls her eyes at her cousin. "It'll only take five minutes! I'll run over to the guys' cabin, show them who really knows how to play beer pong, and head back. Besides, we're all here because Maisie met the love of her life. What if the love of *my* life is just through those woods, and I pass up the chance to meet him?"

"What if there's poison ivy in the woods, and you pass up the chance to meet that?" I ask, causing Rose to toss a marshmallow at me.

"You know what, guys? I think I've had enough campfire time. And I think everyone's had more than enough punch. Come on." Maisie loops one arm through Jenna's and another through Rose's and tries to guide them toward the cabin, but it's like herding cats.

The men erupt into a chorus of laughter, and Rose swivels her head in their direction and breaks loose from Maisie's grasp. "I'll be back in a flash, I swear."

"Rose, don't you *dare* go over there! It's not safe," Maisie insists.

Rose flashes a grin at her. "Poor choice of words."

"I'm serious," Maisie says, gripping Jenna's arm tighter. "You don't know those men. Not all guys are like Finn. The last thing any of us should be doing is traipsing into the woods to meet strangers."

"We're in Hocking Hills, not the middle of a war zone," Rose says. "Anyway, if you're so worried, then come with me."

Maisie crosses her arms over her chest. "No way."

"Suit yourself. But Rose Jackson never turns down a dare." She grabs a flashlight, and before Maisie can say another word in protest, she darts into the woods.

"Jesus Christ," Lorene says. "We really need to revoke her drinking privileges."

"Rose!" Maisie yells after Finn's cousin like she's disappeared into thin air. "Rose, come back!"

"It's okay, Mais," Lorene says, patting the bride's shoulder. "You know how she is. Give her five minutes of adventure and she'll be right back."

"No. It's not safe." Maisie's tone is panicked, strained. Like she thinks there might be a monster out there in the woods, thirsting for the blood of carefree yoga instructors. I watch as she shivers despite her layers of clothing, and the pained expression on her face spurs me to action.

"You go inside," I tell her. "I'll check on Rose, okay? She'll probably just say hi to those guys and come right back."

I grab a flashlight and head for the dense patch of woods that separates the two cabins. I can see Rose making her way through the trees, her figure a dark outline in the moonlight. The sooner I can get her home and get Maisie's party back on track, the better. I take careful, measured steps, trying not to let my feet come into contact with any shrubbery. If I'd known chasing a drunken bridesmaid through the forest would be part of my job description this weekend, I would have packed hiking boots instead of sandals.

"Rose!" I call after her. "Hurry up and finish your dare before I get bit by something!"

"Hush," she teases, slowing her pace so that she's only thirty or so meters ahead of me. "You and Maisie are such worrywa—fuck!" She lets out an animalistic cry of pain and crashes toward the ground, sticks snapping beneath her.

"Rose!" I sprint toward her, my heart pounding out of my chest. Leaves crunch beneath my feet, and the sound of laughter floats into the woods from the bachelor party cabin. When I reach Rose, who's curled up in the fetal position beneath a towering pine tree, I drop to my knees and place my hands on her arms while she writhes in pain.

"I fell," she whines, reaching for her ankle. "I tripped on that fucking branch and I think I broke—fuck, that hurts! I think I broke my ankle." She curses again and wraps her hands around her right foot.

"Okay, let's get you back to the cabin," I say, taking a deep breath to slow the pounding in my chest. Maisie was right. This wasn't a safe decision at all. "Come on."

Rose whimpers as I hoist her off the ground. She can't bear any weight on her right foot, and it takes us five minutes to cover the distance to the cabin. By the time we stumble inside, Rose crying in pain, my arm feels like it's going to fall off.

Color drains from Maisie's face when she sees us, and she leaps up from the couch and rushes over. "Holy shit, what happened?"

In spite of the commotion, I'm shocked by her use of the s-word. It's only the second time I've heard Maisie curse in my month and a half of knowing her, and the sound of it jars my ears.

"Have you been crying?" I ask, noticing the slight mascara stain beneath her eyes. "Are you okay?"

She wipes her face with her sleeve. "I'm fine. The smoke from the campfire makes my eyes water like crazy."

Rose releases a howl of pain, demonstrating that *she* is anything but fine.

"It's her right foot," I explain. "She tripped, and she thinks she broke her ankle."

Maisie gasps and covers her mouth like I've announced that Rose's foot was gnawed off by a rabid raccoon. "I told you, Rose. I *told* you not to go into the woods."

"That's not very helpful right now," Lorene points out, helping me guide Rose to the couch. I prop her injured foot up on a pillow, and she grasps my arm so tightly that I cringe in pain.

"She probably needs an X-ray," Lorene says, squinting at Rose's rapidly swelling ankle. "We're about ten miles from the hospital. Is anybody sober enough to drive her? Because I'm definitely not."

"I'm not." I regret drinking all that punch. Like me, the others have enjoyed more than their fair share of adult beverages tonight. Well, everyone except the bride-to-be.

"Maisie can drive Rose, right?" I ask. "You didn't have anything to drink."

Maisie, wiping under her eyes again, shakes her head firmly. "I don't drive at night. I can't."

"C'mon, Maisie, please," Rose begs. She's in so much pain that she winces with each word. "It hurts so, so bad. I can't take it!"

"I'm sorry." Maisie, perching on the edge of an armchair, wraps her arms around herself and rocks forward slightly. "I can't, I'm sorry. You know how bad my night vision is."

"We'll go with you," Lorene offers, clutching Maisie's hand. "We'll help you watch the road. I'm not that drunk, really. I'm just too tipsy to steer."

"Please," Rose repeats. "It *hurts!*"

"I can't," Maisie whispers. "I can't do it."

Her shoulders are hunched over, and she looks so small and scared that it makes me want to cry. Maybe I was wrong about her not having anything to drink. Maybe she downed some punch when no one was looking. Maybe what those women were whispering to each other at her bridal shower wasn't so far off. I feel guilty as soon as the thought strikes, but whatever's going on with Maisie, I'll have to figure it out later.

Rose, racked with sobs of pain, clutches my hand and pulls it toward her like she's about to bite.

"We can call an ambulance," I suggest. "We can call 911."

"We can't call an ambulance for what might just be a sprained ankle," Jenna says.

I resist the urge to reach across the coffee table and smack her. If it weren't for her stupid suggestion to play Truth or Dare, I'd still be eating chocolate by the fire—or even better, curled up in bed.

"Well, I can't just listen to her scream," I argue back. "We have to get her to a doctor, and we have to do it fast."

As soon as the words are out of my mouth, Rose grips my hand harder. "Liam," she says, moaning like she's on her deathbed. "Liam's at his cabin this weekend."

Liam. A jolt of electricity runs through me at her mention of his name. I vaguely recall Liam mentioning something at dinner about spending his weekends in the Hocking Hills, and my heart rate quickens.

"You have to call him," Rose utters, gritting her teeth. "Get him here. Please, Willa."

The prospect of calling Liam fills me with excitement, and then trepidation. What if things are awkward between us now? What if he wants to kiss me again, thereby endangering my secret with Maisie? Or worse—what if he doesn't?

"Willa!" Rose repeats. "Please. For the love of God, call him!"

The agony in her voice sends me running for my phone. Now isn't the time for me to be thinking about myself, or about the softness of Liam's lips. I grab my iPhone and find his number, the one I haven't called or texted since our kiss, in my contacts. But when I try to call, all I get is a No Service alert.

"Fuck," I say as Rose howls in pain from the living room. "Fuck, fuck, fuck."

"There's a landline," Lorene says. "In the kitchen."

I brace my hands against the cool granite counters, trying to quell the urge to vomit. Two White Claws, plus punch, plus sprinting through a forest do not equal a happy stomach. And the thought of talking to Liam only makes it worse.

But he'll know how to help Rose, so I have to put on my big-girl pants and get it done.

I find a cordless phone and dial his number again. It rings once, twice, three times, and by the fifth ring I'm cursing Liam Rafferty to hell in my head.

"Pick up, pick up," I mutter. *Pick up and help us. Pick up and tell me the kiss meant something to you, too.* I shove the thought away and take a long swig of water from a bottle on the counter.

"Hello?" Liam's voice is gruff, and I'm so surprised that he finally answered that I drop the phone.

Thanks to the White Claws, my reaction time isn't great, and it takes me a few seconds to retrieve the phone from the ground and stand back up.

"Hello?" Liam's repeating when I press the phone to my ear again. "Can I help you?"

"It's me," I announce, and then I mentally kick myself. How should Liam know who "me" is? A few banter-filled conversations and one dinner date haven't exactly bonded us for life.

"It's Willa," I say. "Sometimes you call me Sparkles." *Sometimes you kiss me and make me forget that I no longer believe in love.*

The whole thing comes out so awkwardly that I wish I could crawl into the kitchen floor and live there forever.

"Willa?" he asks. "It's almost midnight. Are you okay? Is something wrong with Kaya?"

His concern for me, and especially for Kaya, softens my resolve not to think about his lips anymore. "Yes, I'm okay. And Kaya's fine. She's doing great, actually."

"Good. That's good." He pauses. "I haven't heard from you in a while."

I wish I could tell him every thought that's racing through my mind: *I haven't heard from you, either. I wanted to text you. I want to eat tacos with you again. I want to feel your body against mine again. I want . . .*

But I can't.

"Willa, is this a booty call?"

I can hear the teasing in Liam's voice, but my face heats up with embarrassment anyway. "No!" I say quickly. "No, of course n—"

I'm interrupted by Rose howling in pain and unleashing an impressive string of curse words when Lorene tries to touch her injured foot.

"What was that?" Liam asks.

"That was Rose. You know, Finn and Lorene's cousin—"

"Yes, I know who Rose is. What's going on?"

"We're at Maisie's bachelorette party," I explain. "In Hocking Hills. Rose tried to crash a bachelor party during Truth or Dare, but she tripped over a tree stump or something, and she thinks she broke her ankle. And I'm pretty sure Maisie's having some kind of panic attack. And nobody can drive Rose to the hospital, because we all drank too much, except for Maisie. But she can't drive because of her vision issues. I want to call 911, because I'm worried that Rose will need an amputation or something if I don't."

When I finish my long-winded explanation, Liam stays completely silent on the other end of the line.

"So should I?" I ask impatiently. "Call 911? And do you think her ankle's broken?"

"Willa," Liam says, his voice calm and measured. "I need you to take a deep breath, slow down, and repeat what you just said. Skip the part about Truth or Dare."

I take a deep breath and do as instructed. "So," I say when I've repeated the important stuff. "Should I call 911? Or can you pretty please come help us?" Did I just say *pretty please*?

"Of course I'll help. What's your address?"

I hear barking in the background of his line as I rattle off the cabin details Lorene is holding in front of my face.

"I'll be there in ten minutes," Liam promises. "Just rice Rose's foot until I get there."

"Rice her foot?" I ask, my ears tingling from the very high pitch of Rose's hollering. "I don't think we have any. We brought a lot of snacks, but not rice. I think Lorene packed quinoa, though. Do we just dunk it in there?"

"No, Willa. *R-I-C-E* it. Rest, ice, compression, elevation. And don't let Lorene examine Rose's ankle, no matter what. I taught her how to use a stethoscope once, and she thinks she's a doctor now."

"RICE it," I repeat, wishing I hadn't drank quite so much. "Oh, yeah. Of course." Before I can say anything else, he hangs up.

26

I jog back into the living room with a bag of frozen peas I lifted from the freezer. "Good news, guys. Liam's on his way."

"Thank God." Rose yelps when I press the bag to her swollen ankle, but I hold it there anyway. I glance at Maisie, who's watching the action unfold from her armchair, and notice that she's shivering.

"You okay, Maisie?" I ask, grabbing a blanket from a basket near the couch and passing it to her. "Can I get you some water?"

She sniffles and shakes her head. "I'm okay. I just can't stand seeing Rose in pain. And I think those pre-wedding jitters are finally making an appearance."

"The jitters are a real thing," Lorene agrees. She presses a cool washcloth to Rose's head as if her cousin is dying of consumption. "I was so nervous the week before my wedding, I decided to cut my own hair. *My own bangs.* It was hideous. My mom freaked out when she saw me, and I had to keep my veil on for the whole reception. It was a gorgeous wedding anyway. Not that it matters now."

Rose, still wincing in pain, wraps her hand around Lorene's. "It'll be okay, Lor. I promise."

Lorene squeezes Rose's hand and glances at me. "Divorce is anathema in our family. I keep trying to work up the courage to file, but I'm scared, you know? I wish Wes would just do it himself. At least that way my mom might pity me instead of disown me."

Maisie's eyes widen at Lorene's comment, and she pulls her knees to her chest like she's trying to disappear into the chair. I remember what she told me in the car about her relationship with her parents, and I wonder just how rocky things are between them. I want to ask Maisie, to tell her it's okay if not everything in her life is sunbeams and rose petals. That people will love her anyway; that *I'll* love her anyway.

The feeling of protectiveness that comes over me as Maisie wrings her hands together unnerves me. I used to feel that way about Sarah, back when I had a best friend to look out for. But I can't go down that path again. Besides, I'm Maisie's employee, not a real friend, as difficult as that is to remember sometimes.

"You think Wes might file?" Maisie asks. Her voice is small, quiet, and I wonder if Lorene or Rose notices.

Lorene shakes her head. "Why would he? He has everything he wants: a wife who takes care of his kids and his house and his dinners, and a lineup of girlfriends to keep him entertained. If I could go back in time, trust me: it wouldn't be my hair that I'd cut off."

"Maybe you should just be honest with your mom and tell her you want to split up with him," Jenna suggests. "She's your mom, after all. She's supposed to love you no matter what."

Maisie's jaw tenses and she leaps up from her seat with the agility of a housecat. "Sorry," she says when her sudden motion startles everyone. Her cheeks redden as we all watch her curiously, and she pulls the blanket around her like a shawl. "I just . . . I . . . I mean, does anyone want tea? I think we could all use some."

"Tea?" Lorene asks, like Maisie's suggested that we do lines of cocaine. "Now?"

"I don't need tea, I need painkillers," Rose moans, pushing the bag of frozen peas off her ankle.

"Willa?" Maisie asks. Her voice trembles, and she clears her throat. "Tea?"

"Shoot," Lorene says as her phone buzzes. "Speaking of the literal devil, it's Wes." She frowns at her phone and wanders out of the living room to answer it. I watch her disappear down the hallway, and I watch Rose fumble with the peas, and Jenna swipe through OkCupid matches on her iPad. And suddenly, it makes more sense why Maisie hired me. Because her friends and future sister-in-law, as well-intended as they are, are too wrapped up in their own worlds to notice the shakiness of her tone and the way she's clutching the blanket like she hopes it'll swallow her whole.

That's what Sarah and I did for each other all those years. We noticed the little things about each other. The changes in voice and body language and facial expressions that only a close observer—only a best friend—would pick up on. Maisie has people who care about her, but she doesn't have that. And I know how crushing that absence is. I know better than anyone.

"Come on," I say, taking Maisie's hand. "Tea sounds nice. I'll help."

Her hand is clammy and cool against my own, and I guide her past the now-deflated penis balloon and into the kitchen.

"Maisie," I whisper when we're alone, "what is it? What's wrong?"

She shakes her head and presses her fingers to her temples. "It's everything. It's Rose and her ankle, and the fact that Mrs. Forsythe won't stop texting me about how tacky my wedding favors are, and I ate so many pieces of pie tonight that my last fitting will be a disaster on Monday, and—" She pauses to take a shaky breath. "I'm overreacting. Like I said, it's just wedding jitters. And I'm PMS-ing, too." She gives me a small smile, but it's a fraction of its usual wattage. "It's the perfect storm, but I'm fine, I swear. It'll pass."

Maisie's a good liar—I watched how easily she lied to Finn and the others about our friendship—but I saw the way her face fell when Lorene talked about her mother, how her shoulders trembled when we asked her to drive Rose to the hospital. That's not wedding jitters or PMS.

That's something else.

"Maisie," I say.

She spins around and opens one cabinet, then another. "There has to be a teakettle somewhere." With twitching fingers, she flings open the pantry door. "There just has to be."

"Here." I slide a chair out from the butcher-block table and gesture for her to sit down. "You sit. I'll find a kettle."

"I can't sit." She rabbit-taps her foot against the floor and flings open another cabinet, revealing an elaborate collection of spices. She reaches up to peek behind a ceramic jar, but her clumsy motions knock it over and send it flying off the shelf. It lands on the floor and shatters, spilling a thick layer of sugar dust onto the hardwood.

Maisie covers her mouth with one hand, staring at the mess like she's looking at the broken fragments of the Hope Diamond.

"Hey, it's okay. Just watch your step until I find a broom."

"It's not okay." Her voice is small, choked, and the last shred of calm leaves her body as she breaks down into sobs. "None of it is okay."

"Maisie," I say, gathering her into my arms without hesitation. "Mais, it's okay. Whatever it is, it's okay. I promise."

She shakes her head but leans in to my embrace, and I run my hand over her hair and squeeze her tighter. Her chest heaves with sobs, and the sight of sweet, kind Maisie in so much pain tears my heart in two. "Shh," I whisper, patting her back the same way Stacey patted mine when I cried in bed all those days and weeks after The Incident. "I've got you. You're okay. Breathe, Maisie. Just breathe."

It's a role reversal of the time I wept in her arms at the bridal shop, and I wonder what's causing her to erupt into sobs at her own bachelorette party. Whatever it is, I want to help her fix it. Because despite all my efforts not to, I care about Maisie. She rabbit-tapped her way into my heart, a place I thought was sealed off forever after Sarah nuked our friendship, and I'm worried for her.

"Whatever's wrong, we're gonna fix it," I tell her. "You and me. I promise. But I need you to tell me what's going on."

She takes a long inhale, then straightens her shoulders and in classic Maisie fashion pulls a handkerchief from her pocket and blows her nose into it.

"I don't think I can," she whispers, wiping away her tears and squeezing the hanky into a tight ball. "I don't—"

A knock at the door cuts her off, and Maisie's eyes widen. "That's Liam. Quick, do I look like I've been crying?"

I try to keep my expression neutral. Maisie's clearly not wearing waterproof mascara, and red, angry blotches circle her eyes. "Um, maybe a little. Or maybe a lot."

She sniffles and dabs at her eyes with her handkerchief. "I'm gonna sneak upstairs and fix my face while you let Liam in."

I don't understand why the state of her makeup matters right now. We need to fix whatever's weighing on Maisie's heart, not her stupid mascara. "Lorene can get the door. Let's go upstairs and sort everything out."

"Willa, please." Her voice is pleading, like it was the first time she asked for my help at Espresso 22. "If Liam sees how upset I am, he'll mention it to Finn. And I want Finn to think the bachelorette party was perfect. I don't want him to worry."

Maisie's fervent dedication to keeping up appearances for Finn seems to have no bounds, and I don't understand why she's hiding things from him. "But Finn's your fiancé. If you love him and he loves you, and you feel safe with him, why can't he know that your party was a total shitfest? Why can't he know the truth?"

"Because I don't want him to know the truth," she answers. "Because it's mine, okay? Not yours, and not Finn's. *Mine.*"

It's the first time I've heard even a trace of sharpness in Maisie's voice, and it's like witnessing Mr. Rogers kick a puppy. Jolted, I take a step backward.

I hear Lorene open the front door to greet Liam, and Maisie bends down and starts to frantically pick up the broken pieces of the jar. "I'm okay," she tells me, not looking up from the sugar disaster. "I promise. Please just go and help Rose. I don't want anyone to know I broke down."

I want to kick the jar fragments away from Maisie's hands, to tell her it doesn't matter what anyone thinks of her breakdown. That I'm her friend, and that means I'll help her sweep up the broken parts of her life, whether it's a sugar jar or a relationship or the rough edges of her heart.

"Please, Willa," she repeats. "Go help Rose. I promise I'm okay."

I don't think she's the least bit okay, but I nod anyway. I may not have read all the self-help books Stacey tossed at me over the past few months, but even I know that I can't help Maisie until she's ready to let me. And she's the one who signs my paycheck, which means if she wants me to go help Rose, I should do it.

"Okay," I say, handing her the broom and dustpan from the pantry. "As you wish."

"Hey, Willa," Maisie calls after me as I start to leave the kitchen. When I turn back around to face her, her cheeks are still red and patchy, but a small smile, her real smile, has replaced her tears. "Thank you."

I'm way more concerned about Maisie than I am about coming face-to-face with Liam again, but my stomach flutters anyway when I see him standing in the foyer. Wearing a pair of gray joggers, a black T-shirt that shows off his arms, and a baseball cap, he waves a hand in greeting. Dark stubble spreads across the lower half of his face, and his shirt is rumpled, like he just got out of bed. Makes sense, considering that it's midnight.

"Hi," I say, trying to sound like the bride-to-be didn't just lose her shit entirely—and like I haven't been imagining the feel of his lips on mine every hour of every day. I don't know what to say next, so I fold my hands together and shift my weight from side to side to give myself something to do. "Fancy meeting you here."

"Uh, yeah," Liam says while Lorene gives me some serious side-eye. "How's Rose?"

I want to sink into the welcome mat, but Rose defuses the awk-wardness of the moment by howling in pain.

"Guess she's in there." Liam follows the sound of her cries into the living room, and Lorene and I trail after him.

"Li, thank God you're here. My ankle hurts like a bitch," Rose says, reaching her hand out and locking her fingers around his. She's sprawled out on the couch like Kate Winslet in *Titanic*, and I half expect her to ask Liam to draw her like one of his French girls.

"Have you tried putting weight on it?"

"I can't. It hurts too much."

Liam is all business as he examines her ankle. She winces when he touches it, and he places a reassuring hand on her arm.

"Well?" Rose asks, her voice small. "Is it broken?"

Liam sighs. "I think so, Rosie. But we need an X-ray to be sure. Come on, let's get you to the car."

He slides his hand under Rose's body, and in a move that makes the estrogen levels in my body skyrocket, he lifts her up in one smooth motion.

"Come on," he says, looking right at me. "Let's go."

I glance behind me to see if Lorene is suddenly standing there. "Who, me?"

"Yes, Willa, you. Help me with the door, please."

Uneasiness overwhelms me. I'm already exhausted from the alcohol and the drama of the evening, and I want to stay put and make sure Maisie's okay. Plus, I'm anxious about being in close quarters with Liam. What if he thinks I ghosted him after our kiss, and he's annoyed with me? What if he tries to kiss me again, and I'm tempted to break my vow? What if he doesn't? What if—

"Go ahead, Willa. We'll be fine here." Maisie steps into the living room, and the inky mascara trail that ran down her face is gone. Her cheeks are rosy instead of covered in patchy blotches, and her voice carries its usual level of pep. If it weren't for the trace of sugar on the knee of her leggings, I might have thought I'd dreamt the events that unfolded in the kitchen.

"I can't," I say. "I'm . . . busy."

"Busy with what, exactly?" Liam asks.

I scramble to come up with something. Anything. *I'm worried about Maisie* obviously isn't a reason I can share with him. *I'm obsessed with your forearms, but I'm not who you think I am* probably won't cut it, either. "I promised Maisie I'd help her make tea."

"Tea?" Rose stares at me like I said I'd promised to help Maisie bury a body. "What the hell is it with you guys and the tea?"

"Well," I say, "I just think it would be better if Lorene went—"

"Willa," Rose interrupts, her tone agitated. "I love you, but I need you to shut the fuck up and help Liam get me to the hospital, okay? *Okay?*"

I thought that five thousand dollars was a lot of money, but there aren't enough Benjamins in the world to make this worthwhile.

"March, Willa," Rose commands, letting out a shriek of pain when Liam readjusts her weight. "March!"

"You heard her," Liam says. "And I'd appreciate it if you hurried, because I'm carrying a full-grown human here."

Wishing I could down another round or two of punch, I take a deep breath and imagine myself a month from now, on a sunny, quiet beach somewhere far from all this.

And then I march.

27

Two and a half hours later, my right butt cheek is fast asleep in a plastic chair in the Hocking Valley Community Hospital's ER waiting room. I rock back and forth on my seat, trying to regenerate blood flow to my ass and wishing I were home in my bed. It's literally painfully clear to me that Liam doesn't need me here. He disappeared into the ER with Rose as soon as we arrived, leaving me to wonder why the hell he wanted me to tag along. He practically ordered me to accompany them, so why isn't he at least popping out every hour or so to give me an update?

It's not that I expect him to ditch Rose in favor of making out with me in the waiting room, but part of me hoped that he asked me to come because he wanted to spend time with me. Stupid, I know. I tell myself that it's better this way; the less time Liam and I spend alone together, the less I'll be tempted to break my vow and kiss him again. The less I'll be tempted to believe that I could fall in love with someone again.

To distract myself, and also because I'm worried about Maisie, I pull out my phone and shoot her a text. How are you?

She responds within seconds. Good. Eating a Hershey bar and getting ready for bed. How's Rose?

There's no mention of her breakdown in the kitchen, but I don't press her to say more. There will be plenty of time for that on the ride home tomorrow. Getting x-rays. No word yet.

How's Liam? Maisie writes back, her words followed by a fire emoji.

Nowhere to be seen, I start to respond before I hear the sound of footsteps from the hallway. Liam strides into the waiting room like he owns the place, and I shove my phone into my purse like I've been caught red-handed.

"She fractured her tibia."

I'm annoyed by the fact that he doesn't even bother to greet me. Why didn't he let Lorene come instead of me? I try to brush off my frustration and remind myself that tonight is about Rose, not me. But when Liam takes off his baseball cap to run a hand through his hair, I find the action so ridiculously sexy that all thought goes out the window.

"Willa?" he asks. "Did you hear me?"

I snap out of Liam-taking-off-his-hat-in-slow-motion land and back into reality. "Yes, I heard you. Rose fractured her tibia? What does that mean for her?"

He sits in the chair next to mine, accidentally bumping my arm with his. The touch sends shivers down my spine, and I scoot farther away, remembering my vow. "It's a clean break, so she doesn't need surgery. They're sending her home in a cast. And with pain meds."

"Poor Rose." I think of how excited she was for her upcoming yoga retreat in the Mojave Desert. "She's gonna be miserable."

Liam nods. "She doesn't have an easy time sitting still, that's for sure. The attending said she'll be good to go in ten minutes or so. They're just finishing up some paperwork."

"Okay."

I stretch my legs out, then fold them under me. The waiting room is quiet except for an elderly woman in the corner who keeps clearing her throat. I don't speak, and neither does Liam. Instead, I lean forward and back in the chair, trying to get my butt cheek to wake up. I want to ask Liam why the hell he dragged me to this middle-of-nowhere ER when Lorene or Jenna could have easily come instead, but I'm afraid the answer won't be the one I want to hear. Maybe he insisted that I come because I seemed the least drunk, except for Maisie. Maybe his reason for wanting me here had nothing to do with our kiss at all. The Liam sitting beside me now, his spine ramrod straight and his tone serious, is light-years from the man who called me strong and cupped my face in the palm of his hand.

And I want to know why. But instead of asking, I get up from my seat to stretch my legs. Because I'm Maisie's bridesmaid, and Liam's Finn's best man, and that's it. His inner thoughts are no concern of mine. *Should* be no concern of mine.

"Why didn't you text me?" Liam asks suddenly, as I'm fishing through my purse for change for the vending machine.

His question catches me completely off guard, and I drop a handful of loose quarters into my purse. "What?"

He scratches his cheek, and I try very hard not to stare at his facial hair. "Last week, after our date, I gave you my number. But you didn't text me. How come?"

His words hit me like a brick. Holy shit. Liam Rafferty sat by his phone waiting for me to text him. Maybe he checked his phone in between seeing patients at work, hoping to find a message from me.

Maybe he scrolled through his texts while watching Netflix with Frodo, double-checking to see if he'd missed anything. The thought fills me with such joy that I could perform a happy jig in the waiting room, but I restrain myself.

"I was . . . busy," I answer, reclaiming my seat. What am I supposed to tell him exactly? *I couldn't text you because I'm only pretending to be Maisie's friend. We made up an elaborate backstory to trick everyone, and Camp Wildwood doesn't even exist. Oh, and by the way, I couldn't call you because you touched a part of my heart that's no longer open for business.*

"Geez, Sparks. You could have at least said you had to wash your hair." Liam's tone is playful, but his usual smirk is nowhere to be seen. He really is disappointed, I realize. He really did want to hear from me.

"I wanted to text you," I tell him, despite the fact that I should be keeping my big mouth shut. "I really did." I can't bear to let him think that our kiss meant nothing to me. Not when I've dreamt of it, of the way he made me feel, every single day since.

"I bet." Liam's jaw tenses, and he leans back in his seat and crosses his arms over his chest. A tiny vein pulses near his temple, and I have to stop myself from reaching out and brushing it with my fingertips.

"You could have at least texted to let me know you got home safe," he continues.

I stare at him, confused. "Why? I'm an adult. Of course I got home safe."

"*Why?* Are you serious?" Liam turns to face me, eyes blazing. "I know you're an adult, and you're very independent, but it was late when we headed home, and you'd had a long day. It would have been nice not to worry."

"You were worried about me?" No one besides Stacey and

Glory—and, in recent months, Maisie—has worried about me since The Incident. And certainly no one like Dr. Dreamboat. The thought of Liam looking out for me feels warm and welcome, kind of like the feel of his lips against mine. Which is the last thing I should be thinking about right now, considering that his body is mere inches away.

"Why do you sound surprised?" Liam asks, his tone revealing his frustration.

"Why do you sound mad?"

"I'm not mad." His voice is as tense as the line of his jaw. "I just don't understand why you're shocked at the idea of me caring about you. I know we got off to a rocky start, but I thought . . . I thought things would be different after our date. Do you still think of me as the asshole who laughed at you? Because I'm not that guy, Willa."

The vulnerability in his voice softens my resolve, and I want nothing more than to nuzzle against him and tell him I know he's not that guy. That he's Dr. Dreamboat to me now, not the Worst Man. The person who'd made me feel proud of what I'd overcome, and hopeful for what I could do next.

"I know," I tell him. "I don't think of you like that at all. I know who you are." His gaze meets mine, and my words ring in my ears. *I know who you are.* I might know who Liam is, but he doesn't have a clue who I am. Not really. I want to tell him, to explain to him why Maisie and I lied, because maybe he'd understand. Maybe he'd like me anyway. He's been through pain like I have, and lived to tell the tale. Maybe he wouldn't judge me for what I did to make it through my darkness.

But Maisie's secrets aren't mine to tell, and I can't open myself up to Liam. It's only a matter of weeks until I have enough money saved to move away, and I refuse to let any entanglements make me second-guess my plan.

Liam leans toward me, and I inhale his now-familiar scent of pine and balsam. I could cut the sexual tension with the heel of one of Ruthie's stilettos, and I tilt away from him in my seat. "In case you were wondering," I say, eager to fill the air with words instead of my hormonal longing, "I'm not mad at you either."

"Why would *you* be mad at *me*?" Liam narrows his eyes. "Are we still fighting about whether you flung that chair over your head at the party? Because I know it's a sore spot, but it's true. You did."

I grit my teeth and decide to ignore the throne comment. "Why would I be mad? Oh, I don't know. Maybe because you dragged me to a hospital in the middle of the night so I could sit here—alone—while you took care of Rose."

"She was in a lot of pain, Willa."

"I know. I'm the one who helped her get back to the cabin, re-member? And I feel awful for her. But you didn't have to drag me all the way out here and then desert me. I could have stayed at the cabin and slept."

Liam suddenly looks less deflated. "Holy shit, Sparks. You're jealous."

"I am *not* jealous. I'm just exhausted, and I'm worried about Maisie, and I wish—" I pause. I wish I could tell him how I really feel about him. How much I wish I could throw my vow and my secrets out the window and kiss him again. But I can't. "—I wish that vending machine had Diet Dr Pepper."

"Why are you worried about Maisie?"

Shit. I've let my fatigue and my frustration get the best of me and I accidentally let my real worries slip out. I can't exactly tell Liam that Maisie had a mini-breakdown at her own bachelorette party. "She's just getting nervous as the big day gets closer," I say quickly. It's not a total lie. "You know, normal bride stuff. Nothing she and I can't handle."

I don't know any normal brides who hire a stranger as their bridesmaid and hide it from their groom, but Liam seems to accept my answer. "I know how much the wedding means to her. It's got to be a ton of pressure. It's good she has you to look out for her."

I'm not sure if anyone besides Maisie, myself included, understands just how much the wedding means to her. I'm not sure if she'll ever let me know. Besides, Maisie deserves more than a hired hand to look out for her. She deserves a real best friend, the kind who bakes you a confetti cake on your birthday, and on just-because days, who keeps your secrets and your hair ties and knows every line of *You've Got Mail* by heart because it's your favorite movie and she's watched it with you on fifty different Friday nights. She deserves the kind of friend I used to be before my world crumbled.

As if on cue, my phone vibrates, and I reach into my purse and pull out my phone to find a text from Maisie. Tell him how you feel about him. Bride's orders.

I scramble to cover the screen before Liam catches a glimpse of it, but he's distracted anyway as a nurse in blue scrubs enters the waiting room. She has a clipboard tucked under one arm and pushes a wheelchair carrying a very sleepy-looking Rose toward us.

"Rose!" I jump up from my seat and hurry over to her. Her right foot is covered in a cast that extends from the top of her shin to the base of her toes. "How do you feel?" I ask, giving her hand a squeeze. "Do you want anything from the vending machine?"

She shakes her head. "I just want to go home and sleep."

After Liam speaks briefly to the nurse, we head back out to the car. I'm relieved that we finally get to return to the cabin; another ten minutes alone with Liam, and I might have lost control of myself and obeyed Maisie's orders. But longing still consumes me as Liam helps Rose stretch out on the back seat and I claim shotgun. Sitting in the passenger seat of his car again, the headlights illuminating the space in front of us, is like returning to the scene of a very sexy crime. This very seat is where I threw caution to the wind and kissed him. This is where I traced the lines of his tattoo with my fingertip. This is where he ran a hand along my collarbone.

This is where my feelings toward him—and some of my feelings toward myself—changed.

When Liam climbs into the driver's seat, it's all I can do to stop myself from reaching out to touch him. I slide my hands into the sleeve of my sweatshirt, determined to keep them to myself.

"You okay?" he asks, perhaps noticing how I've scooted as close to the passenger door as possible.

I want to tell him that I'm not okay at all. That I thought about him every day after our kiss and wanted to text him more desperately than my sister wants Glennon Doyle to do a live show in Columbus. I want to curl up in his arms and tell him the truth and share with him my concerns about Maisie and my own future. I want him to look at me again and tell me that I'm strong, that I'm a good friend, that I'm someone I can be proud of being. I want him to know who I am.

But I can't do any of those things, so I just nod and lean my head against the passenger window. The glass is cool on my forehead, and I take a deep breath and close my eyes. "I'm fine."

It's not the first lie I've told him, and it breaks my heart that it won't be the last.

28

Back at the cabin, Liam and I help Rose get settled on the couch. I set a glass of water and a bowl of crackers on the coffee table next to her, and Liam gives her the next round of painkillers.

"Thanks," Rose whispers to us, nestling into her pillow.

The cabin, so full of activity earlier in the day, is quiet now. Maisie snores on the love seat, and the upstairs lights are off, so everyone else must be in bed. I adjust Maisie's blanket to cover her feet, and when I'm done, I look up to see Liam watching me.

"I think my work here is done. Time for you to get some sleep, huh?"

I nod. I don't want him to leave, but I can't exactly spill my innermost desires and tell him to stay. "Yeah. I'll walk you out."

I certainly don't need to escort Liam outside, but I tell myself I'm not doing it so that I can soak up another few precious seconds of time with him. I'm just doing it to be polite. He did save the day, after all. Again. I follow him onto the front porch, letting the screen door creak shut behind me. Mosquitoes and moths flutter around the hanging lantern just outside the door, and I swat a gnat off my arm.

Shadows darken Liam's face when he turns to face me. "G'night, Willa."

"Night, Liam." He's so close that I could eliminate the distance between us in an instant, but I keep my feet firmly planted on the welcome mat. "Thanks for coming to help."

"It was a pleasure. Really." He pauses, like he wants to say more, then nods at me and turns to head to his car.

He's only halfway down the porch steps when the words I've wanted to say all night come tumbling out of my mouth. "I really did want to text you."

My heart skips a beat when I realize what I've said, but it's too late. My confession is out there, hanging in the air between us, thick as the humidity of the night. Liam pauses midstep and turns back toward me. "What?"

I know he heard me the first time, but I repeat the words anyway. Even though I know I shouldn't. "I wanted to text you. I thought about texting you every day."

He trudges back up the stairs to meet me on the porch. "So why didn't you?"

I don't know what to tell him. *Because I can't let you find out that Maisie's paying me. Because I'm worried that falling for you means signing up for a world of hurt. Again.* To buy time, I pull myself up to perch my butt on the crossbeam railing, my legs dangling beneath me. "It's not easy for me to let people get close," I say finally. "After everything that happened."

Liam nods and removes his baseball cap, then puts it on again backward. I would normally consider it a douchey move, but he looks deep in thought when he does it. The same way Maisie looks when she rabbit-taps her foot. "I've noticed. But it's not easy for me, either. Considering."

I think of the pain Liam probably endured when his marriage ended, how he lost friends he trusted and the person he'd vowed to love forever. "Does it ever get easier?" I ask.

"It's easier with you." He takes a step toward me and reaches out like he's going to touch my leg but stops. "Look, Willa, if you're not interested in going on another date with me, I get it. You don't have to feel awkward because we're both in Finn and Maisie's wedding. The last thing I would ever want is to make you feel uncomfortable."

I almost laugh at his statement. Liam doesn't make me feel uncomfortable; he makes me feel alive. The idea of going on another date with him unleashes a swarm of happy butterflies in my stomach. "I am interested. In going on another date. And in doing . . . what we did after the date."

"You mean kissing?" Liam asks, taking another step toward me.

It's dark outside, but I can feel myself blushing. "Yes. Kissing."

He smiles, and the swarm of butterflies goes wild. "That's good. Because I like you, Willa. I like standing in line at a bakery with you, and eating tacos with you, and arguing with you about whether you threw that chair. And I really, really like kissing you."

"I didn't throw the ch—throne. And I like doing those things, too. Especially the kissing. It's just that . . ." I trail off and look down at my lap, trying to find the right words to explain myself. I don't know how to tell Liam that I've been blindly stumbling through my own life since The Incident, and that I don't know how to trust anyone anymore. I don't have the words to explain how hard it is to believe that someone could like the new Willa, the Willa with no blog and no forty thousand Instagram followers and no big Saturday plans. And I don't know how to tell him that he might think he likes me, but he doesn't actually know me.

What I do know is that I like the way he's looking at me right now, his body tensed and his muscles taut. I like the way he takes a step toward me, and the way he stands between my legs and tucks a strand of my hair behind my ear.

"It's just what?" he asks.

I don't answer him with words, because I don't know what to say. Instead, I finally let myself reach out and touch him, cupping his cheek with my hand. His stubble is rough under my palm.

"It's a simple question, Sparkles." Liam's voice is quiet, guttural. "Either you like me, or you don't. Either you want me to touch you, or you don't. Either you want me to kiss you, or you don't." He leans his body closer and nuzzles his face against my hair. He smells of balsam and campfire, and my fingers can't help but graze the soft cotton of his T-shirt.

"Which one is it?" he breathes. His words are warm against my ear, and I shiver when his lips graze my neck. "Do you want me like I want you?"

Leaning in toward Liam, encircling him with my legs while he runs his hands up my thighs and under my shirt, his touch hot against my bare skin, feels as natural as breathing. He presses his forehead to mine and we pause there for a moment, together. I press my hand against his chest and feel the hummingbird-beat of his pounding heart. My hands somehow snake their way around his neck, and Liam presses his weight against me. I feel solid and safe, like his nearness to me is a fortress that keeps all the bad things out: the memories I try to forget. The lie I'm telling him. My wish that I really were friends with Maisie and Rose and Lorene.

With Liam in front of me, all I see is him. All I feel is elation. All I want is all of him.

"Willa Callister," he whispers, "can I kiss you now?"

In answer, I lean forward and press my lips to his. They're as soft and warm as I remember, and his tongue tastes like peppermint. My arms, still wrapped around his neck, pull him closer until there's no space between us. Our lips meet and part and meet again, and I let out a soft moan when Liam pulls back to kiss the exposed skin of my neck. When he brings his lips back to mine, I reach up to run my fingers through his hair and accidentally knock his hat off. His hands slip higher beneath my shirt, stroking my back, and it's so delicious that I can't believe it's happening. I can't believe that we're here under the moonlight, the chirp of crickets and the hush of the forest all around us, creating electricity with our lips and our tongues and our hands.

"Take me home with you," I tell him. "Take me to your cabin."

"Are you sure?" he asks, his lips pressed against my temple.

I shouldn't be kissing Liam. At the very least, I should tell him that I'm leaving after the wedding. Leaving him, and all the pain I've carried with me since The Incident, behind.

But I kiss him anyway. And I don't tell him those things. Because when I'm kissing Liam, I feel more like myself than I have since my world fell apart.

I press my mouth against his ear. "I'm sure," I whisper. "Take me home."

29

We don't sleep the whole night. We touch each other over and over again, with our hands and our mouths and every part of us, and then we lie awake in Liam's bed. He lies on his back and I lie on my side, one leg wrapped over him, while we talk for hours. Liam tells me about his favorite patients and the hardest cases he's had to deal with at work. I tell him what life was like for me after The Incident, how my whole identity—fiancée, best friend, blogger and reporter—vaporized, and how I tried to mend the pieces of my broken life with booze and men and terrible reality TV. He tells me how he eats Lucky Charms for breakfast every Saturday. He tells me that when he was a kid and his parents weren't around a lot, he spent every waking moment he could at Finn's house and pretended Finn and Lorene were his brother and sister. I tell him about Stacey's obsession with self-help books and Maeve's fascination with dinosaurs. I tell him I worry that I'll always be a disappointment to my sister and, eventually, to my nieces. He runs his thumb over my earlobe as he listens.

When we get hungry, he makes us scrambled eggs, and we eat

them with strawberry Pop-Tarts and sliced cantaloupe. When I get up to put my plate in the sink, Liam wraps his arms around me from behind and presses a series of kisses to my neck. We stand there like that for a long moment, just touching and breathing together.

With my body pressed against Liam's, and my stomach full and happy, I remember what Ruthie told me about Herman being the exception. Maybe Liam is the exception, too. Maybe he'd understand why I agreed to take Maisie's money in exchange for being her brides-maid. Maybe he'd understand why I didn't tell him before now. Maybe he'd believe me when I tell him that I understand what his tattoo means to him. That I don't want to pretend anymore, either.

I turn around to face him, and he grabs a lock of my hair to twirl between his fingers.

"You're interesting," I tell Liam. "And you're kind."

"I agree." He laughs when I roll my eyes at him. "I mean, thank you, Willa. You're interesting, too. And you're mostly kind, except for when you're calling me a butthead."

I laugh, remembering how much he annoyed me in the begin-ning. "I called you a butthead one time, when we were in line at Mrs. Yummy's. And you were being one."

"I know."

"Liam, I . . ." I pause. I want to tell him the truth so badly, so he knows I'm not a liar like his ex, or like Max and Sarah. But telling Liam about how Maisie hired me would be betraying Maisie, and I can't do that to her. Not just because she's technically my boss, but because I care about her so much. "I need to be back at the bachelorette party before anyone wakes up."

Even though everyone was asleep when I left, ditching a bache-lorette party overnight to spend time with a guy isn't a great look. And I don't want anyone to know that Liam and I spent the night together. It might draw attention away from Maisie, and I want to keep what happened between us private.

Liam nods and glances at his watch. "It's almost five a.m. I really doubt anyone will be up before nine, but I understand if you want to play it safe."

We crawl back into his bed and cuddle for ten minutes, not saying anything at all. When I feel my eyelids get heavy, I kiss Liam's forehead and get up to gather my clothes from his bedroom floor. When we're dressed, he hands me a steaming thermos of coffee and we head outside. It's still dark out, and I inhale the fresh forest air and listen to the cacophony of pre-sunrise bird calls.

It's a ten-minute drive on a long, winding road from Liam's cabin to the Airbnb, and he keeps his hand on my upper thigh the whole time. I trace the numerals of his tattoo with my index finger, then interlace my hand with his.

"What time are you guys heading back home?" he asks when we reach the cabin, his engine idling.

"Well, we were planning on yoga, breakfast, and a nature walk. So maybe around one or two, I'd guess." Although I doubt there'll be any nature walking after Rose's injury.

Liam nods. "Can I take you to dinner? And just so we're clear, I am asking you on a date."

I laugh. "I could be persuaded. Did you have a particular place in mind?"

"Have you been to Third and Hollywood? They have incredible short ribs and a great patio."

I almost decline immediately. Third & Hollywood was one of Max's favorite places. I haven't gone there since The Incident, even though I miss their truffle ricotta and toast like no other. I stopped going to so many places I used to love since The Incident. And I've stopped doing things I once loved to do, because they made my stomach churn with memories I'd like to forget.

"We can go someplace else if you'd prefer," Liam says, reading the expression on my face.

Maybe it's time to stop avoiding the places and things I love because of what Max and Sarah did. It wasn't just an engagement and a friendship I let them take from me. I lost a piece of myself. And it's time to take that piece back.

"No," I tell him. "Third and Hollywood sounds great."

30

Liam's estimation that no one would be up before nine a.m. was overly generous. It's almost eleven before half the group is up and moving around, and it's noon when Lorene finally threatens to yank the last sleeping Forsythe cousin out of bed. My body refuses to move faster than a snail's pace from my lack of sleep, but my brain is exhilarated, like a new chapter of my life is beginning. Not so much a chapter with Liam, even, but a new chapter of me.

Thanks to Rose's broken ankle, she's in no shape to lead us in a yoga session. We could still do the nature hike without her, but everyone's too hungover for anything besides stuffing our faces with waffles and cinnamon rolls. By the time we eat, do the dishes, and clean up the state of disarray the cabin's in from the night before, it's time to head home.

I try to corner Maisie a handful of times to make sure she's okay after how upset she was last night, but she's always with one of the other women. When I think I have a private moment with her in the kitchen, Rose hobbles in with a Sharpie and demands that we both sign her cast. Armed with her usual smile and braid lying across one shoulder, Maisie looks perfectly herself. Like last night never happened.

I don't get any one-on-one time with her until we're in the car and on the road back to Columbus. "So," I say after she chatters on for several minutes about how delicious Lorene's banana bread waffles were, "how are you feeling?"

"Great. Just a little tired. I'm gonna take a crash nap with Pippa the second I get home."

When she doesn't offer more, I try a more direct approach. "I wanted to talk to you about last night."

Maisie fidgets in her seat, tugging on the strap of her seat belt. "Yeah. I know I got a little weird. I'm sorry about that."

The fact that she thinks she needs to apologize for displaying emotion breaks my heart. "There's nothing to be sorry for, Maisie. Do you remember what you told me when I lost my shit at your dress fitting? You said it's okay to have feelings, and it's okay to show them. It's okay for you to do that, too, you know."

She nods but doesn't look at me.

"Was there something in particular that upset you? I noticed that you got kind of emotional when Rose agreed to do that stupid dare, and then when Lorene was talking about her mom—"

"I started my period this morning," Maisie says, fiddling with the air-conditioning vent. "So that explains a lot of it. And like I said, all this wedding stuff can make me a little nutty. But other than that, my bachelorette party was perfect. It means a lot to me that you were here."

Maisie's clearly trying to shut this line of conversation down, but I can't let her. I care too much about her to let my concerns be washed away by her cheery demeanor and sweet expression of gratitude. I wonder how many times I've heard Maisie say the word *perfect* since I've met her. The bachelorette party was *perfect*. Her wedding has to be perfect. The cake from Mrs. Yummy's and the long gown Mrs. Forsythe loved and the four bridesmaids and groomsmen all have to be perfect. Everything has to be perfect. But that's not how life works, and I can't help but wonder why Maisie feels compelled to achieve all that perfection.

"I know you think it was PMS and jitters, Mais, but I have to be honest. It seemed like more than that."

Folding her hands in her lap, Maisie finally looks in my direction. "What do you mean?"

"I mean, I know stress affects everyone differently, but I've had PMS symptoms plenty of times. And I remember what it's like to plan a wedding. I had jitters, too. But you seemed . . ." I remember the frantic tone of her voice as she insisted on making tea, and the desperate look on her face as she bent over the spilled sugar, trying to clean up the broken jar fragments. "It seemed like whatever was bothering you was deeper than that. A lot deeper."

Maisie looks out the window as we cruise down the freeway, watching trees and McDonald's billboards roll by. "I get really bad anxiety sometimes."

That doesn't surprise me one bit, but I prod her for more. "You do?"

"Yeah. I manage it pretty well, but it gets the best of me occasionally. And when it does, I get this terrible feeling that something awful is gonna happen. When Rose decided to go into the woods, it was like I couldn't breathe, you know? Like my lungs were just collapsing on themselves."

"Like a panic attack?"

She nods and pulls her feet toward her chest. "Something like that. I know it sounds crazy."

I consider the depression I went through after The Incident. "It doesn't sound crazy. I've had my own mental health struggles, so I get it. Besides, you weren't far off in thinking something awful was going to happen to Rose in the woods. She did get hurt."

Maisie shakes her head. "That's not really the kind of awful I'm talking about."

She speaks so softly that I want to reach over and grab her hand, to comfort her, but I don't. This is the most freely she's ever spoken to me, and I don't want to do anything to derail it. "What kind of awful are you talking about?"

She shrugs. "Who knows. My mind is a crazy place sometimes. But I'm working on it."

I smile at her, wanting her to know that it's okay to keep talking. That she can show her real self to me. "Aren't we all?"

"Remember that first time I came to your sister's house and I asked you to be my bridesmaid? You asked you where I went on Mondays, when I tell Finn that I'm going to the coffee shop."

I nod. "You said that was something only a bridesmaid gets to know."

Maisie busies herself tugging on a loose thread of her blouse. "Well, here's something nobody knows, not even my bridesmaids: the real place I go is my therapist's office."

She delivers the line like she's announcing that she attends a weekly Satanic cult meeting. She glances sideways at me, as if she's expecting my jaw to drop in shock.

"You go see your therapist? That sounds pretty normal, Maisie. It sounds healthy." It's the hiding it that's abnormal. "Why is that something you have to keep from Finn?"

She sighs. "It's not something I *have* to keep from him. It's something I want to keep private. He'd worry about me. He'd ask questions when I got home. Like, *Hey, honey, how was therapy today? Learn any good coping mechanisms? Anything that'll help you not act like a psycho at your own bachelorette party?*"

I'd give her some serious side-eye if I weren't driving. "Do you really think Finn would ask those kinds of questions?"

"No. But he'd want to help me. And some things . . . some things not even Finn can fix."

I want to know what sort of things she's talking about, so that I can help her, but before I can say anything in response, Maisie turns on the car's Bluetooth to link my Spotify playlist to the sound system. "Anyway, I'd rather focus on good things today. Like the fact that in just a few weeks, I'm going to be Mrs. Maisie Forsythe. And then I'll never have to have another conversation with Mrs. Forsythe about whether personalizing the champagne flutes is tacky or not."

Something tells me that Mrs. Forsythe's influence in Maisie's life isn't going to lessen once the wedding's over. "I know you want to appease her, but remember, it's *your* wedding. Not hers. You can still change your mind and wear a rockabilly dress. You can still make Pippa a bridesmaid, like you wanted."

She grins. "Can you imagine? When I mentioned that idea to Mrs. Forsythe, she acted like I was insane. You would have thought I'd suggested that Pippa cater the wedding. But none of that stuff really matters to me. What matters is that at the end of the day, Finn and I will be husband and wife. If doing it in a certain dress makes his mom happy, then I'm not gonna complain about it."

Her tone is so resolute that I don't bother disagreeing with her. "Okay. But just so you know, if the anxiety and the champagne flute drama ever get to be too much, all you have to do is tell me. And we'll turn this car around and flee straight to Mexico. I swear to God."

Maisie smiles at me, and there's no trace of the worry I saw in her eyes last night. "Thank you, Willa. But right now, I'm ready to go home. And while we're on our way there, you get to tell me what happened between you and Liam last night."

When I glance over at her, she's grinning at me like the cat that got the cream. "How much do you know?"

"I know you weren't quite as quiet sneaking into the cabin this morning as you thought you were." She smirks and claps her hands together, and her delight over my dalliance with Liam is almost enough to make me forget my worries. "We've got an hour left on the road, which is plenty of time for you to tell me what happened without leaving out a single detail."

"Fine," I say while Maisie waits with bated breath. "But first, where are the Twizzlers?"

"Twizzlers." She passes me the bag like I'm a surgeon and she's handing me a scalpel. "Now go."

31

Stacey, Glory, and the girls aren't home when I get there. They're probably off on one of their Sunday afternoon adventures to the zoo or the Columbus Museum of Art. I head straight for my bedroom, eager to take advantage of the peace and quiet and get some writing done. I haven't published any of my recent blog posts, but I'm feeling more inspired to write with each passing day. And after this weekend, I feel like myself for the first time in months. Not like old Willa, exactly, but closer to her.

Dear Waywards, I type, fully aware that there aren't any Waywards anymore, and so I'm writing to an echo chamber of myself, major update to report. I spent the night with Dr. Dreamboat! (Cue tsunami of confetti.) When I told the Animal Whisperer, she made me sit in her driveway for twenty minutes just so she could ask me about every—and I mean every—detail of my adventure. I forgot how good it feels to have a friend like that, someone who squeals and laughs and reacts in all the right places while I tell them a story. Who is so interested in me, and in my life, that she ignores her border collie barking its head off to listen to me talk.

I forgot how it feels to have a best friend. And the fact that I think of the Animal Whisperer as a best friend terrifies me. But I can't lie to myself any longer; our friendship feels real. I don't know how, or when, but somewhere along the line, my heart—my scarred and broken heart—opened to make room for her. And it's opening to make room for Dr. Dreamboat, too.

Before, all I wanted was an escape. But now I find myself wanting to be a real part of the Animal Whisperer and Dr. Dreamboat's world, and to stay in that world after her wedding. To be her real friend, and maybe eventually Dr. Dreamboat's girlfriend. (I mean it about the confetti.) I want to be there for the Sister-in-Law when she finally decides to file for divorce, and for the Yoga Fairy to teach me that ridiculous soulful breathwork she's always talking about. I want Dr. Dreamboat and me to go on double dates with the Friendly Lumberjack and the Animal Whisperer, and I want Kaya to look up to her and see that her secret frog projects can take her all the way to a thriving career at the zoo. I want Dr. Dreamboat to come to game night at Ruthie's, so that maybe someone will pick me as a charades teammate for once. I want him to come to family dinners, where Stacey and Glory can complain about how much butter I cook with while Maeve hunts dinosaurs and Lucy tries to eat hair. I don't want to leave them.

I don't want to leave them.

And that scares the shit out of me. Because my entire goal was to leave, to save up enough money to pay off some debt, and move to a new place where no one knows me or Princess Sparkleheart. Before the Animal Whisperer's bachelorette party and my night with Dr. Dreamboat, I was hell-bent on ending up in a beach town somewhere. I was imagining the feel of gritty sand beneath my toes and the loud caws of seagulls overhead as I transformed into someone different. Someone new.

But now, Waywards, I'm not so sure that I want to be someone else. Despite everything that's happened, there's a part of me that wants to stay here.

There's a part of me that wants to stay me.

32

Third & Hollywood, aptly located at the intersection of Third Avenue and Hollywood Place, is a simple, modern building with a slant-roof patio. Liam and I agree to meet there at seven for dinner. At six fifty-five p.m., I park and examine myself in the overhead mirror. I decided to wear a violet sundress and wedge sandals, and I kept my makeup simple and fresh. I apply a layer of ChapStick and tuck a flyaway hair back into place. It's so humid that I don't even dare to wear my hair down, so it sits in a loose bun at the nape of my neck.

I'm so excited to see Liam again that I practically skip from the car to the restaurant. Inside, I'm greeted by exposed-brick walls, dark wood, and an aroma that makes my mouth water. Lit candles at each table give the restaurant a cozy, romantic vibe, and Liam waves to me from a table toward the back. I focus very hard on walking toward him at a normal pace, refusing to give in to the temptation to sprint over, leap into his arms, and start another round of adult activities right here and now.

"You look beautiful," he says when I reach him. He stands to wrap me in a hug, and I almost—*almost*—like it as much as a kiss. I feel safe and cared for in the cocoon of his arms, and I linger there for a moment before I lean back.

"You look beautiful, too," I say.

Liam laughs and sits back down. "I just started scanning the appetizer menu. I knew you'd probably break a chair over my head if I went ahead and picked one without you."

I glare at him, and he raises a hand in apology. "Sorry. I couldn't resist making that joke one more time."

"Hope you enjoyed it," I retort. "Because if you want a repeat of what happened last night, you'll kiss that joke good-bye."

Liam smiles and reaches for my hand across the table. He traces my palm with his index finger and then wraps his fingers through mine.

"I was worried you might not show," he says quietly.

Since I practically ghosted him after our taco date, I can't say I'm surprised, but I play it off easily. "And miss out on the short ribs you talked about? I think not."

He smiles. "I just meant, I know we left things really uncertain after our first kiss. I don't want you to think last night left me questioning anything. I'm not uncertain about you, Willa."

A little explosion of happiness radiates in my chest, along with something else—a compulsion to tell him the truth about me and Maisie. But out of loyalty to Maisie, I keep my mouth shut.

"I'm not uncertain about you, either." And that's the honest-to-God truth.

⌒⌒⌒

The ribs are even more delicious than Liam promised, and I love the cauliflower-and-cashew soup so much that I could consume an entire vat of it.

"What do you think about dessert?" Liam turns the menu toward me. It's not a question of whether we want dessert but which one. "We could get the apple brown betty or the pecan pie sundae. Or we could go for the chocolate pot de crème. Or we could get all three and then roll ourselves home."

My stomach is already full from dinner, but I can always somehow manage to make room for dessert. "Apple brown betty, I think. Because it has an adorable name."

"It does have an adorable name. So do you, Sparkles." Liam leans across the table to kiss me, and I'm very annoyed by the nickname, but not as annoyed as I am by the thought of not kissing him back.

Our PDA is interrupted by the sound of glass breaking, and I pull back from the kiss to see that a waiter has dropped a fully loaded tray a few tables over from us. The overturned tray rests on the ground, surrounded by broken bits of glass, a pile of mashed potatoes, and an escaped stack of short ribs.

"Sorry," the waiter apologizes, bending down to clean up the mess.

"It's no problem," the woman at the booth nearest him says. "Here, let me help."

I freeze. I'd know Sarah's voice anywhere. *Here, let me help,* she used to say when Stacey came to visit us at our college apartment, my sister's arms full of Kaya and organic groceries. *Here, let me help,* she said when I came down with the flu on my twenty-first birthday, and she ran to CVS for medicine and came back with two varieties of cough syrup and three bottles of wine.

My heart stops as the waiter moves to the left, no longer blocking my view of the booth. I can only see the top of Sarah's head as she reaches down to help him, but when she straightens up again, her gaze locks onto mine.

"Willa," she says, blinking like I might be a figment of her imagination.

Max, who's been scrolling through his phone in the seat across from her the whole time, oblivious to the waiter's struggle, snaps his head up at her use of my name. "Willa," he repeats. "Hi." He looks from Sarah to me, but he doesn't look me in the eyes. Instead, he glances toward the door, probably trying to estimate how many seconds it would take him to escape.

"Willa," Sarah says again. I could almost find their repetition of my name comical if it weren't for the sinking sensation in my stomach, or the heavy thud of my heart in my chest, so loud I think Liam can hear it.

Seeing Sarah's profile picture on Facebook, with the two of them beaming in front of a fireworks display, was painful enough. That felt like someone had thrust a knife into my chest, leaving me bloody and breathless. But seeing them together in real life, at the restaurant where Max took me out to dinner whenever we felt like celebrating, is so much worse. It's like someone reaching inside me and twisting the blade of that knife over and over again, until my insides are mush.

And I know what Sarah's going to do before she even does it, because I know her. Or I thought I did. She's going to make a beeline for our table, just like she did at Chloe's disastrous birthday party. But this time, I won't run. I won't let myself. After The Incident, I thought I was utterly alone in the world. Alone in that crushing, all-encompassing heartbreak. But I was wrong.

I'd had Stacey, always, and Glory and the girls. And now I have Maisie and Liam.

I'm not alone. I'm not alone. I repeat the thought like a mantra as Sarah gets up from the booth and steps over the spilled plates. I repeat it as she hurries toward me, her face pleading, desperate. I repeat it as she places a hand on her belly, which is rounder than it was at Chloe's party. Much rounder.

I'm not alone.

"Willa," she repeats as she reaches our table. She starts to extend a hand as if she's going to embrace me, but she draws it back toward her stomach suddenly, like I'm a dog that might bite. "Please don't leave this time."

I stare at the curve of her stomach, hugged in a floral-print blouse I would have steered her away from if we still did our shopping together. "I'm not going anywhere."

"Willa?" Not even looking at Sarah, Liam reaches across the table to grasp my hand. "You okay?"

His voice is the only one that should be saying my name. I appreciate the fact that he's prepared to launch into bouncer mode on Max and Sarah, but I don't need him to. I squeeze his hand back, and the warm pressure of his fingers in mine helps to slow the pounding in my heart.

"I'm Sarah," she says to Liam, her voice barely above a whisper. "I'm . . . Willa and I used to . . ."

Liam doesn't take his gaze off me. "I know who you are."

Sarah nods, and her eyes fill with tears when she glances at me again. "I miss you," she says. "I miss you so, so much."

In my darker moments, I'd imagined that Max and Sarah would

break each other's hearts like they broke mine, and the thought of them distraught and miserable brought me comfort. But Sarah standing in front of me with tears streaming down her cheeks doesn't bring me any pleasure. Despite what she did to me, I still feel the urge to reach out and wrap my arms around her, to rub her back and promise her that everything will be okay. Because I was truly Sarah's best friend, even if she was never really mine.

"I miss you every single second of every single day," she continues, her voice catching. "I know you hate me, and you should. I deserve it. But I'm so sorry, Willa. God, I am so, so sorry."

I believe her. I've known Sarah almost my whole life, which means I know that the tears streaming from her eyes and the trembling of her hands are genuine.

"I'm sorry," she whispers again.

I know she means it. But sorry doesn't undo the damage she caused. Sorry doesn't erase the fact that she took the most consistent, loving bond we had in our lives—our friendship with each other—and ripped it apart for a man.

"You're pregnant," I say.

Sarah glances down at her baby bump as if she's forgotten that it's there. "I . . . yes. I wanted to tell you about it. I've wanted to tell you so many things."

I've wanted to tell her so many things, too. How it almost killed me when I found her with Max. How I couldn't eat or sleep or write or feel anything other than grief for months afterward. How I met Maisie and started, slowly, to heal. How I'm not there yet, not completely, but I'm getting better every day.

"Willa." Max, no longer content to hide in the booth with his filet mignon, starts to get up, too. "I just want to say that I'm also—"

The sound of his voice saying my name again almost makes me snap. "No," I say. "You sit down, and you stay quiet. You don't get to speak to me."

Patrons at other tables are watching us now, but I don't mind. It's Max and Sarah who should be embarrassed, not me.

Max holds his hands up in front of him. "Okay, you got it. All I wanted to say was—"

"No," Liam interrupts, his voice low. "She told you not to speak to her. So you sit down, and you stay quiet." His whole body is tensed, like he's about to leap up from the table and pounce on my ex-fiancé. My heart thuds in my chest again, but it's a different kind of thud this time.

"Who's he?" Max asks, still directing his attention to me as he nods toward Liam.

I'm all set to scandalize the other diners by telling Max to fuck off, but Sarah beats me to the punch. "Dammit, Max! For the love of God, *stop fucking talking.*"

He looks from me to Liam and back toward me, then mutters under his breath and strides for the exit, leaving Sarah—and presumably their bill—behind.

"What a charmer," Liam observes, watching Max scurry out the door. "You really dodged a bullet, Willa."

"I'd say." The situation is the opposite of what happened the day of The Incident. Instead of me running away, barely able to see straight because of the rage pulsing through my veins and the tears blurring my vision, it's Max fleeing the scene with his tail between his legs.

"I'm sorry about him," Sarah says, brushing a tear from her cheek. When she seems to realize the double meaning of her words, she cries harder, and I can't stop myself from removing my napkin off my lap and handing it to her. Not because she deserves it, but because I'm strong, like Liam said. And sometimes strength means having the grace to hand your pregnant ex–best friend a sauce-covered napkin while she's in hysterics in public.

"Thanks," she whispers, dabbing her cheeks with the cloth. "I know you don't want to see me. Or talk to me. I just . . . I want you to know that if I could go back in time, if I could . . ." Her shoulders tremble, and she takes a deep breath to steady herself, like she's practiced this speech in the event that she ever ran into me. And, knowing Sarah, she probably has. "Hurting you is the worst thing I've ever done. The worst thing I'll ever do. And the consequence— not having you in my life anymore—is the worst pain I've ever known. But none of that matters. All that matters to me is that you're okay." The waiter, the one bringing our apple brown betty, has stopped to watch Sarah, too, but she keeps her gaze on me. "I don't deserve to know—I'll never deserve to know, but are you okay, Willa? Are you okay?"

She's crying so hard that my napkin is incapable of helping her, and I feel tears spring to my eyes, too. Because even though our friendship ended, the love and affection I held for her didn't just die a clean death. That's what made her betrayal so excruciating: it wasn't just my engagement that I lost. The tragedy of The Incident was never about Max. It was about our future together, mine and Sarah's. I lost the grasshopper brownies she made for me whenever I was feeling down, and I lost her voice on the other end of the phone after I got into an argument with Stacey, reassuring me that everything would be all right. I lost her in-depth recaps of Tinder dates and *The Bachelor* episodes and our annual *Harry Potter* movie marathon sessions, complete with the homemade butterbeer we could never get to taste right. I lost her standing beside me on my wedding day, and on all the days afterward, big and small.

And I lost my chance to know and love her child. To be Aunt Willa to her baby. I lost her, and in losing her, I lost a part of me.

The reality of that loss sweeps over me like a tidal wave, and it's all I can do not to drown in it. I've held it together for this whole public reunion so far, but the realization that Sarah will be a mother without me there to witness it threatens to push me over the edge. I'm flooded with memories of the two of us playing house, one of us playing the mom and one playing the baby and her childhood dog, Rupert, playing the dad. I remember our '90s pop-star phase, where we decided that I'd one day give birth to a baby boy and Sarah would have a girl, and we'd name them Justin and Britney and they'd grow up to fall in love and have babies of their own.

I know Sarah's remembering all of it, too. I can see it on her face.

"Willa," she whispers. "I am so, so sorry."

I believe she is. And I'm sorry too, for myself, and even for her, and for her baby that I'll never know and love. I felt like I was finally getting better, and maybe I was. But this revelation is like a new branch on the tree of hurt that's been blooming inside my chest since The Incident, the one I've tried to cut down for months, at first with booze and locking myself in my bedroom and then, eventually, with being Maisie's bridesmaid.

But I can't. And I can't sit inside this restaurant a second longer, with Sarah and Liam and twenty random diners watching me. I have to go, like I always intended to. And not just go home—I have to go *away*. To start over.

"Willa, I'm gonna get the check," Liam says. He waves to our waiter, who's still standing there with the apple brown betty, looking utterly lost.

But I don't wait around for the check. And I don't answer Sarah's question. Instead, I grab my purse from under the table and do what I've been intending to do since the start of the summer, long before I found out about Sarah's baby.

I run.

33

Liam tries to call me twice on my drive home, but I don't pick up. I'm embarrassed by the fact that I'm pretty much ghosting him again, but I don't want to talk to him right now. I don't want to talk to anyone. So that he doesn't worry about me, I fire off a quick text after I park in Stacey's driveway: Just got to my sister's. Sorry for ditching. I'll call you soon.

I'll call him once I'm on the road out of Columbus, when his pinewood scent and muscular forearms seem farther away. When I'm not tempted to change my mind and turn back.

When I enter the house, I can hear Stacey, Glory, and the girls playing Candy Land in the family room. Like a teenager out past curfew, I tiptoe upstairs as quietly as possible. The last thing I need is Stacey discovering what I'm doing and locking me in my bedroom to stop me.

In my room, I dig out the suitcase I bought for myself when shopping for Maisie's bridal shower present. I toss it onto the bed and start throwing in anything I can get my hands on: a top, jeans, leggings, and enough underwear to last a week. I don't know exactly where I'm going yet. I'll probably drive south, toward Myrtle Beach. Our mom took Stacey and me there once when we were kids, and it's enough of a tourist trap that I can at least find a job selling hermit crabs or spray-painted T-shirts until I land a writing gig. I'll call Stacey when I've been on the road for a few hours and I'm far enough away that she can't reach through the phone and strangle me.

"Aunt Willa, look! Behind you! It's a varaptor!"

I turn around to see Maeve standing in the doorway, carrying Kaya's T-ball bat in her arms.

"Behind you!" she repeats. "A varaptor!"

My niece's insistence that there's a velociraptor in my bedroom usually strikes me as adorable, but not today. Today I just need to escape. I don't have time for velociraptors or other distractions.

"Get it!" she shrieks, her tone practically earsplitting. "It's hungry!"

"Maeve, I don't have time—"

"GET IT!" she screeches, her little lungs probably about to explode from the strain. "GET IT NOW!"

"*Maeve*," I reply, my voice sharper than intended. "I don't have time right now, okay?"

Stacey appears in the doorway with a mug in one hand and a book tucked under her arm. "Don't have time for what? What's going on?"

"Nothing. I'm just . . ." I glance from my sister to Maeve, who looks deflated. Her little chin trembles as she lowers the T-ball bat. I sigh, wishing I could take my words back. "I snapped at Maeve. I'm sorry. I'm just in the middle of something."

Stacey pats the top of Maeve's head. "In the middle of what?" She peers around me to my half-full suitcase on the bed. "Are you donating more stuff to Goodwill?"

I sigh. There's no point in lying to my sister now. Or in hiding the fact that I've wanted to leave all along.

"I'm leaving," I say.

"But the *varaptor*," Maeve insists. "It's gonna *eat* you."

Stacey narrows her eyes at me. "What do you mean, leaving? Like you're going to Maisie's for the night?"

"No. Like leaving leaving." I toss a pair of heels into the suitcase in case I need them for a job interview.

My sister crosses her arms over her chest. "What do you mean, 'leaving leaving'? Can you stop riffling through your damn shoe collection and look at me, please?"

I drop a pair of running shoes into the suitcase and turn to face my sister. It's time to rip the Band-Aid off. "I mean, I'm moving to Myrtle Beach."

"Myrtle Beach?" Stacey looks at me like I've declared that I'm going to Hogwarts. "The one in South Carolina?"

"Yes. What other one do you know?"

Stacey rubs her temples like her brain hurts. "What? Are you going on vacation or something?"

"No, I'm moving there. To live."

"You're going to *live* in Myrtle Beach? Why? What are you going to do there, Willa? Manage a mini-golf course? Sell some freaking hermit crabs?"

I don't appreciate the cold dose of reality she's trying to give me. "I'm going to write."

Her shoulders, which are practically up to her earlobes, drop in relief. "Okay, writing is good. Very good. Myrtle Beach? Not good. You can write here."

"I can't, though." I can't stay someplace where I keep getting accosted by Sarah, and worse, by my memories.

"But why? I've seen you on your laptop the last few weeks, working on blog posts. Of course you can write here. And if the girls are too loud in the playroom, we can get you some of those noise-canceling headphones."

"I don't mean I can't write in this house. I mean *here*, as in Columbus. Where Sarah is." I sit down on my bed, exhausted. "I ran into her today. Again."

"Oh, Willa." Stacey scoops Maeve up and deposits her on the bed, then sits down across from me. Maeve scoots into my lap, tapping her bat against my pillow. "Did she chase you around again?"

I laugh at the absurdity of it all. "Yeah. And guess what? She's pregnant."

My sister gasps, and her hand flies to her chest before she collects herself. "Jesus. Who's the dad?"

I shrug. "Max, I guess. They were together."

Stacey stares up at the ceiling and presses her hands to her cheeks. "Holy shit. No wonder you want to leave."

I do a double take at her admission. She so rarely agrees with me that it catches me off guard when she does. "Yeah."

"You can't, though." She reaches over to place a hand on my calf and squeezes. "You know that, right?"

Frustrated, I motion to the suitcase beside us. "Clearly not."

Maeve, suddenly noticing the suitcase, attempts to climb inside it, and Stacey wraps her arms around her to stop her. "Look, I fully agree that what happened to you sucked. It beyond sucked. What Max and Sarah did was horrible, and there's no getting around that. But getting hurt is a part of life, and yeah, it sucks and it's terrible and sometimes it's so painful that you think you can't go on for another single second."

Tears fill my eyes as my sister speaks. I've never actually heard

her acknowledge that life can suck sometimes. She's usually so focused on flinging self-help books at me that I thought she'd forgotten what it's like to have your heart broken. "Is this supposed to be
inspiring?"

"*But*," Stacey continues, "people survive. They get through it.
And eventually, days or months or even years later, they come out
the other side. Maybe a little damaged, or a lot, but they get through
it. And they find happiness again. But you have to deal with your
heartbreak, Willa. Moving to Myrtle Beach isn't dealing with it. It's
giving up."

I know that Stacey isn't entirely wrong. She can't be after all
those goddamn wellness podcasts she listens to. "I just thought it
would help me to be somewhere Sarah isn't."

Stacey nods. "Maybe it would, at first. But what would it really
change? If you move to Myrtle Beach, Sarah and Max still did that
hideous thing they did to you. She'll still be pregnant. They'll still
be together, even if we both know their relationship is probably completely miserable."

I laugh despite the tears in my eyes. "He did skip out on her at
the restaurant today. Skipped out on the check, too."

"Of course he did. He's a coward. But you, Willa, you're brave.
You clawed your way out of your depression. You're writing again,
and you help me and Glory with the girls so much now. Just look at
how well you handled things when Kaya got sick."

"Raptor," Maeve says, as if to remind us that she's there.

"If you move to the beach, you won't be able to come to Ruthie's
game nights anymore. And you're getting so much better at charades, Willa! And you won't be able to read the girls their bedtime
stories, which will really suck, because Aunt Willa is their favorite
storyteller. When you were gone for the bachelorette party, Kaya

wouldn't even let Glory or me read *The Paper Bag Princess* to her. It's her favorite book, but she wanted you."

The thought of Kaya wanting to read with me chips away at a little bit of the ache in my heart.

"And what about Maisie? You two were becoming such good friends. You can't just leave her because of what Sarah did. She's not Sarah. She doesn't deserve that."

I think of Maisie wrapping her arms around me at the bridal shop and carrying stacks of casseroles into our kitchen and listening with rapt attention as I told her about my night with Liam. "No, she's not. And you're right. She doesn't."

"And what about Dr. McDreamy?" my sister continues, on a roll now.

"Dr. Dreamboat," I correct her.

"What?"

I blush. "Never mind."

"You've practically been skipping around the house since you guys went on that date. I bet there's no Dr. Dreamboat in Myrtle Beach."

I don't think there's a Dr. Dreamboat anywhere else in the world. But that's one of the more shameful reasons I wanted to move: if I don't stay in Columbus, Liam never has to find out that I lied to him. I'll never have to own up to my deceit.

"But Liam doesn't know the truth. That Maisie's paying me. If he did, he wouldn't want to be around me anymore. He'd hate me."

Stacey pats my leg. "How do you know that? How can you ever know if you don't give him a chance to understand?"

She has a point, but I think I know Liam better than my sister does. I know his tattoo and what it means. I've traced it with my fingertips.

"Talk to Maisie about it," Stacey says. "I'm sure she knows Liam well. She can help you figure things out."

"But Maisie's not my real friend. She's my boss, remember? And I'm her employee."

My sister gives me a dubious look. "I watched that woman carry six Pyrex containers of food into this house the day after Kaya's surgery. Don't try to tell me she's not your real friend."

My heart soars at the thought. "But she's still paying me to pretend. Which means our friendship isn't real."

"So don't let her pay you anymore. And voilà! Problem solved."

It's not a solution I'd considered. If I don't take the second half of Maisie's money, which I'm due to receive after the wedding, then I won't be her fake bridesmaid anymore. I'll be a real one, and my lies to Liam won't be quite as extensive. Plus, if I decide to stay, I won't actually *need* the rest of Maisie's payment. "You make it all sound so easy, Stace."

She shakes her head. "You've already been through the hard stuff. This part? Staying with your family, who loves you and needs you? Being there for Maisie and Liam, who are good people—people who might actually deserve you, Willa—that's the easy part. But you can't stay in Columbus for me, or for Dr. Dreamface, or even for Maisie. If you stay, which you should, you have to stay for you." She taps my chest with her index finger to drive the point home.

For me. For so long, I'd thought the only way to take care of me was to run. To pack up a suitcase and my broken heart and get the hell out of Dodge. But meeting Maisie and Liam challenged that belief, and even though I backslid into my old, defeated mind-set after seeing Sarah today, I haven't run away yet. My suitcase is still unzipped, and my middle niece is still curled up in my lap, poking at my belly with her index finger.

It's not too late to change my mind. It's not too late to be the woman I want to be.

"Aunt Willa," Maeve whispers. "The *raptor*."

My sister has a point. She has a lot of points, actually. If I move, it won't be because of me. It'll be because of Max and Sarah. And sure, there would be no pregnant Sarah to run into on the beach. There'd be no chance of running into Max and suffering an epic meltdown. But there would be no Stacey, either. There would be no Kaya talking my ear off about frogs, or baby Lucy pulling my hair, or Maeve shooting at me with her Nerf gun like I'm a T. rex. There would be no Ruthie to call me Wilhelmina and disapprove of my fashion choices. There would be no Liam. And there would be no Maisie.

"The raptor," Maeve repeats, still undeterred from her mission.

I'm done running, I realize. I'm going to stay, even when it's hard. Even when it's painful. I'm going to stick it out.

Because I'm Willa Callister, and this is who I am.

"You're right," I tell Stacey.

My sister's eyes widen. "I'm *what*?"

"You're right. Myrtle Beach isn't going to solve my problems. No beach is. Besides, who's going to help Maeve hunt the velociraptor if I'm not around?"

Maeve roars and holds her hands up like little dinosaur claws.

"So you're staying?" My sister's face glows like a sunbeam. "For real?"

The megawatt smile on Stacey's face radiates love, and it's strong enough to drive out the hopelessness I felt earlier. I can't help but think of how much Maisie seems to miss Clara, when here I am with a sister who's stuck with me through all the bullshit I put her through. It was Stacey who gave me a home when I needed one, who gave me a job and a shoulder to cry on, literally, and then gave me the tough love I needed when it was time to stop crying and start carrying on with the rest of my life. The day I walked in on Max and Sarah, I thought I'd lost my fiancé and my best friend all in one day. But Sarah wasn't my best friend. She never was. It was Stacey all along. It just took me a hell of a long time to realize it.

"Yes," I say. "Thank you, Stace. For talking some sense into me."

Stacey covers my hand with hers. "We both know you would have turned around before you got to seventy-one. Because you belong here, with us." She winks at me. "All I did was save you some gas money."

"Aunt Willa!" Maeve yells, pointing toward the closet. "A T. rex! Come on!"

"Better get it, Aunt Willa," Stacey agrees. "I've heard the T. rex has pretty big teeth."

"Huge teeth!" Maeve says with a roar.

I slide my suitcase away from me and get up to wrap my niece in my arms. "Okay, little hunter. Let's get him!"

Maeve squeals with delight as I swing her around. With her in my arms, I don't feel the urge to run away and be someone else, or any of the crushing heartbreak I felt just hours earlier. For the first time in months, I feel like I'm exactly where I should be.

I feel like I'm home.

34

The next morning, after I've showered and made scrambled eggs for the girls, it's time to face the music. I pick up the phone to call Liam, hoping to catch him before he gets to work. I'm not sure how he's going to react to the fact that I ditched him at the restaurant last night, and I won't blame him if he's upset. And after Liam, I'll call Maisie to tell her that I can't accept the rest of her payment. That I want to be her real bridesmaid and her real friend.

Liam answers on the first ring. "Willa?"

I have to force myself to get the words out. "Hi. Hey. Look, I'm so sorry for leaving you like I did. I know it was really—"

"Are you with Maisie?"

Confused, I shake my head like he can see me through the phone. "No, I'm not. I was going to call her in a little bit."

"She's missing, Willa." He sounds frightened, and the anxiety in his tone sends a chill down my spine. I've never heard Liam worry, not even when Rose broke her ankle or Kaya needed surgery.

My heart drops to my stomach. No way is that possible. "What do you mean she's *missing*? I dropped her off at home yesterday, right after we got back from Hocking Hills." I watched Maisie wave good-bye to me as Finn helped her carry her gigantic suitcase into the house.

"I just spoke to Finn. He said she went out for milk around ten last night, and she didn't come back."

I pull the phone away from my ear to glance at the time. It's almost eight a.m., which means Maisie's been gone for nearly ten hours. *Ten hours.* "What do you mean? Where else would she go?"

Liam's voice is strained. "I don't know. Finn fell asleep on the couch and woke up around six. That's when he realized she wasn't there."

My mind races through possibilities that might explain Maisie's absence. "Maybe he just missed her. Maybe she left early for work, and he was still asleep. Maybe—"

"Her work stuff is at home. And she and Finn always have breakfast together on Mondays. She insists on it. Says it gets the week started off right."

That sounds like Maisie, but not coming home sure doesn't. She wouldn't do that. My pulse races, and my heart pounds in my chest like a caged animal trying to break free. I've listened to enough episodes of *Crime Junkie* to know that "going out for milk" and not coming home is a bad, bad thing. "Well then, where the hell is she?"

"I don't know. I hoped she was with you." I hear the sound of an engine revving to life. "I'm headed to their place now."

"Okay," I say, my voice shaking. "I'll meet you there."

I break the speed limit the whole way to Finn and Maisie's. I try to call her, but it goes straight to voice mail, and so do my next two attempts. At a red light, I send her a text—Where are you? Please call me—and hightail it onto Garden Road. I can't let my brain start to imagine something bad happening to her.

Her driveway is full of cars, so I park on the street and jog across the yard. The door is open a few inches, and I knock briefly before pushing it open and hurrying inside. Pippa greets me with a wagging tail, oblivious to the worry that's pulsing through my veins.

"Willa," Finn says, striding toward me in the hallway. "Have you heard from her?" He's wearing sweat pants and a ratty T-shirt, and I'm pretty sure I can spot crumbs in his normally well-combed beard.

"No. I tried to call her but—"

Finn's phone rings and he presses it to his ear and answers it before I can finish my sentence. I follow voices into the living room, where I find Rose, Liam, Lorene, and Mr. and Mrs. Forsythe gathered. Mr. and Mrs. Forsythe, looking stern and fatigued, sit on a gray sofa. Rose sits in an overstuffed reading chair, her cast-bearing leg extended in front of her as she whispers to Liam. Lorene, wearing a pair of running shorts and a hoodie and looking less Lorene-like than I've ever seen her, paces the room with her arms at her sides. She hurries over when she spots me.

"We've all tried to call her," she says. "Her phone's either dead or turned off."

"Lorene, what the hell is going on? Where is she?"

"I don't know. No one knows." She glances out the window, as if she expects Maisie to pop into view at any moment. "Finn says she told him she was going to get milk. He was watching a baseball game when she left. When he woke up, she'd left him a voice mail apologizing for not coming home. I listened to it. She sounded like she'd been crying." Lorene shakes her head. "He should have gone with her. Who cares about a fucking baseball game?"

"It's not your brother's fault, Lorene," Mrs. Forsythe says, narrowing her eyes at her daughter. "Besides, you didn't mention what else she said in the voice mail." She turns her gaze toward me. "Maisie told my son she was getting cold feet about the wedding and needed a day or two to think things over. So she's not actually *missing*. She's just being a flighty bride."

It takes all my restraint not to reach out and choke Mrs. Forsythe with her anchor-print scarf. "Maisie's not flighty."

"Agreed," Rose says. "Anyone can get cold feet, I guess, but it doesn't make sense. She was more excited to marry Finn than she was about anything, ever. She was more excited for her wedding than she was to help design the sea lion exhibit at the zoo. And she freaking loves sea lions."

Mrs. Forsythe nods. "I understand, dear, but you've never been a bride. It's a lot of pressure on a woman. Perhaps Maisie just needed a moment's peace. Remember when Lorene cut her own bangs right before her wedding?"

"Jesus, Mom," Lorene says, scowling.

I bristle at Mrs. Forsythe's words. She has a lot of nerve to talk about putting pressure on anyone. I consider how many details of the wedding Maisie changed to please her: her dress, the cake, the venue, even crossing Pippa off the bridesmaid list. "I don't think we should be comparing a missing person to a bad haircut," I say, trying not to grit my teeth.

Mrs. Forsythe presses her hands into the fabric of her seersucker pants. "Once again, she's not actually missing. She told Finn she needed time to think things over. So let's give her that. When she decides to come home, they can talk things out and he can decide whether he wants to proceed with the wedding."

"Whether I want to proceed with the wedding?" Finn asks, his tone disbelieving as he enters the living room. "Of course I do, Mom. Maisie's my fiancée. She's going to be my wife."

Mrs. Forsythe nods. "I know you love her, honey. I'm just saying that Maisie doesn't always think things through."

I can't bite my tongue while this woman insults my friend. "What do you mean? She's the most thoughtful person I know."

"Well, the horse and carriage, for one thing. She hired someone to bring her to the wedding in a horse and carriage. But did she mention it to any of us? No. Did she fill out the proper permit? No. Imagine my surprise when I got a call from the gentleman she hired, inquiring about whether there would be an appropriate place on my property to dispose of the horse's waste." Mrs. Forsythe presses a hand to her chest like it's horse waste, and not the fact that *Maisie is fucking missing*, that's the scandal of the day. It's all I can do not to pull a Lorene and find a salad fork to stab her with.

"That's not a big deal," Finn says. "She just didn't know about the permit. And why the hell are we talking about horses right now? They can shit wherever they want, as long as Maisie comes home."

Liam, quiet until now, holds his hands up for silence. "Let's just focus on finding her. Finn, have you noticed anything different about her lately? Any changes in behavior, clues that might help us locate her?"

Finn sits down on the armchair next to Rose's and buries his face in his hands. "The money," he says when he lifts his head up, his voice muffled.

"What money?" Liam asks.

Finn wipes his eyes with the back of his sleeve. "I checked the joint savings account. Maisie's been withdrawing large sums of money over the last few months. Withdrawals she didn't tell me about."

"Oh my God," Mrs. Forsythe says, the color draining from her face. "She's on drugs."

"What?" Lorene looks at her mother like she suggested that Maisie's a hippopotamus. "Don't be ridiculous, Mom. She doesn't even drink."

"And why doesn't she drink?" Mrs. Forsythe asks, looking at her daughter like she's equally ridiculous. "Maybe it's because she's a recovering addict. She's from a small town, right? And you know how it is in those places. They don't have anything to do, so they do opioids. Maybe Maisie was doing well until the stress of the wedding made her relapse. It all makes sense, doesn't it? The disappearing, the missing money. It all fits."

"Excuse me," Lorene says, putting her hands on her hips. "Did you just say they 'do opioids'? Who told you that, Laura Ingraham?"

Mrs. Forsythe ignores her. "Finn, I know you love Maisie. So do I. But if she's stealing from you, that's something you can't forgive."

"Maisie would never steal." I realize that my fists are balled up, and I have to force myself to relax them. "And if you knew her, even a little bit, you'd never say something like that."

"Willa's right. It's our joint account, Mom." Finn's tone is sharper than I've ever heard it. "That means the money in it belongs to both of us. Maisie didn't steal a cent."

"Well, she didn't tell you about it, either," his mother says. "You can't have a healthy relationship when one of you is keeping secrets."

"Wes keeps a ton of secrets from me, Mom." Lorene paces the floor so fast I think she might burn a hole in it. "But when I told you about that, you told me to be patient with him. So where the fuck is this advice coming from?"

"Lorene." Mr. Forsythe opens his mouth for the first time, sounding decidedly bored. "Don't curse at your mother."

"Let's get back to the matter at hand," Mrs. Forsythe says, her tone softer this time. "We can discuss your relationship with Wes another time." She turns her gaze toward Finn. "I know you don't want to consider the fact that Maisie might be using, honey, but why else would she withdraw money without telling you? What else would she need it for?"

My heart thuds in my chest. The last thing I want to do is betray Maisie's trust. It was so important to her that Finn believe she had a friend like he did in Liam, a real friend from childhood. Maisie would die if he discovered the truth about our friendship.

"And how much money are we talking?" Mrs. Forsythe asks. "Because I'm not sure how much heroin costs, but—"

"Maisie is not on heroin!" My outburst comes out loud, *really* loud, and Mrs. Forsythe blinks at me.

"I'm sorry, what?"

"Maisie Mitchell is not on heroin," I repeat. "Have you *met* her? She carries an actual handkerchief and gets excited about wombat exhibits. She's the only adult I know who actually uses the word 'gosh.' She's as straightlaced as they come. And I don't mean any disrespect, but your suggestion that she's stealing money from your son to fuel her drug habit is the most ridiculous thing I've ever heard. And I have three nieces under the age of seven, so I hear a lot of ridiculous things."

Mrs. Forsythe stares at me with wide eyes. "I'm sorry, who are you, again?"

I clench my jaw. "I'm Willa Callister. Maisie's friend. You and I met at her bridal shower, *Victoria*."

She gives me a look that could freeze hell. "Okay, Willa. Since you know so much about Maisie, why don't you tell us what she's been spending all that money on?"

I tuck my fingernails into my palms, hard, and think of Maisie rabbit-tapping her foot against the café table while she waited for Finn. I think of her wolfing down Stacey's pancakes in my sister's backyard and hugging me in the bathroom at White of Dublin. I think of her helping Ruthie pick out date outfits, and talking about her sister Clara at the cabin.

I think of how Maisie might never trust me again once I say what I'm about to say. But I'm worried to death about her, and we need to find her. And Finn can't find her if he doesn't have the right information.

If I tell Maisie's secret, it'll make me a horrible bridesmaid. But I can't worry about being her bridesmaid right now. I need to be her friend instead. And right now, being Maisie's friend means telling the truth. It means laying Mrs. Forsythe's bullshit bare.

"Me," I say finally. "She's spending the money on me." I glance at Liam, knowing he might never want to speak to me again once I'm finished. Let alone kiss me.

"Do *you* have an opioid habit?" Mrs. Forsythe asks, looking bewildered.

"Mom," Lorene hisses. "Shut the hell up about opioids."

"No. Of course not. I . . . Maisie is . . ." I interlock my fingers, as if holding my own hand will give me the strength I need to keep going. My heart thuds in my chest, so loud I swear I can hear it, and I know there's no turning back. "Maisie hired me to be her bridesmaid."

"She *what*?" Rose asks, her eyes wide.

The secret Maisie and I have worked so hard to protect is out, and all because of me. Because I had to. I cross my arms across my chest as if to hug myself. "She hired me," I repeat. "To be a bridesmaid."

Liam looks at me in disbelief. "Maisie *hired* you? Why? You're friends."

"Yeah," Rose says. "From Camp Anawanna. So why is she paying you to be a bridesmaid if you're friends?"

The way Liam and Finn are looking at me, like I've morphed into a complete stranger before their very eyes, makes me want to melt into the floor.

"We're not friends," I say quietly. "I mean, we are now. We really are. I love Maisie. But in the beginning, we were strangers. She needed a fourth bridesmaid, and I needed money so I could leave town. That's how it started."

"And Camp Anawanna?" Rose repeats.

My eyes brim with tears. "There is no Camp Anawanna. I mean, there is, but it's fictional. And so is Camp Wildwood. I never went to summer camp, and I don't think Maisie did, either."

"So you didn't steal Hershey bars from boys' cabins?" Lorene asks, trying to follow.

I shake my head, tears spilling out of my eyes. "No. And we didn't run into each other years later at the library and reconnect. We met at a coffee shop. Maisie ran inside when I was waiting for my date to show up, and she offered to pay me to pretend we were friends." I glance at Finn, who looks so crestfallen that I almost can't bear it. "She wanted you to think she had friends so badly, Finn. She just wanted you to think highly of her. That was all she wanted."

He shakes his head. "I don't understand. So that day I met you at Espresso 22, when you were there with Maisie . . ."

"That was the first time I met her."

Finn leans forward in the armchair, his posture tense. "So where does Maisie go when she says she's meeting you at the coffee shop? And why in God's name did you let her pay you thousands of dollars to be in our wedding? That's just cruel, Willa. You took advantage of her."

I wipe my eyes with the back of my hand. "I'm sorry. That's not what I was trying to do."

"And on Mondays?" he asks, his voice choked. "Where does she go on Mondays?"

I remember Maisie's confession in the car on the way back from Hocking Hills, how embarrassed she was to admit that she met with her therapist on Mondays. I can't divulge that to Finn, or to anyone. I've already spilled her biggest secret, and I won't tell any more.

"I'm not sure." It's not a total lie; I don't know her therapist's name, or where they practice.

"Fuck." He buries his head in his hands, and Liam wraps an arm around him. "I should have talked to her more. I knew how stressed she was about the wedding. I shouldn't have let things get to this point."

"It's not your fault, honey," Mrs. Forsythe says. "Some girls get so worked up about the wedding that they forget about the relationship. If Maisie was willing to pay this total stranger to be her bridesmaid and make up stories about how they knew each other, she has deeper problems than you could have known."

Fury burns inside me. I hate Mrs. Forsythe. I hate her for demeaning Maisie, and for making her think she wasn't good enough to be her daughter-in-law. I hate her for poisoning Finn with lies.

"You're wrong," I say. "Maisie may have problems, but so do I. So do you. So does your precious Finn. And the only reason Maisie got 'worked up' about the wedding is because she wanted to impress you. Because she wanted *you* to accept her into your perfect family. That horse and carriage she ordered? She knew you had a horse and carriage at your wedding because you talked about it all the freaking time. She probably just wanted to surprise you! She had me sprint to Mrs. Yummy's bakery because getting a cake from there was make or break for her. Because you had one at your wedding, and Lorene had one at hers. And she didn't even want the dress she picked out! It's not even her style! But she went with it because you oohed and ahhed over it. And how did you treat her in return? By letting your asshole friends gossip about her being an alcoholic. By sitting here in her living room and accusing her of being on drugs."

I wipe away a tear, my fingers trembling. "Maybe Maisie shouldn't have run away, but that doesn't give you the right to judge her. She's the only person who's been a friend to me in a long time. She's kind and she's thoughtful and she would never, ever do anything to intentionally hurt anyone. Especially your son. You don't deserve her, Victoria. And neither do I."

Mrs. Forsythe looks taken aback. She opens her mouth and closes it again, like a baby bird waiting for food from its mother.

"I agree with Willa," Lorene says. "Instead of sitting around hypothesizing about what drugs Maisie's on, we should be out there looking for her."

"I'm gonna call the police," Finn says, leaping up from his chair. "And then I'll check the zoo. Liam, can you check the Olentangy Trail? We usually pick it up at the Antrim trailhead on our walks."

"I'll check the yoga and barre studios she goes to," Rose says. "Yoga is the first thing I do when I'm feeling down."

Lorene nods. "We can start there and then check all the bookstores. You know how much Maisie loves getting lost in a book. I'll go with Rose."

"Perfect," Rose says, trying to put all her weight on her left leg as she clambers up from the armchair. "Because I can't walk on my own."

I watch as Finn and Liam and Rose and Lorene—Maisie's real friends and loved ones, the people who actually have a right to be here—spring into action. I lean against the wall, feeling horribly unwelcome and out of place, and I miss Maisie so much right now I'd pay a million dollars just to make sure she's okay.

"I'll stay here with your father in case she comes home," Mrs. Forsythe tells Finn. "We'll take care of Pippa."

He nods and hustles out the door toward his car, his phone glued to his ear. Rose trails after him on a set of crutches, and Lorene and I end up side by side in the hallway.

"I'm sorry," I tell her, tearing up again.

Lorene shakes her head. "I should have noticed something was up. The way she brought you into the fold so quickly, so close to the wedding. And the story you told me about the bees. I just thought you'd confused them with wasps, like Maisie said."

"I'm so sorry for lying," I tell her. I'll repeat my apology as many times as she'll let me. "I really do care about Maisie. I care about all of you."

Lorene's eyes soften, and she puts her hand on my arm for the briefest of moments. "I know you do. And honestly, if I hadn't been so preoccupied by all the bullshit with Wes, if I'd just paid more attention, I would have noticed something was wrong." She tugs at the sleeves of her hoodie. "We'll figure everything out, okay? But first, we gotta find our girl."

I follow them outside, and my eyes are so blurry with tears that I almost trip over the threshold. When I turn around to close the door, I find Liam standing in front of me. His expression is hard, flinty, and his eyes bear none of the playful flicker I've grown to love.

"Liam." I don't know what to say to him, but I have to say something. I want to reach out and put my hand against his stubble-covered cheek. I want to take him into my arms and tell him that everything will be okay, and have him tell me the same. But I can't. Because he's looking at me like he doesn't recognize me. Like I'm a total stranger. Because maybe, to him, I am.

"Excuse me." He steps right past me, not giving me a second glance.

His coldness breaks my heart, and I feel like the wind's been knocked out of me. "Liam, wait. Please." I reach for his arm, but he yanks it out of my reach.

"What, Willa?" His voice is as sharp as a razor blade. "What do you want to say? That you're sorry for disappearing on me last night? That you're sorry for lying to me all this time? For making up stories about the little adventures you and Maisie had at your nonexistent summer camp?" He runs a hand through his hair, mussing it up so he looks like he just rolled out of bed.

I wipe a tear from my cheek. That's exactly what I want. To say I'm sorry, but that everything between us was real. That I'm still Willa. I'm still me. "Yes."

Liam focuses on Finn's car as it reverses out of the driveway. He won't even look at me, and the frigidity of his demeanor makes me feel like I'm looking at a stranger, too. "I told you that I don't do lies. I told you how important honesty and integrity were to me, and you lied to me anyway. You lied to all of us."

"I wanted to tell you. So badly. That's why I didn't text you after our kiss. Because I couldn't stand lying to you! But I had to. I didn't want to betray Maisie."

"You didn't want to betray her?" Liam's tone is incredulous, and the words coming out of his mouth ring foreign and hollow in my ears. "How did that work out for you, Willa? Because she's missing. And instead of being out there looking for her like I should be, I'm standing here wasting time listening to your bullshit excuses. Well, I'm done. I'm done with all of this."

He turns away from me, his jaw set in a firm line.

I can't just let him walk away, thinking I'm a liar like his ex, or like Max and Sarah. I remember tracing his tattoo with my fingertips, and the memory almost breaks me. "Liam," I say as he slides into the driver's seat of his car. "Wait. Please. Just let me explain, let me—"

Just let me explain. It's the same thing Sarah said to me when she followed me out of Max's apartment, and I don't blame Liam for slamming his car door shut before I can finish. He starts the engine, but hits the brakes before he pulls onto the street. His gaze meets mine, and my heart swells when I think he might let me come with him. But just before I take a step toward the car, he pumps the gas and backs out of the driveway, accelerating down the street.

Fuck. I run my hands through my hair, trying to get a grip on my emotions. I need to stay calm and focus on what's most important: Maisie. Liam might hate me with the fire of a thousand suns, but I can cry about that later. I wipe my face with my sleeve and jog toward my car. Right now, the only thing that matters is my friend. She changed my life when I was at rock bottom, and I'll be damned if I don't try to do the same for her.

35

I wish I knew more about Maisie's therapist. She was vague about the details; even telling me that she saw one seemed like a momentous step for her. I have no idea if her therapist is male or female, or where Maisie attended sessions. But since Espresso 22 is in the small suburb of Powell, and a desperate Maisie barged inside that particular coffee shop on the day we first pretended to be friends, it makes sense that her therapist might work nearby. I Google therapists in Powell, Ohio and scroll through the resulting list of twenty-five people. It's a starting point, but thanks to privacy laws, it's also a dead end. I can't exactly call each office and demand to know if Maisie's a patient.

Undeterred, I attempt to call Maisie again while I start driving toward Powell. I might not be able to contact every therapist, but I can drive around the neighborhood in hopes of finding her. When my call goes straight to voice mail again, I hang up and offer a silent prayer to the universe to help me find my friend, and then I decide to drive straight to the place where this all started: Espresso 22. Weaving in and out of traffic, I drive across town like a maniac, and I almost run over the curb when I pull into a spot. I hop out of the car and run into the café like I'll die if I don't get caffeine into my bloodstream.

I've changed a lot over the last couple months, but the café hasn't. The aroma of freshly brewed coffee fills my nostrils as I scan the interior, my heart pounding in my chest. There's a Bible study group in the far corner, its middle-aged members holding mugs of coffee over their holy books. At the table near the door, a yawning teenager turns a page in her textbook and lifts a can of Diet Coke to her lips. And there, perched at the table where I sat to wait for Zachary all those weeks ago, is Maisie.

I'm so relieved to see her that my eyes well with tears again. She sits facing away from me, her long auburn hair hanging loose down her back. I'd recognize that hair anywhere, just like I'd recognize the sound of her foot tapping against the table leg.

"Maisie." I jog toward her table, tripping over the teenager's backpack and muttering an apology. "Maisie!"

Her eyes widen when she turns to face me, and I take one look at their red, bloodshot color and know that she's been crying.

"Willa." Her voice is soft, breathy. "What are you doing here?"

The question is so outrageous that I do a double take. "What am I doing here? What are *you* doing here? Everyone's worried sick about you!"

She shakes her head like she doesn't understand. "What do you mean? I told Finn I was okay. I just needed a few days to think. Did he not get my message?"

Speaking to this version of Maisie is like talking to a stranger, and I want to reach out and shake some sense—and some life—into this alien woman in front of me. Instead, I pull the chair across from her out, the legs scraping against the hardwood floor, and I sit. "I'm sorry, but *what do I mean*? Are you serious? You randomly run off for milk a couple weeks before your wedding, and then you tell your fiancé that you have cold feet and aren't coming home, and you don't expect people to worry? You don't expect Finn to send out a search party? Everyone's freaking out, Maisie! Lorene and Rose and Liam are all out looking for you. And so was I, obviously. Finn called the police."

Her chin trembles. "Oh no. I hoped he wouldn't worry. That was the last thing I wanted."

Her lack of faith in Finn—did she truly think there was a shred of possibility that he wouldn't worry?—is so out of character for her that I reach across the table and squeeze her hand just to make sure she's real. "What did you think was gonna happen? He'd listen to your voice mail and think, *Cold feet? No problem. See you in a few days, maybe!*" I'm so worked up that I smack the table with my palm, and Maisie pulls her hand away like I've hit her.

"I didn't . . . I guess I didn't think." She gathers her hair in a ponytail, lets it fall down her back again, then repeats the motion. "Is he angry?"

I remember Finn's stern words to his mother. "Not with you. But he's terrified, Mais. As was I." I watch as she wipes her brow with her handkerchief and balls the cloth up in her fist. "Where did you go last night? Why'd you run away? Because there's no way in hell you got cold feet."

Her chin trembles, and she grips the edge of the table. "Yes, I did."

I know Maisie can sell a lie when she needs to, but I'm not buying this one. "Why run away, then? Why not just talk things out with Finn? Why not call me? You know I'm always here for you, right?"

She looks away from me, focusing on the untouched lemon muffin that sits on a yellow plate in front of her.

I want her to say something, to tell me what's going on, but I remember all the times Stacey held me in her arms after The Incident while I refused to talk. I needed her then, and Maisie needs me now. "Okay," I say, sliding the plate toward her. "We can sit here as long as you want, but I'm not leaving. Because you're my friend. And maybe it's been a while since I've had friends, but I'm pretty sure one of the basic rules is that you don't let another friend suffer alone."

"You won't want to be friends anymore," Maisie whispers. "Not if you know who I really am."

The weariness in her voice breaks my heart. "I know exactly who you are. You're the woman in the blue dress who barged into my life and changed it completely. You rescued me from my own misery and made me believe in friendship again. You made me believe in *myself* again. So if you think there's something about you that can scare me away, go ahead. Try me. Because I promise you, there's nothing you can say that could make me stop being your friend."

She shakes her head. "There is, Willa. And once you know, once Finn knows, I'll be alone."

I'm not sure what terrible secret she thinks will send Finn and me running for the hills, but I have to confess to her that the secret of our friendship is already out. "Finn knows that you hired me."

The color drains from her face. "What?"

"I was so worried about you, I had to tell him the truth. He knows that you hired me, and that you haven't been meeting me here on Mondays. And guess what, Maisie? Finn doesn't care about any of that. He's still out looking for you. He's probably sprinting around the zoo right now, sweating his butt off because he's terri-fied. Because he loves you. And so do I."

"But he won't," she insists. "And you won't. Once you really know me."

I reach for her hand again, and this time she doesn't pull away. "And who is that, Maisie? Who are you really?"

Her face crumples, and I squeeze her hand harder. "I'm not . . . I'm . . ."

"Mais," I whisper, "it's okay. You're okay."

"I'm a bad person, Willa."

Her admission is so absurd that I almost burst into laughter. Maisie, the queen of casseroles and handkerchiefs and southern hairy-nosed wombats, is anything but bad. "I promise you you're not. Whatever it is that's making you believe that, you can tell me. I promise. I won't even flinch."

She tucks her hair behind her ears, and I notice that she's shaking. "Yesterday, after you dropped me off, I went through the mail that came on Saturday. I found . . ." Her voice is so soft that I have to lean closer to listen. "My family isn't coming to the wedding."

I'm certain I've misheard. "What?"

"My parents. Clara. They aren't coming. None of them."

I stare at her in confusion. How could they all just cancel on her like that? How could they bail on the biggest day of her life? Fury shoots through my veins when I see the tears spilling onto her cheeks. Nobody hurts my friend on my watch. *Nobody.* "Why the hell not? It's your wedding! They're your family! They can't just not come. They can't."

Maisie shrugs, her shoulders trembling. "They can, and they are."

"Hell no, they're not. I will drive to West Virginia and drag their asses into my car if I have to! They're your family, and they better act like it. You deserve—"

"They don't consider me family anymore, Willa."

Her words cool my tirade. "What do you mean?"

Maisie's voice is flat. "My mom hasn't returned my calls in years, but she took the time to respond to my invitation. They aren't coming."

I remember how strange I found it that Finn hadn't met her

parents. I remember our conversation in the car on the way to her bachelorette party, when she told me they didn't approve of her choices. I'd known something was off, but I never imagined they'd treat Maisie like this.

"You want to know the truth about me? Well, I really did grow up in a small town in West Virginia. Hummel, to be exact. I really do have a mom and a dad and a sister named Clara. I used to, anyway. They disowned me a long time ago."

I don't understand. Disowning wonderful Maisie, with her colorful headbands and her love for animals, would be like disowning a litter of kittens. "Why the hell would they do that?"

She takes a shaky breath and looks down at her hands. "My family is . . . my family isn't like Finn's. Or yours, even. My dad was strict. The children-should-be-seen-and-not-heard type. My mom was afraid of him. And they were both religious. I was less so." She traces a circle around her plate with her index finger, not looking up. "I was a rebellious teenager. I didn't want to go to church or stay home on Friday nights helping my mom around the house. And I had a boyfriend. Sam. My dad didn't like that."

None of those things sound particularly rebellious to me—God forbid a teenage girl have a *boyfriend*—but I keep my mouth shut.

She pushes the plate away from her. "This one night, when I was supposed to be grounded for talking back to my dad, I snuck out to go to a party with Sam. It was at some guy's house who was friends with Sam's brother. It was backwoods shit. You know, Bud Light and lame music and people sneaking off into the woods to fool around. Stuff I wasn't supposed to be around. Stuff that good, God-fearing girls wanted no part in."

"Sneaking out to a party sounds like pretty standard teenage behavior, Maisie. I don't see how that makes you a bad person."

She glances out the window, avoiding my gaze. "For the daughter of a woman who refused to even cook with white wine, I was a pretty big drinker. I just felt so good when I was buzzed, you know? So okay with myself. And when you've got parents who think you're a whore for hiding copies of *Cosmo* in your bedroom, feeling okay with yourself is hard to come by."

I try to picture Maisie drunk, but it's like trying to conjure up the image of a stranger. "A whore for reading *Cosmo*?" I ask in disbelief. "Seriously?"

"In one of the magazines, I'd circled some information about the pill. My dad lost his shit when he saw it. You would have thought I was reading about satanic rituals instead of sex ed." Maisie shrugs. "Honestly, he might have been less pissed off that way."

I imagine what it must have been like for her to grow up in a family that shamed her for doing perfectly ordinary teenage-girl things, and I just want to reach across the table and hug her.

"Anyway, that night at the party, I did what I always did when I snuck out: smoked a little bit and drank a lot. I drank even more than usual that night, after everything that happened at home. I should have stopped way before I did, but the beer just kept flowing, and I felt so good, Willa. Like I didn't even care anymore that I was going to hell for mouthing off to my parents or yawning at church or whatever heinous sin I'd committed that week."

"Hell? Are you kidding me?" I ask, unable to hide my incredulity. I lower my voice when the barista glances over at me. "Hell isn't for nice people who bake cookies and have an endless supply of cute hair accessories, Maisie. You're not a bad person, no matter what your parents taught you. You're one of the best people I've ever met. You're *the* best."

She hunches forward as if to make herself as small as possible, still avoiding eye contact. "I'm not. I promise you I'm not."

"Why, because you drank beer before you were twenty-one? It sounds like you were in a hard place and just trying to let off some steam. There are better ways to do that than Bud Light, sure, but you were a kid. It's not like you could trot off for a matcha smoothie and a spin class."

Maisie turns away from the window, and the faraway look in her eyes sends a chill down my spine. "No, it's . . . it's more than that. When the party was dying down, Sam drove me home. We should have sobered up first, but I knew I had to sneak back in by three a.m. That's when my mom usually woke up to pee, and I didn't want to get caught. Like I said, I was already supposed to be grounded, and I was afraid of getting in even more trouble." She lets out a dry laugh, and the joylessness of it unnerves me. "It was three miles from the party to my house. That's a longer drive than it is from here to the zoo. I thought we'd be fine. I was wrong. I was so, so wrong." Her voice barely rises above a whisper, and her chin trembles as she speaks.

"It's okay, Mais. Whatever it is, it's okay."

Tears stream down her cheeks, and she doesn't bother to wipe them away. "It's not okay, Willa. It wasn't okay. Sam hit someone with his truck on the way home. A girl, around my age. Elizabeth. She was walking home from the same party, and he didn't see her until it was too late." She lets out a little gasp, like she's been holding her breath all this time. "She came out of the woods, and I thought she was a deer at first. Sam tried to stop. He really did. But one instant the road was empty, and the next there she was, and we didn't . . . we didn't . . ."

"Maisie," I whisper. "It's okay. Look at me. It's okay."

She shakes her head. "I can still hear the sound of the brakes shrieking. When I go to sleep at night, I swear I can smell the burnt rubber from Sam's tires against the asphalt. I swear I can still hear Elizabeth scream. It all happened so fast, in a fraction of an instant, but for me, that moment stretches on forever, you know? Like a part of me still lives in it." She wraps her arms around herself, and I notice the goose bumps dotting her skin. "She survived, but barely. The impact of the accident broke her pelvis, and she had internal bleeding, too. She had to get so many surgeries, and she missed her entire senior year."

I think of how much effort Maisie's put into keeping all of this a secret. I think of all the times she's probably lain in bed with Finn at night and wanted to tell him, wanted to free herself of the burden weighing on her heart. I think of the nightmares, and the guilt, and the shame that's weighed her down for a decade.

"Maisie," I say, my tone gentle, "it was an accident. Yes, you and Sam made a dangerous choice, and it's terrible that someone was hurt. But nobody died, thank God. And people make mistakes. Teenagers make mistakes! You're careful now. You're thoughtful. And you're much, much kinder to other people than you are to yourself." The tears running down her cheeks make me want to cry, too, and I wipe my eyes. "Don't you think it's time to forgive yourself? Finally, after all these years?"

She tugs at the neckline of her T-shirt and pulls it up to wipe her face. "Elizabeth wasn't just someone. She was the pastor's daughter. When we ran into her, Sam I and might as well have crashed into Jesus himself. The whole town hated us for it. And the shame I brought to my family . . . my dad kicked me out after that. He called me an insult to the church and our family and said I was an awful example for Clara, that it was dangerous for me to be around her lest she follow my lead. He actually used the word 'lest.'" Maisie buries her head in her hands. "I was stupid to think my parents might come to the wedding. But I still wanted them there, you know? They're my parents. I thought maybe if they saw this big, beautiful ceremony, if they saw what I'd made of myself, they might not be ashamed anymore. They might forgive me."

The brokenness in her tone makes me want to drive straight to West Virginia and set her parents straight. "You weren't stupid. You were hopeful. And it's not your fault that your parents are punishing you for their own shortcomings. You deserve unconditional love, just like you did when you were a teenager. And you don't deserve to be ashamed." I want nothing more than to wrap my arms around my friend, to hug away the pain and the hurt and the years of feeling like there was something bad about her. "I'm so sorry that you've felt so alone."

Sniffling, she taps the tabletop with her fingers. "I thought about telling you that night at the cabin."

I remember how worried I'd been after her breakdown in the kitchen that night. "I'm glad you feel able to tell me now."

"I've thought about telling Finn so many times. About that night, about my family. I think maybe he'd understand. He's Finn. But I just wanted . . . I just wanted to leave it all behind. Forget that it ever happened."

I understand wanting to leave it all behind. My problems are a drop in the bucket compared to what Maisie endured, but I know what she means. I spent the whole summer dreaming of an escape.

"Therapy's helped, but I still have a lot of work to do. And I still think about my parents and Clara, and Elizabeth, all the time."

I remember the longing way she spoke about her sister at her bachelorette party. "Have you tried to reach out to Clara?"

She nods. "Yeah. But I can't find her on Facebook or Instagram or anything. I'm sure my parents don't let her use social media, so if she has any accounts, they're secret. She always was smart."

"Maybe one day, when she leaves for college, you can find her."

Maisie shifts in her seat. "I'm not sure she'd want to hear from me. My parents probably talk about me like I'm the Antichrist, if they even mention me at all. She probably thinks I'm awful."

"Maisie," I say, my tone fierce, "you are the kindest, most loving human being I've ever met. I'm sure Clara remembers that. Trust me, she'll want to hear from you. You said it yourself, she's smart. She'll understand."

She shrugs. "I really hope so."

"And in the meantime, you won't be alone. Not ever. I will always be here."

She gives me a half smile, and the sight of it makes my heart jump. "Even if I'm a crazy person who disappeared on her fiancé?"

"Even if you hit Mrs. Forsythe over the head with your wedding bouquet." I pause. "*Especially* if you hit her over the head with your wedding bouquet."

Maisie laughs.

"When I met you," I say, "I was looking for a way out of Columbus. All I wanted to do was run away. You made me realize that I could have a friend again, that I could *be* a friend again. I saw Sarah and Max last night, and you know what I realized? That I'm okay without them because of you, and Liam and my family. I thought about running away, but I don't want to anymore. I want to stay. And I'm hoping you'll stay, too."

She shrugs, spiritless. "I don't know. Running away is a very convenient option."

"Running away is convenient, but it won't make you happy. Take that from an expert. You have so many people here who love you. Don't give up on us because your parents are too blind or stubborn to realize what they're missing by not wanting to be a part of your life."

Maisie sighs and pushes her hair away from her face. "I really thought you wouldn't want to be my friend anymore after I told you what I'd done."

I slide her muffin toward her. "You're rarely wrong, Mais, but you were wrong about that. I love you no matter what. And I know Finn does, too."

She raises the muffin to her lips and takes the smallest of bites. "I can't believe I ditched him like that. I don't know what I was thinking."

I shrug. "You were scared and sad and thinking that you were alone. But you're not. You never were."

Maisie straightens her shoulders as if preparing for battle. "What am I gonna do now? How do I fix this?"

I watch as she takes another bite. "Well, that's up to you. Do you love Finn? Do you still want to marry him?"

"Oh, my gosh, yes."

"Okay." I sit back in my chair, the tension draining from my shoulders now that I know Maisie is back to being her sensible, optimistic self. "Then you're gonna eat your muffin and call your fiancé. And you're going to tell him what you told me, or at least as much as you feel comfortable telling him."

Taking a deep breath, Maisie nods like a soldier who's just been given orders. "And you'll stay with me? The whole time?"

I smile at her. "I'll stay with you the whole time, Maisie. We'll face all of it. Together."

36

Dear Waywards,

It's been a long time since you've heard from me. Eight months, two weeks, and four days, to be exact. For most of those months, I hid from everyone, including you. Including myself. I thought no one would be interested in a Willa who didn't have a fiancé or a best friend, but I was wrong. I'm still me. I'm still worthy. And I've got a lot to say.

Over the last two months, I wrote a few posts that I wasn't ready to publish until now. You might be surprised when you read them. There's none of the woo-hoo, isn't-my-life-in-Columbus-great, aspirational content I used to post. Instead, there's honesty and humor and a couple of curse words. And it's okay to be honest, even when it's ugly. Even when it hurts. I learned that this summer. (See the posts I've just added for the full story, and for a picture of me in my Princess Sparkleheart costume. I promise you it's worth it.)

Before I met the Animal Whisperer, I was a shell of my former self. I quit writing and running and painting my nails. I spent more hours than I'd care to admit wrapped in an actual Snuggie, Waywards. A Snuggie.

Because I thought I was alone. But I was wrong. I was never alone; and in your darkest moments, neither are you. There's someone out there who understands your pain and won't judge you for how you choose to overcome it. Maybe that person is your overbearing but well-intentioned sister, or the next-door neighbor who loves you almost as much as she loves critiquing your outfits. Or maybe it's someone you haven't met yet: a bouncy-haired stranger who crashes your pity party at a coffee shop, or a swoony doctor whose insane forearms are rivaled only by his good heart.

And maybe the way you cope with your pain isn't the same as mine. Maybe it's not wine and endless Netflix and a plan to move to a different state and never look back. Maybe it's a Roman numeral tattoo, or a Silver Singles profile, or the decision to hire a stranger as your brides-maid. Whatever you have to do to find your way back to yourself, do it. And forgive yourself for it. Because you are not alone.

You aren't. Not when you have flashbacks of that terrible thing that happened to you all those years ago, or when you discover that your former best friend and ex-fiancé are having a baby. Not when you have to file for divorce from the spouse who betrayed you, or when you think the only way to make things better is to pack up a suitcase and run.

I ran into my former best friend the other day, and she asked me if I was okay. I couldn't respond in the moment, because I was over-whelmed, but the answer is yes. I'm okay. I'm better than okay. I'm closer to my family than ever before, and I've formed a friendship that will last a lifetime. I was so afraid of sharing my struggles on this blog because I thought it meant I was publicly admitting to failure. But it doesn't. It just means I'm human. And because you're human, too, I think you can relate. Even if you've never destroyed a three-hundred-dollar cake while looking like Glinda the Good Witch's unhinged sister.

So here we go, Waywards. I'm back. And just remember: you're never really alone, even when life is at its worst. Good things are just around the corner—or just inside that coffee shop.

No matter what happens, you've got me. The real Willa.

And I am here to stay.

⌒⌒⌒

Once I hit *post* on my blog updates, I text a link to Liam. Three bubbles appear on my phone screen, and my breath catches when I think he's typing a response, but then they disappear. To cheer me up, Maisie takes me on a behind-the-scenes tour of the zoo, where I finally catch a glimpse of the infamous Glen the wombat.

Maisie and Finn postpone the wedding from September to October. It's Maisie's idea more than Finn's; she wants to attend couples counseling before they tie the knot, and she decided to have the small, offbeat wedding they actually want—not the black-tie affair in Mrs. Forsythe's two-acre backyard. Mrs. Forsythe nearly had a seizure when Finn told her he was still marrying Maisie, apparently, but that was small potatoes compared to Lorene's announcement that she was filing for divorce.

In the month after she tried to run away from her own wedding, my friendship with Maisie only deepens. We meet several times a week to hang out. We talk about our days over tacos, and she comes over to Stacey's to eat dinner with us. Maisie tells me about what Clara was like when they were younger, and every so often, she talks about Elizabeth, too. Sometimes, we really do meet for Monday coffee at Espresso 22 before she comes to game night at Ruthie's, and I finally have someone willing to be my charades partner.

Lorene and Rose, who I worried might hate me forever, accept my apology for lying with grace and an invitation to join them for girls'-night-out karaoke. When the four of us get together, sometimes we talk about Maisie's wedding plans. Sometimes we talk about the bad shit that happened in our pasts. And sometimes we just sit around and make fun of Mrs. Forsythe. It's one thing that really binds us all together.

❧

Maeve's fourth birthday party is a blowout affair. It's not quite as elaborate as Chloe Wellington's, but Stacey and Glory lean hard into the dinosaur theme. There's a blowup T. rex that stands over six feet tall next to the playhouse, and Glory bakes a chocolate cake shaped like a brontosaurus. The girls' friends dart back and forth across the backyard, finding "dinosaur eggs" hidden in the grass, and nobody shouts at Maeve to put down her Nerf weapon.

"I'll never get this image of you out of my mind, Wilhelmina," Ruthie says when I emerge from the house in my Princess Sparkleheart attire. At Maeve's request, Princess Sparkleheart, Dinosaur Hunter, will lead everyone in the singing of the "Happy Birthday" song. "It's priceless."

I glare at Ruthie and adjust the folds of my pink skirt. "This lace itches like you wouldn't believe."

"Oh, I believe it," Maisie says, snapping a picture of me with her iPhone. "This one should definitely go on the blog."

"Oh, it definitely will," I promise. From now on, my readers will know the real Willa—itchy ball gown and all.

"Aunt Willa!" Maeve calls, holding up a large gold dinosaur egg. "Look!"

I admire her egg, and Stacey and Glory herd the guests around the picnic table, where Stacey lights the candles on the cake. I take my position at the head of the group, sporting my princess flower crown and wielding the dinosaur-hunter Nerf gun Maeve insisted I carry.

"Happy birthday to you," I sing, motioning for everyone to join in. "Happy birthday to you . . ."

Children's little, off-key voices pair with the off-key ones of the adults, and it's all I can do to keep myself from covering my ears until the song ends. Maeve blows out her candles in one long whoosh, and I clap for her as Maisie takes another sixty pictures.

"Hey, Princess Sparkleheart," a voice calls out to me as I turn away from the cake. "Seen any seismosauruses around here?"

I look up to see Liam Rafferty grinning at me, dressed in a pair of jeans and an Ohio State T-shirt. A mob of butterflies swarms inside my chest, and I blink a few times to make sure I'm not hallucinating him. "What's a seismosaurus?" I ask finally.

He scoffs at me. "Come on, Sparkles. Everyone knows the seismosaurus was the largest of the sauropod dinosaurs."

I'm so happy to see him, to hear his voice, that I want to fling my flower crown into the air in triumph. Instead, I force myself to play it cool. "Everybody who's a nerd, maybe."

"Takes one to know one, Sparks."

I adjust my crown, trying to look as nonderanged as I can, and take a step toward him. "What is it with you and children's birthday parties? Are you just a big fan of cake and piñatas?"

Liam grins. "I'll have you know that your sister invited me. She still credits me with saving Kaya's life, so I'm pretty sure I'm invited to Thanksgiving, Christmas, and Arbor Day, too."

I've never loved Stacey more than in this moment. The thought of Liam's presence at every family holiday is almost too wonderful to imagine. "Well, we don't do anything for Arbor Day, so you're gonna be pretty disappointed."

Liam takes a step toward me. "I think I'll be okay."

When we're next to each other, I have to stop myself from reaching out to wrap my arms around the back of his neck. "It's really nice to see you, Liam."

He smiles, and my stomach does that fluttery thing it does whenever he's within a ten-foot radius of me. "It's nice to see you too. I'm sorry I didn't respond to your text. I just needed some time."

His words are like a balm to my soul, and I can't resist the urge to touch him anymore. I reach out to brush his tattoo with my fingertips. "I understand."

He reaches up to straighten my crown, and the nearness of him makes me dizzy. "But I need to ask you something."

"If it's a dinosaur-related question, I guarantee you I won't know the answer."

Liam laughs, a real, full-throated laugh, and the sound of it is pure magic. "There's this wedding coming up next month. My best friend's gonna marry the love of his life. I was wondering if you wanted to be my date." He brushes my cheek with his thumb. "I promise it'll be fun. I won't even call you Sparkles."

I laugh and wrap my hand around his. His skin is warm against mine, and I trace my fingers over his knuckles.

"Well? Can I have an answer? You're leaving me hanging here, Willa."

Dropping my Nerf gun, I lean forward to press my lips to his. "In case it wasn't clear, that's a yes," I say. And then I kiss him again. Just because I can.

37

On the day of Maisie's wedding, the trees that surround the Africa Event Center at the Columbus Zoo and Aquarium pop with brilliant reds and oranges. Early afternoon sunlight speckles the leaves, and somewhere in the distance, I can hear the howl of a gibbon. I only know the sound is from a gibbon because Maisie taught me.

"How's my hair?" she asks, flicking her fishtail braid over her shoulder. She traded the gown Mrs. Forsythe picked out for a taffeta vintage dress with a sweetheart neckline and lace overlay. The full circle skirt ends midcalf, and her gold flats feature a bow at the heel. It's very nontraditional, and very, very Maisie.

"It's perfect," Lorene says in admiration.

"It's gorgeous," I agree.

"Hell, *I'd* marry you looking like that," Rose says. "Hot damn."

The four of us, plus Pippa, stand inside the event center while we wait for the ceremony to start. Pippa, wearing flowers around her collar, looks almost as stunning as her mom.

"Okay, Wil," Maisie says, fluffing out her skirt. "You're sure you're good to walk Pippa down the aisle?"

"Are you kidding? There's no one I'd rather have escorting me." Except maybe Liam, but I'll see him at the end of the aisle. Pippa wags her tail and licks Maisie's hand.

Fifty guests sit outside near the giraffe pasture, waiting for Maisie to emerge. To her credit, Mrs. Forsythe showed up, and she even made a point to admire Pippa's flowers.

"Is it true there will be penguins at the reception?" Rose asks, fingering the end of Maisie's braid.

"Rose, *focus*," Lorene scolds.

"Sorry for liking animals," Rose mutters, facing forward with her bouquet. Her crutches are gone, but I suspect that she misses having everyone sign her cast.

Maisie laughs, and I reach behind me to squeeze her hand in mine. She's decided to walk down the aisle herself, and Mrs. Forsythe didn't say two words about it.

"You're the most beautiful, wonderful, fantastic bride of all time," I tell her. "Are you ready for this?"

Maisie nods, and the opening notes of Journey's "Don't Stop Believin'" cue the bridal party to begin our grand entrance.

"Positions, everyone!" Lorene commands. "Backs straight, smiles on, eyes forward. Let's do this."

"It's a wedding, not a military march," Rose grumbles, but she adjusts the skirt of her lavender dress and does as instructed.

I wait my turn as Finn's college-aged twin brothers, Reed and Whit (short for Whitaker, I shit you not) escort Jenna and Rose down the aisle. Liam, looking good enough to eat in his charcoal-gray suit, walks Lorene down the aisle next, and I try to hide my jealousy over the fact that Pippa gets to pant freely.

"Hot damn," Maisie whispers, winking at me, but before I have time to whisper back, Pippa and I are up. Finn's high school buddy

Kyle was supposed to escort me down the aisle, but he knocked back one shot too many in the hour leading up to the ceremony, so he's waiting at the end of the aisle instead.

"Here we go, Pip," I whisper, and she licks the inside of my palm in encouragement.

As the two of us exit the event center and step into the sunshine, nerves threaten to overtake my stomach. But they quickly disappear when the crowd oohs and ahhs at Pippa and her adorable flower collar, and I realize no one's paying attention to me—no one except Liam, anyway. He grins at me from the end of the aisle, and it takes every ounce of restraint I have not to tug on Pippa's leash and sprint toward him. Next to Liam stands Finn, looking handsome as hell in his suit, with a green-succulent, Maisie-approved boutonniere fixed to his lapel. He's beaming so widely that I think his face might crack, and Pippa lets out a bark of excitement when we reach him.

"Doggy!" Maeve cries from the third row of the audience, and I have to stifle a laugh as Stacey and Glory both lean toward her to shush her.

After Pippa and I take our place next to the other bridesmaids, the music switches from Journey to the Beatles' "Here Comes the Sun." Maisie's boss, a red-haired woman in a green pantsuit who's doubling as wedding officiant, motions for everyone to stand. I turn to watch as Maisie emerges from the event center, clutching a bouquet of blush-pink peonies. Her auburn braid catches the October sun, lending her her very own spotlight, and I'm close enough to Finn to hear his sharp intake of breath.

"Here comes your wife," Liam whispers to his best friend, and I'm not sure whose eyes well up with tears first—mine or Finn's.

Maisie's steps down the aisle are smooth and confident, with the poise of a woman who knows exactly who she is and exactly what she's doing. Pippa's tail thumps against my leg when her mom reaches the end of the aisle, and Finn wraps his arms around his bride and kisses her.

"Hey now," the wedding officiant says, "you're supposed to save that for later." Everyone laughs and cheers as Maisie and Finn kiss one more time, and the gibbon calls again from somewhere across the zoo.

Once the bride and groom are able to take their hands off each other, the ceremony begins. Rose squeezes my hand in hers as Maisie and Finn promise to spend the rest of their lives together, and Pippa wags her tail and lets out a single warning bark to the Masai giraffes roaming in the pasture behind the officiant. I watch as Finn slides a ring onto Maisie's finger and she slides one onto his, and I spot Liam wiping away a single tear that he'll probably deny later. I grin at Stacey and Glory holding hands in the audience, my nieces clustered between them.

"I now pronounce you married," the officiant finally declares. "Finn, you may now kiss your wife. Maisie, you may now kiss your husband."

Applause and cheers ring out from the crowd as the newlyweds embrace, and I realize how lucky I am to be surrounded by the most precious, tender thing that exists in the world: love.

❧

"I was *not* crying," Liam insists, tightening his grip on my waist as we shuffle around the dance floor. "It was one singular tear. Not that there's anything wrong with showing emotion."

"Hush, Rafferty." Rose, who's spent the last hour cuddling up to one of Finn's friends from college, a dark-haired gentleman with an Italian accent and excellent shoes, shakes her head at him from a few feet across the dance floor. "Whitaker told me you sobbed like a baby before the ceremony started."

"Damn it, Whit," Liam mutters, his jaw tightening.

I laugh and press a kiss to the side of his neck, his skin warm under my lips. Liam makes a soft murmuring sound and lowers his lips to meet mine. I wrap my arms tighter around his neck, my body tingling in response to his nearness, and Liam seems to have the same idea.

"Think anyone would notice if we disappeared for a few minutes?" he asks, his lips against my ear.

The proposition is tempting as hell, but I laugh and force myself to peel my body away from his. "I'd love to, but I'm on duty here. Don't forget." Even though I'm at the wedding as a real bridesmaid now, not just a hired one, I still take my position very seriously. I've already had to help the newlyweds locate a missing grandparent (Finn's maternal grandmother, whom I found trying to sneak a joint near the giraffe yard) and dissuade a very persistent penguin from pecking at the hem of Mrs. Forsythe's floor-length gown. That penguin is my hero.

"You're really good at this," Liam says, his hands resting on my lower back as Taylor Swift's "Lover" blares from the speakers. "The whole bridesmaid thing."

I flush with pride like I do whenever he praises me. "Thanks. It's easy when Maisie's the bride."

He nods. "What you did for her . . . I bet you could build a business out of it."

It's an idea that's crossed my mind, too. I'm certain there are more brides in Columbus like Maisie—brides who could use a helping hand on their wedding day. I probably wouldn't become best friends with all of them, but then again, there's no one else like Maisie.

"You think?" I ask, cupping Liam's cheek in my hand.

He grins. "I think you can do anything you want, Sparks."

I swat his arm at the use of my old nickname. "Hey, you promised you wouldn't call me Sparks!"

"My bad, you're right. I did." Liam pulls me closer toward him so that his mouth is against my temple. "I'll make it up to you later. And *that's* a promise I intend to keep."

Before my dress can automatically start to unzip itself in response, Maisie intervenes. "Sorry, lovebirds," she says, cutting in between Liam and me as the DJ cues up a faster-paced song, "but I need a dance with my bridesmaid here."

"As you wish," Liam says, taking her hand and giving her a little spin. "I'll go get us a round of cake."

"Didn't you already have two pieces?" Maisie asks, laughing.

"Hey, Willa and I nearly died for that cake. I think that entitles me to at least four servings." He waves and ducks out of the way as Rose and her suave dance partner shimmy into his path.

"Mrs. Yummy did an amazing job," I tell Maisie as she takes Liam's spot. "That Belgian chocolate flavor was totally worth surviving a stampede of brides." Maisie and I wiggle our hips around in time to the beat, observing the flushed, happy faces of the dancers around us. Closer to the DJ table, I spot Kaya and Maeve skipping around in circles. "This is the best wedding I've ever been to, Mais. And I'm not just saying that because it's yours."

She beams. "It's everything I dreamt it would be. And more, thanks to that penguin who really had it out for Mrs. Forsythe." Maisie laughs as Lorene glides past us, her kids dancing after her, and then she turns her gaze toward me. "I couldn't have done any of it without you, Willa. And I'm so grateful."

I think of how far we've both come since that day we met at the coffee shop, and I can't help but reach forward and take Maisie's hand in mine. "I couldn't have done any of it without you, either. That's what friends are for."

She smiles and squeezes my hand, and I realize there's no place in the world I'd rather be right now than here with her.

"Maisie!" Finn calls out from the cake table. "Willa! Come here. It's almost time for the Cha Cha Slide!"

"There is nothing that man loves more than the Cha Cha Slide," Maisie whispers, rolling her eyes good-naturedly.

"Except for you," I correct her.

She blushes, nodding. "Except for me."

"Seriously, hurry!" Finn calls again. "It's the next song up!"

"C'mon," I say, giving Maisie's hand one last squeeze. "You don't want to keep your husband waiting."

She laughs and taps the floor, just once, with her shiny gold flat. "Okay," she agrees. "Let's go."

And so we do. Toward love and family and whatever else the future holds for both of us.

Acknowledgments

The publication of this book is a dream come true and I am grateful for the support and encouragement of many people who helped make it happen.

Endless thanks to my agent, Jessica Watterson. You're an absolute powerhouse and a wonderful human being, and I'm so happy we're a team. Thank you to everyone at Sandra Dijkstra Literary Agency, including Andrea Cavallaro and Jennifer Kim. Thank you to Dillon Asher of the Gotham Group.

Berkley is the perfect home for my book. I am so grateful for the hard work and expertise of everyone who worked on it, especially my editor, Angela Kim. From that initial phone call while I was on my honeymoon, I knew my manuscript was in the best hands. Thank you for the support you've shown me on both a personal and a professional level. Additional thanks to the entire Berkley team, including Jennifer Myers and Amy J. Schneider.

I participated in Pitch Wars in 2017 and 2019, and without it, I don't think this book would exist. Thank you to Brenda Drake and the Pitch Wars committee, Melissa West, Kristin Rockaway, Alexa

Acknowledgments

Martin, and Laura Heffernan. I am eternally grateful for the support, camaraderie, and friendship of the PW classes of 2017 and 2019.

Susan Bishop Crispell, your mentorship changed my life. You taught me so much about how to craft a novel and deepen my characters, and I can't thank you enough.

Valerie Sayers, your fiction writing class at the University of Notre Dame helped me find my voice.

Thank you to my husband, Chris Rea, for being my best friend and my partner in all things. You are everything I like in the world wrapped up in one person, and I love you beyond measure.

Kelly Reardon, "thank you" doesn't begin to cover it, but I'll try anyway. You are the most incredible sister and best friend, and you have been my rock since day one. Thank you for loving me fiercely. Here's to puppy chow and PWA forever.

Mom, thank you for being my number one fan. You've worked so hard your whole life to make mine special. Thank you for showing me the magic of reading and for all those trips to the library and Little Professor. I'm so lucky that you're my mom.

Dad, thank you for giving me my Irish sense of humor and for your support and love. And many thanks for letting me check out all those books on your library card. Sorry about the late fees!

Audrey Roncevich, my best cousin-friend-sister, thank you for being you. Your loving heart is the safest of places, and you bring me so much joy.

Thank you to my friends and family, including Kim Rea; Tyler, Paige, and Greyson Rea; Aaron and Tristen Rea; Jim Rea and Denise; Bella and Gunnar Rose; Brittany Angarola; Taylor Nichols; Isabella Reardon; Angela Lontoc; Julia and Harper Hanna; Veronica Jenkins; Mary Collins; and Josh, Jess, Ollie, and Remy Reardon. Thanks to my extended Reardon, McVey, and Corletzi families. I love you all.

Raiden, Maya, Nash, and Bree, thank you for the snuggles and companionship. All dogs are the best dogs, but you're the best-best dogs. I know you can't read this but I couldn't bear to leave you guys out.

During the editing process for this book, I was pregnant with my son, Ciaran. He passed away when I was forty weeks along. I want to thank the labor and delivery nurses at Dublin Methodist Hospital, who cared for us with the utmost compassion and respect. You are my heroes.

After Ciaran's passing, I was supported by other loss moms who showed me that I was not alone, and that hope lives on. To the parents who shared their stories of miscarriage, stillbirth, infant loss, and infertility: I'm sorry we're in this club together, but I cherish your support. Thanks also to Star Legacy Foundation, which supports research related to stillbirth and perinatal loss and provides resources for grieving families.

To anyone who might read this book while going through a hard time: you are very brave, and I'm proud of you. The bad times won't last forever, but it's important to ask for help when you need it. Please remember that you are never, ever alone.

And mostly, to Ciaran: I miss you more than words can say. Thank you for making me a mom—for making me *your* mom. It is the honor of my life.

The Wedding Ringer

Kerry Rea

Discussion Questions

1. Willa loses her fiancé and best friend after they both betray her. What do you think you would do if you were in Willa's position? Would you also want to leave town?

2. If someone came up to you the way Maisie did at the café, what would you do? Would you agree to be a stranger's bridesmaid?

3. *The Wedding Ringer* brings up a lot of themes: female friendships, the importance of family, past mistakes, and more. What speaks to you the most? Why?

4. Willa keeps a huge secret from Liam throughout most of the book. Would you tell Liam about it or would you find it difficult like Willa does? How do you think Liam would have reacted if Willa told him in the beginning?

5. Have you ever been in the wedding party? What were the highlights? Did you run into any issues or chaos (e.g., the cake situation)?

6. Do you think Willa will ever speak to Sarah again? Would you if you were in her shoes?

7. Willa never planned on being a children's birthday party performer, but life took her in a surprising direction. Have you ever had an unusual job? Did you enjoy it, or did you struggle with it like Willa did?

8. Willa's blog is an important part of her identity. Have you ever written a blog? What are some of your favorite blogs to read?

9. When Willa's feeling down, she turns to episodes of *The Golden Girls* and *The Office* to lift her spirits. What are your comfort shows?

10. Willa and Liam disagree on the importance of social media. She views it as a way to connect with people, while he doesn't participate in it. What's your relationship with social media like? Are you more Team Willa or Team Liam?

Keep reading for an excerpt from

Lucy on the Wild Side

Kerry Rea's next novel from Berkley!

I wish I were a Humboldt squid.

Everyone thinks chameleons are the best camouflagers, but a Humboldt squid can change its colors as fast as four times a second. If I could do that, I'd transform myself into the rain-cloud-gray shade of my office walls. That way, Elle wouldn't be able to find me and remind me of my four p.m. assignment.

But I'm not a squid, and I jump when my office door bangs open.

"Lucy." My best friend, Elle, pops her head inside the doorway, with a mass of black curls framing her face. "You cannot hide from the children."

I sigh and shut my laptop, where I've been updating the daily feeding log. The gorillas ate their regular afternoon snack of popcorn, cereal, and sunflower seeds, with peanuts added in as an extra treat. As a keeper, part of my job is keeping detailed records of the gorillas' dietary intake, social interactions, sleep habits, and vital signs. I've got at least an hour of data entry left today, but that will have to wait.

I don't want Elle to kill me.

"I know you hate doing the Critter Chats, but they're important. I've got twenty-six second graders out there who can't wait to learn about primates," she says, sticking her neck farther into my shoebox-size office. It's so tiny that between my cluttered desk and stuffed mini fridge, I can't lean more than three inches back in my chair without smacking my head against the door. Elle has no chance of getting in.

"Did you say twenty-six?" I ask in disbelief. "That's a fuck-ton of kids."

When she raises an eyebrow at me, I grab a fresh can of Diet Coke from the mini fridge and pop the tab open. I'm going to need a serious caffeine fix to make it through the next half hour.

"And it's not that I hate the Critter Chats," I continue, letting the cold deliciousness of my drink soothe me. "It's that I hate the *four o'clock* Critter Chats."

Three times a day—nine a.m., one p.m., and the dreaded four p.m.—a zookeeper from the primates department hosts an educational Q and A in front of the outdoor gorilla exhibit. I enjoy the Chats most of the time, since they're a great way to share my passion for gorillas with the public. During the morning and early afternoon sessions, the kids who attend are in cheery, inquisitive moods. It's early enough in the day that the zoo is still fun for them, and they've got a day full of camel rides and ice cream flamingo pops to look forward to.

But by late afternoon, the excitement and sugar highs have faded, and the exhausted children have sunk into cranky moods. If they're little, they've gone all day without their usual naps; and if they're teenagers, it's late enough in the day that their phone batteries are dead and they have to suffer through the oppressive June heat without access to TikTok.

It's not a great situation.

"I know they can be challenging, but you're the only primate keeper available today. Jack's assisting over in Asia Quest, and Lottie has to go to her grandmother's funeral. Plus, it'll get you extra brownie points from Phil."

I clear my throat. "It's Lottie's grandmother's *cat's* funeral," I clarify, narrowing my eyes at Elle. "And I bet she could make it back in time."

Elle's dark brown eyes flicker with exasperation. "You know I don't assign keepers, Luce. I just make sure that somebody's out there to educate the children."

She's laying it on a little thick with that whole *educate-the-children* line, but she's not wrong. As an associate activities director, Elle's responsible for coordinating events for the public, including Zoo Camp, the painting-with-penguins fundraiser sessions, and Critter Chats. If I refuse to be a good sport, I'll be making her job harder. And since we've been best friends since the first day of Zoo-Teen volunteer orientation twelve years ago, that's not an option for me. Plus, she has a point about my boss, Phil. He's looking to promote a junior primate keeper to senior sometime this year, and I want that job more than anything.

"Okay, okay," I relent, standing up from my chair to stretch my legs. At five-nine, I tower over Elle's five-one frame, and I bounce on my heels to increase blood flow to my long limbs. "Just tell me, this second-grade class—are there any girls with flower names? You know, Tulip, Rose, Iris? Because girls with flower names always give me the hardest time. Along with boys with bougie names, like Brantley or Oakley or Banks."

I'm not pulling those names out of thin air. Last week, a five-year-old named Tulip tried to stick gum in my hair, and a six-year-old Banks screamed at me when I explained to him that gorillas aren't monkeys. I've learned to maintain a ten-foot distance between myself and children at the afternoon Critter Chats, lest any of them have a tantrum and decide to fling a Capri Sun at my head.

Elle scrunches her nose. "Who names a kid Tulip? Anyway, it's almost four, so let's go, please. And if the kids get too rowdy, just tell them that filming starts next week, so if they come to the zoo again over the summer, there's a chance they'll get to be on TV. Kids love TV."

Kids love launching full juice boxes at innocent zookeepers' heads more than they like TV, in my experience, but I don't argue. Elle's mention of filming inspires a flutter of excitement in my stomach. Next week, the Columbus Zoo and Aquarium will be the site of a months-long documentary project produced by wildlife expert Kai Bridges, host of *On the Wild Side with Kai Bridges*. *Wild Side* has taken viewers like me—I've seen every episode, including the famous one about the last grizzly bear in a small Montana county— from the ice shelves of Antarctica to the volcanoes of Hawaii, show-casing animals in every biome. Now his production company wants to show audiences the magic of wildlife right in their own backyards, starting with our zoo.

I'm so excited about the docuseries that not even the memory of Tulip and her aggressive bubblegum antics can lessen my enthusi-asm. I'd rather die than be on camera—my fellow keepers, Lottie and Jack, can have that glory to themselves—but I'm looking for-ward to meeting Kai. He's the son of famed primatologist Dr. Char-lotte Kimber, who's half the reason I'm a gorilla keeper, and meeting her offspring is probably the closest I'll ever get to meeting my idol herself. Plus, at least on TV, Kai looks like Tom Hardy's twin, if said twin wore a Crocodile Dundee hat and said *wowza!* in a South Af-rican accent every time an apex predator appeared.

The docuseries will put our zoo on the map, and my heart skips a beat when I imagine people all over the world getting to know the gorillas I've dedicated my career to.

But first I have to survive the Critter Chat.

"All right, let's go," I say, taking another swig of Diet Coke and surrendering to the inevitable. "But I swear to God, if any second graders launch spit wads at me, I can't promise not to retaliate."

Elle shakes her head but smiles as I follow her out of my office and through the administrative section of Ape House. She loves kids, which is a good thing, since she and her husband, Nadeem, are expecting their first baby in six months.

"C'mon." She lifts her employee ID to grant us access to the hallway leading toward the gorillas. "And while I have you, don't forget about that benefit picnic this weekend. You don't have to wear a dress, but you *cannot* wear your work uniform."

I sigh. Like the Critter Chats, attending zoo fundraising events is part of my job, but I don't enjoy it. It's the actual *work* part of my career that comes easily to me: building relationships with the animals, researching advances in gorilla care, keeping impeccable records of every aspect of their lives so that conservationists can use the data to bolster outcomes for gorillas in the wild. But making agonizing small talk and eating tiny appetizers at a rich donor's house doesn't appeal to me. I'd much rather be knee-deep in hay getting real work done.

"What's the picnic for?" I ask, trying not to let my annoyance show. It's not Elle's fault that zoos, like other nonprofits, rely on the support of the community to thrive. "And I wouldn't wear my work uniform. I'm not a moron."

As we approach the behind-the-scenes animal area, the unmistakable odor of hay and gorilla fills my nostrils. It smells like a barnyard exploded, and it's my favorite scent in the world.

Elle rolls her eyes. "It's to raise money for a lemur rescue in Madagascar. And I'm not saying you're a moron. I'm saying that sometimes, you're so focused on work that things like general self-care fall to the wayside. Remember that gala at the art museum? The one for the giraffe blood bank? You showed up in khakis and a polo shirt. With gorilla shit on your boots."

I glance down at the black polo, khaki shorts, and hunter green rain boots I'm currently wearing. There's not a cloud in sight today, but the boots are essential footwear for a long day scrubbing exhibit floors.

"Piper was born the night of the gala," I explain, remembering the night the zoo's youngest gorilla entered the world. "So excuse me for not missing the birth of a *critically endangered creature* so I'd have time to shower."

"Nadeem and I had to sit next to you at that gala, so you are not excused." Elle reaches an arm out to give me a friendly swat, and I hop sideways to miss it.

"Point taken."

I push open the heavy metal door that leads us out of Ape House and into the warm June sunshine. We emerge on the keepers-only side of Gorilla Villa, the twenty-six-thousand-square-foot outdoor viewing area. Currently, the members of silverback Ozzie's troop roam the space, enjoying what's left of an afternoon scatter feed. Ozzie, the four-hundred-pound leader of the group, rests on a wooden platform above us while he munches on a head of lettuce.

"Hi, handsome," I say. Ozzie's eyes dart toward me, but he continues enjoying his snack. With the distinctive smattering of red hair on his forehead, the proud, observant look in his eyes, and trademark silver hair on his massive back, Ozzie never fails to stop me in my tracks.

"He looks so majestic," Elle says, craning her neck to look up at him.

"That's because he *is* majestic." The silverback, the dominant male of a gorilla family, is the cornerstone of a troop's survival in the wild. He mediates conflicts, leads his group to feeding sites, and will even sacrifice his own life for the safety of his kin. Ozzie, in all his lettuce-munching glory, is no different.

The rest of Ozzie's troop is scattered throughout the Villa. Thirty-one-year-old Zuri, my favorite member of the troop, basks in the sun on an overhead ledge. Her fellow females, Tria and Inkesha, doze on a beam tower in the center of the exhibit while Tria's daughter, one-year-old Piper, sleeps on her mom's chest. On the public side of the Villa, youngsters Tomo and Risa engage in a wrestling session, and young male Mac sticks his head into the opening of a tunnel on a grassy hill, probably foraging for more greens.

The outdoor exhibit, a massive structure of interconnected beams and wire mesh, serves to give the gorillas as much choice in their whereabouts as possible. Overhead transfer chutes connect the outdoor space to Ape House, allowing the troop members to move freely between their indoor and outdoor habitats, and a labyrinth of ropes, ladders, and tunnels provides opportunities for playing and napping out of the public eye.

"Ready?" Elle asks, passing me a headset mic and sliding hers on.

"No," I mutter as we approach the shaded viewing area where a crowd has gathered to watch Risa and Tomo's playful antics. My stomach drops when I see that the twenty-six kids Elle mentioned are wearing matching purple T-shirts with *St. Thomas Day Camp Superstar* printed on the front.

"Dammit, Elle. You didn't tell me they were day camp kids!"

She bites her lip in guilt. She knows as well as I do that a four o'clock Critter Chat with day camp kids is the worst scenario of all. Not that I have anything against camps—I'm not a monster, and I was a child myself once—but the sheer ratio of exhausted teachers to unruly, even more exhausted kids is a recipe for disaster.

"It'll be great," Elle whispers as we approach the group. "I promise."

I shoot her a dark look but take my place at the glass window in front of the exhibit. The thick humidity in the air does no favors for my wavy, white-blond hair, and between the frizz and the loose pieces of hay stuck in my ponytail, I probably look like a deranged Targaryen.

"Welcome," Elle says, waving her arms at the assembled group of children and flashing them her perma-watt smile. Between the kids' chatter and the birdsongs floating through the air from the nearby aviary, her voice is lost in the commotion.

"Welcome!" she repeats, louder this time. For a petite person, Elle can really project.

"For this afternoon's Critter Chat, we've got junior keeper Lucy to teach us about the gorillas who call our zoo home. And if you use your very best listening ears, I bet she'll even answer some questions for you."

I try not to hold my breath as Elle winks at the crowd. Something tells me their listening ears got switched off somewhere around lunchtime.

"And remember," Elle continues, "no tapping the glass, please." She smiles and motions toward me with a dramatic sweep of her arm, as if we're on a game show and I'm the prize behind door number three. "Let's listen up while Lucy tells us all about gorillas!"

"Hello," I say, taking my cue. I swallow hard, and my gaze darts from Elle to the group of purple-shirted children. I know I'm not about to deliver the Gettysburg Address, but my palms have already grown slick with sweat. Public speaking, even when it's about my life's passion, has never been my strong suit. I'm great at chatting with small groups of zoo guests, but any more than that triggers serious stage fright. I'd rather shovel gorilla dung.

"Your mic," Elle mouths to me, motioning to her headset.

It takes me a second to realize my mic isn't turned on, and my cheeks heat up as I correct the error. I spot my boss, Phil, making his way toward Ape House from the bonobo exhibit, and he stops to observe the Chat.

"Hello," I repeat, trying to calm my nerves. "I'm Lucy, and I've been a keeper here for four years. Right now, you're looking at Ozzie's troop. Ozzie is the big, beautiful guy chowing down on lettuce over there."

I point to him and introduce the other members of his troop. The crowd listens as I go through my educational spiel, telling them about troop social structure, what makes a healthy gorilla diet, and how western lowland gorillas are faring in their native lands (hint: not well).

Just before I can launch into the most important part of my speech and explain how people can support gorilla conservation in the wild, a gap-toothed boy from St. Thomas Day Camp raises his hand.

"Do gorillas fart?" he asks, prompting a roar of laughter from his classmates. His teacher rolls her eyes and gives me a sympathetic glance. I'm guessing gorillas aren't the only thing he asks that question about.

"They do, actually." I answer his question smoothly, as if it's no big deal. And it isn't. Kids are naturally curious, and I've found it's best to give them simple, honest answers. "Most animals experience flatulence. Except for octopuses. And birds. And, according to researchers, sloths."

Elle side-eyes me as if to ask how I know that as another St. Thomas kid raises her hand.

"Why did you become a keeper?" she asks, shifting her weight from one skinny leg to the other.

I smile at her. It's a question I could spend hours answering.

"Well, when I was little, my grandmother bought me an incredibly special book called *Majesty on the Mountain* by Dr. Charlotte Kimber. She wrote it about her experience studying mountain gorillas in Rwanda. I loved that book so much that I took it with me everywhere. In fact, I'd spend hours in the woods pretending I was her research aide."

I remember stuffing my Lisa Frank backpack full of Goldfish crackers and twist-cap Sunny Delights and traipsing into the woods outside my grandmother's house. I'd gather leaves and sticks and even dead bugs and glue them into my "research notebook," where I'd write detailed logs of my outings. I couldn't exactly track gorilla dung or observe their behavioral patterns like Dr. Kimber. So instead, I counted elderberries and made meticulous notes about the urinary patterns of the neighbor's poodle, Clancy.

On Friday nights, when my grandmother Nona microwaved popcorn and let me pick a movie, I always chose the film version of Dr. Kimber's book. At the end, when the actress playing Dr. Kimber sobbed over the death of her favorite gorilla, Nona and I would cry our eyes out until she swore never to let me watch it again. But she always relented, and if she thought I was weird for stalking around in the woods with a Dr. Kimber-like braid in my hair, she never let it show.

"That book introduced me to the magic of gorillas," I continue. "I'd go through *National Geographic* magazine and cut out pictures of gorillas and monkeys and chimpanzees and put them up on my bedroom wall." I'd also displayed seven posters of a *Titanic*-era Leonardo DiCaprio, but that's neither here nor there.

"When I was old enough, I joined the ZooTeen program right here at our zoo." I explain how I studied biology in college and did several internships before landing my dream job. "For me, it all really started with Dr. Kimber's book. I wouldn't be here today without it."

Unmoved, the gap-toothed kid from St. Thomas raises his hand again. "Do gorillas puke?"

After I assure him that gorillas share 98 percent of our DNA and thus have the same basic bodily functions, Elle twirls her finger subtly to get me to wrap things up. I breathe a sigh of relief. Nobody's tossed so much as a gum wrapper at me, and Phil was here to witness every second of my successful Critter Chat.

Forget camouflaging myself like a Humboldt squid. I'm proud as a peacock.

But before I head back inside to my sweet, sweet Diet Coke, I want to drop a line or two about conservation. "Dr. Kimber, who the mountain locals called *Nyiramacibiri*—the woman who lives alone in the forest—wrote that the building block of conservation is love. Love for gorillas and the earth that sustains us all. We don't have to be 'people who live alone in the forest' to make an impact. We can do that right here in Ohio, whether we're keepers or second graders."

I describe the zoo's partnerships with international conservation programs, and how global demand for palm oil has accelerated the deforestation of great ape habitats. I encourage them to download the zoo's palm-oil shopping guide so they can ensure the products they buy, from cooking spray to ice cream, contain sustainable palm oil.

The boy who asked about gorilla bathroom habits pretends to

snore loudly, but I'm satisfied with the session. If I've done my job right, and I think I have, the kids will go home with a little more knowledge about gorillas and compassion for their plight in the wild.

And I'll go home without gum in my ponytail.

Elle turns off her mic as the crowd disperses. "Great job, Luce." She glances at her smartwatch and frowns. "Shoot, we went five minutes over. I've gotta run to the Tasmanian Devil Chat next. Text me when you're leaving, okay? Sam mentioned getting dinner at El Vaquero tonight."

The prospect of enchiladas with my best friends is almost enough to make my stomach growl, and I wave good-bye as she trots off. I still have a lot of data to work on today, along with drafting plans for Ozzie's upcoming birthday.

Remembering that I've got a question for Phil about Ozzie's cake, I scan the crowd for him. I spot him next to the surly faced, six-foot-tall bronze statue of Rock, one of the zoo's original gorillas. He's deep in conversation with an auburn-haired man who's an inch or two taller than the Rock statue, and looks about as pleased.

"Lucy!" Phil calls when he notices me observing them. "Come here. I've got somebody for you to meet."

Following my boss's orders, I approach the pair. Phil, with his salt-and-pepper hair and all-khaki outfit, looks like he could pass for Steve Irwin's dad. Unlike my neatly groomed boss, the auburn-haired man looks like he hasn't seen a razor in months. His full beard bears streaks of blond, and a scar over his right eyebrow leaves a half centimeter of it bare.

"Hello," I say, trying not to stare at the scar. "I hope you enjoyed the Critter Chat."

I'm used to making niceties with the occasional donor who stops by for a behind-the-scenes tour with Phil. But instead of the awestruck expression most people wear when they're up close and personal with gorillas, his lips are curled into the deep frown of someone who just stepped in dog shit.

His gaze shifts from Phil to me, and I force myself to look into his hazel eyes instead of at his eyebrow.

"I'd hardly call a gorilla a critter," he says in a deep voice.

His words bear the trace of an accent, but I can't quite place what it is, and his gruff tone catches me off guard. I glance sideways at Phil, but he doesn't seem to pick up on any tension.

I shrug. *Critter* is probably a better term for a pygmy slow loris than a great ape, but I don't name the programs.

"Well," I say, "I hope you found the talk informative. Education is a big part of what we do here at the zoo."

Phil beams, and I award myself a mental brownie point. Take that, Jack and Lottie.

The bearded man says nothing in response. Phil glances from me to the sour-faced guy and clasps his hands together, and I start to wonder if he called me over to help him escape from this dreadful conversation.

I should get double brownie points for that.

"So, Phil," I say, giving him a meaningful look, "when you're done here, I wanted to talk about Ozzie's birthday cake. He didn't like the pumpkin puree frosting last year, so I was thinking we could try strawberry this time."

Before Phil can respond, the grumpy man turns toward me again. "You were wrong, you know."

He watches me with a steady gaze, and I blink at him in confusion. What the hell's he talking about? Wrong about what? I wasn't wrong about any of the facts I laid out during the Critter Chat. I know more about these gorillas than anyone, except for maybe Phil.

I spend upwards of sixty hours a week tending to them and researching every possible method for improving their care. I miss family
dinners and nights out with friends because my work with the gorillas always comes first. I love it. I love them.

And I know my shit.

"Wrong about what?" I ask. I manage to keep my tone calm, even
though I want nothing more than to reach out and yank his stupid
beard. I've dealt with enough mansplainers who think watching a
single documentary on Animal Planet makes them a zoologist.

He nods toward the spot where I stood to lead the Critter Chat.
"You said the locals called Dr. Kimber *Nyiramacibiri*. The woman
who lives alone in the forest. They didn't."

It takes real effort to keep disdain from crossing my features. My
cheeks have a tendency to go fire-engine red when I'm annoyed, and
I don't want to give this guy an inch. I force myself to take a deep
inhale and think about enchiladas.

"I'm not wrong." I've read *Majesty on the Mountain* at least twenty
times and watched the movie way more than that. I know everything
there is to know about Dr. Kimber, down to her favorite color (green)
and what she liked to cook for dinner in her tiny mountain hut (jas-
mine rice). While other kids my age collected Beanie Babies and
played Nintendo 64, I sent my Barbies on gorilla-tracking expedi-
tions and had fake conversations with Dr. Kimber in my head.

So Mr. Eyebrow Scar can take his know-it-all attitude and his
stupid beard and shove it. Hard.

"You are wrong," he insists, running a hand through his thick
waves of hair. If I didn't loathe this dude so much, I'd ask him what
conditioner he uses.

Instead, I run my fingers over the zoo badge on my waistband, as if to remind myself that I'm the one in charge here. Technically Phil's the one in charge, but I refuse to be condescended to in front of my boss by a mid-thirties man-baby who never learned to double-check his facts. Especially when I'm gunning for a promotion.

"I'm not, actually," I reply. "And I'm one hundred and ten percent confident in that." I lift my chin slightly, trying to look as proud and noble as Rock, the gorilla statue.

He raises his eyebrows and opens his mouth to respond, but a chiming noise stops him. While he grabs his smartphone from his pocket and presses it to his ear, I glance sideways at Phil to see if he's picking up on the serious douchecanoe vibes. But Phil just smiles at the dude like he's the second coming of Jane Goodall.

Whoever this asshole donor is, he must be worth a lot of money.

"I've gotta give someone a lift from the airport," he says to Phil after the call ends. "We'll talk more next week."

"Looking forward to it." Phil sounds almost breathless with excitement, as if this guy just handed him fifty-yard-line tickets to the Super Bowl.

I glance from a radiant Phil to the surly bearded man and back to my boss. What in the world am I missing here?

The man turns to leave, but before he reaches the walkway toward the main zoo path, he pauses. He turns back to give me a curt nod, as if he's remembered to at least *act* like someone who has manners.

I don't nod back. Instead, I fix him with a steely glare.

Because I'm not wrong.

After a moment, perhaps when he realizes I'm not going to back down, he turns away. I breathe a sigh of relief and utter a silent prayer that he trips on his way out.

"What a jerk, huh?" I ask when he's out of earshot.

Phil, still staring after the man like he's about to walk on water, doesn't seem to hear me.

"Can you believe it?" he asks. "Kai freaking Bridges! It's going to be quite a summer, Lucy."

My heart drops into my stomach. "What did you say?"

Phil grins at me. "That was Kai Bridges. He stopped by to get a feel for the zoo before production starts next week. Sorry I didn't give you a proper introduction."

I'm so surprised that I take a step sideways, as if to regain my balance. "*What?*"

That was Kai Bridges, son of my all-time, number-one, I'd-die-to-meet-her idol? That's the guy whose wildlife programs have won three Emmys? That's the guy whose docuseries about our zoo is supposed to make the world fall in love with Ozzie and his troop?

What. The. Hell? The onscreen Kai Bridges is a chipper, clean-shaven adventurer who's always saying *wowza!* and flashing a trademark toothy grin. The onscreen Kai has a strong South African accent and isn't a major asshole.

"Where's his accent?" I ask Phil. "Why's he look like he hasn't shaved in a month?" *Why is the incredible Dr. Kimber's son a total, colossal jerk?*

Phil shrugs. "I'm sure he presents himself differently for the show. I met Lady Gaga in an elevator once, and she looked really different than she does in her music videos."

I'm surprised that my boss is familiar with Lady Gaga's videos, but not as surprised as I am by the man I just met. Minutes ago, I was beyond excited for *Wild Side* to start filming. Over the last month, I'd put together spreadsheet upon spreadsheet of data and created a seventy-slide PowerPoint to help the production crew get acquainted with each of our gorillas.

But the man I just met doesn't seem like a PowerPoint kind of guy. He seems like a cocky, ignorant jerkface who tried to embarrass me in front of my boss and doesn't know basic facts about his own mother. And there's no way I can trust him to capture the magnificence of the gorillas I love so dearly.

Forget wanting to be a Humboldt squid, or even a peacock.

I wish I were a great white shark.

Image by Simon Yao

Kerry Rea lives in Columbus, Ohio, with her husband and their small army of dogs. She grew up in Youngstown, Ohio, and graduated from the University of Notre Dame. She believes that a happy ending is always possible.

Connect Online

AuthorKerryRea.com
AuthorKerryRea
KerryMRea

Ready to find
your next great read?

Let us help.

Visit prh.com/nextread